A
FRIEND
IN
BARCELONA

A
FRIEND
IN
BARCELONA

SCOTT
MACKAY

HarperCollins*PublishersLtd*

Toronto

First Edition

Canadian Cataloguing in Publication Data

Mackay, Scott
   A friend in Barcelona

ISBN 0-00-223499-8

I. Title.

PS8575.K393F74 1991   C813'.54   C91-093155-0
PR9199.3.M2438F74 1991

---

91 92 93 94 95 RRD 5 4 3 2 1

To my mother, Claire

Chapter 1

Three sailors pitched a dead Ludendorff off the bow of U-512 into the Atlantic. It was September, 1943. Commander Hermann Paul Goerlitz, no longer in charge, sat on the edge of the catwalk, his face peppered with a week-old beard and his eyes red and sore from chlorine gas fumes. A British Hudson flew a figure-eight pattern above them, making low sweeps over the U-boat once every third turn. Poor Ludendorff, he thought. There was no eulogy or singing, no *Auf einem seemansgrab da blühen keine rose* or blowing of the boatswain's whistle. Just a corpse wrapped in a blood-stained sheet — no match for that Hudson — sinking slowly beneath the sea.

Goerlitz looked up at the Hudson, wondering how the gunner felt, or if he could even see their high-seas burial of Ludendorff. He wondered how much fuel the British aircraft had left. Maybe it would run out and crash into the ocean before reinforcements could arrive.

Waves rolled toward them one after another, breaking against the side of the U-boat in a wash of bubbles and spray. They were nothing like the crew of U-93.

1

There was no one like Commander Weiss, Lieutenant Frischauer, or Petty Officer Ballerstedt. All this because of some chlorine fumes, he thought. He looked at the storm clouds on the horizon. It would rain soon.

He had to make them listen. But Bergen had his gun.

He got to his feet and walked toward the conning tower, gazing at his crew. He couldn't let this happen. They sat around the conning tower and the catwalk as if they were in a beer garden, drinking the champagne and smoking the cigarettes the Lady's Guild of Wilhelmshaven had scrounged up for them before they had weighed anchor.

As he approached the tower, his face was grim and set. The crew stopped telling jokes, stopped drinking, and one by one turned toward him, fearful and wary. He climbed the companionway to the top of the tower where Bergen and Heusinger, one of the boat's quartermasters, shared a fifth of champagne.

Bergen put his tin cup down and raised Goerlitz's gun.

"Captain?" said Bergen, not sure what Goerlitz wanted.

Goerlitz clenched his fist, drew back, and punched Bergen as hard as he could in the mouth. Bergen fell back, knocking the bottle of champagne over, surprised, but still clutching the gun. He touched his fingers to his mouth, where blood seeped from his lips, then raised the gun and pointed it at Goerlitz's head. They looked at one another with pure hatred. The Hudson made another low sweep over the U-boat.

"Go ahead, Bergen. Shoot. I'd sooner be dead than surrender a boat like this."

Bergen held the gun unsteadily, looked as if he were about to fire, then lowered it, losing his nerve. He took out a dirty handkerchief and dabbed at his lip.

"You bastard," he said, his upper class Prussian accent

becoming pronounced. "You fucking, fucking bastard."

"Go screw your mother, pig," answered Goerlitz.

Goerlitz turned around and looked at his men.

"Listen, all of you."

If they no longer obeyed him, at least they still feared him. They turned. Lieutenant Bergen looked on warily.

"Men, what is happening here is unworthy of the *Kriegsmarine*, and especially the *Unterseewaffe*. Lieutenant Bergen is capitalizing on your fears to save his own worthless skin. We sank a tanker and that's something you can all be proud of. Then we were attacked. We were depth-charged. We sustained battery damage. And we stayed under for twelve hours, and that's something you can be proud of as well. But we had to surface, and that Hudson was there, waiting for us, and Ludendorff was killed. Bad luck, but we must fight against our bad luck now. When you joined the *Unterseewaffe* you all took an oath, and though the conditions of our search and destroy mission have been difficult, I must remind you of that oath."

He paused to look at his men then glanced up as the Hudson resumed its watch pattern.

"I know you've only had two months training instead of the usual six," he said. "That's a direct executive order from Hitler and we cannot question the Fuhrer's decision. But now it's time to get a grip on ourselves and avoid the humiliation of capture. We can't let this boat fall into enemy hands. You know how special it is. You know how much went into it, how much depends on it. That plane can do absolutely nothing. His reinforcements haven't arrived. If we're quick we'll be able to escape."

"Wonderful idea, captain," said Bergen. "Why don't we all go below and choke on chlorine fumes for another twelve hours?"

"Bergen, the engineers have almost solved the chlorine problem. And it wasn't that bad, not with the respirators."

There was a disapproving murmur among the crew. He turned to his chief engineer, Staudinger, who was taking a few minutes away from the fumes below, puffing dolefully on a cigarette, his eyes bleary with the exhaustion of eighteen straight hours of work on the battery block.

"Staudinger, how long?"

Staudinger shook his head slowly and flicked his cigarette into the ocean.

"It's worse than we first thought, captain. We've fixed most of the leaks, but there's at least a half dozen we haven't been able to find."

"You said less than two hours."

"I'm afraid it will be at least eight now, captain. And then we'll have to drain the bilge. That's another four."

Goerlitz gazed steadily at Staudinger.

"Are the electric engines operable?" he asked.

Staudinger shrugged and looked at the spot where they had dropped Ludendorff overboard.

"We can make one or two knots underwater for about eight hours."

Goerlitz turned to his crew.

"Did you hear that?" he said. "Did you hear what Staudinger just said? We can do it. We can really do it. That Hudson can do nothing to us. If we act now, we'll have a chance to escape."

"Captain," said Bergen, "we'd all sooner stay alive in a prison camp than die in a U-boat. The electric engines may be operable, but we're not going back down. I don't care how special this boat is. Those fumes almost killed us. We won't be able to do our jobs. There's five in sick bay already. We're not going back down. We're going to surrender."

Goerlitz kept his eyes focused on Bergen for several moments then looked at his crew. They looked so young to him. This was pointless, he thought. He didn't have

4

time to argue with them any longer. The Hudson's reinforcements would soon be here. He had to salvage what he could out of this.

"Bergen, I must destroy the code books. Don't try to stop me. I must destroy the manuals. Let's not give it all away. And I must signal the High Command to let them know we've been captured."

Bergen looked first at Heusinger, then at Neumann, who was the radio operator. A large wave slapped the side of the U-boat, sending a fine spray to the top of the conning tower, polishing the 3.7 centimetre flak gun with a slick coating of seawater.

"Neumann," Bergen finally said, "you go with him. Make sure he doesn't try anything." He gave Neumann the commander's gun. "And don't tell the High Command of our little disagreement with the captain." Bergen scratched his chin, thinking. "Tell them . . . tell them we were attacked by two British frigates the moment we surfaced, that we were boarded only after a valiant fight, and that we were finally overrun." Bergen turned his gaze to Goerlitz. "And I mean it, Neumann. If the captain tries anything, shoot him."

Neumann and Goerlitz descended the conning tower companionway through the air-lock into the control room, where a skeletal crew manned the U-boat. Of all the boats in the fleet, why did it have to be this one, the new special trans-Atlantic ocean-going Type IX C. God knows what secrets the British would learn from it. He took the code books, manuals and grid-coordinated maps from the drawers under the navigating table while Neumann held the gun to his head. Then he went down the bunk-lined passageway toward the engine room, got his duffel bag from his bunk, put the manuals, maps and code books inside, and slung the bag over his shoulder. He turned and looked at Neumann.

"I'm surprised at you, Neumann. Mutiny never turns

out well. That's something you should have learned by now. Why don't you give me the gun? Don't you see how easy it would be? Dive. Dive now. That Hudson can do nothing to us."

"It could strafe us, sir."

"Not if we dive. We can take a little more chlorine. If we dive now, by the time reinforcements get here we'll be halfway to Lorient. Now give me the gun. Give me the gun and I'll go kill Bergen."

Neumann gazed at Goerlitz for a moment, then raised the gun, pointed it with a steady strong arm at his chest, and shrugged, his face expressionless.

"I'm sorry, sir. Lieutenant Bergen is in charge of this vessel now. I must follow his orders. Please, could you stand over there, hands at your sides, while I send this signal to the High Command? Your death would be a waste at this point."

Using his left hand, Neumann put the head-set on, turned the dials to the proper frequency, and began tapping out the message to Lorient, keeping his eyes trained on Goerlitz. When he was finished, Neumann listened for several moments, then hung the head-set over the back of the chair.

"Well?" said Goerlitz.

Neumann shrugged.

"They've acknowledged," he said. He waved the gun in the direction of the conning tower. "Please, captain, could you climb the companionway now."

They climbed the companionway to the conning tower. The sea was growing rougher and pitched ceaselessly against the U-boat's starboard side, sending up a sticky spray, and the wind was picking up, bringing the storm clouds closer. The British Hudson continued its figure-eight pattern, its engines bellowing over the waves. Goerlitz looked at Bergen with cool contempt then went down to the edge of the catwalk and emptied the manuals, maps and code books out of his duffel bag into the ocean.

•

Around seven o'clock two Catalina seaplanes appeared in the sky. The Hudson, now low on fuel, headed east and disappeared into the clouds.

The Catalinas circled until nine that night when a British trawler, unarmed except for a gun on both the stern and bow, appeared out of the fog to the north plowing through the high foam-flecked waves. A civilian vessel, thought Goerlitz, a mere stick of a ship that couldn't have cost more than ninety thousand marks to make. The boat ran up alongside U-512 and the white lettering stencilled on the bow, Goerlitz saw, said *Purvess. Purvess*, he thought. What kind of name was that for a ship?

Because of rough seas the *Purvess* didn't come closer than fifty yards at first. It was dark now and the rain was growing heavy. Goerlitz saw movement aboard the *Purvess*. Officers gathered outside the bridge, several holding binoculars to their eyes. One raised a megaphone to his mouth.

"Do any of you know English?" boomed the man's voice across the waves.

"What's he saying, captain?" demanded Bergen. "And you'd better damn well tell the truth."

"He wants to know if any of us speaks English."

"Neumann, give Goerlitz the megaphone."

Neumann handed the megaphone to Goerlitz.

"Wave your hand like a good volunteer," said Bergen. "And don't try anything." The trawler's spotlight went on and scanned the submarine. "Because I really will kill you."

Goerlitz got up, took the megaphone, and lifted it to his mouth.

"I speak English," he called.

"The captain of your submarine is ordered to board

my ship immediately. Otherwise I will fire and sink you."

Goerlitz glanced at Bergen, who stared at the officers of the *Purvess* with complete incomprehension. All they had to do was man the 10.5 centimetre deck gun and the *Purvess* would be shot to pieces. A bunch of old English farts, he thought, scared out of their wits because they actually had a German U-boat.

"The sea is too rough," he called. "It is impossible."

"It's up to you to find a way," replied the *Purvess*, the voice echoing over the waves. "We'll try to draw closer. Your captain has five minutes to come aboard or else we fire."

The guns of the trawler were suddenly trained on U-512.

"Captain, what are they saying? And don't lie to me."

"They want me to go aboard."

"Then go aboard."

"I'd like to get a few of my things."

"They're not going to hold their fire all night. Neumann, you go with him."

Goerlitz went below, Neumann at his back again, and packed his razor and a few items of clothing into his duffel bag. He unscrewed his bottle of schnapps and, ignoring Neumann and the gun that was pointed at his head, took a large sip. What unfortunate fate had ever given him such a crew? He took the color-tinted photograph of Ute from under his pillow. Her blonde hair was braided in a bun at the back and now that he studied her, she seemed no more than a child. She belonged to another lifetime, when the war was still new, and there had been nothing but victory after victory, nothing but hope. He wondered if she had stayed in Munich, in the second-floor apartment on Liebigstrasse with the window-box of geraniums, or if she had moved to Berlin to live with her parents, as she said she might in her last letter. A lifetime away, he thought. He found his knife. It glinted in the dull oily light of the U-boat. He threw the knife into his duffel bag and then he and Neumann climbed topside.

The *Purvess* had drawn within twenty yards of U-512, a dark clumsy shape rolling with the roughening seas. Somewhere in the night sky above, the Catalina seaplanes circled and circled, and Goerlitz thought that the pilots must be puzzled, scared that it was some kind of trick, that at any moment U-512 would send up a wall of fire with the four 2 centimetre antiaircraft guns. Goerlitz turned to Bergen. The lieutenant's face gleamed a pale yellow in the *Purvess*'s spotlight.

"Captain," said Bergen, "you'll try and arrange the best possible terms for us."

Goerlitz didn't say anything. There was more movement aboard the *Purvess*. In the fitful glare of the bridge lights the captain of the trawler put the megaphone to his mouth.

"The five minutes are up. Either your captain comes aboard immediately or we open fire."

"What's he saying, captain?" asked Bergen.

"He says if I don't come aboard immediately he'll open fire."

"They shot over a line and the raft's down there, by the port saddletank."

"I see that."

"Captain," said Heusinger. "We're serious about throwing you overboard if you don't go willingly. There's no point in fighting any more. Get in the raft."

"Heusinger's right," said Bergen. "Get in the raft, captain. It's over."

"If I ever see you again, Bergen, I'll kill you."

"Captain, please, get in the raft."

He turned from his Number One and descended the companionway to the catwalk, loathing every step. The black rubber raft butted gently against the side of the submarine. Most of the crew had gone below to get some rest, now that the boat had begun to air out, but there were still a half dozen loitering on the catwalk, curious about what was going on. The ocean heaved and swelled all around the sleek form of the U-boat. His boat. His first command. Mutiny. He couldn't believe this. He tossed his duffel bag into the raft, slid down to the saddletank, and got into the small rubber dinghy. As the sailors aboard the *Purvess* began to drag him across the storm-tossed water, a gust of wind blew his white cap from his head.

•

Soon, through the efforts of the seamen aboard the *Purvess* and U-512, they had the *unterseeboot* in tow behind the trawler. The captain and first mate aboard the *Purvess* questioned Goerlitz, but as he gave them only his name, rank, and serial number, they finally gave up.

He sat in a chair on the bridge, tired but unable to sleep. The first mate held a Webley revolver trained at his chest. He was an older man, perhaps in his forties, and looked as if he weren't used to handling a gun. They were taking him to the only prisoner-of-war camp for German U-boat officers in England, Triggsdale Hall, where through the personal word of Admiral Karl Doenitz he knew his old crew, Commander Weiss, Lieutenant Frischauer, and Petty Officers Ballerstedt and Schla-brendorff were imprisoned.

As the hours passed, and the *Purvess* drew nearer to England, Goerlitz had a chance to sleep. In the hours he was awake, sitting in the chair on the bridge watching U-512 in tow behind them, he went over the events of the last forty-eight hours again and again, analyzing them, trying to figure out what went wrong just in case he should ever be in the same situation again.

It was well past noon the next day when the Irish coastline came into view. The last time he had been in the Irish Sea had been on the night U-93, his old boat, had gone down under the prow of the Polish corvette, *Krajenka*. He watched the crew members of U-512 walk around the catwalk.

At twelve o'clock they were joined by two British frigates and one American destroyer. How would Weiss have handled it, he wondered? Weiss would have shot Bergen even at the merest suspicion. Then again, Weiss had never had to deal with such an inexperienced crew. But would Weiss have used the trans-Atlantic boat for its trans-Atlantic purpose of sinking shipping up and down the American seaboard, or would he have taken the opportunity to destroy a twenty-four-thousand-ton tanker in mid-Atlantic, the way Goerlitz had? True, it had brought repeated depth charge attacks, chlorine fumes, and the death of Ludendorff. The crew had been shaken after that. If only they had all been real U-boat men, not green recruits. If only Bergen had been like U-93's Frischauer and not just a German trying to make the best of a bad situation. They would have been free long ago.

It was just after four when Liverpool came into view. They battled a swell past Liverpool, kept heading north, the weather disagreeable and moody. If only the fools would dive, even here in the Irish Sea, he thought. In this rough water no one would ever find them. Just dive. Break the hawsers tying her down, and dive. It would be so easy.

The *Purvess* and its escort shouldered U-512 eastward. As they got closer to shore, he saw, in the fading light of day, the east and west harbors of what couldn't be, had to be, was unmistakably Barrow-in-Furness. Were his eyes playing tricks on him? He knew Barrow-in-Furness well, at least as well as any U-boat officer could know it from the pre-war maps of the area the

Unterseewaffe had obtained around 1935. At that time it had been simply a merchant port of little significance. Now it was a major naval base, and had been long considered a prime target of the U-boat High Command. Goering had claimed his reconnaissance planes hadn't the range for Barrow-in-Furness. He needed them all for the Eastern Front. But the view among many naval officers was that Goering feared his vaunted Luftwaffe couldn't penetrate the thick air defenses around Barrow-in- Furness. Goering had always preferred excuses when confronted with the risk of failure. And so the *Unterseewaffe* had no accurate picture, and only the most unreliable information about Barrow-in-Furness. For the moment he forgot about U-512 and the dismal events of the last forty-eight hours. The trawler captain didn't understand the grave mistake he was making, allowing him to stay above. Goerlitz couldn't believe his luck. He was being given a guided tour of one of Britain's premier naval bases. The tips of both east and west harbors floated on a misty sea and looked alive through the fog and rain. Destroyers, frigates, and corvettes lay at anchor. There was a lot of merchant shipping. He knew Barrow-in-Furness as well as any U-boat captain, which wasn't much, but now he would gain a first-hand tactical knowledge. There was a large staging area for convoys to the northwest. They approached the east harbor in a series of zig-zags, around the mines and submarine nets. Goerlitz memorized everything he saw — a series of small submarine pens, a road, a hill leading up to a sheep pasture, a slate fence, and another road beyond the fence. He glanced back at U-512, then kept looking around until she was dragged into port. They might have U-512, at least for now, but he had something that in the long run would be far more valuable.

Chapter 2

Major Raymond Hatley, commandant of the officers'
prisoner-of-war camp at Triggsdale Hall, reclined on his
sofa at home the night they marched Goerlitz ashore,
smoking a Wild Woodbine and drinking the tidy Glen
Orley his wife, Marjorie, had fixed for him. On the radio
they played a comforting rendition of *I'll Be Around*. The
smell of fast-fry steaks and eggs — their weekly treat —
wafted from the kitchen. With a whimsical almost
dreamy movement, he scratched the back of his head and
smiled. It was that night again. The night he spent alone
with his wife, the blinds shut, and the radio playing softly, the night he didn't have to worry about the camp. He
drained his glass, took the bottle from the coffee table,
and poured another. Bing Crosby records littered the
floor — Marjorie was a great fan — and the newspaper
lay draped over the wingback chair.

She came in with the steaks and eggs. At thirty-five
she was eight years younger than he was. Her hair had
been freshly done, and though it was still a little stiff, it

nevertheless made her look attractive. She put the plates on the table and sat next to him. She curled up, lifting her knees, exposing a tantalizing inch or two of thigh, and put her slender arms around his neck.

"So, Marjorie," he said, "here we are again. You know, when I'm here with you like this the whole world seems so far away. It's a damn shame I have to spend so much time at the camp."

"Oh, now, Ray, you know you're needed there. Who else would be able to run Triggsdale Hall as well as you?"

"Carberry's a competent assistant. They could at least give me two nights off a week." He smiled. "I'm a married man now, aren't I?"

She stroked the side of his head with the back of her fingers.

"We all have to do our bit, don't we?" she said. "We have to be conscientious in whatever small way we can if we're going to beat the Germans. An enemy's an enemy."

Hatley shrugged and cut into his limp little piece of war-ration steak.

"Actually, they're not a bad lot. You have to be around them for a while before you see that."

They were halfway through their meal when the telephone rang. It was a man by the name of Gerald Laurie, an inspector from the Naval Intelligence Department calling from London. As Hatley listened to what Laurie had to say, his stomach slowly went sour from the annoyance of it all. There was a new prisoner, Laurie said. A U-boat commander. And a U-boat as well, such as they had never seen before, captured two-hundred-and-fifty miles off the southeast tip of Iceland. The commander of this new U-boat, *Korvettenleutnant* Hermann Paul Goerlitz, would be brought to Triggsdale Hall. His crew had mutinied on him. This astonished Hatley. He knew what U-boat men were like. They were disciplined.

They would not mutiny, and he felt his interest growing. Laurie told Hatley to ask Goerlitz about the mutiny. Goerlitz had been a crew member aboard Georg Weiss's U-93. The prisoner would be there in two hours. Laurie himself would come to Liverpool tomorrow and would be in Barrow-in-Furness by the day following. Oh, damn and rot, thought Major Hatley, hanging up. This war did make life inconvenient at times. His only night off. Couldn't the bloody navy blokes in London understand that. He put the receiver back on the cradle.

"Bad news?" said Marjorie, leaning forward.

"I'm afraid I'm going to have to go to the camp. We've got a new prisoner. Rather an important one. They've got his U-boat. Brand new. Never seen the likes of it before. I'd like to have Carberry attend to it, darling, but I really feel as if it's a matter I should see to myself."

"Oh, darling, you know Carberry doesn't have the expertise you do. He wouldn't know what questions to ask. Heavens, he doesn't even speak German."

Hatley looked at his watch.

"He's not due for another two hours."

They looked at each other, each knowing what the other was thinking.

"How bad is the road?" she asked, her voice taking on a conspiratorial tone.

Hatley shrugged.

"It's no hell, what with all this rain."

They gazed at each other steadily.

"It could take me two hours to get there," he said. He was no match for the longing he saw in her wide blue eyes. "Or maybe even two-and-a-half."

"You could always say you had trouble getting in because of the road," she said, and they both knew they had used this excuse several times before.

"That's true." He was caving in, as he always did. "And the blokes from Barrow are bound to be late with him anyway. They always bloody are."

"That's true," she said.

And that was all it took. The steak and eggs were forgotten, So were the drinks. She put her arms around his neck again and kissed his earlobe. Even after three years of marriage she was as affectionate as ever. He considered her his mid-life miracle. He never thought it possible that anybody as attractive as Marjorie could love him quite so much, nor after forty-three years of bachelorhood that he could actually be a married man. Dinner could wait. The camp could wait. The whole damn war could wait. He turned and kissed her on the lips, then raised his hand to her breasts. The rain beat outside their Barrow-in-Furness flat, and over the rain they could hear the sound of the surf. On the radio, ever so softly, the announcer forecast tomorrow's weather.

She reached down and loosened his belt, unbuckling it. She slipped her hand beneath the waistband of his boxer shorts, her fingers feeling like velvet. She was sure of herself, knew exactly what she was doing, and wasn't shy about it. Did it naturally and with a great deal of skill. She finally hiked her skirt above her hips. On these nights she did without the encumbrance of underwear, wore only a garter belt and stockings. She sat astride him on the couch. She was as good a lover as she was a dancer, he thought. The way she moved was electric, the subtle control of her hips and pelvis hypnotizing. As her rhythm increased he began to smile uncontrollably, showing the space between his front teeth he never liked to show. She was his mid-life miracle, the woman who had finally given some meaning to his existence, and he loved her, and had assured her that he would make every effort to stop looking at the other women when they went to the pub, and to stop boozing so much.

•

Much to his consternation, when Hatley got to Triggsdale Hall, deep in the misty vales of England's Lake District, they were indeed late with the prisoner. As he sat in the green leather club chair by the window in his office waiting, his legs crossed, a cigarette burning lazily in the marble ashtray beside him, he poured a long satisfying two fingers from his special bottle of Glen Orley, and looked out beyond the yard where the moon, showing itself for the first time after a week of bleak weather, shone brilliantly on the pasture-covered hills to the east. Nothing really to do, he thought. He looked at his watch. 7:30. Out in the yard, a strong wind rippled all the mud puddles and shook the branches of the oak trees. He heard a truck crossing the parking lot, and leaning forward in his chair, saw the truck's painted-over headlights. He screwed the lid on his bottle of scotch and walked to the mirror. Nose not too red and eyes not too glazed. Now if only he could suppress the persistent urge to hiccup. His cheeks were still flushed from his lovemaking with Marjorie. He popped a mint into his mouth, stood to attention, and put his hands crisply behind his back. You're in fine form, Ray. There's no need to worry. Tell him the rules, show him the duties, and then dismiss him. He's just another Jerry commander.

He heard boots thumping up the corridor as the guards brought the new prisoner to his office. Major Hatley cleared his throat, scratched his mustache, and smiled in the aloof way he used when dealing with prisoners.

"Here he is, major."

"Thank you, Patterson. At ease. You and the private stand by the door while I talk to our new friend."

"Yes, sir."

The corporal and the private walked to the door.

Well, here goes, thought Hatley. One of the reasons he had this job in the first place was because he spoke German.

"Ich glaube dass ich mit Korvettenleutnant Hermann Paul Goerlitz spreche?"

"I would sooner you speak English, major, than endure your crippled pronunciation."

Major Hatley gazed at Goerlitz for a moment. He had the half-crazed look they all had when they were just dragged in from battle. Goerlitz was filthy. He had a broad and strong-boned face and just the slightest hint of a receding hairline, looked around thirty-five. Hatley didn't like the expression on Goerlitz's face. Usually when they came here they were resigned, and some were even thankful, but he could see that Goerlitz was anything but thankful.

"I understand it was mutiny, captain."

"It was."

"I'm suppose to ask you about that."

"There's nothing I have to say, major. Nothing whatsoever."

Major Hatley frowned. He just wanted to go back home to his lovely Marjorie.

"What about this battery problem? There was a battery problem, wasn't there?"

"Hermann Paul Goerlitz, *Korvettenleutnant*, 032619."

"I see, captain. Well, as you wish. I haven't got the patience for you right now. Mind you, if you cooperate, you'll get better treatment. Now, then, here is a list of camp rules in German, and this is a schedule of camp duties. I appreciate your right to give me only your name, rank, and serial number, but I sincerely urge you not to break any of these rules or I will have to be very firm with you. If you accept your lot gracefully and make the best of the situation, then we'll get along just fine."

Major Hatley looked at the German U-boat commander. Goerlitz gazed straight ahead, stiff to attention. His
face looked like hardened clay.

"Is that understood, captain?"

Goerlitz didn't answer. He kept looking straight
ahead.

"You might as well try and be polite, Captain
Goerlitz. Here in England we find it helps lubricate
things. And if it's any consolation, you have my sympathy. It must have been terribly unpleasant having your
own chaps turn on you like that. I can hardly imagine
how it could have happened. I thought U-boat men were
known for their discipline."

"I don't want your sympathy, major."

"That's not the right attitude, captain. You'll find my
sympathy is a very good thing to have. Ask any of the
other German officers in my camp."

Major Hatley rubbed his mustache. His nose felt
numb from too much scotch.

"Now, I suggest you read the rules carefully. Reveille at
0600 hours and lights out by 2100 hours. Rotational details.
We find that works best. We can't have the same men
cleaning the latrines all the time. Cigarettes are allowed
only in certain areas. Other areas are completely off limits.
And those sheds to the west are strictly out-of-bounds.
And I do mean that, captain. Any prisoner caught within
fifty yards will be shot. Is that understood, Goerlitz?"

Goerlitz remained silent.

"Very well, captain. We'll give you six months. Then
you might talk. Are there any questions? I don't think
there should be. The rules are very precise. You're in
Building C. That's just down the way by the mess hall.
That's Captain Weiss's building. I understand he was
your old commander."

Goerlitz didn't reply. The major looked away from
Goerlitz's stony face. Perhaps he hadn't made it clear

enough to the German that there were benefits to cooperation.

"Good chap, Weiss," said Hatley. "He's cooperative. We appreciate that. And we like to show our appreciation." He paused. "My censors passed a letter only this morning that his wife, Helga, I think, was going in for an operation. Something to do with the intestine. I told him myself. Said I'd personally let him know when word arrives on how it turned out. He was most grateful."

Goerlitz looked at Hatley, his eyes showing cynical amusement.

The major felt his altruistic grin disappear, and a weary frown came to his face. Goerlitz was beginning to annoy him.

"Corporal Patterson, take the captain to Records and have him photographed and fingerprinted. Then take him to the shower-house and give him a shave and a haircut. And for God's sake, get that grease off his face. He looks like an Ethiopian." He gave Goerlitz a contemptuous look, an expression he had practiced in the mirror at home, and sighed, as if he were indifferent to Goerlitz. "Dismissed, captain."

•

Commander Weiss sat on the window sill of Building C, one foot pressed firmly against the floor, the other dangling over the ledge, his chin resting in his large hand while he gazed out at the yard. Triggsdale Hall, the manor of the late Lord Selby, glowed a sombre shade of brick red in the dull light of the half moon, and its slate shingle roof was slick and satiny after a day of rain. On the table beside him lay a copy of the morning edition of the London *Times*, one Ballerstedt had stolen from a prison guard. He had read the story several times. Goerlitz had surrendered U-512, a fully operational ocean-going Type IX U-boat, without a fight.

Weiss stood up, took the newspaper in his hand, and read the story once again. The basic information had been radioed three days ago from the eastern Atlantic by the capturing aircraft and had been printed only today. He allowed himself a smile, marveling at the speed with which Doenitz had once again implemented the Helga project. He had acted pleased at Hatley's misplaced compassion concerning Helga in order to stifle any suspicion at the outset. There had been four U-boats in the Irish Sea that night, with four candidates, Goerlitz among them. And four commanders — only one would be picked — waiting for their specified code words. He had been picked. The name Helga had come over the radio. And now here it was again, too coincidental to ignore. At last he was being given another chance.

He turned to page six of the newspaper. There was a column about what the capture of U-512 might possibly mean to the British. But he didn't bother to read it a second time. He kept thinking of Goerlitz. Goerlitz had been an outstanding U-boat man when he had been the chief torpedo officer aboard U-93, had as much nerve, if not considerably more, as much skill, strength, and ingenuity as any of the rest of them. When U-93 had finally been rammed by the Polish corvette, *Krajenka*, and split in half, and they all had to abandon ship in a sea of burning oil, Goerlitz, rather than allowing himself to be taken prisoner, as all the rest of them had in that desperate hour, breast-stroked away, avoiding the patches of burning water, to a large broken crate.

Weiss tossed the newspaper down and looked out the window at Triggsdale Hall again, more particularly, Hatley's office. Goerlitz was in that office right now listening to Hatley's traditional welcoming speech. He had caught a brief glimpse of Goerlitz as he had emerged from the truck and mounted the broad slate steps of Triggsdale Hall.

Goerlitz had joined the U-boat arm against his father's wishes. His father had tried to get his son a safe job as a cryptographer with Canaris's *Abwehr*. He had been so promising. Doenitz had even said so in that final meeting before the last patrol of U-93, when Doenitz and Weiss had discussed the Helga project, as it was code-named, in total secrecy. Admiral Karl Doenitz, commander of the U-boat arm, had been most impressed by his young chief torpedo officer. Now it would seem Goerlitz was his choice, and the presence of the captured commander could be the only explanation for Doenitz to decide, after all this time, to activate the dormant Helga project. Now it was up to Weiss to make it work. Even if it meant some unexpected discomfort to Goerlitz.

It was strictly forbidden, especially in the *Unterseewaffe*, to surrender a fully operational vessel to the enemy. And Goerlitz would have a debt to pay. He tapped his fingers irritably against the window sill. He thought of the possible opportunities before him, and of the things he would need.

There was going to be a soccer match between the Triggsdale Hall football team and the team from the naval base in Barrow-in-Furness, and something might possibly be done there. And the prison inspectors were coming the day afterward and something might possibly be done there. Weiss began to formulate his plan, a way to cow Goerlitz into complete obedience and to fulfil the difficult mission he and Doenitz had imagined over a bottle of schnapps in the map room at Lorient more than three years ago.

Chapter 3

Inspector Gerald Laurie of the Naval Intelligence Department had just finished his telephone conversation with Major Raymond Hatley when his assistant, Donald Taylor, came into his office carrying the evening edition of the London *Times* under his arm.

"Had a chance to read the paper today?" asked Taylor.

"You know I've been much too busy, Don."

"I think you should take a look at this," said Taylor, dropping the paper on Laurie's desk. "You're not going to like it."

Laurie put on his glasses and read the story Taylor had circled in pencil. It recounted the surrender and capture of U-512, described the boat as ten times more technically advanced as anything they had in the British Fleet, and told how experts would be arriving all this week in Barrow-in-Furness to study and learn its secrets. It described the capture as a major victory for the Royal Navy. The story was brief, to the point, and from a security standpoint, mishandled so badly that Laurie couldn't believe the Admiralty had allowed it to be printed. Were they really so incompetent? He looked up at Taylor with wide mystified eyes.

"Don't they realize the Germans are going to read this?" he asked. "We might as well send them a detailed map. Don't the stupid bastards ever think of these things?"

Taylor shrugged. "Apparently not."

Laurie put his glasses back in their case and gazed across the room where his coat and hat hung on a coat-tree.

"I suppose I'm going to have to go up and see Carson about it. We certainly can't have any more of it. Do you know if he's still in?"

"I believe his secretary said he would be working late tonight."

"Good. I'll see you at the airfield in the morning, then, Don."

After Taylor had gone, Laurie climbed the stairs, the newspaper under his arm, to the fifth floor. His blind eye was bothering him tonight, as it did whenever he was over-worked and over-tired, and his stomach ulcer was making him irritable. It would be a long day yet. He still had to visit Heather in the hospital, and then he would have to spend some time with his four-year-old son, Ted, before he finally retired for the evening. He had to be up early to catch his plane to Liverpool.

Dorothy, Carson's secretary, was surprised to see him.

"Thought you would have gone home ages ago, sir," she said.

"We're lucky if any of us gets home much before nine these days. I understand Leo's still here. Do you mind if I sneak a few minutes with him? It's rather urgent."

Five minutes later he stood in front of Carson's desk watching the grand old man of Naval Intelligence read

24

the story in the newspaper. Carson didn't seem in the least bit surprised. He looked up over the rims of his bifocals.

"Yes, well, I meant to tell you about that, Gerald. I know we issued a gag order, but the boys in the Admiralty thought it might be a good idea to release it."

"In heaven's name, why? Don't they understand the importance of this submarine? Don't they realize that all information about it should be strictly classified? Especially its location, Leo, especially its bloody location."

"I tried to tell them that. But they thought it would be good for public morale. It's not every day we capture a fully operational U-boat, especially one as technically advanced as U-512. The Admiralty thought they'd thumb their nose at the Germans publicly. Good for propaganda."

"It's not good for propaganda. If it's good for anything, it's good for Hermann Goering. He'll mount a strike by the end of the week."

"Nonsense, Gerald. Goering's got the stomach for a lot of things, God knows, but I don't think he has the stomach for Barrow."

"You and I both know that's rubbish, Leo."

Carson rubbed his chin between his thumb and forefinger. He leaned forward and folded his hands on his desk.

"Now, look, Gerald, there are some things the Admiralty decides to orchestrate every now and again, and I'm afraid this is one of them."

"I thought you gave me absolute authority over the U-512 investigation."

"I did. And you still have it. Heavens, you're our top inspector. Of course you have absolute authority. Only we can't fight the boys in the Admiralty, can we, because they have absolute authority over us. And I think they've made the right decision in this particular circumstance. I think it's good for morale, don't you? It's a definite concrete victory that we can show the public. And you have to admit, the likelihood of a strike by the Luftwaffe is very remote."

"That's not the way I see it," said Laurie. "That they should write anything at all about Barrow-in-Furness shows a sorry and unjustified lack of prudence. You can be sure the Germans know how important that base has become to us over the last eighteen months. It's our main receiving point in the Midlands for both food and weapons. This is just sending them an engraved invitation."

Carson shrugged and leaned back in his chair.

"For the record I've already lodged a formal complaint with the Admiralty expressing our concerns. I don't know what else I can do."

Laurie thought for a moment.

"Well, let's try and minimize the damage, then, shall we?" he said, trying to keep his irritability under control. "I want our carpenters at the site first thing in the morning. They've got to build an upper works over U-512. Tell them to get some netting. I want that boat to look like a fishing trawler from the air, and I want it done by the end of the week."

•

When he left Naval Intelligence for the night Laurie drove up Whitehall in his second-hand Hillman and veered left past Trafalgar Square under the Admiralty Arch then down The Mall toward Buckingham Palace. How he hated this beastly little car. But Heather had totalled the Bentley two months ago, drove right into the back of a parked lorry, and was now in St. Mary's Hospital with a broken leg and broken arm. She still wouldn't admit to attempted suicide, said it was just an accident, but Laurie knew better. There had been two other times, one with pills and the other with the gas stove. And yet the accident, strangely enough, seemed to have cleared her mental fog, lifted enough of her years-long cloud of depression to begin to reveal the woman he had once known. Was it possible that by crumpling the front end of his Bentley, a car he had doted on, she had seen that life was really worth living after all, that she had a husband who loved her and that she had son who loved her?

He turned north past Hyde Park, his painted-over headlights casting weak beams on the pavement before him. He smiled. Whatever the explanation, for the first time in years he could honestly say that he had a happy marriage, and that the future looked bright. There had been enough bloody disappointments in his life. His grandfather had been a navy man, his father and uncle had been navy men, it was the only thing Laurie had ever wanted in his life, but when he applied for active service, hoping that some day he would be in command of his own ship, they turned him down. Can't take you, mate. You're blind in one eye. Try rear echelon. Not much action, but they're always looking for people. And so he had joined Naval Intelligence, and had worked his way up to Chief Technical Inspector.

He drove along Knightsbridge. The streets were dim. There was a blackout in effect. Well, he had spent his time in the wilderness, knew a thing or two about life, and now they listened to him, sometimes, now that he had a little clout. Ahead he saw St. Mary's Hospital looming through the wet plane trees.

He turned into the hospital's small parking lot and found a spot near the admitting entrance. One thing about the Hillman, you could fit it in anywhere. With all the window shades pulled the hospital had a dismal aspect at this time of night. But that didn't stop his spirits from lifting. He was here to visit Heather, a Heather he hoped he would never have to take to Dr. Unsworth again. Whatever had been wrong — a chemical imbalance of the mind brought on by severe stress, Dr. Unsworth had called it — seemed to be a thing of the past.

He found her reading the latest novel by J.B. Priestley when he entered her room. That was a good sign. She never read books and for the last three years hadn't had the concentration to read more than a sentence or two of the newspaper. A great smile came to her face.

"Gerry," she exclaimed.

"Hello, darling," he said. He leaned over and gave her a kiss. "And how are you getting along?"

She put her book down and brushed her hand through her light auburn hair.

"The nurse took me out in the wheelchair around the grounds today. The sunshine this morning was ever so beautiful."

"Well, I'm glad you got some fresh air. This place smells like rubbing alcohol too much of the time. Here. I brought you something." He took an orange out of his pocket. "Westmoreland brought a dozen to the office this morning and passed them around. Says he knows a grocer over in Camden Town who sells them under the counter, no coupons needed."

She took the orange in her good hand and looked at it.

"It's been a long time since I've seen one of these," she said. "All we get around here is apple sauce. Have you made the arrangements with Mrs. Moss for tomorrow?" she asked.

"Yes. She says Teddy can stay as long as need be. She's a dear old girl, isn't she?"

"She's absolutely wonderful. Have they given you any idea when you'll be back?"

"We really don't know. It's a very complicated piece of machinery. It could take a week, it could take two. It might even be as long as a month."

She looked away, disappointed by this news.

"I don't know whether I can do without you that long, Gerry," she said, in a quiet but steady voice.

He took her chin in his hand and kissed her on the lips.

"You'll do just fine. You wait and see. They'll look after you well here. And I'll be back just as soon as I can."

•

It was well past eight when he picked up Ted at Mrs. Moss's. His son sat in the seat next to him as they drove in the Hillman to their small house in Golders Green. Laurie was happy. He had complete authority over U-512, or at least as complete as the Admiralty would ever allow, and that was enough.

"Will I be able to see mommy tomorrow?" asked Ted.

Laurie nodded.

"I've arranged with Mrs. Moss to take you to the hospital tomorrow afternoon. You won't be lonely staying with Mrs. Moss for a while, will you, Ted?"

"Oh, no, not at all, daddy. I like Mrs. Moss."

"There's a good lad."

They had a little bit of hot milk together when they got home, then he settled Teddy into bed and went to his den. The walls were adorned with nautical instruments. There was a glass cabinet filled with the medals his grandfather and father had earned during the Great War — his grandfather had medals going back to the Boer War — and there was a framed photograph hanging above his roll-top desk of himself, Taylor, and West-moreland standing in front of a captured German E-boat. He gazed at the photograph for a moment. He must have been tired that day. His left eye was off center.

Now it was time to forget, he thought. He poured a

glass of port from the decanter he kept on the table, put his glasses on, and looked at the volumes of naval books he kept in his bookcase, finally choosing one by Admiral John Graydon Puddicombe, Retired. Now it was time to forget the disappointments of his career, how crushingly nerve-wracking it had been managing Heather for the last three years, and how exhausting it had been raising a little boy single-handedly. It was time to imagine, time to pretend, time to visualize just what might have been if he hadn't been born with one blind eye. He sat down and began leafing through the book, stopping a few moments at the engravings he particularly liked, reading the stories he had read so often before. If only, he thought. Those were the two biggest words in his life. If only he could have been there, not stuck behind a desk at the NID, but in battle, commanding the action, such as always had been his dream, from the bridge of a magnificent battleship.

Chapter 4

The uniform they gave Goerlitz was too big and hung from his shoulders. As Patterson escorted him across the yard to Building C, Goerlitz kept his eyes to the ground. A cold September wind blew from the north. In his duffel bag he carried what few possessions they hadn't taken away from him. His knife, of course, was gone. Patterson climbed the wood steps of Building C and opened the door. Goerlitz mounted the steps slowly.

Inside, Commander Weiss, Lieutenant Frischauer, and Petty Officers Ballerstedt and Schlabrendorff of U-93 waited for him. Though Commander Weiss was only thirty-seven he looked closer to fifty, his forehead deeply scored by wrinkles and his close-shaven hair starting to turn grey. Frischauer still had the same sunken cheeks and deep-set eyes, though he looked much older as well. Ballerstedt still reminded him of the sad clowns at the circus in Munich, and Schlabrendorff was as tall and skinny as ever. As Patterson closed the door, Commander Weiss's eyes burned through Goerlitz. Goerlitz tried to hold the commander's gaze but he finally looked to the floor.

"It is customary for me," said Weiss, "as ranking officer and moral leader of this camp to welcome our unfortunate comrades who have been taken in battle. Eyes front, Goerlitz, and stand to attention."

"Yes, captain."

"Step forward."

Goerlitz walked forward, leaving his duffel bag at the door, until he was within a yard of his old commander. He kept his eyes front, as he had been ordered. The commander's lips bunched, his cheek muscles tensed, he took a deep breath, and spit as hard as he could into Goerlitz's face.

Goerlitz closed his eyes but opened them quickly and looked ahead of him while the commander's spit dripped around his nose.

"That is the welcome I give you, Captain Goerlitz."

Goerlitz looked at his former fellow crew members. His gaze finally rested on Ballerstedt. He was a short man with large round glasses and had a smallness and agility that were well suited to submarine life. Aboard U-93, Ballerstedt, the armaments and explosives officer, had been his closest friend. But Ballerstedt's eyes were neutral. Goerlitz brought his face forward and looked at Commander Weiss. What could he have expected? In their view, he had committed a crime.

"Permission to wipe my face, captain."

"Permission granted."

Goerlitz pulled a rag from his pocket and wiped his face.

"We know all about it, Goerlitz. All officers of the *Unterseewaffe* hold you in universal contempt. We shall conduct an inquiry, Goerlitz, in fact more trial than inquiry." Weiss handed him an English newspaper. "Read the article. I imagine you read English better than any of us."

Goerlitz read the article quickly. It recounted the mutiny aboard and the capture of U-512.

"Turn to page six. There's commentary."

On page six the editorial suggested the capture of a fully operational Type IX U-boat, undamaged except for a number of minor battery fractures after a depth-charge attack, was the greatest naval intelligence coup of the war.

"They think it might be the turning point," said Ballerstedt.

"Before we start, Goerlitz," said Weiss, "I just want you to understand one thing. I personally never, absolutely never, would have surrendered as you did. The very fact you're alive proves you're guilty. I think suicide is eminently preferable to the surrender of an operational U-boat, especially one as technically advanced as U-512. As prisoners-of-war we have only a limited means of implementing punishment, but I'll tell you one thing, Goerlitz, we'll make a special effort with you. I'm surprised at you, Goerlitz. In fact we're all surprised. Of all people, we should have least expected this from you. Do you have anything to say?"

Goerlitz looked at his old crew, remembering all the horrors they had lived through, then turned back to Weiss.

"I never wanted to surrender. I was willing to fight."

"We're sure you were, Goerlitz," said Lieutenant Frischauer. "But you know as well as any of us that mutiny's not an excuse. No excuse, Goerlitz. You're directly culpable for the surrender of U-512. Why didn't you scuttle? Why couldn't you stop the rebellion with your firearms?"

"I think in the present circumstances those questions are hypothetical, Frischauer. It's an established fact. My crew mutinied. The boat was surrendered. And now I am standing here before you."

Weiss ran his large hand over his bristly grey hair. His dull, purple lips crinkled.

"And you have nothing to say in your defense, commander?" he asked.

"I'm not going to sacrifice my dignity by defending what I consider an undefendable position, sir. I understand the gravity of my crime. However, I feel it my duty to inform you that the training period for U-boat crews has been reduced from six to two months by a direct order from the Fuhrer."

Weiss's lips tightened and his eyes narrowed. He looked at his crew members, who had shed their impassive faces and now showed either alarm or disbelief.

"Two months?" said Weiss. "How does the Fuhrer expect a crew to man a U-boat in a combat situation after only two months of training? Was it made clear to him just what the implications of such a drastic measure would mean? I find this entirely incomprehensible, Goerlitz."

"I believe Doenitz conferred with the Fuhrer at Berchtesgaden two days prior to the release of the order. Unfortunately he was unable to convince the Fuhrer just how foolhardy and potentially disastrous the order would be. Be that as it may, the boat was under my command and I was responsible, even with an undertrained crew, and I shall accept whatever punishment you decide is appropriate."

He examined Weiss closely. There was something going on behind those glassy eyes, a calculating and sly appraisal such as he had seen so often during those tense moments of combat aboard U-93. There was a conspiratorial undercurrent to this meeting, he could feel it. Weiss shoved his chair aside and walked to the window where Triggsdale Hall could be seen looming beyond the mist rolling up from the late Lord Selby's trout pond. He turned and stared at Goerlitz. Goerlitz tried to decipher his old commander's expression but it was unreadable. What was Weiss thinking?

"Very well, captain," said Weiss. "We accept the situation as you have described it, and that it was a situation for which you were not entirely responsible. But you couldn't have forgotten the code of the Kriegsmarine. We never, never surrender any vessel to enemy forces. Not even in the case of mutiny. You must have realized the surrender of U-512 would reveal countless technological secrets to the enemy. And you must have understood the surrender of your vessel would mean the deaths of countless German seamen."

"Yes, commander. I have nothing to say in my defense. Do you understand? Nothing. I will neither plead nor make excuses. I hold myself responsible, and I fully expect, when the war is over and we return to Germany, to pay for the consequences of my mistake."

Commander Weiss walked to the window, gazed at Triggsdale Hall, and began tapping his fingers against the sill, just as he had tapped them against the navigating table in the control room of U-93. Goerlitz again got the feeling there was something going on, that Weiss's censure was half-contrived, that somewhere behind his unexpressive eyes there was a hidden motive. Whether the other crew members got this feeling, he wasn't sure. Weiss turned around and looked at Goerlitz. Weiss was a man to be admired, and certainly a man to be feared. His old commander walked to his chair, put his left foot on it, leaned forward, and crossed his arms over his knee, his long-fingered hands dangling on either side.

"Very well, captain," said Weiss, focusing his cold grey eyes on Goerlitz. "I'm glad you appreciate the magnitude of your crime. It's what I would have expected from one of my crew." Weiss glanced at Ballerstedt, then Frischauer, his former Number One, stood up, put his hands behind his back, and squared his shoulders. "You will live in complete isolation," said Weiss. "You will take meals alone at the far end of the mess hall. You will be excluded from the life of the camp. No one will speak to you. From this moment on, Goerlitz, you don't exist as far as we're concerned. When Germany invades England, we will turn you over to the occupation forces and recommend a sentence of execution."

•

That night, while the occupants of Building C fell asleep, Goerlitz remained awake in his bunk thinking. His punishment in this camp didn't bother him, nor did the sentence of execution. What bothered him was that he had lost the respect of his former crew, especially Commander Weiss. He sat up and looked across the row of beds toward the window. Weiss lay in the second bed to the left. Ballerstedt lay next to him. Who would have thought that he would have ever seen them again, especially here in Triggsdale Hall, where he himself should have come after they had been rammed by the *Krajenka*.

He remembered that night, when Weiss had mysteriously changed course for the Irish Sea, ignoring the High Command's order to wolfpack with Cremer's U-333 off the coast of Morocco to attack an incoming convoy. Even then the Irish Sea had been dangerous, yet the captain had behaved in his usual calm way. Nor did any of them doubt his decision to get as close to shore as possible. They all knew their commander had a reason. He always did.

He felt a strong attachment to these men, different than he felt toward Ute and his father. A bond that had been built in the face of death, with men who knew what despair and hopelessness were, and who knew sudden salvation. The things they had gone through.

36

But now U-93 was on the bottom, and these men were in an English prisoner-of-war camp, and despite all the times they had saved one another's lives, had consoled and humored each other through the long dismal stretches of boredom, they no longer respected him. And that bothered him.

He swung his feet quietly out of bed and stood up. In some small way it was a pleasure to stand on a dry floor. He walked over to Ballerstedt's bed and gazed down at his old friend. They were the same age. Thirty-two. Ballerstedt lay with his head turned to one side, breathing softly, his black wool cap pulled over his curly hair. He couldn't have been more than five-foot-three and, with his beakish nose, reminded Goerlitz of Napoleon. And now they were no longer friends.

Through the course of the next day Goerlitz was ignored. Some of them looked at him out of curiosity, the way people do when they see a legless man pushing himself on a cart, but none of them talked to him.

At the mess hall that night he sat at the far end, as he had been instructed, and looked at the others, as a caged animal in a zoo might look at visitors. Then, as if pre-arranged, two officers of the *Kriegsmarine* got up from their table with their trays, approached the end of the hall, and sat next to him without saying a word. His muscles hardened. He glanced at Commander Weiss, who sat at the front of the mess hall. Weiss pretended not to see. The blond man, whose hair was combed back in a reflective shell, ate with his mouth open, and looked as if he knew some joke no one else knew. He glanced at Goerlitz and smiled, still chewing. Goerlitz was puzzled. The smile appeared half genuine.

"I'm Meissner," said the man.

"My name is Goerlitz," he replied, his muscles still hard, waiting for the confrontation he knew was inevitably going to come.

The man nodded. "You're an asshole."

Meissner continued to eat, sawing into his whitefish patty, dabbing it with a scoop of mashed potatoes. It was something new for Goerlitz to be told he was an asshole by a petty officer. He looked at Weiss, who continued to eat, then at Ballerstedt, Frischauer, and Schlabrendorff. What was going on? Whatever it was he didn't want any part of it. He was going to act like a decent sailor. He lifted his tray and stood up. Meissner grabbed him by the arm and pulled him back to his chair.

"Where do you think you're going, asshole?"

"Some place where the smell isn't so bad, asshole."

Meissner let go of Goerlitz, continued to eat, then glanced at the black-haired *Kriegsmarine* sailor across the table. Goerlitz rose once again. He could accept his punishment but he wouldn't be taunted. Meissner again grabbed Goerlitz's arm and tried to force Goerlitz back into his chair.

"Let go."

When Goerlitz tried to pull his arm away, Meissner smashed Goerlitz's tray upwards, flinging the dinner into his face.

With a sweep of his arm Goerlitz dumped the petty officer's dinner into Meissner's lap. Meissner looked down at his prison uniform, now wet with coffee and water, his eyes slowly widening as anger reddened his face. Then he looked at the black-haired man sitting across the table and nodded. The black-haired man rose suddenly, upsetting his chair, and swung out with his fist, punching Goerlitz in the side of the head. Goerlitz stumbled, stunned, and looked around.

All the others pretended not to see, went on eating their dinners as if nothing had happened. Meissner stood up and put his hand on his hips, grinning, baiting Goerlitz. All his anger came out and Goerlitz swung at the man, punched him in the left eye, then broke his lip with a firm jab to the mouth. Meissner lurched backward, falling over his chair, his legs splaying as he toppled to the floor. Petty officers didn't do this to commanders, thought Goerlitz. The black-haired man, picking up his chair, smashed it over Goerlitz's back. It was a strong oak chair and thudded mercilessly against his spine. He went down with a grunt as the air whooshed out of his lungs. Meissner took the opportunity to kick Goerlitz in the stomach several times. He lay there gasping for breath as the camp guards marched down the aisle with their pistols drawn and their clubs ready.

"All right, all right, break it up," shouted the British sergeant, pulling Meissner away. "Break it up." The sergeant turned to one of the guards. "Wish I knew how to speak Jerry. I'd tell them where to go awfully bloody fast."

•

The camp guards took the three men to the detention block and put them in separate cells. Goerlitz sat there for five hours before someone brought him a glass of water for the night.

He was summoned early the next day, before reveille, and marched to Triggsdale Hall. Though the sun wasn't up, the sky was brightening, and dew covered the grass. A lark flew across the yard in a series of dips, and mist rose from the artificial trout pond. Major Hatley's battered old Morris was parked under the portico and lamplight shone from his office. The camp guards escorted Goerlitz up the steps and down the hall past the bulky pieces of furniture and mahogany panelling. A curious British officer glanced out the staff lounge then went back to drinking his coffee. From somewhere upstairs he heard a radio playing.

He found Major Hatley standing in front of his desk, prepared as he had been the other day, hands behind his back, smiling in that cheerful way all the British seemed to have, though in the major's case the smile was artificial. He sucked a mint. Even at this early hour he smelled of scotch.

"Good morning," said Major Hatley.

Goerlitz kept his eyes forward, looked at the portrait of Lord Selby above Hatley's head.

"All right, captain, if that's the way you want it. You know, we all try to be chummy around here, but I can see you're not the chummy type. Since it's obviously your wish I'll keep our meeting as brief and formal as I can. I won't even offer you any toast and marmalade. Wouldn't that have been nice?" The major stopped and waited for a reply, but Goerlitz remained silent. The major shrugged and went on. "My guards tell me there was a disturbance in the mess hall last night. They tell me you were the one who started it. Do you have anything to say?"

Goerlitz thought for a moment.

"I wasn't the one who started it."

"Sergeant Saville talked to Commander Weiss last night," said the major, "and Weiss said you threw the first punch."

"Meissner threw the first punch."

"Come, come, you can't expect me to disbelieve Commander Weiss," said Hatley. "I want you to know, Goerlitz, that we simply don't tolerate this kind of behavior in my camp. I'm surprised to have to tell you this, a man of your rank."

Major Hatley dropped his hands to his sides and let out a small disappointed sigh, as if Goerlitz's behavior were beyond comprehension. His khaki uniform looked as if it hadn't been washed or ironed in weeks and hung around his bony frame like a crumpled paper bag.

"Do you understand?"

Goerlitz only half listened to Hatley. So that's the way it would be, he thought. The sentence of passive punishment was now to become a campaign of active punishment. Was this what Weiss had been thinking during those strange silences in Building C before passing sentence? Was this part of their plan?

"Futhermore," continued the major, "this kind of behavior is unseemly, and I'm afraid I must take steps to discipline you. Starting today you'll be on reduced rations for five days, and you'll spend those five days in the box."

The major paused.

"Can't you at least try to be little more cooperative, commander? I know you've been under a great deal of strain, and you must resent capture because it means, after all, that you've lost, hasn't it? And nobody likes to lose. If you would just accept things the way they are, captain, then everybody would get along a lot better. In fact, you might even find Triggsdale Hall pleasant after a while. However, if you misbehave, I can make your life very miserable, just as I'm going to make it miserable now. You've probably heard of the box by now. It's that small grey building made of slate at the end of the fairway. I'm sure you'll enjoy your stay. Lovely old building. Seems Lord Selby made it to store a few odds and ends. Awfully small. Don't know what the martinet had in mind. But it suits our purposes wonderfully. I might add it gets terribly cold in there at this time of year."

Major Hatley put his hands behind his back once again, striking a feeble military pose, and gazed at Goerlitz with vague and dissipated eyes. "If you don't behave yourself after this, you might see yourself in there well into autumn, possibly winter. Am I making myself clear, captain?"

Goerlitz hardened his stare, his lips stiffening into a wry hateful grin, frightening Hatley.

"As clear as piss, major."

The major's face reddened. "Patterson, take this man to the box," he said.

Chapter 5

A warm Mediterranean breeze blew from Barceloneta
Beach through the windows of Ribalta Shipping Services
Incorporated. Miguel Ribalta, president of the firm, sat in
his black leather swivel chair filing his nails with an
ivory-handled nail file. There was nothing like the sweet
breeze from Barceloneta Beach to make a man feel that all
was right with the world. Satrustégui, all three-hundred-
and-fifty pounds of him, sat on the couch opposite
Ribalta's mahogany desk, taking up over half of it, and
next to him sat the girl, Anna Liebel, the young Jewess
they had smuggled — for a price, always for a price —
out of Vichy-controlled Marseilles.

Ribalta lifted his newspaper and glanced through the
first few pages while he waited for the bank representative to telephone. On the bottom of the second page there
was a story about a new kind of German U-boat the
British had captured southeast of Iceland. He read further, how the U-boat had surrendered to aircraft without
a fight because of a battery leak and a mutiny. He continued to read because the story suggested a name he had

once known, one of four code names given to him a few years ago by an *Abwehr* agent in Barcelona. He carefully tore the small story out of the paper, took out a stub of pencil, jotted the name *Helga Weiss* beside it, and pinned the story to the bulletin board above his desk.

He looked at the girl. Anna Liebel was pale and frightened, had expected to be in America, where she had rich relatives, over two weeks ago. But Ribalta had kept her here until he had been certain there would be no better offers from the Gestapo.

Satrustégui ate fried shrimp out of a newspaper cone, a confection he had found on the Ramblas just up the street from Plaza de Cataluña. He offered some to the girl but the girl just shook her head and turned away. She had lost fifteen pounds since she had been in Ribalta's safe-keeping. Ribalta spoke in French to the girl. Ribalta was Spanish, or as he preferred to think of himself, Catalonian, and Anna Liebel was a German Jew. But they both happened to speak French; Anna, a highly cultured Parisian French she had learned in finishing school, and Ribalta the gutter French he had learned in the harbor taverns of Marseilles.

"Come, now, Anna, you should eat. We've done everything possible to make you comfortable. What are your relatives in New Jersey going to say?"

She looked at him, her dark eyes narrowing with hatred.

"You are a pig," she said. "*Cochon*! You are a liar. And I would sooner starve than eat what the alley cats have pissed on."

"Ah," he said. "Ah, ha, such spirit." He switched to Spanish and turned to Satrustégui. "She says she would sooner starve than eat what the alley cats have pissed on. She probably learned that at her school, where all the girls are whores."

Satrustégui laughed.

"I don't know why you waste your time with her," he said. "If she doesn't want to eat, she won't eat. If she doesn't want to drink, she won't drink." Satrustégui wiped his greasy hands on his pants. "There's no explaining Jews."

The telephone rang. Ribalta glanced at his watch, then lifted the receiver.

Ribalta heard what he expected to hear. A man named Tellsen, Fritz Liebel's bank representative in Europe, told him the money, ten thousand American dollars, had been conditionally transferred into the shipping company's account that morning, and that complete anonymity had been maintained through the various transactions, both on this side of the Atlantic and in New Jersey. A representative from the bank's branch in Barcelona had been telephoned a few moments ago and was on his way to the shipping office. If the girl was dead or harmed in any way, the transfer would be cancelled and the bank would call the *Guardia Civil* to arrest Ribalta immediately. If the girl was well, the representative would call the bank from the shipping office and the money transfer would be final.

"I assure you, my friend, the girl is perfectly safe."

He hung up. Of course the girl was safe. Whether it was guns, jewels, or refugees, he always delivered his goods unspoiled, and always to the highest bidder. Did the man think he had no experience? This was just another deal in a long series of deals. And war was the best time for those who understood the value of money; he was sure that was something Tellsen would understand. Even as a soldier in the Spanish Civil War Ribalta had understood the value of money. He sat back in his swivel chair, adjusted his sunglasses, folded his hands across his stomach, and looked at the girl. Her breath quickened. She hadn't understood his conversation with the bank representative, but she knew something was going to happen. He felt sorry for her. He hated making victims out of people whom he liked. And he liked Anna Liebel. He liked young girls, even if they were a little crude. And he liked Anna so much he would light a devotional candle in her honor at Valencia Cathedral tonight to bless her heathen Hebrew soul. He still wasn't going to say anything to her about the telephone call. Let her wait, he thought. Let her pay for what she had put him and Satrustégui through.

•

Inspector Gerald Laurie stood at the window of his temporary field office overlooking Morecambe Bay in Barrow-in-Furness, anxious to get started but frustrated because he had to wait. The water was choppy, flecked with white-caps, and small high-flying cumulus clouds floated across the sky. Numerous boats of every description were docked at the many piers of the naval base, and several more — destroyers, frigates, and corvettes — lay at anchor in the bay. Laurie was frustrated because he usually got things done so efficiently, so quickly, and now he had been forced to wait because of the inefficiency of others.

Directly below him in a concrete-bordered submarine pen lay U-512. She was sleek, black, lethal. There was a swordfish with a serrated nose painted on the side of the conning tower. Unfortunately the carpenters had just started camouflaging the upper works. He could hear Taylor talking on the phone in the other room. Taylor was looking after the tools and equipment needed to disassemble certain difficult sections of U-512.

Laurie lifted his grey flannel jacket from the back of his chair and pulled it around his shoulders. They were having problems getting the equipment. A delay was understandable with the technicians, but not with the equipment. He wanted the best people, and the best people, naturally enough, were on other assignments, and schedules had to be changed and replacements found for them. Lieutenant Commander Murray Simpson-Beale, the hydroplane, ballast and control panels specialist was in Siam working with a team of Americans on a partially damaged Japanese sub the U.S. Navy had towed in, and wouldn't get back to England until the end of the week. And Chief Engineer Curtis Fine, the structural expert, was in Edinburgh on a research project to develop a submarine hull capable of withstanding seven hundred meters, and he couldn't possibly get away, he said, for at least another two days. Then there was Captain John Hopcraft, the munitions, armaments and explosives technician, who was on a purchasing assignment in Halifax, and who wouldn't be back much before Thursday. Because it was a Type IX submarine, unlike anything they had ever seen before, he thought the Admiralty would have made special arrangements to get these people to Barrow-in-Furness as quickly as possible. But the Admiralty had handled this situation much the way they handled any other situation, with a slow bureaucratic mismaneuvering that was far more counter-productive than effective.

He pulled his tartan scarf around his neck, put on his fedora with the small turquoise feather in the hat-band, pulled out his cigarette case, and stuck a cigarette in the corner of his mouth where there was a perpetual nicotine stain. He adjusted it so it would hang there comfortably while he smoked, so he wouldn't have to use his hands, and struck a wooden match, just as Taylor walked in. Taylor was a tall thin man, well over six feet. Laurie lit his cigarette and exhaled a cloud of smoke into the room.

"Well?" said Laurie.

Taylor shrugged.

"Did you get my message at the hotel?" asked his assistant.

"What message?"

"It seems some of these larger tools are going to have to be made at the foundry in Glasgow. The German's haven't standardized the sizes yet. We're running into all kinds of exceptions."

"You mean to tell me that in the whole bloody British Fleet, Carson can't find any of these larger tools? I find that hard to believe, Don."

"Sir, I might remind you that the Royal Navy uses Imperial measurements. And we've never seen anything like the Type IX before. Now, if you'd like to talk to Admiral Carson yourself, I can get him on the telephone."

"I'm amazed we're actually starting to win this war, considering what we've got to work with."

"I'm sorry, sir, I've done all I can."

Laurie knew that when Taylor used the deferential "sir" it was more from a shared frustration than respect. He stared at the portrait of King George beside the window, trying to suppress his anger. He twitched his lips, letting the first bit of ash from his cigarette tumble to the linoleum floor. His stomach ulcer was bothering him.

"Yes, I suppose you have, Don," he said. "Well, all right, go ahead and do what you have to, but try and hurry them, will you? Who knows how many Type IXs they have out there? And the sooner we know their strengths and weaknesses the sooner the Royal Navy can destroy them."

"It will involve a requisition, sir," said Taylor, unfolding an official form. "I'll have to get your signature."

"Requisition? A requisition for what? Shouldn't we have priority?"

"A requisition for the necessary steel."

"Oh, for God's sake." Laurie snatched the requisition from his assistant, scratched his signature on the appropriate line, then handed the form back to Taylor. "Get it off as fast as possible. Have you shipped the designs to the foundry?"

"They received them early this morning, sir. Westmoreland called."

"And what did he say?"

"That they'll be able to forge the tools easily with the designs we've given them. But not until they get the steel."

"That's great. That's just great." Laurie frowned and adjusted his scarf. "If anybody wants me, Don, I'll be down on the boat."

"Yes, sir."

Laurie followed the terraced pathway down the hill through the woods then walked along the east harbor road to the submarine pen. It wasn't anything like the submarine pens the Germans had in Lorient, with their forty-foot-thick reinforced ceilings and even thicker bomb-proof walls, but simply a concrete enclosure in the water with a ten-foot barbed wire fence all around. Security was poor, and though Laurie had argued about this with Carson, the admiral maintained that they were too short-staffed already and couldn't possibly afford any more people than they already had. A two-man watch during the day and a one-man watch during the night. The admiral argued, rightly or wrongly, that no one was going to steal a U-boat, and that an extra guard or two wouldn't stop the Germans from making an air attack on U-512 if by any chance they decided to risk the deadly gauntlet of antiaircraft defenses surrounding Barrow-in-Furness. Nevertheless, the pressure was on to get this boat moving as quickly as possible. The sooner they had U-512 out in open seas the better Laurie would feel.

A guardhouse and a large blockhouse stood outside the submarine pen, as well as a parking lot with a couple of jeeps and a few trucks. He spat his cigarette from his mouth as he approached the guardhouse. He saluted the sailor who stood watch at the gate.

"At ease, sailor. Could you let me in, please?"

"Yes, sir."

The sailor slung his keys from his belt, unlocked the gate and swung it open on creaking hinges.

Laurie went inside and walked slowly along the pier, gazing at the U-boat. It was longer than the Type VII C, the more common German U-boat, with a larger conning tower and much heavier armament. He hopped aboard and made his way along the catwalk past the big flak gun and climbed the companionway to the top of the tower. The winter garden, as he had heard some German sailors call it. On top, he twisted open the conning tower hatch and descended the companionway into the control room, the heart of the boat, the smell of seawater and grease wafting up at him. The chlorine gas fumes, he noted, had long since dissipated.

At the bottom, he looked around. There were dials, switches, valves, and panels everywhere. The radio operator's headphones hung over the back of a metal chair that was screwed into the floor. All was quiet except for the tinny lapping of the waves against the side of the U-boat. He would have loved to have been the commander of this boat. This Goerlitz had been a lucky fellow. At least until his crew had mutinied on him. He would have to talk to Goerlitz once Goerlitz became more cooperative. He had phoned the camp commandant, Major Hatley, again. An interview at this time would be completely unproductive, the major had said. In fact, the prisoner was in solitary confinement and wouldn't be out for five days. That didn't bother Laurie. In five days the technicians would have a much better idea of the kinds of questions they would want to ask Goerlitz anyway. What bothered Laurie was the muddling incompetence of the people he had to push in order to get things done.

Laurie reached for one of the switches on the control panel and flicked it upwards. The white lights disappeared and the control room was bathed in a misty red glow, battle stations. He pressed a lever forward and the state-of-the-art periscope rose smoothly out of its sheath with a gentle hum. He had to give the Germans credit. Their machinery was always of the highest quality. He pulled the periscope handles down on either side and brought his eyes to the viewing piece.

Through the calibrated sighting scope he saw the hill, and turning slightly to the left, the building where his temporary field office stood. He kept swinging left, scanning the east harbor section of Barrow-in-Furness. What a time Goerlitz must have had with this submarine, this wonderful instrument of death, he thought. He kept turning left, out over the white-flecked waves of Morecambe Bay until he finally had the battleship HMS Baron squarely in his sights. She was a large battleship with a deadly armament, and Huff-Duff submarine detection antennae crowded her bridge. Laurie's lips stiffened and his brow settled into an even lethal line.

"Bearing four-five-zero," he said. From out the conning tower hatch, he heard a plane pass by overhead. "Steady. . .steady. . .steady as she goes. Flood tubes one through four." He waited, concentrating on the battleship. "Open bow caps."

An imaginary torpedo officer told him that the bow caps had been opened.

His face broke into a smile.

"Fire," he whispered.

•

Goerlitz walked through the damp night. Patterson and another guard held their bayonets to his back and marched him up the fairway Lord Selby had once used as an archery range but which Major Hatley now used to practice his golf. Patterson was a thick-set man with red hair and a red mustache. They passed the trout pond where the mosquitoes, the last of the summer, hovered in clouds above the water lilies. Goerlitz was tired. He just wanted to go to sleep.

The box had a steel door and a barred window. Patterson gave him a couple of blankets, a pitcher of water, and a chamber pot. The other guard shoved him in, closed the door, drew both steel bolts across, then locked the padlock. Goerlitz heard them walk away.

When he was sure they had crossed the fairway he tried to push the door open but it wouldn't budge. He looked around but couldn't see anything because it was too dark. So he felt his way along the wall until he came to the corner, spread out one of his blankets, pulled the other around his shoulders and sat down. Besides the barred window there was only a small slot in the door that had to be opened from the outside. All in all, it reminded him of a submarine with a lighting failure, only it smelled of earth, not seawater. He lay down on his side, and tried to sleep.

He pulled the blanket closer around his shoulders and gazed at the squat grey walls as his eyes slowly grew used to the dark. The walls were rough and unfinished, and there were hooks at the interstices, where garden implements had once been hung. So this was where he would spend the next five days. On reduced rations.

He had suffered far worse privations. He was tired, so miserably tired, and his body was beginning to feel the strain of the last three weeks. He would have to rest, and then he would be able to think clearly and decide what he was going to do. He shifted position, lay on his side, folded part of the blanket to make a pillow, and soon fell asleep.

The morning birds woke him several hours later.

Light filtered through the chinks in the slabs of slate and shone through the window. He got to his feet and peered through the bars. The forest stretched up the hill away from the fairway. In and among the saplings he saw a deer with white spots on its back. It jumped away suddenly at the sound of approaching boots and darted up the hill. In a moment, the slot opened and a guard shoved a tray of food in. Scrambled eggs made from egg powder and a piece of bread fried in fat. Both cold and a little damp. He took the tray, the slot closed, and the guard walked away. He sat down and ate his breakfast in small tentative bites.

When he got out, he thought, Weiss would arrange something else and he would be in for ten days. Then Weiss would arrange something else and he would be in for twenty days. Oh, well, he didn't mind being alone in the dark, at least not yet. What bothered him was the captain's disapproval. He nibbled at his piece of bread. He should have killed Bergen before he had lost every opportunity. He should have been more sensitive to the mood of his crew. He should have opened the ballast tanks when Neumann had taken him below to get the maps, manuals and code books. Overpower Neumann, just as he had been overpowered, and drowned the whole lot of them. There would be forty-three men dead, but at least the British wouldn't have U-512.

He spent much of the morning thinking about what he should have done, pacing occasionally, picking a slug off the wall and squashing it in the corner away from where he had made his bed. He went over the events leading to the capture of U-512 again and again, getting angrier and angrier as the morning wore on.

He expected lunch but none came. His stomach growled continually and he felt light-headed and nauseated from lack of food.

Around three it rained hard, some of it seeping

through the chinks in the slate, and he began to shiver. He pulled both blankets around him but he still couldn't stop shivering, so he tried to think of something warm. He thought of U-93's patrols off Sierra Leone in 1941, and how they had been able to go swimming in the tropical water because there had been virtually no sea or air cover in those days, thought how they had all wandered around on the catwalk in their shorts, and how they had been able to rendezvous with other U-boats. Then he thought of Ute, and how she felt so warm in bed lying next to him. She was still a child, true, and the gap had widened with four years of battle aboard U-boats, yet now he wanted to take her in his arms. As he drew his blankets even more closely around his shoulders, he wanted to feel her warmth, wanted to see her blue eyes. Had there ever been love in those eyes, he wondered? Was the eight-year age difference too great to establish anything so capricious as love? And would she ever be able to forgive him for the abominable way he had treated her after she had suffered her miscarriage, as if it were her fault? He thought of their honeymoon, two weeks alone in his father's country house outside Munich, when she had been only eighteen.

That had been a month before the final patrol of U-93. The weather had been at its autumnal best in those first two weeks of October, and the last apples on his father's orchard trees had ripened to a rosy fullness. Sweetly remembered images came back to him, her pale and finely shaped hand resting on his knee while they watched the sunset from his father's gazebo, the wreath of wild flowers she had made and draped haphazardly over his head, the piece of burlap spread out on the pile of wood chips in the wine cellar the day they had gone down to taste the wine and ended up making love.

His father, Otto Goerlitz, more than approved of her, and hoped that she at last had induced some common sense into Hermann. His eyes caught sight of a slug squirming along the wall and he watched it for several moments as it left a reflective trail of slime on the slate wall. When Ute had become pregnant, that had made his father's arguments stronger. Now you have someone more than just yourself to live for, he had said. Hermann, please, for your own sake, for Ute's sake, for your child's sake, apply for a transfer. You've done diligent work in the *Unterseewaffe*. But you've also had the necessary *Abwehr* training. They would make you a cryptographer just like that. A nice safe easy desk job.

But Goerlitz had scorned his father. His father was a heretic and an intellectual. Goerlitz wanted the blood and honor, the awesome reality of combat. Yet now he wasn't so sure. He was homesick. He wanted to tell his father that perhaps after all they did agree on certain things, that blood and honor weren't the best way to run a country, that a nation as great as the Fatherland might be better run on cool reason and open, free discussion. He longed for home, for Ute's warm touch, and for the wonderful talks he had with his father. He wished he was sitting with them right now in the gazebo, or in the apartment in Munich, sharing a pot of tea, safe, warm, and peaceful.

Outside, he heard trucks on the camp road, and gazing out one of the chinks, he saw a convoy with a heavy motorcycle escort drive past Triggsdale Hall to the explosives sheds. Triggsdale Hall doubled as an ammunition dump. The motorcycles with side-cars splashed their way through the mud puddles on the camp's dirt road. If there were only some way he could speak to Ute, to ask her to forgive him, to tell her he had been a fool. The sad picture kept coming back: Ute with her resplendent blonde hair down and something fading from her blue eyes when he told her only farm animals had miscarriages. It was as if something had turned off.

Moments later she had stumbled against the wall, her leg dripping blood, and he had helped her to the bedroom.

The last of the trucks disappeared on the left side of the fairway. How could he have been so hard, and what had disappeared from her eyes? If only there was some way he could reach her. But she was so far away.

The slot in the door opened just past six and a bowl of thin soup and more eggs from egg powder appeared on the tray. There was also a cigarette and a wooden match. He knocked on the door, the slot opened, and the guard looked in. Goerlitz saw a pair of eyes. It was Patterson.

"Yes?" said Patterson.

"Who brought me the cigarette?"

Patterson's eyes smiled. "Don't tell anybody, mate, but I did. Hope you enjoy it."

The slot closed and he heard Patterson walk away. He brought the tray to his blankets and sat down. The cigarette was dry, as was the match. He put the cigarette and the match in his pocket to save for later. The soup had a few meager vegetables in a broth of beef powder. He considered the eggs more a protein ration than food. Still, he was hungry, and he ate everything in less than a minute. He resisted the cigarette as long as he could. It would give him something to look forward to.

Rain fell again just past nine. Except for the single thought of the cigarette his mind began to empty. He fell asleep. When he awoke several hours later the rain had stopped and the chinks in the slate shone with a pre-dawn light. He sat up, hoping he hadn't crushed his cigarette, and was glad to find it in one piece. He checked his match to make sure it was dry. He wasn't a regular smoker, mainly in Paris, when a pack of Gauloise could disappear in a night. As he looked for a dry spot to light the match, he couldn't wait for the smoke's first kick to hit the back of his throat.

He finally found a dry patch of slate, stuck the cigarette in his mouth, lit the match, and pulled hard.

He gulped down the smoke, taking note of the brand in the light from the match. Wild Woodbine. The kind the major smoked. Not the asphyxiating smoke he was used to in a French cigarette, but strong enough, and flavorful. If only there were some way he could get out of here sooner than the five days. He held the smoke in for a moment then let it flow slowly out his nose. He watched the match burn down, thinking he might start a fire to keep warm, but there was nothing dry enough in the box to catch. He held the match, warming his hands around it until it burnt down to his fingers. He took another drag of his cigarette and smiled.

His head swam. The nicotine, he thought. How pleasant. The chinks in the wall slowly brightened. He had to destroy U-512. He knew it was the only way he would be able to exonerate himself in front of Weiss and the others. He knew it was tied up in Barrow-in-Furness, less than twenty miles from Triggsdale Hall.

When Patterson came with his breakfast several hours later, Goerlitz waited at the slot.

"I must speak with Major Hatley," he said.

He saw Patterson's eyes appear in the slot.

"Major Hatley? What for?"

"I want to apologize. I want to tell him I'll behave myself now."

"Now, now," said Patterson, "you've got five days, and five days it's going to be."

"Could you please tell the major I wish to see him?"

"I'll mention it, mate. But I don't think it will do any good. He was awfully miffed at you."

Chapter 6

Major Hatley walked up the fairway with Corporal Patterson. Goerlitz wanted to see him. He had learned the news early in the day. Let Goerlitz wait, he thought. Make him sweat. Two days in the box and already he wanted out. Couldn't blame him. Nasty in there, with all the damp and rot.

He found Goerlitz sitting with his back to the wall on his blankets. Patterson shone his flashlight at Goerlitz. The commander stood to attention and saluted crisply. My, what an improvement. Wonders what the box did.

"At ease, captain. Patterson tells me you've had a change of heart."

"Yes, commandant, I have. I've been thinking over your advice and I'm beginning to see some sense in it." Goerlitz glanced at Patterson. "I see now that you have only the best interests of your prisoners at heart, and seek only our best welfare."

How wonderful, thought Hatley. "Yes, that's very true, captain. I believe in cooperation."

"I want to tell you personally, major, how sorry I am for the way I have behaved. I should know how to surrender honorably and take my imprisonment gracefully, as a real officer would. But I wasn't thinking clearly."

Hatley looked around the box, noted how Goerlitz had arranged his pile of blankets in the corner and how a lot of the ground had been swept clear of slate and cedar chips.

"Is that all you wanted to say to me, captain? I have this chap from Naval Intelligence who's been after me about you. These battery fractures, for instance. Is this a common thing for the new Type IX U-boat, or does it just happen to be a problem with your particular submarine?"

The U-boat commander turned away, his broad face bunching, as if he had tasted something sour.

"I would like to be a chum, major, as you call it," he said. "I would like to play by the rules, but I would also like you to play by the rules as well. I've given you a fully operational U-boat. What more can I do?"

"I accept your apology." Hatley twisted his chin a notch higher. "But I get the feeling you're up to something, Goerlitz. I'm quite a bit older than you," said the major in a friendly but somewhat patronizing tone," and I've been commandant of this camp since the beginning of the war. I've seen prisoners come and go and I know when I smell something in the wind. I don't know what you have in mind with this sudden turn around," he said, smiling now," but you might as well forget it."

He looked at Goerlitz, measuring his reaction, how his eyes went blank and his shoulders sunk a bit.

"Sir, I felt I owed you an apology, that's all."

"What is it, Goerlitz? I don't know what you're trying to prove, but whatever it is you won't get very far. In any case you've got five days in the box, Goerlitz. Is that too long? An apology after two days is fine, but you're still going to be in here for five." Hatley looked out the small barred window and shrugged. "Is there anything else, captain?"

"No, sir."

"I find your sudden civility contrived, Goerlitz. You don't really mean it. You've got to have a lot more for me if you want out of the box right now. For instance, what's this we keep hearing about a hydrogen peroxide powered underwater engine?"

"Major, please, I made a mistake."

"You wouldn't believe how well we treat our friends, captain. Would you like a steak and kidney pie tonight and a nice warm bed?"

But Goerlitz didn't answer. He was red with suppressed anger. Usually that didn't bother Hatley, but as he studied the commander, how his big-lipped mouth was slightly open from exhaustion, his eyes bleary, and his brow fighting an urge to frown, he thought Goerlitz might be more a problem prisoner than he had originally anticipated.

"Well, you just sleep on it. As I said, I don't know what you have in mind, but whatever it is, you won't get away with it. Put the war behind you, Goerlitz. It's over. At least for you it is." Hatley looked around the box one more time. "And while you're trying to keep warm in here, why not think about what you might be doing five or six years from now? Because I think that's how long it will be before you get out of Triggsdale Hall."

•

When the sound of Hatley and Patterson's boots had disappeared down the fairway, Goerlitz went back to his blankets and slumped in the corner. What had ever given him the idea that he would be able to outsmart the major with a simple apology? Was it the films he had seen when he had been in the *Jungvolk* ten years ago, always portraying the British as slow and dim-witted? He remembered one clip in particular, where Londoners were compared to the pigeons in Trafalgar Square, dirty, grubby, living in squalor, and always shitting themselves. A film similar to the one he had seen about Jews: hordes of rats overrunning Europe. Sitting in this slate shack, had he lost the ability to separate the wish from the fact? His father had told him those films were rubbish, that they stereotyped and distorted, and deep down, Goerlitz had known this. But Goerlitz had been too full of the dream of a new Germany, too fervently loyal to Hitler to ever truly listen to his father. Hitler had given them all an excuse to feel proud about being German. And what was so bad about that? Pride in nationality. What was so bad about that? It had been a pleasure to show the world just how good they could be. Not that the Britons were any better or worse, nor that the Slavs were inferior, because he knew everybody was really the same, but he wanted to be proud to be a German, wanted to be proud of Hitler, at least for the most part, and proud of many, if not all, of the things he had done.

He got up and looked through the window down the fairway. It was almost dark. The spotlight swept the far end of the yard. The British were in his boat right now, dismantling this and that, taking notes, finding U-512's strengths and weaknesses. And he was in the box and couldn't do anything to stop them.

He gripped the bars on the window and tried to shake them loose, then picked up a piece of slate and chiseled around the concrete frame. But the slate splintered and fell apart even before it made so much as a chip in the concrete. He swore at the window and threw what was left of the slate to the ground.

He had to get out of here. He had to somehow destroy U-512 before the British got a good chance to study it. But how? He had to escape. It was a matter of honor. It was a matter of loyalty and allegiance not only to the *Kriegsmarine* but also to Doenitz. Who was he kidding? Separate the wish from the fact? Six years with the *Unterseewaffe* had made him cynical about the Reich. But it was a fact that he wanted to prove himself to Frischauer, Ballerstedt, Schlabrendorff, and especially to Weiss, wanted them to see him again as their old comrade, and as someone they could respect.

He got down on his hands and knees and dug through the rocky soil. Maybe he would be able to dig his way out. What a fool he had been to apologize to Hatley. It had never occurred to him that he might actually raise the commandant's suspicion with his sudden apology.

He dug for the next three hours until he was so hot his prisoner's uniform steamed in the damp cool air. His fingernails were ragged and bleeding. He had been under the impression that with this kind of building the slate would go down only six inches below the ground. But he dug a sizeable hole, well over three feet deep, before he decided it was useless, and that it would take him over a week to dig himself out.

He brushed the dirt off his hands and walked back to his blankets. He couldn't believe he had failed so miserably in his first command. Was the war really over for him, as the major suggested? Was the Fuhrer really as infallible as he had once wanted to believe? Were the British truly slow and dim-witted, and were the Jews really like rats? He had a headache. He felt feverish. These questions were no longer even worthy of consideration. He just wanted to go home, home to Munich and Ute, especially Ute, to try and save what had become an extremely fragile marriage.

•

A little past midnight he was awakened by a German voice at the window.

"Goerlitz," the voice whispered. "It's me, Baller-stedt."

"Ballerstedt?" Goerlitz thought he was dreaming. His mind cleared and he sprang to the window. Ballerstedt peered in on him, his round glasses astride his hawkish nose, his wool cap covering his hair. "Ballerstedt, how did you get here? Aren't the dogs out?"

"There are no dogs. I came through that copse over there." Ballerstedt cast a cautious glance over his shoulder. "Here, I brought you a cigarette."

"Ballerstedt, listen, I have to get out of here. I must destroy U-512. We can't let them learn any more than they already have. You've got to help get me out."

"Calm down, Goerlitz. Here, take this cigarette. It will do you good."

Goerlitz took the cigarette, lit it, and inhaled deeply. Yes, that was better, calm down. Try and convince Baller-stedt rationally and calmly.

"Patterson brought me a cigarette yesterday," he said.

"That doesn't surprise me. He's well liked by every-body in the camp. A German soldier saved his father's life in the Great War. He likes the whole lot of us. He takes mail for us. He actually takes mail for us."

"Ballerstedt, really, I have to get out of here."

"Forget it. There's no way out of the box. We've all been in, we've all tried to get out, and believe me, it's impossible without the key."

"But you don't understand, Ballerstedt. You must tell Captain Weiss that I have a plan."

The spotlight swept by the end of the fairway.

"What kind of plan?"

"A plan to destroy U-512."

Ballerstedt smiled sadly and shook his head.

"Listen to me. I've learned a lot in the two years I've been here. I've learned to distrust grand and noble schemes, especially from those who have just been captured in battle."

"Please, Ballerstedt, I only care about German lives. Call it grand and noble, but Weiss is right when he says the technological secrets the British will uncover from U-512 will cost the lives of hundreds of German seamen."

Ballerstedt sighed once more and pressed his lips together. He looked down the fairway.

"I should get going. They run a guard up here every half hour."

"Listen, please tell Weiss that I have a plan. In fact I order you to tell Weiss I have a plan."

"We're in a remote corner of England in a prisoner-of-war camp, Goerlitz, and the old rules don't apply here."

"Ballerstedt, please, I implore you, as my good friend, please tell Captain Weiss I have an idea."

From down the fairway Goerlitz heard the crunch of boots.

"I'll mention it, Goerlitz, but it's not going to get you out of the box any sooner. I've got to go."

"You have a meeting with him," said Goerlitz. "You, Frischauer, and Schlabrendorff."

"Goerlitz, I've got to go."

•

It was dark inside Building C, well past midnight, and Commander Weiss again sat on the window ledge gazing out past the yard at Triggsdale Hall. The spotlight on the Victorian mansion's main turret turned round and round, scanning the fairway, the copse beside the fairway, the parking lot, Buildings A through E, and the latrines before it lost its intensity in the misty shadows of the shut-down slate quarry at the far end of the camp. Frischauer and Schlabrendorff sat on their bunks nearby, waiting for Ballerstedt to return from his visit with Goerlitz. Today's edition of the London *Times* lay on a chair beside Weiss, something Schlabrendorff had stolen from the staff officers' lounge while he had been sweeping the carpet there this morning.

There wasn't much on U-512, just ten or eleven lines on the bottom of page eight. A technical crew, the story said, was being assembled by Naval Intelligence, and would arrive in Barrow-in-Furness by the end of the week, or possibly the beginning of the next.

"Do you see him?" asked Frischauer.

Weiss peered into the darkness near the copse.

"Not yet. Saville should pass by in another two minutes."

The spotlight made a complete sweep of the camp, dancing over the copse before Sergeant Saville finally came on his round down to the quarry and back, his rifle slung over his shoulder, a cigarette in his mouth. Weiss watched until Saville had disappeared into the mist beyond the latrines, then turned his attention back to the copse. A single shadow emerged from the copse and detached itself from the jumble of shadows among the trees. Weiss turned around.

"He's coming."

Schlabrendorff and Frischauer went to the back window. The spotlight passed Building C, filling the room momentarily with light, then moved on.

They pulled Ballerstedt up through the back window. Ballerstedt took off his wool cap and wiped his forehead with the back of his arm. Weiss moved to the center of the room.

"Well?" he said.

"He's frantic," said Ballerstedt. He stopped for a

moment to catch his breath. "More frantic than I've ever seen him."

"Good, good."

"But he wants to destroy U-512."

The commander straightened his back and put his hands on his hips, a frown coming to his face. The officers of U-93 had been surprised by Weiss's revelation last night, how he had been ordered by Doenitz to set a course for the Irish Sea on the fateful night U-93 had gone down under the prow of the Polish corvette, *Krajenka*, how they were to put a man in England to at last gain accurate information about the crucial naval base at Barrow-in-Furness, how this man would have been a last minute selection by Doenitz himself from four candidates, of which Goerlitz was one. Weiss had declared that this new Helga message could only be the signal from Doenitz that he knew of Goerlitz's capture, that the plan was still alive, and should now be activated. They discussed at length last night how they now had the chance to motivate Goerlitz, through his shame and dishonor. As usual, Weiss had the absolute support of his crew. He was a man who inspired obedience.

"I knew he would," said Weiss. He shook his head slowly from side to side and walked forward into the room. "But I'm afraid it's out of the question. We'll have to explain to him that we have far more important things for him to do. He must know, beyond doubt, that the only way he can regain our respect is if he completes the mission as outlined three years ago by Admiral Doenitz. I admire his determination to destroy U-512. But we must make him realize that it's far more crucial to get information about Barrow-in-Furness back to the High Command." He walked to the window and gazed out at the dark yard.

"There will be very specific things I'll want you to do over the next week or two. We'll be working on a schedule. I've already sent word to my contact in Spain. We'll have to get Goerlitz a suit, a map, some money, all the things he'll need on the outside, even some identification if we can manage it. With any luck he could have those dispositions to Doenitz in three weeks time."

•

Three days later they let Goerlitz out of the box. He was pale, shaky, had lost ten pounds, but when he finally saw Commander Weiss in the games room of Building E, he stood stiff to attention, clicked his heels, and saluted with hard fingers. His old commander stared at him sourly. Ballerstedt, Frischauer, and Schlabrendorff looked on from their bunks.

Goerlitz told Weiss the basic outline of his plan to destroy U-512.

Weiss stood up, walked to the window with his back ruler-straight, his head held high, and looked out the window at the yard for several minutes, where a few prisoners flattened old tin cans under the watchful gaze of a camp guard. He turned around, his eyes wide, gleaming, as if he had just seen something none of the others could see. With measured steps he walked back to the table. He sat down and turned a pencil end on end with a slow movement of his hand. He suddenly smiled in the most peculiar way, an expression Goerlitz had never seen on his old commander's face. Frischauer kept his eyes to the floor. Schlabrendorff shifted uneasily and Ballerstedt peered through his round glasses with a half-smile on his face. There was something odd here, thought Goerlitz, something extremely odd. This didn't feel like the old crew of U-93.

"You speak like a true son of the Fatherland." He looked at Goerlitz, his grayish eyes focusing on some seemingly distant point. His eyes were different, thought

Goerlitz. They were too controlled, too guarded. "A true son of the Fatherland, Goerlitz, but you will go nowhere near U-512."

Goerlitz's face darkened. "I beg you pardon, commander."

"It's not enough, is it, Goerlitz? They've had U-512 for almost a week, and what they haven't learned by now they'll learn very soon. And we don't know whether she's still tied up in Barrow-in-Furness, or if she's already been recommissioned. She could be sailing with the British Fleet by now. She could be destroying German shipping this very moment. And if she's still tied up, well, what with all this publicity, it's simply a matter for the *Luftwaffe* now, isn't it?"

"The captain's right, Goerlitz," said Frischauer. "Perhaps if you had escaped on the first day, when the British had yet not had time to study U-512, the risk might have been worth it. But now, after six days, we have to ask ourselves if the objective is worth the risk."

"Sir," said Goerlitz, addressing Weiss, "I think the destruction of a German U-boat in enemy hands is a very worthwhile objective."

"I agree with you, Goerlitz, but we have something far more important we wish you to do. We admire your drive and your patriotism, and your apparent determination to destroy U-512, but sometimes these things blind us. The larger goals of the Reich, Commander Goerlitz. That's what you must think of. Germany, captain. Germany. If you want redemption, you must think of the final victory of the Reich."

This was the kind of rhetoric that had always moved Goerlitz, ever since his last days with the Hitler Youth, when he had decided to join the *Unterseewaffe* against his father's wishes. Yet now he was impatient.

"And you'll get a chance to have your redemption, Goerlitz," continued Weiss, "but you'll do it my way, under my orders. My orders, Goerlitz, and you know what that means. The only reason we choose you and have been so generous in giving you this opportunity to regain your honor is because we believe you are the man most qualified for the job. You have *Abwehr* training. You speak English more fluently than any of us. And because you have been disgraced, your motivation will be unwavering."

Goerlitz frowned. What could be more important than destroying U-512?

"Yes, we will help you escape, Goerlitz. But you must understand that to destroy U-512 would only jeopardize your chances of accomplishing what really needs to be done, a larger, more important mission that Admiral Doenitz himself has given the highest priority. You will escape and go to Barrow-in-Furness to carefully record the dispositions of Allied merchant and naval shipping at anchor in Morecambe Bay, its lanes of approach and departure, the location of all surface-floating mines, and any submarine nets or man-made barriers in and around the naval base at Morecambe Bay. Then you will go to Liverpool. There is a ship, the *San Julian*, owned by a man in Barcelona. His name is Ribalta, and the captain is Marcelo Gil Robles. Ribalta is a good friend of the Reich. The *San Julian* will be in Liverpool in about two weeks time. From there you will go to Barcelona, then to Marseilles, and then to Lorient, where you will present the dispositions and other information to Admiral Doenitz for a full scale combined U-boat and *Luftwaffe* attack on Morecambe Bay which will permanently cripple all of England and win us the war."

Chapter 7

The sky was cloudless over Barcelona. Miguel Ribalta was on his way to the Ramblas to collect the weekend take from Satrustégui. The temperature was in the eighties. Everybody moved slowly. A tram clanked by, crowded with midday passengers. It was good to be in Barcelona, with its filth and litter, its dank smell from the harbor, and decrepit old buildings. People weren't as rich as they had once been, but if a man were smart enough he could survive comfortably here. When a man reached forty, comfort mattered more, he reflected, than war and politics. His old friends, the Falangists, couldn't understand. To say he had grown sick of suffering and now wanted to enjoy the fruits of all those long hard years was an over-simplification. He smiled sadly as he reached the Gothic Quarter. Had something died inside? Sometimes he thought so. Sometimes he thought his soul was a calloused little nub.

The Ramblas, a wide boulevard dissecting the Gothic Quarter, smelled of donkeys and diesel fumes. At one time this street would have been crowded with Spanish and German sailors, but most of the Germans were gone now. Franco didn't want them in Spain. And the Nazi banners had been removed. He stopped at a fruit stall and bought an orange. That's what he liked about Franco. Franco was adaptable. Ribalta took out his army knife, something he had saved from his soldiering days, and began peeling the orange, making a long green and yellow spiral. Was it the hardness of his soul that made him adaptable like Franco, or had he simply come to understand the value of money? Fanatics like Enrique and Ramon would never understand the value of money. Of the old crowd, only Marcelo Gil Robles, captain of the *San Julian*, understood money and what it could do.

Satrustégui sat at the front desk sweating, his shirt open and his stomach hanging over his belt. Ribalta took out his handkerchief and wiped his forehead.

"You don't look well, Satrustégui. Are you hungover?"

"Just a bit, Señor Ribalta. A big weekend."

"Well, good, lots of money."

Satrustégui gave him an envelope full of pesetas. Ribalta smiled. The envelope was thicker than usual. What would he buy, he thought? He needed a new pink shirt, and a pair of alligator shoes. He needed a new pair of sunglasses for the beach.

"All right, thanks. Don't work too hard. How are the girls?"

"Sore," said Satrustégui.

"Ha," said Ribalta. "I imagine so."

The bulk of pesetas was conspicuous along the Ramblas, and as the Ramblas was infested with pickpockets and thieves, he kept a sharp lookout. Most of the pickpockets knew him and stayed away. More than one had been slashed by his knife. They could spot him a mile away because he was the only one on the Ramblas who wore a pink shirt. They didn't come near him any more unless they wanted their noses nicked.

He collected his mail at the nearby post office where he had a box, and continued up the Ramblas, then turned off into the Barrio Chino. There weren't too many Chinese left and that suited him fine. He didn't like the Chinese. All the old Chinese signs had been torn down and the Barrio Chino, though it still retained the name, was just as Catalonian as any other part of the city.

He went to his favorite cafe in a street so narrow he could spit across it. He sat at his preferred sidewalk table and tried not to let the donkey shit squashed between the cobblestones bother him too much. The waiter brought him a croissant and a glass of wine. He lit a cigarette, tossed the match into the gutter where it sputtered briefly, and began opening his mail.

Mostly bills. A formal wear shop? Ah, yes, the new cummerbund and bow-tie. Then a bill from the garage for repairs on his Seat. Another one from the yacht club and another from the telephone company. And then there was the monthly notice from the *Asociación de la Derecha Falangista*, Barcelona chapter, telling him the date of the next meeting and that his quarterly dues were late. Why did they still bother him? Enrique and Ramon knew he hadn't come to a meeting in three years. Enrique and Ramon should know by know that Spaniards couldn't discuss politics in a civil fashion. The meetings always degenerated into drunken shouting matches. And now that Franco was in power politics didn't matter anyway. Oh, well, he thought, just send them their two-hundred-and-fifty pesetas and forget about them. And what was this? Postmarked in England. Perhaps from MI5, whom he sometimes sold his services to? The envelope was too grubby for a British government office, looked as if it had been folded in someone's pocket for a long time. The end had been taped up with that special government recycling tape they were using in Britain now and was postmarked in Barrow-in-Furness. That rang a bell. He slit the end of the envelope and took out a single folded sheet. On it was a single name. Helga Weiss.

•

Goerlitz pushed a large wheeled bucket up the camp road toward the shower-house with a mop. In the yard below the Triggsdale Hall football team and the naval base team played a game of soccer in the warm September sunshine. A group of spectators, bussed in from Barrow-in-Furness, crowded the hill, cheering and clapping as the players kicked the ball around the field. A number of prisoners stood in grey striped uniforms at the end of the field following the game, and several staff officers sat on the steps of Triggsdale Hall. Ballerstedt was at the back of the shower-house, out of sight. Goerlitz smiled. It was good to be fighting this war again, even in this small way.

Sergeant Saville stood guard outside the shower-house door, smoking a cigarette, drinking a bottle of brown ale, watching the game from afar. As Goerlitz approached, the sergeant pulled his shoulders back and put his bottle of beer on the shower-house step. Saville was an older man, forty-five or fifty, who had been called up from the reserve and who looked as if he might have been a clerk in civilian life. He was somewhere between five and six feet, closer to five, had a beer-nurtured paunch, and a sanguine complexion. His blue eyes bulged as Goerlitz neared him. There was a little bit of beer foam on his stiff grey mustache. Goerlitz stopped and saluted.

"Permission to enter the shower-house, sir."

Saville looked Goerlitz up and down. Goerlitz pretended to be bored, his eyes straying to the game.

"I wasn't told about this," said Saville. "I thought

Schlabrendorff was on maintenance detail this week."

"He is. He's got the flu and I've been ordered to take over."

Saville considered this, his blue eyes bulging even more. A sudden cheer came from the field. Saville looked past Goerlitz, distracted.

"Well, I suppose it's all right. Go ahead. You know where the hose is, don't you?"

"Yes. Schlabrendorff told me."

He had expected to find the shower-house empty, that everybody would be watching the game, but he found a player from the naval base team sitting on a bench in the locker room adjoining the shower-house. He was a young man, no more than twenty-five, with curly, sweat-soaked brown hair and a wiry muscular build. Goerlitz walked past him. The man was bare-chested, with the arms of his shirt tied around his neck. He was wearing cleats. His pant leg was rolled up and he was tying and retying an elastic tenser bandage around his calf, trying to get it just right. Goerlitz wheeled the bucket around the side, gazing at the wall where uniforms and a few suits hung from brass hooks. Damn, he thought. How was he going to do this with that sailor in the room? There were only about ten minutes left in the game, then this room would be crowded with sailors. He continued to wheel the bucket into the shower room where eighteen shower spouts stuck out of the green-tiled wall in a long neat row. At the end of the row there was a thick partition, and behind this, shelves of cleaning supplies and a utility sink built into the floor. A long rubber hose was attached to the tap. He turned it on full, letting it run to cover the sound of his movements.

He walked back to the end of the shower room where there were some long narrow windows placed high in the wall. He opened one of them, the top pulling outward like a transom above a door, then climbed on the bench and pulled himself up. Outside he saw the hill behind Buildings A through E, and at the top of the hill through the sparse plane trees, a long stretch of concertina barbed wire.

"Ballerstedt," he whispered.

Ballerstedt's head appeared below him, coming out from the wall where his friend had been waiting. Ballerstedt nodded, then disappeared beneath the edge of the window again. Goerlitz dropped lightly to his feet, walked back to the utility sink, and filled the tin basin with water. While it was filling he crept back and looked around the doorway into the locker room. The man was still there tying his tenser bandage. Goerlitz scanned the line of uniforms and suits hanging on the hooks. Only three suits to choose from. Two grey ones and a brown one at the end right next to the man. But the man would have to go if he was going to do anything.

Goerlitz hurried back to the utility sink, turned off the tap, and looked at the boxes and bottles of cleaning materials. His instructor at the *Abwehr* training school outside Hamburg, Colonel Peter Hashagen, had always taught them to use, as weapons, any materials that came to hand. There was bleach, powdered cleanser, liquid soap, hydrochloric acid, bar soap, ammonia, industrial floor polish and a number of other cleaning supplies. Ammonia, he thought. He took the bottle of ammonia down, opened it, sniffed it, flinched, and began pouring it into the tin bucket. The fumes were strong but he continued to pour until they were almost unbearable, then put the cap back on the bottle and the bottle back on the shelf. He wheeled the mop and basin into the shower room, his eyes squinting at the powerful fumes, and started swilling the strong solution around on the floor in the corner with his mop. Almost as bad as the chlorine fumes from battery damage on a U-boat, he thought.

At first the naval base team player didn't notice but

in a few moments he coughed softly, turned to Goerlitz, and stood up.

"Hey," he called. "Hey, you. What the hell do you think you're doing?"

Goerlitz stopped working, and, pretending he didn't understand English, put on his politest smile, and using his politest voice, said, in German, "I'm cleaning the floor, you stupid English bastard."

The man stared uncomprehendingly at Goerlitz.

"Oh, for Christ's sake, couldn't you have waited to do this? That stuff smells to high heaven."

The man picked up his shirt, and, tenser bandage dragging along the floor, marched out of the shower-house, cursing quietly. Goerlitz continued to mop the floor until he was sure the man was safely out of the shower-house, then abruptly let go of the mop, allowing it to clatter to the floor, and hurried to the row of uniforms and suits. Oh, God, he had only seven minutes to do this.

He pulled the jacket of the first grey flannel suit around his shoulders. There were pale green pinstripes through it. Too tight around the shoulders, and the arms were a little short. He coughed into the ammonia and his eyes watered, irritated by the stinging vapors. He pulled the jacket off and went to the next grey suit, of a heavier tweed material. The jacket was still snug, but at least it was a reasonable fit, so he took off his prison trousers and tried on the suit pants, afraid that at any moment Sergeant Saville might walk in. Pants too short and too tight. He pulled the suit off, hung it up quickly, then moved onto the brown one. If worst came to worst, he would just have to take the second grey suit and make do with it.

He tried on the brown jacket first. A much better fit than the others. The arms molded comfortably up around his shoulders and the sleeves hung evenly at the wrists. But the lapel was slightly torn. Oh, well, that didn't matter so much. He glanced toward the door, then, sitting on the bench, quickly pulled on the pair of brown pants. Not exactly perfect but much better than the others. He secured the belt at the last hole. Ballerstedt would be able to shorten the legs the inch or two they needed with a needle and thread. He pulled the suit off and got back into his prison uniform as fast as he could, sweating with effort. Another cheer came from outside. The game was almost over. He dashed around the corner into the shower room, the suit rolled into a ball under his arm.

"Ballerstedt."

He listened. Nothing.

Then Ballerstedt began to whistle *Lili Marlene*. That meant wait. That meant keep quiet, that one of the guards was passing. There were only three minutes left.

Goerlitz dropped the suit on the bench in the shower room and hurried back to the locker room, where he started going through the shoes — loafers, Oxfords, and brogues — pair by pair until he found some old brown brogues that fit.

He went back to the shower room and listened at the window. Ballerstedt was still whistling *Lili Marlene*, but in a few moments he stopped.

"Heinz," whispered Goerlitz.

"It's all clear, Goerlitz. I'm waiting. Saville is wandering down to the field. The game is almost over. Hurry up."

Goerlitz climbed up onto the bench and dropped both the shoes and the suit out the high window. Ballerstedt stowed the articles into a thirty-gallon pail, one of the pails the prisoners used to carry flattened tin cans, slate, sewage, water, firewood, coal, and so on, and walked slowly away. Yes, it was good to be fighting this war again. Good to be following Weiss's orders again. He watched Ballerstedt carry the pail to the far end of the yard and leave it where the municipal garbage truck from Barrow-in-Furness came to pick up their garbage. In a few moments Schlabrendorff came by and carried it into Building C, just as Weiss had planned.

•

The navy blokes began to come on strong only toward the end of the game. Major Hatley, playing goalie at the far end of the Triggsdale Hall yard, was in fine form. The score was 3-0 for Triggsdale Hall, and he was determined to keep it that way. His wife, Marjorie, and her girl friends sat drinking tea on the hill leading up to the parking lot. Patterson, who played forward, was tiring, and so was the defense. There were only seconds left in the game. The navy blokes were getting their second wind and coming at him from the other end of the yard. Hatley crouched and got ready. The big man with the red mustache kicked the ball to the small chap with the black hair, and the small chap took a long shot at the net.

Hatley ran for the ball and it bounced off his shoulder. A cheer rose from the hill. The fellow with the mustache came around the side and tried to kick the ball into the unguarded corner at the right of the net. The ball skidded along the grass. Hatley stretched his leg as far as he could and stopped the ball.

He saw Patterson halfway down the field running furiously toward him. A third sailor caught the rebound and tried to kick the ball into the Triggsdale Hall net once again, and this time the ball went high. Hatley jumped for it and angled his head. The ball bounced off his head and flew far out into the field. Hatley was amazed. He had never made a save like that in his life. He laughed out of exhilaration.

A few guards ran by. "Great save, sir."

"Great?" he said. "It was fantastic. We're going to shut the bloody bastards out, I tell you." He called across the field to Marjorie. "Hey, Marjorie, did you see that save? Save of a bloody lifetime."

The referee blew the whistle and the game was over. The major jumped into the air and punched at the sky.

"A shutout," he cried.

He ran out to the field. He had clearly been a star. He had never played so well in his life. McDonald, Linholm and Archer lifted him onto their shoulders as the ladies on the hill clapped for him. Hatley raised his arms in the air. His men cheered him. Navy blokes thought they were so good. Teach them a lesson. Couldn't get the ball in even if the net were as wide as the channel. Teach them all a lesson.

They put him down and slapped him on the back. He glanced over his shoulder. Marjorie had left the hill and was waiting for him with her friends in the parking lot. He jogged across the yard and up the hill.

"Oh, Ray, you're sopping wet," she said.

He kidded along with her in front of her friends.

"Is that all you can think of, Marjorie, when I've made the save of the century? Of course I'm sweaty." He chuckled and gave her a kiss. Tonight was their night, and now, to make it better, they had something special to celebrate. "I've been preserving the honor of Triggsdale Hall."

"You did marvelously, Ray." She kissed him.

"Didn't I, though?"

"You certainly did. Now, come on, you'd better get washed up."

"You go home with one of the girls, Megs. I'll be home shortly. I have a few odds and sods to arrange in the office."

"All right, dear. I'll start dinner. But do hurry."

"Can't wait to get the meat in the oven, eh?" he said,

squeezing her, smiling just enough to reveal the space between his teeth. "Off with you now."

He jogged across the field to Triggsdale Hall.

In his office he found his assistant, Lieutenant Carberry, waiting for him.

"Dr. Duncan was up from town during the game, sir," said the lieutenant.

"Was he?" said the major, wiping the sweat off the back of his neck. "Well, it took enough nagging, didn't it? He's two weeks late."

"He says there's been an outbreak of influenza. Four men altogether."

"Who?"

"Meissner, Frischauer, Schlabrendorff, and Hoetll."

"Building C, in other words."

"Yes, sir. Dr. Duncan suggests rest and isolation for a few days. No details or duties."

"All right. Anything else, Carberry?"

"That's it, major."

"Did you see any of the game?"

"Only bits and pieces. I had a lot of paperwork to do."

"We won."

"Did you really, sir?"

"It was a shutout."

"A shutout. Well, Grey must feel proud of himself."

"No, Grey wasn't playing goalie this time. I was."

"Good show, sir, good show."

Hatley smiled at Carberry. "I thought I might give those navy blokes a few lessons."

He heard the sound of cleats approaching from down the hall.

"I wonder who the devil this could be," he said.

Two members of the navy team entered the office. The curly-headed one spoke first.

"My name's Bendersky. Captain Bendersky."

"Major Hatley," said Hatley. "Good game, sir. You were playing defense, weren't you?"

"Yes, I was. This is Ensign Beaumont."

The ensign saluted.

"Is there a problem, captain?"

"The ensigns's suit is missing," said the captain.

"Is it really?"

"We can't find it anywhere," said Ensign Beaumont.

The major smiled. Sour grapes. He should have expected it from the navy blokes.

"Where did you leave it, ensign?"

"In the locker room, sir."

"And you're sure it's not there?"

"Major," said the captain, "we've looked everywhere. We think one of the prisoners might have stolen it."

"I hardly think one of my prisoners would steal it. This is an officers' prisoner-of-war camp, captain. They simply wouldn't do something like that. Maybe your friends are hiding it on you for a joke."

"With all due respect, sir," said Ensign Beaumont, "they're not in a very joking mood."

The major smiled then chuckled. "No, I suppose they're not."

"Sir, the suit cost me fourteen pounds."

"Fourteen pounds? Is that all?"

"That's quite a bit for the ordinary enlisted man, major," said Captain Bendersky.

"Yes, I suppose it is."

"And we would appreciate it very much if you had the camp searched."

Hatley thought of the evening's plan, how Marjorie would be waiting to hike her skirt above her hips, and how disheartened his men would be after their resounding victory to have to search the camp right now. But sour grapes was sour grapes, and he could see it written all over Bendersky's face. More than likely the suit hadn't even been stolen, because after all, they had bumped the navy team from their second place standing. Well, if that's the way Bendersky wanted it, he had no choice. Might as well teach them a thing or two about good sportsmanship too.

"Of course, sir. I'll have the camp searched at once."

He had Carberry run to the locker room.

Soon his men were back, still in their shorts and jerseys, standing in the yard, sullen and disgruntled. He walked forward, hands behind his back, cleats gripping the grass.

"I'm sorry about this, men." He looked toward the sidelines, where Captain Bendersky and Ensign Beaumont stood waiting with a few of their team mates, out of earshot. "But I'm afraid Captain Bendersky insists on this search. And you know I've always done everything by the book. Strictly routine. Don't bend over backwards. You know the procedure. Patterson, take your men down to the quarry. Saville, you check the buildings. And Ridout, take your men and have a look around the pond and the box. Carberry, have the prisoners rounded up in the yard under armed guard."

"Aren't you overdoing it a bit, sir?"

"Just do as I say. I want to show Bendersky just what kind of fool he's being. By the book, lieutenant."

"If you say so, Ray."

Carberry took five of the men and soon all the prisoners were gathered in the yard, one-hundred-and-seventy-two U-boat officers, shuffling figures in striped grey and black uniforms. Bendersky and Beaumont began to approach Hatley from the far side of the yard, but stopped and gazed at the prisoners for several minutes. Hatley's eyes were drawn to Goerlitz. He was so pale. Hatley supposed that's what happened when one spent one's life in a submarine. Goerlitz glanced toward him. Hatley looked away, focused on Weiss. Weiss kept his head down, looking straight ahead. Ballerstedt was talking to Schlabrendorff, and Frischauer gazed at Bendersky and Beaumont, as if he were somehow astonished by them. How bleak their grey prisoner uniforms looked against the brilliant blue sky, he thought.

Bendersky and Beaumont stood watching the prisoners for a few more moments, then walked toward Major Hatley. Hatley turned in their direction, unsmiling. He wasn't going to let them believe he was happy about this.

"We didn't mean for you to go to so much trouble, major," said Bendersky.

"Standard procedure, sir. I won't say my boys are thrilled. But they'll do it. I still doubt one of the prisoners has taken it. They hardly look as if they're going dancing, do they?"

"Well, Ensign Beaumont appreciates it, Hatley. You're a good sport. A damn good sport."

Saville was the first to report back. He took the major aside.

"Look at this. Look at what we found in the games room of Building E."

Saville showed Hatley a series of photographs, nude women in garter belts and stockings.

"How do you suppose they got hold of these?" asked the sergeant.

"I've known about this for a long time, Saville. And frankly, I've turned a blind eye. Obviously there's someone on staff who's helping them, and it's harmless enough. Terry, we're both married men, we can get it whenever we want. But think of these poor buggers."

Sergeant Saville reflected for a moment.

"That's true, sir. That's very true."

"I just prefer to keep it quiet. If it will let some steam off, who cares how they're getting into the camp?"

"That's a good point." Saville glanced warily at Bendersky and Beaumont. "What should I do with the photographs, sir?"

Hatley smiled, once again revealing the space

between his teeth. "Give them to me," he said. "I'll look after them."

Patterson and Ridout finally reported back ten or fifteen minutes later. They hadn't found the missing suit either. Hatley approached Bendersky. The captain looked uncomfortable.

"I'm sorry, sir," said Hatley, "but we can't seem to find the suit."

"Really, Hatley, I didn't mean you to go to so much bother."

"Oh, no bother, sir." Yes, he would teach them a thing or two about good sportsmanship. "No bother at all. I'm sorry about the suit. The best I can do for now is write the ensign check on the camp account for fourteen pounds, and he can buy a new one." He turned to Beaumont. "I'll search the camp again tomorrow and call you if your suit turns up. If you want a prisoner's uniform in the meantime, sergeant, there's a few available."

The captain nodded, embarrassed.

"How's that sound, ensign?"

"I'm sure McDonald and Archer have taken it," said Ensign Beaumont. "I don't trust those two. They're a couple of jokers."

"Maybe they have. If they have, they're just having fun. I'm offering you fourteen pounds for their fun, ensign. Take it or leave it. I think I've been more than cooperative."

"Yes, you have, Hatley," said Bendersky.

"I suppose I'll take it," said Beaumont. "Though I don't know where I'll find a suit like that for fourteen pounds these days."

Chapter 8

By evening, the spotty showers had turned to a steady drizzle. Commander Weiss leaned the shovel he had been using to spade the shrubbery gardens of Triggsdale Hall against the balustrade. He walked quietly around what had once been the conservatory but what had now been converted into a greenhouse to grow tomatoes and cucumbers, stopping when he came to the windows of Major Hatley's office. Weiss grinned. The prison inspectors had arrived a half hour ago and were sharing a drink with the commandant before inspecting the camp. He kept going toward the portico, stopping when he got to Major Hatley's rusted out Morris. He looked around. A guard patrolled the far road by Buildings A through E, and there was another down by the quarry, and one up by the half completed wall at the end of the fairway.

He crouched behind the car and listened. No boots coming. Only the sound of the rain and wind through the trees in the hills. He opened the door, the clumsy old hinges clunking enough to make him wince, leaned across the seat, and snapped open the glove compartment. The compartment was packed with a pile of disorganized junk; papers, old bills, a couple of screwdrivers. He took it all out and began sorting through it quickly. After a few minutes he found what he was looking for, a dog-eared map of Barrow-in-Furness and the surrounding Cumbrian countryside. He put the rest of the junk back into the glove compartment, got out of the car, closed the door as quietly as he could, took off his left shoe and lined the instep with the map, then put the shoe back on.

He walked with his usual prisoner's gait across the yard, avoiding puddles so the map wouldn't get wet, then followed the camp road past Buildings A through E to the mess hall where prisoners had started to gather for the evening meal. Weiss walked to his crew's table. Frischauer, Ballerstedt, Goerlitz, and Schlabrendorff were waiting for him. He nodded.

"I've got it," he said. He looked at the *Kriegsmarine* officers, forty-five or fifty of them, sitting around the mess hall. "Have you told them what to do when the prison inspectors get here?"

"They know," said Ballerstedt.

"And Frischauer, you're ready?"

"It should be easy," answered his Number One.

"Goerlitz, you just stay out of the way. The last thing we need is you back in the box right now."

"Yes, captain."

"When do you think they'll come to the mess hall?" asked Schlabrendorff.

"I'm not sure. But Patterson said certainly while we're eating."

The prisoners were halfway through their potato and celery stew when the prison inspectors, accompanied by Major Hatley, and Hatley's assistant, Lieutenant Carberry, entered the mess hall. The chief inspector was an older man with a brown bowler derby and a watch chain hanging from his vest pocket. The junior inspector was a much younger man, and though Weiss could see he didn't have the same broad shoulders Goerlitz had, he was roughly the same height and about the same age. The older inspector leaned over to the nearest table and spoke to one of the prisoners. Apparently he knew some German. The prisoner took out a package of cigarettes and gave one to the inspector. The inspector lit it, inhaled, blew smoke toward the dim incandescent bulbs, then moved on, looking around the hall. Weiss looked at Frischauer.

"You know who you want."

Frischauer nodded.

Weiss looked around the hall, catching furtive glances everywhere. He lifted his spoon, held it in the air for a second or two, and dropped it to the floor. Immediately, down the table, prisoners started pushing and shoving each other, and the pushing spread through the hall quickly. Sailors got to their feet upsetting chairs and tables, causing a horrible noise, yelling and shouting while Hatley, Carberry, and the inspectors looked on, unsure of what to do. The fracas, as if it had a mind of its own, enveloped Hatley, Carberry, and the inspectors. Frischauer, who before he had joined the *Unterseewaffe* had lived in the St. Pauli district of Hamburg on the Reeperbahn, and who possessed many street-wise skills, insinuated his way into the crowd of fighting U-boat men. Weiss watched his Number One carefully. Within seconds Frischauer was next to the junior inspector. Suddenly there was a lot of jostling among the prisoners. Even Weiss couldn't see Frischauer's hand. Frischauer was quick and accurate. Weiss's Number One moved away just as Sergeant Saville and five guards came in from the other side, blowing their whistles. Frischauer came back to the table.

"Do you have it?" asked Weiss, over the din.

Frischauer showed him a wallet and a National Registration Identity card.

"Good," said Weiss. "Now, get out of here with it."

●

It was raining the night Inspector Gerald Laurie went to see Goerlitz at the prison camp. The light had all but disappeared from the sky. Triggsdale Hall sat like a great brick pile in the gloom. Laurie didn't expect much from Goerlitz, but it was worth a try, and he certainly didn't have anything else to do. Not until Murray Simp-son-Beale arrived the beginning of next week.

Major Raymond Hatley greeted him in the large front hall of the late Lord Selby's country manor. The camp commandant was a tall man whose uniform fit him badly, who had a spot of egg or mustard on his tie, and whose minty breath belied the alcoholic glaze over his dissolute grey eyes. The major saluted, then shook the inspector's hand.

"So pleased to meet you, Major," said Laurie.

"The pleasure's all mine, inspector. We always like to work closely with intelligence in these matters. Could I fix you a drink before we start?"

"No, I don't think so. I know you're a busy man. I wouldn't want to take up too much of your time."

"Quite all right, inspector, quite all right. If you'd come this way, the prisoner's upstairs."

Laurie followed Major Hatley up a wide curving staircase. The wallpaper had a rich burgundy pattern, was old, stained in places and peeling in others. Hatley took him to a large room at the end of the hall, what the major told him had once been the butler's bedroom.

Inside, Goerlitz waited at a bare wooden table, watched over by two guards.

"Thank you very much, gentlemen," said Hatley.

"You may wait outside the door. We shall call you if we need you."

The guards left the room.

Laurie sat in the chair opposite Goerlitz, folded his hands on the table, and studied the German U-boat commander. He had stern keen eyes, and watched Laurie warily. His hair was light brown, almost blond. He had a wide but nevertheless pleasant face, broad shoulders, and a strong jaw. His hair was starting to thin near the front, but this somehow made him appear stronger, wiser. He was around thirty or forty, and looked as if he could ably command a U-boat.

"So, Captain Goerlitz," began Laurie. "I understand you speak English."

"I do," said Goerlitz, his tone neutral.

"I hope they're treating you well here. We do try and make a special effort for German officers. After all, we can fight a war, can't we, but there's no need to be uncivilized."

"Conditions are adequate, inspector."

"Good. And I hope you've had time to rest. And time to reflect."

"Oh?" said Goerlitz. "And what do you expect me to reflect on, inspector?"

"Prison time, captain. It's an idea that takes getting used to. And I should like to talk to you about your boat. I hope you've reflected on that. Of course, the Americans have made several sightings of the Type IX up and down their eastern seaboard, but you've provided us with a rare opportunity to study the Type IX in detail. I'm particularly interested in the hull and the hull supports. I expect the prototype must have undergone rigorous tests. We've never seen so much armor. Just how much blast can she stand? How much pressure can she take? The pressure gauge says 280 metres. But I expect she can stand twice that, judging from the construction."

"Why don't you take her down and find out?"

"We intend to, captain."

The two men looked at each other. Laurie could see clearly that Goerlitz wasn't going to help him in the least. Still, he had come all this way, and he couldn't resist baiting the commander.

"We've had our people question some of your crew in Dorset. I don't know whether you've been told. That's where the rest of them are. They found Lieutenant Bergen most cooperative. He said you kept them down for twelve hours breathing chlorine fumes. Your High Command should figure out some way to stop the battery acid from mixing with the sea water in the bilge. In high concentrations I imagine it becomes fatal."

"Perhaps you should drop Doenitz a note and give him your advice. I'm sure he would appreciate it."

"Bergen also said the training period for U-boat crews has been reduced from six to two months. Is this true?"

"Ask yourself whether Bergen is a man you can believe, and you will have the answer."

"I've never met the man, but my people tell me he's quite reasonable."

"I suppose in England your definition of a reasonable man is one who betrays his country. In Germany we happen to think otherwise."

"He's reasonable enough to understand the war is over."

"Tell that to Russian troops on the Eastern Front. Inspector, I think our conversation has gone on long enough. I have nothing to tell you. I'm sure you'll find out all you have to soon enough without my help."

Inspector Laurie looked at Major Hatley. The major simply shrugged. Laurie turned and smiled at Goerlitz.

"I see, captain. As you wish. I don't know what you think you're going to achieve by struggling against us. But let me just say something before I go. It is 1943. The

Allies will win this war by 1944. Even your own analysts will tell you that. If you help us now, when the war is over, we'll do everything we can to reunite you with your family and help you get back on your feet."

"How very obliging of you, inspector. But the answer is no."

"Very well, captain. But do think about it, won't you? Perhaps you'll change your mind after a month or two."

A few minutes later, Inspector Laurie walked with Major Hatley down to the large front portico of Triggsdale Hall. The rain had lessened though it was still steady and now a faint mist rose from the yard. They stood on the steps for a moment. Laurie tucked his tartan scarf into his overcoat then pulled on his leather driving gloves.

"He strikes me as a problem," said Laurie.

"I personally don't like him inspector. He's certainly stubborn, different from most of the men who come here. But I imagine he'll change. I guess we have to expect this kind of thing at the beginning, especially from a U-boat commander. We had the same problem with Weiss. Now he's a pussycat."

Laurie looked across the yard to the parking lot where Westmoreland waited in their government car.

"You'll give me a call if anything develops, won't you?" he said. "He may decide to talk after a week or two."

"Believe me, inspector, you'll be the first to know. You can take my word on that."

•

The following morning Goerlitz and Ballerstedt were on quarry detail. The sky was patterned with several rows of ridge-like cumulus clouds, allowing intermittent periods of sunshine. Goerlitz stood on a ledge up high against the slate rock-face, a sledge hammer in one hand

and a four-pound chisel in the other. He wedged the chisel into a crack, swung back, and slammed it with the sledge hammer. A sizeable slab of slate tumbled to the ledge, and he heaved it into one of the thirty-gallon all-purpose pails. The pail was now full and he lowered it with a rope to Ballerstedt, who was standing on the quarry road next to two almost full wheelbarrows. Saville, McDonald, and Archer were standing guard at the top of the road, passing around a Thermos of tea, chatting, and smoking cigarettes. Other prisoners were breaking off slabs of slate from the rock-face all over the quarry and the air resounded with the bangs of hammers and chisels. He looked down at Ballerstedt. His friend, in spite of the cool weather, had taken his shirt off. It was hot and heavy work. Ballerstedt emptied the thirty-gallon pail into one of the wheelbarrows then looked up at Goerlitz.

"They're full," he called. "You can come down now. We're ready."

Goerlitz carefully groped his way down the rock-face. At the bottom, each man got behind a wheelbarrow and began to push it up the quarry road. Luckily it was Archer's turn to escort them up to the trout pond with their loads. Archer didn't speak any German at all, whereas McDonald and Saville both had a rough command of basic conversational German. Which meant Goerlitz and Ballerstedt could talk without fear of being understood.

"Well, Heinz?" asked Goerlitz.

"Hermann, I don't like it. I wish you'd drop the whole idea."

"Heinz, in another week the British will feel confident enough with my boat to move it somewhere else. We'll have lost all our chances."

Ballerstedt glanced up the road where the local garbage truck was taking the camp's trash away.

"You heard the captain, Hermann. You are to go

91

nowhere near U-512. If you do, it will jeopardize your chances of getting the dispositions to the High Command."

"Heinz, listen to me. You've got to help me. You're the only one in the camp who knows how to build a bomb. And destroying U-512 is an achievable objective. The captain's plan has too much going against it. Everything hinges on this Spaniard, someone who may or may not have been contacted by an *Abwehr* agent in Barcelona almost three years ago. And how do we know Weiss's message to him last week even got through? He might be dead. Or maybe his firm went out of business. Or maybe he's no longer making his scheduled run to Liverpool." He heaved his wheelbarrow through an obstinate patch of gravel. "Heinz, the odds are a hundred, maybe a thousand to one, that I will ever make it back to Germany. I know that and Weiss knows that. If I'm going to end up with a bullet in my back, or at the end of a rope, let me at least have done something worthwhile for it."

They walked past Buildings A through E up to the parking lot, then turned down the trail leading to the fairway, where through the yellowing trees, Goerlitz saw morning mist rising from the grass. He could sense Ballerstedt was wavering, and he pressed further.

"Suppose I do make it. Suppose I get all the way to Lorient and I give the dispositions and other material to Admiral Doenitz. Penetration of the Irish Sea is virtually impossible these days. It may have been a workable plan at the beginning of the war, when the enemy had nothing to fight us with, and it may have stood every chance of success, but the British have made great strides in submarine detection. All of us here are the proof of it. They have Huff-Duff. They have ASDIC and short-wave radar. To send a wolfpack into the Irish Sea now would simply be sending them to their slaughter."

Ballerstedt had nothing to say to this. His face grew

somber as they came out onto the fairway. A cloud caused a brief shadow to play over the grass, but as they headed toward the trout pond the sun came out again and a gust of wind sent some leaves scurrying across the fairway like a panicked crowd.

"I don't know," said Ballerstedt. "Things can't be as bad as all that. Not after only two years."

"Believe me, Heinz. Why do you think Hitler reduced the training period? Because we're losing crews faster than we can produce them. Now, look, if I get the material to Admiral Doenitz I'm the first to admit he might possibly use it, and he might have some success with it, but only at a great cost both in human lives and materiel to the *Unterseewaffe*. And what will we gain? A year? Maybe two? Maybe nothing at all."

"Weiss says it could turn the tide in our favor."

"They'll mount a massive manhunt for me. And the longer I'm at large the more likelihood there is of me getting caught. How many days to Barrow-in-Furness? I can walk it in a day. But Liverpool? I'll have to buy a train ticket. It could take me three days before I get there, maybe even up to a week. They'll know I've gone by that time, even with the deception Weiss has planned. And then once I get there I'll have to rely on this Spaniard. You see my point, don't you? I can get to Barrow-in-Furness. I can destroy my boat. We'll have accomplished something concrete for all our trouble. But it's highly unlikely I'll ever live to get out of the country with the dispositions of Morecambe Bay."

They reached the end of the fairway and dumped their slate into a pile near the trout pond. Other prisoners were stacking the slabs to make a wall just beyond the pond, in essence, building their own cage. They turned around and began heading back to the quarry, Archer still escorting them from behind.

"Help me, Heinz," said Goerlitz. "Build me the bomb.

Certainly I'll try to succeed with both objectives, but it's better I succeed with only one than with none at all. And we don't have to tell anybody, Heinz. Nobody at all."

"We could be court-martialed for insubordination," said Ballerstedt.

Goerlitz smiled, and the smile was not without irony.

"We're in a prisoner-of-war camp in a remote corner of England, Heinz, and the old rules don't apply here. Remember?"

Ballerstedt looked over to the copse were a group of rooks cawed their way over the treetops. There was another gust of wind and Goerlitz saw a stippled pattern of goose bumps appear on Ballerstedt's bare arms.

"Enough," he said, at last, still gazing at the rooks. "Yes, Hermann, I'll help you."

•

If camp guards at Triggsdale Hall had been more observant they might have noticed a certain number of things had disappeared. But they weren't trained soldiers, just normal good-natured men called up from the reserve, most of them over forty, who wanted to get through the war with as little trouble as possible. All were happy with their assignment at Triggsdale Hall because, as with most officers' camps, it was more of a country club than a prison, and many had grown to be friends with the U-boat men, didn't suspect them of anything. So they didn't notice when a screwdriver, a wrench, a pair of pliers, and a flashlight went missing from the machine shop. Nor did they notice, on the day of the prison inspectors' visit, a piece of metal tubing used in making a seat brace for a Lancaster bomber missing, or a couple of round steel plates, or some sturdy two and-a-half-inch bolts, all of which were secured under the floorboards beneath Ballerstedt's bunk.

And if they didn't notice these things they were unlikely to miss a small piece of wire, a glass vial stolen from the infirmary, and some hydrochloric acid taken from the cleaning supply shelves in the shower-house. As far as they were concerned, these things didn't happen at Triggsdale Hall. The German officers in the camp had too much dignity for theft.

If Sergeant Saville, for instance, had been more observant, he might have noticed how the hose hanging above the utility sink in the shower-house was now half its former length, the other half having been cut off by Goerlitz with a butter knife he had stolen from the mess hall. Nor did the guards of Triggsdale Hall hear the small noises Ballerstedt made in the copse while he went about his preliminary work on the bomb. And if Lieutenant Carberry had kept a sharper inventory of the staff stores in the cavernous cellars of Triggsdale Hall, he might have noticed how three packages of biscuits had disappeared, stolen while Ballerstedt had been cleaning the chandelier in the staff lounge. But none of them noticed anything. Their easy assignment, great sense of well-being, and country club lives blinded them to these things.

It was well past three in the morning when Goerlitz sat up in his bunk. Commander Weiss was sound asleep. So were all the others. He swung his feet silently out of bed, walked across the floor to Ballerstedt's bunk and looked down at his old friend.

"Heinz," he whispered.

Ballerstedt opened his eyes.

"Shhh. . ." he said.

Ballerstedt rolled from his bunk fully clothed in his prison uniform, his shoes on, crawled underneath, pulled some of the floorboards quietly away, and handed Goerlitz the flashlight, screwdriver, piece of hose from the utility sink, small cloth satchel and a box of matches. Ballerstedt slid out from under the bunk and stood up just as the spotlight brightened the room. Goerlitz walked to the back window, which he had left open. Ballerstedt walked to the front window, scanned the camp for several moments, then hurried past the rows of bunks and joined Goerlitz. They climbed out and hopped to the ground.

They stood still. The rain had stopped but the sky was still bristling with luminous storm clouds. Goerlitz carried the hose and the box of matches. Ballerstedt took the screwdriver, flashlight, and cloth satchel, and started for the explosives sheds. Patterson was on guard duty. Goerlitz crept from building to building up to the camp parking lot. The wind was up, promised more rain, and Goerlitz was glad because it would cover any noise they made.

At the parking lot he hid behind a jeep and gazed down at the explosives sheds, where he saw Patterson reading a book by the beam of a flashlight. He waited another minute, just to make sure Ballerstedt was ready, then unscrewed the jeep's gas cap, inserted the hose, and began siphoning the green-colored military gasoline all over the parking lot under the jeep.

When the area around the jeep was soaked with gasoline he pulled out the hose, stepped back, and took out his box of matches. He looked at the explosives shed where Patterson was still reading. He crouched, lit his match, shielding it with cupped hands against the wind, then gently tossed it into the puddle of gas and ran. There was a tremendous poof, and sooty orange flames engulfed the jeep.

Goerlitz didn't look back, kept running until he was in the copse, then felt his way through the trees up the hill until he had a good vantage point.

In the lurid glare of the flames he saw Patterson standing at the explosives shed door, just standing, completely surprised. But in a moment the corporal unlocked the explosives shed, grabbed the fire extinguisher inside, and began running frantically for the parking lot, leaving the door wide open. Patterson started shouting, but the wind was too strong, and Goerlitz couldn't make out his words.

The corporal had just reached the jeep when Goerlitz saw a small crouching figure run into the explosives shed. Other guards came running across the yard from Triggsdale Hall, and they were all too concerned with the fire to notice the vague and fitful glow of a flashlight scanning the boxes and crates inside the explosives shed. Goerlitz heard the sudden windy howl of fire extinguishers. After another minute, Ballerstedt emerged from the shed and ran past the quarry road up to the latrines.

Goerlitz followed the concertina wire along the top of the hill until he came to Building C, then descended the path. He met Ballerstedt at the back of Building C. Both men were out of breath.

"Well?" said Goerlitz.

Ballerstedt held up his small cloth satchel

"Five pounds of plastic explosives, a firing pin, and a percussion cap," he said. "Just what we need."

•

The train jostled through the English countryside. Bower looked at Inspector Douglas, an older man with a mustache like steel wool. The inspector snored. Bower smiled. Why did the inspector always have to bum cigarettes? They had spent the last week inspecting camps and munitions factories in northeast England. At every camp and at every factory the inspector had bummed at least three or four cigarettes. At Triggsdale Hall, Douglas had actually bummed cigarettes from the prisoners. You would think with the money he earned he wouldn't have to bum cigarettes.

Bower waited until the inspector's head tilted forward. The inspector's snore, regular and even, could be heard over the sound of the train. Slowly, ever so slowly, Bower reached in the side pocket of his blazer. He stiffened when all he felt were his cigarettes and lighter. Where was his wallet, and where was his National Registration Identity card? Thank God he still had his Ministry train pass. He checked his other pockets but all he found were a few old envelopes he planned to re-use and a couple of shillings. He had brought over fifty pounds. Damn these crowded trains, he thought. A perfect opportunity for pickpockets. Douglas stirred and opened his eyes. The inspector looked immediately at Bower's cigarettes.

"Going to have a smoke, are you?" he said. "Do you mind if I bum one?"

•

On the Sunday after the football match, the skies cleared and the temperature rose, and everybody in the Lake District spoke of an Indian Summer. Major Hatley felt like a king. The inspectors had come and gone without a complaint, and the Barrow- in-Furness *Observer* had devoted half their sports page to the game. Major Hatley had been mentioned twice. Last night at the pub he had been treated like a hero. He had written his report about the fire in the parking lot and now he just wanted to forget about it.

As the Morris chugged up the low mountains east of Windermere, he put his hand on Marjorie's knee, and began to move it upward, ever so casually, to the lace edge of her panties. They were going for a picnic. He had made a special arrangement to have Carberry replace him for the afternoon.

"Are you sure you know where you're going, Ray?"

"It really doesn't matter, does it? As long as we're lost together, that's fine with me."

She laughed. "Oh, Ray, you're so romantic. But we don't want to go too far. We'll run out of petrol. I'd hate to have to walk all the way back."

"Well, you'd better take a look at the map, then. It's in the glove compartment."

She opened the glove compartment. It was packed with junk.

"How do you expect me to find it in that mess?"

Hatley swung the car onto a spur of the road and stopped.

"Sorry about that, love. Look, here's a beautiful spot." She turned to him for a moment, smiled, and began to carefully unzip his fly. He reached over and gently nudged her toward his lap.

"Isn't it lovely here?" he murmured.

•

Goerlitz and Ballerstedt went for a stroll alone together after evening meal up to the copse at the end of the fairway.

When they got there Ballerstedt lifted an old log and held up what looked like a modified tobacco tin.

"Use this only if the scuttling explosives have been removed," said Ballerstedt. "The scuttling explosives will be far more effective than this, but this should blast a sizeable hole into the hull. Tape these braces onto the hull in a dry spot. When you're ready, break the glass vial on the side here. Acid will eat away this small wire in about ten minutes. That's all you'll have. When the wire's gone the firing pin shoots against the percussion cap and. . . Boom!"

Chapter 9

Because of submarine attacks on Allied shipping in the Atlantic, shortages in Britain were endemic, and there was perhaps nothing in more serious short supply than steel. All over the country, tin cans, old appliances, antiquated boilers, kettles, bobby pins — anything and everything — were collected, melted down, and re-used to aid the war effort. Steel, because of its scarcity, was allotted carefully. Though Major Hatley had asked for barbed wire again and again, an assistant deputy of supply in Whitehall had told him that steel had to be used to make bombs, airplanes, and tanks, that barbed wire for an officers' prisoner-of-war camp in a remote corner of England's Lake District had the lowest of priorities, and that the best he could do was send a hundred-yard roll or two every six months. The assistant deputy added that certain camps, due to the large and recent influx of prisoners, were simply open fields, and that new prisoners slept on rough blankets under makeshift tents while they waited for the engineers to build the camps around them.

Major Hatley had received a roll or two of barbed

wire every six months for the last four years, and now had just over a thousand yards of it. Unfortunately the perimeter of the camp was 2,746 yards, and Hatley had been forced to use his wire sparingly, and in the most strategic locations. There was some wire by the explosives sheds, by the main gate, and on top of the hill just behind Buildings A through E. Lord Selby's trout pond at the end of the fairway provided a natural barrier, as did the closed-down slate quarry at the other end of the camp, though he was now having the prisoners build a slate wall beyond the pond. So he hadn't bothered to put wire in either of those places, and simply ran a guard every half hour, twenty-four hours a day.

His boast that no prisoner had ever escaped from Triggsdale Hall was true. But it was a hollow boast because none of the incarcerated German officers in the camp had ever tried to escape. Hatley assumed, for the most part correctly, that if a prisoner escaped, he would have nowhere to go, that there would be no place to which he could escape.

Since their capture, Weiss and the officers of U-93 had made a thorough study of the security strengths and weaknesses of Triggsdale Hall, and had come to the unanimous conclusion that the safest, easiest way out of the camp was through the quarry under cover of darkness.

Goerlitz had put on the suit and the pair of brogues. He had a wallet full of money and a National Registration Identity card. His name was Michael Harvey Bower. There was a map hidden in his shoe. He also had a contact, Ribalta, and a ship, the *San Julian*, and when he got to Liverpool all he would have to do was go to the harbor office and find out where the *San Julian* was docked, and Ribalta would do the rest.

Goerlitz and his former crew stood in the darkness of Building C, their faces brightened every half minute by the passing spotlight. He could tell just by looking at them that he had regained at least some of their respect.

He said goodbye and took the best wishes of his old crew, then lowered himself out the back window of Building C. He would go through the quarry.

A light mist fell from the dull September sky. His civilian suit felt unfamiliar, and he couldn't remember the last time he had been out of uniform. He crept along the back of the building until he came to the corner, and looked down the side to the camp road. The camp road was deserted. Goerlitz ran past the gap to the back of Building B, then to the back of Building A. He climbed the hill into the forest, and feeling his way among the trees, proceeded toward the latrines.

A few lights burned in Triggsdale Hall and the spotlight mounted on top of the main turret swung slowly by the explosives sheds. He crept out of the forest and ran to the back of the latrines, almost slipping on the grass, cursing his tractionless civilian shoes. He peered around the latrines where not far off he saw a gaping, mist-filled cavity yawning in the earth. The quarry.

The trick, Ballerstedt said, was not to break your neck while you groped through the quarry in darkness, or to knock the bomb around too much. You wouldn't want to smash the glass vial of acid, Ballerstedt said, without knowing it.

Goerlitz waited behind the latrines for fifteen minutes. That was when Sergeant Saville came by with his rifle and shone his flashlight into the old quarry. Jagged outcroppings, sheer bluffs, and dismal little pools jumped briefly out of the gloom as the flashlight passed over them. Saville hooked the flashlight back to his belt, lit a cigarette, and moved on. Goerlitz waited a few minutes then ran the last open stretch to the quarry.

He followed the narrow road down a curving slope, but the road soon became flooded and he was forced to climb the side of the quarry. Much of the slate was loose and slippery, and his brogues didn't help matters. He was afraid that the noise of the rock clattering beneath his feet might attract Saville, or that suddenly the spotlight would be turned directly on him.

The slope on the side of the quarry was gentle, consisting of bits of slate that had fallen from the rock-face. But after five minutes the slope grew much steeper and finally became a hazardous pile of gigantic slate blocks, cut by the quarry workers years ago and just left there, like a jumbled pile of dominoes. He clambered up the first monolith, then lowered himself onto the next. This one sloped away at an odd angle and when he was halfway down he hopped onto another slate block, trusting his feet more than his eyes. There was just enough light from Triggsdale Hall to see the barest outline of the quarry. He jumped, stepped, and climbed from block to block until, abruptly, he came to a large seemingly impassable pool.

He crouched beside one of the big slate blocks and contemplated the pool, thinking he might have to go all the way back and find another route. But finally he took off his shoes and socks, put them in his duffel bag, rolled up his pants, and waded through to the far side, carrying his duffel bag over his head. He walked cautiously because the broken slate under the water was sharp, unpredictable, and covered with algae. He had once been a Roman Catholic, in the days his mother had been alive, and he imagined he was crossing one of the five rivers of hell, the Styx or the Acheron. All was dark and quiet except for the sloshing of his footsteps.

At its deepest, the pool went up to his thighs, and he got the pant legs of his suit all wet, but he kept on, feeling his way along the bottom until he climbed onto a shore of broken rock. He was at the far end of the quarry now. An old derrick used for lifting slate blocks loomed like a forgotten monster further along the small beach. A slate wall, like the cubist sculptures a friend of his father's had once constructed out of chunks of metal, rose before him, and he saw that he had no choice but a long struggle to the top.

He took his shoes and socks out of his duffel bag, put them back on, checked the bomb to make sure the glass vial wasn't broken, then hoisted himself up to the first outcropping. In daylight it might have been an easy climb, but in darkness, Goerlitz had to feel every inch of the way. He was just about to the top when he slipped and fell a few feet, sending several loose pieces skittering to the bottom.

Saville was passing at just that moment. The flashlight went on at the far side of the quarry. Goerlitz lay where he fell, clutching the edge of the rock-face, hoping the flashlight wouldn't penetrate through the mist. The flashlight scanned the quarry, searching with a baleful eye.

"Hallo?" called Saville. "Hallo, who goes there?"

Goerlitz heard the crunching of boots. Saville was coming down the quarry road.

"Hallo? Who goes there?"

The flashlight scanned the jumbled chaos of angles and oblongs and finally rested on Goerlitz.

"All right, you," shouted Saville, "get down off there." Goerlitz heard Saville lock and load his rifle. "Get down off there right now or I'll shoot you through the back."

Goerlitz glanced at his duffel bag on the ledge above him. Leaving the duffel bag where it was, he descended the slate bluff, the flashlight following his every move. When he got to the bottom he turned around. Saville shone the flashlight directly into his face, blinding him to everything else.

"I should have known it was you. You just can't get

enough, can you, Goerlitz? All right, now, put your hands on your head and walk slowly forward."

Goerlitz did as he was told, moving toward Saville, his mind working hard as the sceptre of yet another failure rose before him like a dreaded nightmare. He wasn't going to fail this time.

"Now, stay where you are and don't move. I'm coming down, Goerlitz. If you make the slightest move I'll kill you."

Saville walked to the other side of the quarry, keeping the light trained on Goerlitz, following a much easier and well-used path Goerlitz had obviously missed in the dark, and soon stood on the opposite side of the pond. The sergeant began wading across the pond. The flashlight drew closer and soon he could see the vague outline of Saville's pudgy figure, and finally his face in the peripheral glow of the flashlight. The middle-aged guard was out of breath by the time he got to the other side. He was holding the rifle pointed at Goerlitz's chest in one hand and the flashlight in the other. The fool, thought Goerlitz.

Saville moved cautiously until he was behind Goerlitz's back. Goerlitz still had his hands on his head.

"Now, move," said Saville in a high tremulous voice. "And nothing sudden or you're dead. Do you understand?"

"I understand."

Goerlitz waded into the pool, shoes and all, listening, waiting for the right opportunity. Carrying the rifle as well as the flashlight, Saville's balance on the slippery underwater rock wouldn't be that good. Goerlitz speeded up, hoping Saville would do the same. Which he did. And then there was a sudden splash.

"Damn these rocks," said Saville.

Goerlitz swung around and dived at the man, catching him by surprise. He wrenched the rifle out of

Saville's hand before the guard had a chance to fire and warn someone in Triggsdale Hall, then locked his arm around the older man's head and dragged him below the water. Saville began to flail like a mouse in a trap as he understood what Goerlitz was going to do. The sergeant got in a lucky but misplaced blow, startling Goerlitz, and managed to get his head above the surface long enough for a sputtering and winded cry for help.

Goerlitz punched the man in the temple, stunning him, then clutched his hair with both hands and forced the man's face into the chalky green water. Saville struggled and struggled, kicking, grabbing the rocks below and trying to pull himself away, but Goerlitz had a good hold of him. The struggling grew weaker, but even when it had stopped Goerlitz still held his head under. A trick. Stillness. Then one last frantic attempt for oxygen before the struggling subsided for good. Goerlitz held him under another two minutes, then dragged his limp body to the shore.

Saville's eyes were open and his mouth was oozing water as his lungs began to drain. Dead, thought Goerlitz. Drowned. Just like so many U-boat men he had known. Goerlitz started filling the big baggy pockets on the outside of Saville's fatigues with pieces of slate, opened his shirt and shoved some down his chest, then buttoned it up. This would keep him down, he thought. He dragged the body into the middle of the pool, careless of his suit, and forced it to the bottom with his foot. A useless complication, he thought, so unnecessary, but he had no choice. He reached underwater and started piling slate rocks on top of the dead sergeant. When he was satisfied the body was well-hidden, that both the rifle and the flashlight were on the bottom, he walked back to the shore, his suit dripping.

He looked at the water, the dark mystifying water, his friend, his enemy, for six long years now. He brushed his suit off, noticing he had scraped his wrist. The stiffness had disappeared from his brogues.

He took one last look around then climbed to the top of the bluff, getting his duffel bag on the way.

At the top there was a sheep pasture stretching like a dim green carpet to the valley below. At the top there was a chance to destroy U-512 and to deliver a potentially damaging intelligence document to the U-boat High Command. And a chance to return to Munich, where he would be with his father and his friends, where he could sort out the confusion he had unaccountably found his marriage in, and where, especially, he could be with Ute.

•

Laurie sat in the government car on the east harbor road a little way down from the submarine pen. A cigarette hung from his lip. Westmoreland sat beside him. Taylor was back in the temporary field office writing up a report on a failed Luftwaffe strike against U-512 for Admiral Leo Carson. Clouds marched across the sky and a chill wind flecked Morecambe Bay with whitecaps. From here, he and Westmoreland got a good view of the navy salvage operation. Westmoreland put the binoculars to his eyes.

"Look," he said. "Look, I think they've got something."

He handed the binoculars to Laurie. Laurie raised the binoculars to his eyes — because he was blind on one eye binoculars always gave him a distorted view, and he wished he had brought along his telescope — and gazed out to the salvage barge. Sailors were helping navy divers climb aboard, dragging them out of the water, and the derrick's pulleys were turning, hauling something up from the bottom. A wing-tip appeared, then the hated black German cross, so feared and despised by the pilots of the RAF, then part of the fuselage. The tail section was missing and the cockpit glass was peppered with bullet holes. It had been close, thought Laurie, but not close enough. Except for a few bomb craters in the sheep pastures on the hill above, the *Stuka* had done little other damage. Finally, the propeller emerged from the water, dripping, slung with seaweed, one of the blades bent like a broken rabbit ear.

"Not much left of the rear end," said Laurie. "Did you see the paper this morning? Those blasted idiots in the press have it all over the front page."

"A devil of a way to go," said Westmoreland. "Riddled with bullets a thousand feet in the air."

"Do you feel sorry for him, Westmoreland? I don't. Not one bloody bit."

"Not so much for him, sir. But maybe he had a family. Maybe he had little ones."

"Well, I don't feel sorry for them either. They can all go to the devil as far as I'm concerned. Little Nazis grow up into big Nazis."

Laurie continued to look through the binoculars. The derrick swung the wreckage over the barge and lowered it carefully to the deck, a few sailors guiding it with their hands.

"Any witnesses?" asked Laurie. "I mean beside the anti-aircraft boys."

"A bloke by the name of Bolderson, lives just up the way here. Said it cart-wheeled through the air a half dozen times before it burst into flames and dropped into the water."

The *Stuka* settled clumsily onto the barge's desk. Two of the sailors climbed up onto the wing, opened the cockpit, and lifted the dead pilot out. Rigor mortis had set in and the pilot remained in a sitting position despite the way the two sailors wrenched him from the cockpit. He had been over a mile off target, thought Laurie, but even a mile was too close for his precious U-512. He handed the binoculars to Westmoreland.

"There's a sight for sore eyes," he said. Westmoreland looked through the binoculars. "That's one less blasted German pilot we have to worry about."

Laurie glanced at Westmoreland. Westmoreland obviously didn't have the stomach for war.

"You don't have little ones, do you, Westmoreland?"

"No, sir, I don't."

"Well, you wouldn't feel sorry for that pilot if you did. You'd want the whole lot of them to come crashing down from the sky so your children wouldn't have to live in fear. Believe me, I know. There isn't a week that goes by without my poor Ted crawling into bed with me at night because he thinks the planes are going to come."

Laurie took a pull on his cigarette and started the car. Out in the bay the barge emitted a cloud of black smoke as its engines heaved from aft. "Don't fret too much, Westmoreland. After all, it's not as if he died in vain. At least not from our standpoint. Maybe now the bloody Admiralty will realize just how important U-512 is."

Chapter 10

Goerlitz woke up the next morning with the sun shining through the cracks of a small boarded up window. A shed, he thought, to get out of the rain last night. The door opposite the window was partially open, and he saw a pasture with a few sheep grazing by a slate fence. The rain had stopped but the sky was overcast and the clouds drifted past him in a hundred shades of shifting grey. He looked out the door. He was hungry. Pasture sloped downward into the valley and there was a woods off to the right. He opened his duffel bag and ate one of his biscuits, then took a few swallows from his canteen.

There were cobwebs in the corner, and a rusted rake and hoe leaned against the wall. He walked to the window and peered through a crack in the boards. The land rose toward a farmhouse and a few outbuildings. He couldn't figure out where that noise was coming from. It was close by. The shivery sound of metal on metal. Then, four inches from his nose, he saw the back of a head rise into the window. His eyes widened. Someone had been sitting there all along. The man walked forward into the sun. He was sharpening a knife. He was an old man with a scarf around his neck and a hat on his head. While the man continued to sharpen his knife, Goerlitz backed away, picked up his duffel bag, and snuck out the door.

The ground was wet and slippery and his shoes got caked with mud quickly. His suit was still damp and he was shivering with cold. He hurried down the slope, looking back often, and disappeared into the woods before the old man had a chance to see him.

The hill steepened considerably once he was in the woods, and losing his balance, he slid down the hillside on a bed of lichen and landed at the edge of a small pond. He stood up and brushed his suit, then checked the bomb to make sure the glass vial hadn't been broken. It was intact. He took another biscuit out of his duffel bag, ate it, then looked at his map. He had spent the night walking over the Furness Fells, and the cuffs of his pants were wet and covered with burrs. After a moment's consideration he walked due west.

Soon he came to a river, the Duddon River according to his map, which emptied into the Duddon Sands. He walked south along the river, thinking he would hear dogs behind him, but all was quiet.

A little before noon he came to the bridge leading to Laughton-in-Furness, and he stopped in the bushes off to one side of the road, took a sip of water from his canteen, and wiped the sweat from his forehead.

Goerlitz bent over and started picking burrs off his pant legs. The crew members of U-93 had gone over their plan in meticulous detail. They all agreed Goerlitz had to be Michael Harvey Bower. There was no other choice because it was the only identity card they had. But that left the problem of his German accent. It was slight, so slight it could hardly be detected by the other English speakers in the crew, and it couldn't be readily recognized as a German accent. The cover story had been discussed at length in the games room of Building E. They finally decided Michael Harvey Bower had an English father and a Polish mother. Michael had spent the first twenty years of his life in Poland and had moved to England in 1935. This would account for his accent.

Soon he came to Laughton-in-Furness, a village, judging from its size, of about seven-hundred-and-fifty inhabitants. Many of the cottages along the byway were made of slate, though there were some made of brick and stucco. A handful of people shopped in the dozen or so stores and he was glad to see there was no one in uniform. He was thirsty and hungry. Laughton-in-Furness had been another part of the plan. Stop for lunch, hear what he could hear, acclimatize, then move on.

There was a small lunch crowd in the Brown Derby, the town's only pub, and two or three uniforms among them. Sailors, he thought. Nothing to worry about. Everybody looked at him in their turn, only mildly curious. He found a table by the bar. The waitress, who was in her fifties and who wore an old sweater and a baggy skirt, was behind the bar talking to some of her friends. The publican put his arm around her — they were probably husband and wife — and nodded toward Goerlitz. Prodded in this way, she came to his table and wiped the surface.

"What can I get you, sir?"

"A ploughman's lunch, the potato soup, and a pint of bitter."

"Right you are," she said, and walked away.

She brought his bitter first. It was thin compared to German beer. Soup and lunch came a few minutes later.

"That'll be two-and-six, sir."

He gave her a total of three shillings and told her to keep the change.

"Thank you very much, sir. Thank you very much indeed."

She went back and told her friends at the bar. They all looked at him. Was it such an exorbitant tip? Didn't they tip in England? Perhaps he had been too careless. They were just three harmless old ladies. Sixpence. Was it such a great deal of money? He took a bite of his bread and spooned some of the hot soup into his mouth. Hot. Very hot. He sloshed it around with his tongue, refusing to spit it out in front of the ladies. Of course it would be hot, he thought. This wasn't the submarine or the Triggsdale Hall mess hall.

He ate lunch, looking around the tavern as if he were in a dream. It had been three months since he had been near civilians, and sixteen years since he had been to England. He felt extremely uncomfortable, but he supposed this was what Weiss had meant by acclimatize. Wait until the pressure from within was equal to the pressure without, Weiss said. Watch for a while, and then act. He tried to relax, looked around, studied manners, scrutinized expressions, and listened to the conversations around him the way an *Abwehr* agent might. But all he heard were the exchanges of everyday civilian life. To Goerlitz, much of civilian life seemed pointless and boring.

SUBMARINER INSPIRES JUNGVOLK WITH HIS COURAGE. This small headline on the third page of the *Völkischer Beobachter* popped into his head. He could never think of that newspaper story without thinking of Ute. He had been the submariner, a hero at twenty-seven, and she, at nineteen, had been one of the *Jungvolk*. U-93 was in Wilhelmshaven for repairs. It was 1939, the first months of the war. He was back home in Munich, on leave. The regional editor had approached him and he had agreed to talk to the *Jungvolk* on a pig farm twenty miles from town. A small patriotic article, the editor had said. So he talked, and the successes of U-93 were duly narrated to a crowd of admiring teenagers. He was a hero. What the newspaper never mentioned was that he kissed Ute Frömmer for the first time that night.

He pushed his bowl and plate aside and drained the rest of his bitter. He and Ute had gone to beer gardens together in the months preceding their marriage, and they had always made love afterwards. He wanted her. On the submarine he never wanted her. He had his submarine. She was the only thing in civilian life he really wanted. That, and the long talks he had with his father. It was easier to miss them in a tavern than it was in a U-boat. He had to force the thoughts of them out of his mind in order to concentrate on the task at hand.

When he left the tavern he went back to the bridge and followed the Duddon River south. This wasn't the terrain for civilian shoes and soon they were soaked. He looked up at the sky continually, hoping it wouldn't rain. He felt grimy and he knew he smelled foul from hiking so far, but they had all agreed that it would be best to avoid any public transportation until he had taken down the dispositions.

He followed the rail line south around the Sands. He took a rest at six-thirty and ate a few more biscuits. As it grew dark, an undecided rain began to fall. He slipped into the back streets of Barrow-in-Furness around ten o'clock. He was famished, wet, cold, and he wanted Ute.

Barrow-in-Furness was blacked out. He stopped at the Bull Henry not far from the docks and ordered a quarter chicken, three slices of bread, and a pint of beer. The waiter, a boy of fourteen in a white shirt washed so many times it was as thin as tissue paper, smiled at Goerlitz with bad teeth as he put the chicken on the table.

"Are there any lodgings available here?"

"Not here, sir. Down the street, maybe. We're full up because of that Jerry U-boat in the harbor."

As the boy walked away Goerlitz had to use all his self control to stop grinning. The Jerry U-boat was still in the harbor.

When he was finished eating he walked along the street until he came to a tobacconist's, where he bought a copy of the Barrow-in-Furness *Observer* as well as the afternoon edition of the London *Times*. There was nothing about U-512 in the London *Times*, but the *Observer* devoted a good deal of their second page to the captured U-boat, including more coverage of the unsuccessful *Luftwaffe* strike. As Goerlitz read the various stories under the dim light of a streetlamp he grew more and more excited. The first members of the technical crew Naval Intelligence had assembled to investigate and assess U-512 had arrived in Barrow-in-Furness only yesterday, and work would not begin until this evening, when Lieutenant Commander Murray Simpson-Beale got back from a technical investigation of a captured Japanese submarine in Siam.

U-512, the paper said, had become a tourist attraction, and people from as far away as Carlisle had come to see the U-boat, moored in the Royal Navy's submarine pens on the east harbor road. Most hotels in the area were filled to capacity. So work would begin on U-512 this evening, he thought. Yet by tomorrow night she would be on the bottom.

He went to find somewhere to spend the night.

The Chesterton Hotel, just down the way from the Bull Henry, had a full view of the harbor but unfortunately a shared bathroom, and it wasn't until midnight that he had a chance to bathe. He shaved but kept a small mustache because Michael Harvey Bower had a mustache. Then he went to his room and looked at the harbor. He couldn't see much, not with the blackout in effect. He pulled off his suit and climbed into bed. So good to rest his weary muscles. A lithographed print of a seascape hung on the wall, and there were a few back issues of *Punch* on the side table. He pulled the blind down and turned on the light. He reached for his duffel bag on the floor beside the bed and took out the bomb. Ballerstedt had always been good with his hands. So simple: a section of heavy steel tubing with lids bolted on either end, a glass vial, a wire shaved to just the right thickness, some hydrochloric acid, five pounds of explosives, a firing pin, and a percussion cap.

He put the bomb under his bed and pulled out the photograph of Ute. In the damp sweet smell of the hotel room he could almost feel her next to him, could taste her lips on his. He wanted to rub his hands over her breasts, her naked hips. He wanted to wake up with her in the Munich apartment, sit with her by the window and watch the people go by on Liebigstrasse while they had their breakfast. When breakfast was finished he wanted her to read the paper and smoke one of her five weekly cigarettes while he thrashed his way through the Brahms *Sonata in F Minor* on his clarinet. He smiled as he thought of the squeaking and squawking she had endured. He looked at the photograph for five minutes. Her eyes were lambent, and, in tinted color, a deep frozen blue shining from the depths of her sometimes puzzling character. But the photograph and the pleasant thoughts were spoiled by the darker image of Saville's face, super-imposed, like a double negative, and by the brutal way he had been forced to murder the English sergeant. In a different time and a different place he and Saville might possibly have been friends. Killing had always been done from afar, from the torpedo room of a U-boat, but holding Saville underwater by the hair had been an entirely new experience for him. It was fine to look at this photograph and think about how much he loved Ute, and how he would try to straighten things out with her once he got back, but there was something he didn't feel right about now. He couldn't help thinking of the middle-aged guard's pitiful flailing or his choked cry for help before Goerlitz had forced him down once and for all. Even worse had been the sergeant's underwater grappling. Why did things always have to work out this way? Why had Saville been stupid enough to come after him? He frowned. Had he forgotten how to be ruthless?

He crept down the hall around two o'clock in the morning. He left the bomb in the room and all he carried were a note-pad, a pencil, his wallet, and his identification card. The streets were deserted, and it was so dark because of the blackout he could hardly see three feet in front of him.

Only crucial lights burned in and around the naval base. He had memorized much on the *Purvess* but none of what he now saw looked familiar. So he kept walking south, not sure if there were a curfew. He veered east as the road began to rise. He passed a few sailors coming home from a tavern, but they hardly noticed him. At the top of the road he got a better view of the harbor. Black sky merged with black water, but there was just enough light to see by. The houses ended. He was in the southern outskirts of Barrow-in-Furness. He looked at his watch. It was just past three. At this northern latitude the sun would start to brighten the sky soon.

The land — grassy, rocky, and with a few clusters of trees — sloped downward, and the white shapes beyond the slate fence, he discovered, were sheep. He climbed the slate fence, hurried across the pasture, and clambered over the opposite fence, where the land descended through a wooded hill to the harbor. He climbed down the hill to the east harbor road. He recognised this part. They had driven along this road when they had taken him to Triggsdale Hall. Waves lapped at the rocky shore. He continued south along the road.

At the top of the next rise he discovered the submarine pen and U-512, barely visible in the single covered pen light blackout regulations allowed. A group of technicians stood on the pier. The U-boat was surrounded by eight-foot fences with strings of barbed wire stretched along the top, and he could see they had begun to build a camouflaging upper works, although this was by no means complete and covered merely the stern. He would need pliers to cut the wire along the top of the fence. A single guard stood at the entrance of the pen near the harbor road beside a small parking lot. Goerlitz crept up the wooded hill and found a well-hidden vantage point.

He watched the technicians while they looked at his U-boat. For'ard, aft, and bridge hatches were open. There were lights on inside the U-boat. On the catwalk a torpedo lay half covered by a large piece of brown canvas weighed down with a chain. The 88 mm gun had been removed from the conning tower. He was both angry and humiliated. He felt as if someone were looking up his ass with a magnifying glass. Get off my fucking boat, he thought.

A few technicians climbed out the for'ard hatch, and the lights in the submarine went out. He would need a flashlight. An officer in uniform climbed out of the conning tower hatch. Two sailors stood near the technicians smoking cigarettes. Occasionally he heard their soft laughter. The officer and the technicians jumped off the submarine onto the pier and joined the others, where they all stood talking in a group. The two sailors went aboard, closed the hatches, and made sure everything was secure for the night. When the sailors were finished, everyone filed out the pen gate and nodded a goodnight to the guard. They got into two jeeps, each driven by one of the sailors, and in a moment, drove out of the parking lot back to town.

The guard peered after them until they had disappeared over the rise, locked the gate, and walked to the small wood blockhouse. Goerlitz thought that security might have been tighter. But it was a small out-of-the-way pen, only large enough for two submarines, and no concrete pen gates leading out to Morecambe Bay were closed.

The light went on behind the blackout blinds of the blockhouse. The covered pen light blinked out. Goerlitz looked at his watch. Five past four. The sky was still dark. He got up and crept through the wet foliage to the road. He walked right to the fence and looked at his U-boat. A piece of steel, he thought. A weapon. A killer. But it was his. I'm sorry, Captain Weiss, but I'm going to have to disobey your orders this time and destroy it.

He hurried along the fence around the guardhouse to the blockhouse. One of the blinds was up and inch or two, and he looked inside. The guard smoked a cigarette, read the newspaper, and drank a cup of coffee. Goerlitz started back to the hotel, satisfied.

Chapter 11

Hatley's head hurt. He had never drunk so much wine as he had during Sunday's picnic. He sat at his desk rubbing his temples with his fingers, his face scrunched in pain. Another bloody week, he thought. He heard the annoying thud of boots coming up the hall. Didn't Patterson know how to walk quietly? Hatley rose grudgingly. The sky was clouding over and it looked as if it might rain, so he took his umbrella.

"Ready for roll call and inspection, sir."

"You don't have to shout, Patterson. I'm standing right next to you. All right, let's get on with it."

Most of the prisoners were assembled in the yard for roll call, but there were still a few who were sick.

"Who's on the sick list, Patterson?"

"Goerlitz, Frischauer, and Schlabrendorff."

"Goerlitz now?" The major felt in a foul mood. "Pretty soon the whole Christly camp will have this thing, ourselves included. Maybe we should have Dr. Duncan come up for another look."

"He's out of town until late tomorrow evening."

"That's rotten luck. Oh, well, I guess there's nothing we can do about it." Major Hatley and Corporal Patterson began walking down the row of war prisoners. "We'll give him a shout early Wednesday morning. Were you talking to Goerlitz at all?"

"I just peeked in after reveille. Mind you, just from the door. I wouldn't want to get close to any of them right now."

"And?"

"He was sound asleep. Looked cold. Had the covers right around his head."

"Well, maybe I'll go have a look. He probably caught it in the box, the poor devil."

"If you want a dose of it, sir, go ahead."

Hatley stopped and gazed at the coach-house beside Triggsdale Hall.

"What does Weiss say?"

"Oh, nothing much. Just that Goerlitz seems to be getting better."

"Well, at least that's something."

•

Goerlitz woke with a sour taste in his mouth and sat up quickly. He had slept too long. He had wanted to be up much earlier. He pulled on his pants and, walking to the window, saw that the sky was still overcast, the clouds low, stretching in tendrils eastward over the flat steel-like surface of the harbor. He put on his suit, his still wet shoes and socks, looked in the mirror, and frowned, wondering why his hair was thinning and why he had to be so ugly. What did Ute see in him?

He slipped on his jacket and went downstairs to the breakfast room. The hotel clerk, an orange-haired woman of around sixty, raised her plucked eyebrows when he asked for breakfast.

"Sir, I'm afraid breakfast is long over. Did you not read the sign on the back of your door?"

"No."

"Well, I'm afraid you'll have to get something down the way."

"Thank you, ma'am."

He found a quick bite then walked toward the east harbor road. He bought a flashlight and a pair of pliers at a hardware store, then continued on. Damn, he thought, it was going to rain any minute.

He explored the streets of Barrow-in-Furness until he came to a narrow cobblestone laneway called Tolton's Gate where he found a camera shop. Although he knew German cameras well, having been trained in photography at the *Abwehr's* training school outside Hamburg, he wasn't so sure about English ones.

He went inside, some brass bells jingling against the window pane as he opened the door. The shop smelled musty, of old books, and was cluttered with photographic equipment of every description. A neatly dressed man of well over seventy, wearing grey flannels and a white shirt with the thinnest of grey pinstripes, approached Goerlitz. He had a row of pens lined up precisely in his pocket. He wore thick-lensed bifocals, and a large sash of brown hair was combed across his bald forehead.

"And what might we help you with today, sir?"

"I'm looking for a thirty-five millimeter range-finding camera that will take fast film."

"Is a hundred fast enough?"

"That will do. The focus has to be crisp."

The camera shop owner moved up the counter to the cash register. Goerlitz followed.

"Might we ask what you'll be using the camera for, sir?"

"Landscapes and portraits."

"Very good, sir. I think we have just the thing."

He opened a glass display case beside the cash register. He picked up a thirty-five millimeter camera with an accordion-style lens.

"This is the new Larisa," he said. "Hard to believe they make these little darlings in Manchester. Now, as you can see, the lens is collapsible. You just push it in like so." The man pushed the lens in, the cloth accordion-style sides squeezing together. "And there it is. Snaps shut for easy carrying. Very portable, sir. Very portable. All in all, a versatile little piece."

"How much?"

"Fifteen pounds, two and tuppence."

"And with two rolls of film."

"Another four shillings, sir."

"Good, I'll take it."

He paid for the camera. That left him with just over twenty-one pounds of Michael Bower's money.

He followed the harbor road east, then south, looking out at the bay often, where, among the many fishing vessels and pleasure craft he saw frigates and destroyers lying at anchor. By the time he got to the hills south of the town it had begun to drizzle off and on. He found a spot not far from U-512 just below a sheep pasture on the wooded hill, where he could see the ships come and go.

He opened his notebook. On ten of the small pages there were pre-sketched maps of this particular area of the harbor. He was to observe and chart the courses of five approaching ships and five departing ships to determine the unmined shipping lanes. The pages were yellowed, looked as if they had waited a long time for completion. There were supplementary maps to record any obstacles he might see, such as blockships or buoys marking submarine nets, and a few double-sized maps, taking left and right pages, where he was to record the dispositions of all naval and merchant ships at anchor.

He worked on it slowly through the afternoon, marking the exact locations of the anchored frigates and destroyers, taking numerous photographs and recording the courses of the departing and arriving ships. And the longer he worked, the more he saw a U-boat attack on Morecambe Bay might be possible after all, that his old commander and Admiral Doenitz might have been closer to the mark than he had at first assumed, and that the *Unterseewaffe* could inflict heavy damage if they held the advantage of surprise, plus detailed charts.

There was a heavy concentration of American destroyers. Such a heavy concentration of destroyers in the same waters would make ASDIC useless, but that, of course, was for Admiral Doentiz to decide. The British had scuttled a few large tankers to make barriers around the mouth of the harbor entrance. Blockships. Some of the stacks showed above the surface. In spots, the water was unusually frothy, revealing the location of another blockship. He recorded the positions accordingly. He watched as afternoon changed to dusk and dusk changed to night. When he finally walked back to the Chesterton Hotel he had completed the maps, had ten or fifteen pages of notes, and at least forty photographs. He had what any military intelligence bureau would consider a sensitive and crucial document.

•

Lieutenant Commander Murray Simpson-Beale arrived early that day, and Laurie couldn't have been happier. Finally they could get things going. Under the direction of Simpson-Beale, Fine, and Hopcraft, a crew of twenty-two mechanics, electricians, and engineers would inspect every square-inch of U-512, gain, as quickly as possible, an operational knowledge of her, and test her in the shipping lanes of Morecambe Bay under destroyer escort.

He stood in the control room beside the provisional skipper, Captain Robert Elwood, trying to stop the envy he felt for this man, who would be the first Briton to sail what he had come to consider his own submarine. Of course he couldn't boast the same seamanship or battle experience the captain could. The captain had become a hero of sorts as commander of the X-craft submarine attack on the German flagship *Tirpitz*. There was no better qualified man to test U-512. And yet he found it hard to stop the envy, wanted to take the boat in his own hands and make it do what he ordered.

Still, it was good they finally had the investigation underway. It was good to hear Taylor and Westmoreland arguing with Hopcraft about something in the torpedo room down the passageway — his assistants could be exacting bureaucrats — good to hear Simpson-Beale shouting commands in the engine room as his mechanics removed one of the damaged electric engines from its casing. The portable derrick needed to move the light engine had been one of the tools they had ordered from Glas-gow.

"So, captain," he said, turning to Elwood, "how does she feel to you?"

"She feels sturdy, sir. As if she can take a lot of pressure. Mr. Fine says we'll need more than Torpex to break her."

"Well, then, we'll develop something stronger than Torpex, won't we?" said Laurie. He took out his cigarettes, offered one to the captain, who declined, stuck one on his lip, and struck a match on the navigator's table. "There's nothing the Germans have come up with that we can't break," he said, lighting his cigarette.

"I've never liked to be overconfident, sir."

"Oh, I'm not overconfident, Elwood. I'm certain. We've got them. We've got them by their bloody balls."

"If you say so, sir."

125

"So when do you think we'll be able to take her out?"

"Simpson-Beale says anywhere from thirty-six to forty-eight hours. And that's going to involve a crew in here eighteen hours a day."

Laurie didn't like this news. He had been plagued by too many delays already. But he couldn't question the lieutenant commander's decision.

"Well, I suppose if anyone should know, the lieutenant commander should."

"He's a very brilliant man, sir."

"Yes, brilliant, but entirely lacking in focus. See if you can't prod him a bit, will you? We don't want the *Luftwaffe* down on us again. Let's see if we can take her out tomorrow afternoon."

"I can almost be certain, inspector, that the lieutenant commander will find your request next to impossible."

"He doesn't think it can be done? Well, captain, I beg to differ."

The captain turned away, gazed at the hydroplane control for a moment or two.

"I would have to discuss it with him again, sir."

"Well, you do that, Elwood. You do that. You've read my order from Admiral Carson?"

"Yes, sir."

"Good. We weigh anchor for testing tomorrow afternoon at four o'clock."

"It will be a risk, but, yes sir."

Laurie took a pull on his cigarette.

"Risk is what war's all about, isn't it?"

•

Thunder woke Goerlitz just past eleven that night but he clung to sleep, clung to the dream that he so desperately did not want to end. He and Ute had just had a big roast beef dinner with his father, Ute had sung some

Schubert *lieder*, his father accompanying her on the grand piano in the parlor, and now they were upstairs, in bed together, with their clothes off, their mouths locked, Ute pressing herself against him. He squeezed her in all the places she liked to be squeezed, then kissed her, so passionately, so tenderly, just behind her ear. But then another clap of thunder panned across the sky and he knew that he was awake and no longer in his father's country house outside Munich, and that Ute was over seven hundred miles away. He remembered what he had to do. He had to destroy U-512.

He got up, put his damp suit on, and took everything out of his duffel bag except the bomb, the masking tape, a knife he had stolen from the restaurant down the way, the pliers and the flashlight. Thunder again rolled across the sky, and it began to rain, at first lightly, then more heavily. It was going to ruin his suit. A man in a rain-crumpled suit was suspicious, but he had no choice. Weiss and the others could not maintain the influenza deception forever, and they were bound to find Saville sooner or later, and then the British would be on his trail. He had to act now or perhaps lose his chance.

He waited until midnight. He crept down the well-worn stairs of the Chesterton Hotel past the reception desk and went out into the rain. If only he had an umbrella. He should have thought of that. There was nowhere he could get an umbrella now. A man walking around in the pouring rain after midnight without an umbrella was suspicious as well. The streets were deserted. He began to think the rain might be to his advantage. The town, already cloaked in darkness, was almost invisible in the rain. He wondered if the technicians might quit early because of the rain.

The submarine pen light was still on. All three hatches were open and three stark beams shot up from the U-boat. They were being lax with blackout precautions because of the heavy rain. He waited for at least two hours in the pouring rain. Then the technicians emerged from the bowels of his boat. His boat. He sneered. He wanted to kill them almost as much as he wanted to kill Bergen.

The two sailors boarded the U-boat and made it good for the night. Canvas covers had been attached to the roofs of the jeeps, and with windshield wipers flicking, the technicians, officers, and sailors drove back to Barrow-in-Furness.

A few moments later the guard hurried from the guardhouse, locked the gate, then ran to the blockhouse. Goerlitz picked up his duffel bag and descended the slippery hillside. The rain was so loud he could hardly hear the waves crashing onto the shore. He ran across the parking lot to the blockhouse and peered under one of the blackout blinds. The guard wasn't there, just a table, an ashtray, a newspaper, and a few old magazines. Where the hell was he?

He appeared from the right carrying a cup of coffee and a dish towel. He put the coffee on the table, dried himself off, then sat down and lit a cigarette.

Goerlitz crept away. He walked past the guardhouse. The rain grew stronger and a wind began to blow off the bay. The rain came down in needling sheets. His suit was soaked right through and his duffel bag was drenched.

He found a spot on the other side of the pen and waited. In a moment the pen light went off. He pulled the pliers out of his duffel bag, climbed the fence, and snipped three strings of barbed wire. They fell away like limp spaghetti. He jumped to the ground, picked up his duffel bag, and scrambled over the fence. There she lay, in the pouring rain, like a beached whale. He walked around the edge of the pen, noticed a depth marking of ninety feet painted along the side, then hopped aboard U-512. Ninety feet. He smiled. If she sank that far she might possibly crack.

He went in through the conning tower hatch because it was out of view of the blockhouse. The stench of sea–water was familiar and reassuring. The rungs were greasy. He pulled out his flashlight, turned it on, and descended the second companionway into the control room.

His flashlight floated over the trimming panel and the hydroplane control, then shone briefly on the blowing panel. Some of the blowing panel had been dismantled. He walked through the forward compartment past the wall bunks into the torpedo room. All the crates of apples, canned vegetables, and coffee had been removed. A single torpedo lay half stuck in a tube. The other tubes were open and empty. Where were all his other torpedoes? They were as expensive as small houses. He checked the explosives cabinet and saw that the scuttling explosives were gone. He would have to use Ballerstedt's bomb.

He shone the flashlight over the hull and found a dry spot approximately at the water line. He put his flashlight on the deck, opened his duffel bag, and took out both the bomb and the masking tape. The rain beat on the U-boat in a constant rush of noise. He placed the braces against the steel, wedging them securely against a support, taped them to the hull, then removed the piece of coat hanger Ballerstedt had used to protect, at least partially, the glass vial. He slung his duffel bag over his shoulder and walked back to the companionway leading up to the conning tower hatch.

He stopped, held his breath. He heard someone walking around the catwalk. He stood still and listened. He turned off his flashlight. One set of footsteps. The guard, he thought.

The guard approached from the bow of the boat, came toward the conning tower and paused above where Goerlitz was standing. There was silence for a long time. The guard must have been looking at the open conning tower hatch. To Goerlitz, the open conning tower hatch was like a pale moon where the rain came constantly pelting in. Finally, he heard the guard climb the outside companionway. In a moment he saw the guard's head appear in the hatch, and Goerlitz backed away, stood beside the navigating table while a flashlight beam appeared through the air-lock and scanned what it could of the control room. Then the flashlight went out and the guard listened for several minutes at the top of the conning tower. The flashlight came back on, and the hatch was slammed and twisted shut.

Goerlitz climbed the first few rungs of the companionway into the air-lock and listened. He heard the guard descend the steep steps at the back of the winter garden, stop once again, then walk slowly around the conning tower and along the catwalk toward the bow. The footsteps grew fainter and finally disappeared. Why had he come out here, wondered Goerlitz? Perhaps he had forgotten his cigarettes in the guardhouse.

Goerlitz climbed the ladder, opened the hatch, put his bag on the catwalk and, keeping only his flashlight, looked around the pen. The rain was thick, impenetrable. A sliver of light came from the blockhouse window. There was no sign of the guard.

He descended the companionway through the conning tower into the control room once again, moving faster. Maybe the guard might come out for something else. He gripped the appropriate valve, opened the starboard ballast tank a bit, then opened the port ballast tank. Over the rain he heard water begin to trickle into the saddletanks. He continued on into the engine room. One of the electric engines had been unscrewed from its casing and sections of it were missing. The stench of oil struck his nostrils like a wet blanket. He climbed the ladder and opened the aft hatch. The rain came pouring in through the hatch. He hurried the sixty odd meters back to the torpedo room and, using the end of his flashlight, smashed the glass vial on the side of the bomb. The filament sizzled and a pungent smell filled the torpedo room. He checked his watch. 2:46. At 2:56 the bomb would go off.

He clambered up the companionway through the for'ard hatch, slung his duffel bag over his shoulder, and jumped off the catwalk onto the pier. Because he didn't want anything to break the submarine's fall to the bottom he unhooked the hawsers tying her down and tossed them into the water. The partially opened ballast tanks filled slowly. Already the U-boat was low in the water.

A truck approached on the east harbor road and he lay on his stomach until it had passed. His suit was ruined. He didn't know how he was going to get to Liverpool in a suit like this. He ran around the pier, climbed the fence, and jumped to the other side. The ground was turning to mud, and the rain beat persistently. He glanced at the blockhouse then dashed across the road and up the wooded hill. The trees dripped and his brogues couldn't find any traction. His hair was plastered to his head and he was cold to his bones.

Now to wait, he thought. Could a five-pound bomb destroy a seven-hundred-and-forty-ton Type IX C U-boat? Ballerstedt assured him it could. His watch, waterproof, of *Kriegsmarine* issue, ticked away the seconds. 2:56 came and went. He shifted uneasily against the side of the tree. The bomb obviously hadn't gone off, unless it had been so quiet he hadn't been able to hear it. He hoped to see some change in the submarine, but she stayed steady on the water, with no sign of a list. He thought of the alternative. There was only one. Go back to the boat and open the ballast tanks wide. That meant he would go down with her. A stationary U-boat sank like lead when the ballast tanks were full open. And if he went down with her he wouldn't be able to complete the second part of his mission.

Then, at 2:59, he heard a crunching *pank* from the bow, like a firecracker under a juice can, and saw a geyser of water shoot thirty feet into the air. A small blast. Ballerstedt had called it a discreet bomb. Goerlitz looked at the blockhouse, expecting at any moment the pen light to come on and the guard to rush out. But it soon became apparent the guard hadn't heard the blast over the heavy rain.

Five minutes later the boat began to list to port, and though he was sad to see such an expensive piece of precision machinery go to the bottom, particulary because U-512 had been his first command, he knew he had no other choice. A few minutes later water spilled into the for'ard hatch.

She sank slowly at first, emitting a steady stream of bubbles and oozing a multi-tentacled oil slick across the pen water. A car came down the east harbor road, its painted-over headlights like two dim eyes. It slowed to a halt and the driver, a man, got out of the car and walked halfway to the fence where he peered into the submarine pen.

She drifted to the middle of the pen as she sank. The stern lifted into the air, and the camouflaging upper works the carpenters had constructed tumbled into the water. The driver pointed, though there was no one around to point for, shouted something Goerlitz couldn't make out, then began running toward the blockhouse. On the force of its own weight the rudder clanged to the left. The driver pulled the blockhouse door open, and an obviously startled guard hurried into the pouring rain with his rifle and flashlight.

Because the boat was angling down bow first, the water reached the conning tower and aft hatches at about the same time. The driver and guard walked out onto the pier together, the flashlight playing over the water. The boat began to sink quickly, reeling on its side, revealing a barnacle-encrusted keel, then slipped beneath the surface in a wash of bubbles and kelp. Even if they raised her tomorrow the salt water would have already done its job, and she wouldn't be good for much, certainly not operational any more, and not much good for research either. A few moments later Goerlitz felt an almost negligible thud through his feet. The submarine had hit bottom.

Chapter 12

Major Hatley held the receiver to his ear, listening to the telephone at the other end of the line ring and ring. Corporal Patterson stood before him. This was most puzzling. Sergeant Saville hadn't come to the camp for two days. Finally, he hung up, rubbed his eyebrows with his forefinger and thumb, then looked at Patterson.

"It's not like him," said the major. "It's not like him at all. Saville is a very conscientious man. If he were ill he would have called. I wonder why the devil his wife doesn't answer."

"The sergeant told me his wife was visiting relatives in Bristol for the week, sir."

"Really? You don't suppose he took the opportunity to go on a fling, do you?"

"No, sir. Not like him. He's not a lady's man. And the most I've ever seen him drink is three or four brown ales a night."

The major tapped his lips with his fingers then leaned forward and folded his hands.

"Did anybody see him leave on Sunday night?"

"I'm afraid Ridout got here late, sir." Patterson looked away, embarrassed. "It seems there was no one making Saville's round for an hour or two at least, and I'm sure he went home at his usual three o'clock."

"Well, I'd like you to drop round to his flat for me, Rob, on your way to pick up the doctor. Knock on the door. See if he's taken his mail." He thought for a moment. "And if his landlady's there, ask her whether she's seen him."

•

Windermere, a small village on Lake Windermere in the heart of the Lake District, was winding down for the summer. The village had been made famous in the nineteenth century by William Wordsworth but was now more well known as a summer resort. The summertime holiday-makers were going back to London, Birmingham, and Manchester, getting on with the business of fighting the war. The only people left were the villagers and the rich evacuees who owned the expensive cottages along the lake.

The mail had just arrived at the beach-front cottage of Lieutenant-Colonel Leslie James Gregory. Jillian Gregory, the lieutenant-colonel's wife, flipped through it impatiently, tossing magazines on the table, junk mail in the garbage, until she found the weekly letter from her husband. She lit a cigarette. God, how lonely she was. She poured a sherry, sat down at the big picture window overlooking the lake, the boat-house, and the fountain, and sliced the envelope open.

When she finished reading his two-page letter, she wasn't pleased. At one time she would have been furious but now she had grown used to it, and displeasure was about as much as she could feel.

She picked up her glass of sherry, drained it, and lit

another cigarette, stubbing the old one out half finished. Who the hell did he think he was? Did he think he could just put her away in a gilded cage like this, far away from the war, and forget about her? She hated the way he apologized and boasted at the same time. She didn't know how she could love a man like that, full of himself. He wrote the way he talked, with his nose in the air, a man who thought he knew his own worth. "I'm sorry, darling, but it simply couldn't be helped, and, well, we, you know how it is when there's a war going on, and, well, darling, don't get angry, but I'm afraid Cecilia was a little demanding, and well, we, we, we ... "

There was no reply to a letter like that. Didn't he remember Damon, or had the war destroyed his every sense of family?

She got up, walked around the big glass coffee table, and stood at the picture window. She should count herself lucky. She had a big house on one of the finest lakes in the world, as much food as she could eat, and all the latest fashions from the best designers in New York. Everything would be fine if Leslie were here. And everything would be fine if Damon were alive, and if she weren't so damnably lonely.

What had happened to her life? Why did it no longer feel bright and fresh? Why did it feel as if it were decrepit and decadent, like a teetering civilization in its last days? Twenty-four years ago her life had been so vastly different. There had been nothing but hope for her, when Leslie, only twenty-three, still loved her, hadn't evolved into the chronic adulterer he was today.

She couldn't help thinking of her wedding day, that velvety warm June afternoon in 1920, when she married the heir to the Gregory millions, how she had been the envy of London, in a taffeta and silk wedding dress and a diamond tiara. Why did all happiness have to turn sour after a while and how could she, Jillian Gregory, nee,

Portsmouth, a gem in the constellation of London society, have wound up here, sitting on this couch, overweight, forgotten, and half drunk in the middle of the afternoon? What had happened to the wholesome family holidays on the Riviera and the pleasant drives in the Rolls-Royce through Cumbria during Damon's summer vacations? What had happened to the warmth and tenderness that had once been in Leslie's eyes? She had come to the bitter conclusion some years ago that people eventually lost everything they ever worked hard for. And her loss, in particular, had driven her to a life of dissipation and a cycle of self abuse from which she couldn't seem to break free.

She scratched her ribs, moved from the picture window, and sat down on the loveseat next to Leslie's chihuahua, Ten-pin. A stupid prize in a bowling tournament, she thought. Why had Leslie been bowling in the first place? In their crowd it was considered a thoroughly vulgar sport. And why had he been bowling in London's East End, where many of their friends simply refused to step foot?

Did anybody find her attractive any more, she wondered? Not even those old men in town who drank themselves to sleep at Braithwaite's each night?

She bounced off the loveseat and hurried to the mirror in the hall. She lifted her jersey and inspected her figure. Her big breasts were beginning to sag, and her nipples, in the course of the last six months, had sprouted a hair or two. Her waist was certainly fleshier than it had been a year ago, but she had still retained her general shape.

What she needed was a trip away from here, she thought, to New York. But to get to New York she would have to go on a boat, and knowing her luck the boat would be torpedoed.

When she was alone, she ate too much. That's why

she was getting fat. She ate to alleviate her boredom. And could Leslie blame her? This place was so bloody boring. It made her feel like slutting around, just like Leslie did in London.

Ten-pin whimpered, and as she turned, she saw him shudder. They didn't get along. Whenever she looked at the small dog she couldn't help thinking of used condoms and cheap hotels.

●

Laurie stood on the pier of the east harbor submarine pen the morning after the sinking of U-512. Debris of every description — bunk mattresses, oil drums, pieces of lumber from the partially completed upper works — floated on the surface. Curtis Fine and two members of the technical crew were going down in hard-hat diving gear, just to see what kind of shape she was in. Laurie was furious. He was in an absolutely foul, foul mood.

"Inspector Laurie?" It was Taylor, calling from the small building up the hill that housed his temporary field office. "Your call to the admiral has come through. He's waiting for you."

"All right, Don, tell him I'll be right there."

Curtis Fine and the other two divers descended the ladder through the spectrum-colored skin of oil floating on the surface of the submarine pen. Never had he felt so exasperated in all his life. The three men went down in a ring of bubbles and splashes, knocking small wavelets against the side of the pen. He tossed his cigarette into the oily pen water then turned to go.

He walked out the gate, crossed the road, and climbed the terraced pathway to his field office, knowing he was going to need all his control to deal with the admiral. His stomach was rolling with coffee and he felt he could be cross with anybody, even the Director General of the NID.

"Do you have any idea what shape she's in? Or what caused it?" asked Carson once Laurie had explained the situation.

"It's hard to say what shape she's in, Leo. I hope those bloody bastards in the Admiralty are proud of themselves. Fine's going down just now to have a look. I think we have to conclude it was sabotage."

"Sabotage?"

"Yes. Three strings of barbed wire running along the top of the fence have been cut with pliers. If only the Admiralty would have listened to me in the first place. We should have kept U-512's location highly classified right from the start. If they had maintained my gag order, if they'd taken me a little more seriously, it wouldn't have happened."

"Well," said Carson, "this is a dreadful start to what I know is going to be a dreadful day. Of course the Admiralty never does anything wrong, Gerald. Mark my words, they'll blame it all on us. Now, look, I know you're mainly a technical man, but I don't want to get anybody else involved in this. Let's not stir any more dirt than we have to. We'll quietly tidy up and hope the Admiralty agrees our hands are lily-white."

"And what are your priorities, Leo?"

"First, determine just what kind of shape she's in. See if there's anything salvageable."

"I highly doubt it."

"That remains to be seen, doesn't it, Gerald? Then, if it is indeed sabotage, I want to give you the opportunity to go after the saboteur. You've always said you wanted some action. Now here's your chance. I'll authorize whatever resources you need. If you feel you can't handle it, then that's fine, too. I'll find somebody else. Of course there'll be a certain amount of risk involved."

"A full scale manhunt, in other words."

"Precisely."

Laurie thought for a moment. The idea was appealing and yet he was hesitant. He hadn't been involved in a manhunt since his early days with the NID, when he'd been a liaison officer to the French, Spanish, and Portuguese navies. At the same time it was true what Carson said, that he wanted to see some action, especially now that it was wartime. And yet he had to consider all the wonderful progress Heather had made, progress that was almost too good to be true, and how for the first time it looked as if they might live a happy and normal life. He felt he had to be with Heather now more than ever, to help her, and encourage her in her new condition, to make every effort to insure that the whole problem didn't come crashing down around them again. He didn't want to risk that.

"Leo, I think we should carry it one step at a time. I think we should gather all the information we can about what did or did not happen."

"My thought exactly," said Carson. "And I want you to handle it."

"That I can do."

"They're going to want a report, Gerald. Do you think you could manage one by Monday? I'll have a plane in Liverpool waiting to bring you down."

"Monday should be fine. If I'm delayed for any reason I'll call you."

"Super. And if it is a saboteur? Would you like to head the horses and the hounds and bloody well go after him, Gerald?"

Laurie looked out at the bay where he saw the salvage barge cutting through the waves toward the submarine pen.

"I'll give you my answer when and if it seems like an appropriate course of action, Leo."

"If that's the way you want to handle it, Gerald. I have no argument. I'll see you here on Monday, then."

Laurie hung up, went back outside, and descended the terraced pathway to the submarine pen. The derrick operator began pulling the diving bell out of the water. Laurie went through the pen gate and stood by the edge of the pier. Everything they could have learned from U-512 was now out of reach, and what was to be perhaps his ultimate contribution to the war effort, and possibly the pinnacle of his career, was now gone. Well, he was a man who was used to disappointments, and he could endure this one as well as he had endured any of the others.Curtis Fine and the other divers emerged from the pen, covered with stray pieces of algae, looking like spacemen from H.G. Wells' fantasy. Fine climbed the ladder, and a few sailors helped him off with his round, airtight helmet. The chief engineer walked awkwardly toward him, dripping, shaking his head slowly from side to side.

"Well, you're right," he said. "There's no question about it. It's sabotage. A hole's been blown through the front keel. Must have brought their own explosives because we have the scuttling charges in that shed over there. Whoever it was knew what they were doing."

"What's her general condition, Curt?"

"She's cracked amidships, she's obviously flooded through and through, and her port saddle-tank is crushed. I'm sorry, Gerald, but she's a write-off. I'm afraid there's not much we can do. The salt water will have ruined her controls by now. You might as well have Carson scrap the investigation."

"As bad as all that?"

"I'm afraid so."

Laurie thought for a moment.

"Well, then," he said, "that's that. But we're not finished yet. I'd like Hopcraft to go down and determine what kind of explosive was used. Do you think you could arrange that for me, Curt?"

"I'll see to it at once, Gerald."

That was the first step, thought Laurie. Find out how they did it and what materials were used. Method always mirrored the personality, and if they could determine how the saboteur did it, and what degree of skill and knowledge he possessed, particulary about submarines, they would have the beginnings of a profile. And a profile would at least let them start the process of elimination. If he wasn't actually involved in the manhunt at least he could provide the investigating team with useful information.

•

Corporal Patterson arrived at Sergeant Saville's flat in the west harbor section of Barrow-in-Furness shortly before noon. The landlady wasn't there, though there was a note on her door saying she would be back by three, four at the latest. Saville's mailbox was locked, but peeking through the slot, Patterson saw that there was indeed mail inside. He climbed the stairs and knocked on the first door to his right, Saville's flat. He knocked louder but there was no answer. He frowned. This wasn't like the sergeant. He knocked again.

"Sergeant?" he called. "Sergeant Saville, this is Corporal Patterson."

No answer. He knocked yet again. Finally, he sighed. He took out his small notebook, scribbled off a message asking the sergeant to contact the camp as soon as possible, then went back to his vehicle for the drive to pick up Dr. Duncan in the east harbor section of town.

The morning sky had cleared and a stiff north wind had developed, bringing much cooler temperatures, fringing the leaves of the plane trees with an autumnal rust.

The doctor was a short pudgy man with a perpetual frown on his face who wore a bowler hat and speckled bow-tie. Patterson drove slowly. The unpaved road into Triggsdale Hall was a mess because of the recent drenching rain.

The doctor, as it turned out, had spent a large part of the morning down at the submarine pen with a group of other spectators watching the U-512 salvage operation.

"I overheard some of them talking. They say it was sabotage," said the doctor, in his gravelly voice. "It has all those technicians in a funk. They're still sorting through the debris that came to the top."

"I bet the bloody Jerrys got it."

"Maybe. Maybe not. There could be any number of possibilities. I'm sure your Jerry commander's going to be happy."

"Who, Weiss?"

"No, the other one. The new one on the sick list. It was his boat, wasn't it?"

"Oh, Goerlitz. Yes it was. And I'm sure he'll be overjoyed."

At the crest of the next hill Triggsdale Hall came into view. The red brick cornices and dormers looked fresh from all the rain. The prisoners' buildings gleamed white in the afternoon sun, and the puddles scattered all over the yard reflected the sky with a limpid brightness. Patterson felt oddly happy for Goerlitz. The poor bugger had had a rough go of it right from the start.

"Do they know what kind of shape she's in?" asked Patterson.

"They were just going down when I left. And they're not likely to tell me anything, are they? But I imagine it's not good for much. Scrap metal, that's all. They won't learn anything, if that's what you mean, now that the salt water has had a go at it. Besides, it's going to take them days to raise the thing."

Patterson pulled into the camp parking lot. He and the doctor got out. A few of the prisoners looked at them as they walked toward Building C.

"Is it only this Goerlitz now?" asked the doctor.

"Yes. Frischauer started feeling better last night."

"I don't know why you dragged me all the way up here."

"Commandant's orders, doctor."

"Stuff his orders."

They walked up the slate steps of Building C. No one was inside and all the beds were made.

"Look. You see? He's already up. I told the major that it was just the flu and it would have to run its course."

"He's probably out in the yard. Sorry about that. I'll run you right back."

They started down the steps to the parking lot. Then the doctor stopped. Patterson kept walking.

"Sergeant," the doctor called.

Patterson stopped and turned.

"Sir?"

"As long as I'm here, why don't I check him over?"

"Sir?"

"Goerlitz. He's got to be around here somewhere."

"If you wish."

They turned and went to the yard. Most of the men were gathered around a half dozen picnic tables smoking cigarettes or playing cards. Patterson approached Weiss.

"I say, captain, have you seen Goerlitz around?"

"I think he's still in bed, corporal."

"He's not. We just checked."

"I saw him there not ten minutes ago."

"Well, he's not there."

"All right, all right, Patterson," said Dr. Duncan. Weiss clearly frightened the doctor. "Let's not bother Herr Weiss on such a lovely day. If Goerlitz is well

144

enough to be up I guess you might as well take me back to town."

"He's probably in the Hall. Hang on half-a-sec and I'll see."

Patterson walked across the wet yard, his boots splashing in the grass. He asked the private on duty, Ridout, if he had seen Goerlitz.

"No, sir, not here."

"He wasn't in to see the major, then?"

"Not while I've been here."

Warning bells began to go off in Patterson's head.

"I see. Would you gather some of the others, private, and wait for me in the yard? Just a drill, nothing serious."

Patterson continued on down the hall to Major Hatley's office. He found the major working at the roll-top desk next to the window. The major looked up in a vague and distant way. There was a scotch glass by his elbow.

"Corporal?" he said.

"Can't account for Goerlitz, sir. Doctor came up to see him, and we can't find him, sir. Permission to search the camp, sir."

The major leaned forward, rousing himself from his alcoholic doziness. "What?" He looked off to one side, first toward the ottoman, then out the window, rubbing his knees with his hands. "Are you serious? You can't be serious, Patterson."

"It says in the regulations that if we should ever — "

"Yes, yes. I know the bloody regulations." He lifted his right hand off his knee and stroked his temple. "Are you absolutely certain, Patterson? Maybe he's in the latrines. And have you checked the games room in Building E?"

"Permission to do so, sir."

"All right, all right, permission granted." Hatley rose to his feet. "Search the camp."

Patterson about-turned and marched down the hall. Out in the yard, Private Ridout had gathered at least twenty-five guards from both off-duty and on-duty pools. Should be enough to give the camp a good going over, thought Patterson.

He watched as they formed themselves into a line. They were a mixed bunch, the youngest only fifteen, the oldest well into his sixties. Their faces were solemn. They knew this was serious. No drill this time, despite what he had ordered Ridout to tell them.

"It seems there may have been an escape," he began. "Hermann Goerlitz, of U-512. You know the procedure. McDonald, you take your men and assemble all prisoners in the yard under armed guard. Archer, you search the fairway and out beyond the trout pond, as well as the top of the hill. I'll take my men into the quarry. You know the routine. The minute anything turns up, let me know."

Goerlitz was neither in the games room of Building E, nor the latrines.

Of the twenty-five men available, Patterson took only four, as it wasn't a big quarry, and needed a poking and prodding approach to its search. The five of them descended the quarry road, branching out in all directions, looking behind the huge blocks, in the small trenches, and cave-like lacerations.

Patterson continued straight down into the quarry while the other four broke up into teams of two and searched both east and west bluffs. He stopped and looked around. The warm sunshine and the sudden dry weather had made the quarry an almost pleasant place to visit. The heartiest of the summer's last wildflowers clung to the soil-covered ledges. He knew the quarry well and was able to negotiate his path easily over the field of slate blocks to the huge pool and abandoned derrick at the far end, three or four hundred yards away from Triggsdale Hall. He stared at the methyl green water then scanned the huge haphazard bluff before him. Any number of places to hide there, he thought.

He began walking across the pool, his rifle ready, his ears sharp, scanning the opposite bluff for any movement or sign of escape. The water seeped through his boots and socks. Then he stumbled against something. Something soft. Oh, God, he thought. He slung his rifle over his shoulder and reached under the water, clutching at what he could feel was some sort of cloth. The water was an impenetrable green, and he couldn't see his hand once it was four inches beneath the surface. A body. He yanked on the cloth, pulling the dead weight, and a water bloated and partially decomposed face appeared from beneath the surface. It was Saville. Patterson's throat buckled and he had to take several frantic gulps of air before he could control himself.

"Archer," he cried. "McDonald. Archer. . .oh, my good God Christ. . .Archer. . .McDonald. . .I'm down in the quarry." He looked up at his men who still scoured the bluffs. "You lads, get McDonald and Archer here right away. I've found Saville."

•

Late Wednesday night Goerlitz collapsed in a field outside Windermere. He pulled the map from the inside pocket of his jacket. The map was wet and falling apart, but told him he had just another mile to go before he would reach the village. Then he would sleep in a dry warm place.

Pasture and hills rose all around him, criss-crossed with slate fences. The evening had started exceedingly clear and cold but now clouds moved in from the west and threatened rain.

It was well past two in the morning when he stumbled into Windermere. He was tired. He needed eggs, sausages, and three cups of hot coffee.

But nothing was open. He pounded on one of the hotel doors for several minutes. No one answered. The village had an abandoned look. Some establishments had been boarded up altogether. To make matters worse it began to rain. He shivered. He wasn't going to spend another night in the rain.

He followed the road to the lake, then turned onto a side-street. He finally came to a beach. The sky fermented with cold and wet weather, and heavy drops began to pelt the calm surface of Lake Windermere. He was tired. If he didn't find a sleeping place soon he would just fall down and sleep in the rain.

Small docks jutted out into the lake. He walked along the beach, passing cottages and docks one by one, looking for a shed or outbuilding to sleep in. His eyes slowly began to close. His legs shook underneath him. He stumbled into a lilac bush and clung to it. What was that through the hedge there? It looked like a fountain. A fountain like the fountains in the *Hofgarten* in Munich. Then he saw the boat-house behind it. He stumbled across the lawn past the fountain and to his relief discovered the boat-house door was open. He went inside.

He took his flashlight out of his duffel bag and looked around the boat-house. There was a large motor-boat, oars, fishing tackle, life preservers hanging from hooks, and water skis leaning against the wall. This was a start, he thought. They weren't likely to find him here, thirty-five miles from Barrow-in-Furness and sixty miles from Triggsdale Hall. The *San Julian* wasn't due in Liverpool until Monday, according to Weiss.

He could rest here in safety for a while.

Now, he could forget about the dispositions, about Ribalta and this Captain Gil Robles he would meet in Liverpool, about the *San Julian* and about Barcelona. For now, he would rest, get the sleep he so desperately needed.

He took one of the life preservers down and made a pillow for himself on the boat-house floor. He would sleep. And he hoped he would dream of the sunny days at his father's country house, before the Reich had turned sour, hoped he would dream of peace, not of war, as was so often the case these days, and most of all, that he would dream of Ute.

Chapter 13

By morning it had cleared again and there was a chilly north wind blowing down the lake. Jillian Gregory felt restless. It was only Thursday and Leslie wouldn't be home until late Saturday night. Then he had to leave so soon again on Monday morning. Ten-pin sat on the coffee table gazing out the picture window. At least there was a bit of sunshine, she thought. She plopped another egg, her third, into the boiling water and timed it for three minutes, then put it in her egg cup. She broke the shell and began to excavate, adding salt as she went.

It might be the kind of day to turn on the fountain one last time, she thought. There was nothing bleaker than a fountain turned off for the summer. Across the lake she saw the first colors of autumn in the leaves. Ten-pin kept looking out the window at the boat-house.

She finished breakfast, cleared the dishes, then stripped to her brassiere and underwear. She sat on the living room floor, hooked her feet under the sofa, and did some sit-ups. As elbows reached knees, her stomach dimpled, forming a small roll of white flesh. She was going to lose ten pounds by Christmas. She thought she might go swimming in the lake today but it was too cold and she didn't like swimming in the lake. Something would come up and drag her to the bottom, or shoals of leeches would attack her. She thought she might go for a bicycle ride but there were too many hills and she tired easily.

When she was finished her exercises she walked to the mailbox on the lake-shore road and got her mail and the *Times*. She made coffee, sat down at the picture window, and scanned a few war stories. The Italians had signed an armistice with the Allies. The King of Italy had dismissed Mussolini. The Germans had made the Duce a puppet ruler in northern Italy. There was a small article on how a German U-boat in Barrow-in-Furness had been sabotaged. All boring, she thought. When were the newspaper people ever going to realize war news got boring after a while?

She went to the fireplace and started a fire. Then she put on her shawl, pulled on her boots and, opening the door for Ten-pin, walked across the deck and down to the lake. Ten-pin ran quickly to the boat-house. He sniffed at the door.

She grabbed a handful of small stones, walked to the end of the dock, and threw them into the lake one at a time. She turned around and looked at the cottage. What did she need with all this room, she thought? Three storeys was too much for her, and at night she always thought prowlers crept around downstairs. The taps to the fountain were in the boat-house. Come to think of it, it might be a nice day for the fountain. It might even be a nice day for a boat ride, but she decided against it because it was too much work, especially when the engine was cold. Ten-pin scratched at the boat-house door. Ten-pin liked a boat ride. She spitefully decided against one. But the fountain would be nice. One more taste of summer, she thought, before the long miserable winter came.

She opened the boat-house door. Ten-pin scrambled around the bow of the boat to the other side. Oh, God, a muskrat, she thought, or even a skunk.

"Ten-pin, stay away from there."

She walked around the boat and caught her breath when she saw a man lying on the dock using a life-preserver as a pillow. Ten-pin sat placidly beside the man's head. The man stirred, then moaned. His brown suit was drenched and his trousers were covered with mud.

"Excuse me," she said. "Excuse me, but this is private property. You can't sleep here."

The man looked up, his eyes bleary, his chin covered with two or three days' growth, and gazed at Ten-pin, who stared back, timidly wagging his tail. The man's nose crinkled. He sat up and shivered. He looked frozen to death.

"I'm very sorry, ma'am," he said. He had some kind of accent. "I meant no harm." A gypsy, perhaps. "I got to town late last night and everything was closed."

"Well, this is private property. You can't sleep here, and I doubt you'll find anything in town at this time of year."

"I got caught in the rain last night," he said. He got up and slung his duffel bag over his shoulder. "Ma'am, I'm terribly sorry for trespassing, but I was hard-pressed last night."

"I'm sure you were." He was good-looking, she thought. "Where's all your luggage? You brought more than just that duffel bag, didn't you?"

The man stood up. "There was a mistake with my luggage." He hesitated. "Originally, I was going to Carlisle. That's where I'm from. But I decided to make a — "

"You don't sound Scots to me."

"I'm not. I'm half English, half Polish."

"And so your luggage is on its way to Carlisle. How unfortunate." Losing some hair, she thought, and a little broad in the face, but then all those Slavs had broad faces. "You look positively drenched."

"If you could just tell me where I might find a hotel, then I'll be on my way."

"Well, as I say, you'll have a hard time finding a room at this time of year. Everything closes down around the third or fourth of the month. Braithwaite's is about the only place and he's usually full."

The man's teeth began to chatter.

"Well, I'll be on my way, then," he said.

"You look frozen," she said. "Tell you what, why don't you step inside for a moment and warm yourself by the fire? I'll phone Braithwaite's and see if he's got anything left."

•

Miguel Ribalta sat in his favorite wicker arm chair, the one Captain Gil Robles had brought back from Ceylon on one of his many runs to the Indian sub-continent two years ago. Not that it had been a particularly tiring week but he was sleepy in a lazy satisfied way, and felt as if he deserved a treat. He had told Satrustégui this, and Satrustégui, a bright boy, as loyal as a dog, was scouting the town. With so many Barcelonians living in poverty after the devastation of the Civil War, it was an easy thing to buy anything one wanted.

His house was on a hill overlooking Barceloneta Beach. The stucco had been painted a bright shade of pink and the shutters a deep pine green. He sat on the large balcony above the beach, and in the room behind him he heard his Moroccan maid cleaning up. He heard the steady swish-swish of the ceiling fans. He looked up at the sky. There was perhaps no shade of pink he liked better than the rosy color of the sky over the Mediterranean at this time of the evening, and how, as one looked higher, the pink changed to an unfathomable shade of

153

gold and finally darkened to a uniform canopy of blue. If the sky at this time in the evening were for sale he would have bought it. He liked the cool marble tile on his bare feet, and he liked the silhouettes of the potted palms he had placed at either end of the balustrade. In such a cultivated and what he considered a Catalonian house, he would have his treat and enjoy it to its fullest.

For was there anything so pleasing as young and sweet flesh, or nubile curves and slender limbs? He felt himself growing hard just at the thought of it. The ones Satrustégui brought him were always so pretty, innocent-looking. True, he would have to go to confession tomorrow at Valencia Cathedral, and Father Azana would have him say his customary ten Hail Marys and three Our Fathers. It was always Father Azana. Father Azana was discreet, and was also chairman of the property fund, and knew where his largest donations came from. It was a small price to pay to have whatever hard nub of his soul remain cleansed of its impurities. All was fair in business, but he liked to think he still had a few scruples left when it came to his personal life. And so after a treat he always felt the need to repent. All was fair in business, but the best profits came to those who investigated all the possibilities. Just this afternoon his *Abwehr* contact had finally returned his call about the Helga Weiss operation. They had no record of the operation on file. But they would dig further and get back to him. He should have expected such a mystified response from the Germans. There were always other markets. Nothing firm, and until that time it wasn't worth thinking about. It was time to forget about business, time to think more of its rewards.

From his balcony he saw the small jetties and piers, the numerous pleasure craft and sailboats of the Santa Maria Yacht Club. And if he counted the boats he could spot his own sixty-foot cabin cruiser. Maybe after his treat tonight he would go for a short cruise. He heard the soft tread of his Moroccan maid. He turned around.

Jala had been bought at Tangier's illegal slave market deep in the bowels of the Casbah, and he treated her well, allowed her to practice her Muslim religion because she kept his house so beautifully clean, and was as truly devoted to him as Satrustégui. She made a small bow, the same bow she made toward Mecca each evening, and keeping her eyes averted, spoke to him in a soft respectful voice.

"Satrustégui is here, senor."

"Good, Jala, good," he said. "Send him up."

As he waited, he thought how pleasurable it would be to soothe himself, and how it was important for a man to soothe himself at the end of a hard work week; well, maybe not so hard, but easy days had come after many, many hard years, years of desperation, uncertainty, and worst of all, war. Now it was time to enjoy, to soothe all the hurt, and to forget all the grisly things he had seen, heard, and done.

Satrustégui appeared at the large Moorish doors with the concubine. Beautiful, he thought, one of the most stunning Satrustégui had ever brought, with a blemishless complexion, a curly head of luxuriant black hair such as he liked to suppose the Virgin Mary had, and fine, deftly crafted features. His penis began to twitch with excitement. And young, too, surely no more than twelve, as yet unspoiled by adolescence.

"Very good, Satrustégui. Very good. You may go."

Satrustégui left.

Money in such things didn't matter because a few hundred pesetas meant nothing. He pointed to the marble patio stones where the concubine was to kneel. Such a good life now, he thought. There was opportunity in everything he saw. Barceloneta Beach stretched before him in languid shades of mauve, indigo, blue, and green, and the evening's first stars appeared in the sky. This was his empire. Such a good life now. With a sigh of pleasure he stood up, undid his belt, and unzipped his fly. The girl knelt before him, reached in and released his hard penis, licked the palm of her right hand before grasping it firmly, began pumping it, and slowly opened her mouth. And when it was over, and the divine child turned her face away with a blush and spit into a porcelain bowl, it was time for opportunity again, time to pick up the telephone and call Gil Robles, who was in Dublin at the usual number by this time, making his regular stopover before Liverpool. Helga Weiss. The name kept coming back. He dialled the Dublin number when the girl had gone. It was Ramirez who answered, drunk as usual, and it was several minutes before Gil Robles came to the phone.

"Miguel, Miguel," he cried. "How good of you to call."

Gil Robles wasn't particularly sober himself. Ribalta tried to explain to his captain over the crackling wires that he should expect someone, possibly a German, who would want to leave England. Gil Robles, as usual, sobered up immediately when it came to business. He took a good percentage from these passage brokering deals. There was an identification code, he said, a name, Helga Weiss. Whether the person would be German, or something else, he wasn't sure. Only that Gil Robles should be prepared for an approach in Liverpool.

•

Jillian put the receiver down. The man sat on the raised platform around the fire. He was slim, she noted, with broad shoulders. Ten-pin sat beside him. Ten-pin was glad to have company. She was glad to have company too.

"I'm afraid they have nothing left," she said.

"That's a shame," said the man. "I was hoping to do a little fishing and maybe some boating. I should have called ahead." The man rose. "I'm sorry to trouble you so much, ma'am. You've been more than kind. I might as well go straight on to Carlisle. You wouldn't happen to know when the next train leaves, would you?"

The daily train to Carlisle left in just over an hour. But she wanted the Pole to stay a while. Already she was composing her next letter to Leslie:

Well, you see, darling, I found him in the boat-house and he was cold and wet, and well, we all have to pull together while there's this war going on, so I asked him in. I know it was fool-ish of me, a stranger, but he turned out to be nice, and, well, even Ten-pin liked him, and he was so disappointed when there was no place to stay, and we have so much room, so I told him there was a bed available, and, well, we, we, we, well, darling, you know what it's like when there's a war going on.

"The train left early this morning," she said. "There won't be another until tomorrow."

"Damn. It just hasn't been my week, has it? I suppose I should walk to Kendal and see if I can catch a train from there."

"Oh, nonsense," she said. "Look, I have plenty of room. If you want to stay for a few days, that's fine with me."

"No, I really couldn't. You've been much too gener-ous already."

"Why not?"

"What about your family?" asked the man.

"I have no family. My son's dead and my husband won't be home until Saturday. Now, come on, don't be shy. The lake can be lovely at this time of year. And Ten-pin and I could use the company, God knows, now that

157

all the summer people have gone."

The man hesitated, seemed to be thinking.

"Well, if it's not too much trouble," he said. "I'd be very grateful to you."

Jillian couldn't believe her luck.

"No trouble at all. We all have to help each other with this war going on. My name's Jillian, by the way. Jillian Gregory."

She extended her hand.

"Michael Bower," he said, shaking it.

"Well, now, I suppose you haven't had any breakfast, have you, Michael? What would you like? We have fresh eggs. My husband brings me a dozen from London each week. Or you can have hot cakes."

"I don't expect you to feed me, Mrs. Gregory. I'll try and find a bite in town."

"Don't be silly. And you must call me Jillian. I have plenty of food and it would be a pleasure to cook for someone rather than myself for a change."

•

John Hopcraft and his diving crew ascertained that the hole in the front keel of U-512, five yards in diameter, had been the work of a home-made bomb. This was duly noted in Inspector Gerald Laurie's report. Taylor and Westmoreland were drawing up a list of every serviceman on the naval base who had access to any kind of explosives. Laurie wanted to believe it was a German who had destroyed U-512, but he had to take into consideration the possibility that a fascist-loving recruit had been responsible for the sinking of the U-boat.

But then Major Hatley phoned him.

"I'm afraid Commander Goerlitz has escaped, inspector." The major sounded exhausted, drink-worn. "Killed one of my guards before he got out. I thought I should phone you because I think we have to assume there's some connection between the sinking of U-512 and Goerlitz's escape. And that it might be pertinent to your investigation. I don't know."

Pertinent, thought Laurie? More than bloody pertinent.

"All right, major," he said, trying to hide his frustration. With this new development, the investigation was going to take longer, and he was anxious to get back to Heather in London. "Thank you. We'll be at the camp in a half hour."

Laurie and his assistants arrived at the camp just as a blue navy ambulance was taking the body of Sergeant Saville away. He found Major Hatley sitting in his office, slumped in his chair, a half empty bottle of scotch and a scotch glass sitting on the blotter beside him as Lord Selby gazed down with dour eyes. All in all, the major looked like a defeated man. Hatley rose to his feet.

"Inspector," he said, extending his hand.

"Good afternoon, major. These are my two assistants, Mr. Taylor and Mr. Westmoreland."

"Good afternoon, gentlemen. Please, sit down. Scotch? Gin?"

After the drinks were settled and Lieutenant Carberry had been called in to take notes, the four men sat down and Inspector Laurie began the questioning. He questioned the major gently because he could see Hatley was quite beside himself and agitated as could be.

"I've been commandant of this camp for four years," said Major Hatley, "and not once has there ever been even a suspicion of an escape. We all thought it was impossible."

"Do you have any idea when the escape might have taken place?" asked Laurie.

"We have only a rough idea. The officer from the base's forensic lab says Saville has been dead for about two days. Oh, my bloody Christ, what am I going to tell his wife when she gets back from Bristol?"

"So Sunday night, or early Sunday morning?" persisted Laurie.

"As near as we can make out, yes. We all thought he was sick and in bed."

"Tell me, major," said Taylor, "was there anything unusual in Goerlitz's behavior preceding the escape, anything that struck you as extraordinary?"

"Well, yes, there was. When he first came to the camp he was exceedingly belligerent and uncooperative. As I told Inspector Laurie on the phone, I had to put him in solitary confinement. I assure you, Mr. Taylor, that's very unlike most of the new prisoners who come to Triggsdale Hall. My God, they take one look at their warm bunks and the food they'll be eating, and they wonder how they ever got so lucky. Not with Goerlitz. I knew I had a problem the minute I saw him. I told the inspector as much the last time we met."

The major lifted his scotch glass to his lips and drank studiously.

"Anything else?" prodded Westmoreland.

"The second night he was here he started a ruckus in the mess hall. He's a fighter, Mr. Westmoreland, and I thought I should discipline him. That's when I put him in solitary confinement. I put him in the box for five days. Terribly nasty in there at this time of year but I thought Goerlitz deserved it. Well, he was in there for two days, and then Corporal Patterson told me Goerlitz wanted to see me. I went up to the box and he was a different man. Polite, civil, even docile. Any fool could see it was a ruse. Goerlitz isn't the kind to sacrifice his pride. He had a reason. I could see it in his eyes. He wanted something."

"Are you sure Goerlitz is the one who killed Saville?" asked Laurie.

"No question about that, inspector. Saville was found

in the quarry, which is one of the two likely places a prisoner would try to escape. And he ran guard duty by the quarry on the night he was murdered. I'm afraid we have to put two and two together. Massive bruising on the side of his head. His pockets were stuffed with slate, and he had slate shoved down his shirt to keep him under."

"Commandant," said Westmoreland, "has anything been stolen from the camp, or have you noticed anything missing, say in the last week or two?"

The major looked at Westmoreland. Westmoreland was a gruff blustery man whose voice was unnecessarily loud and whose upper lip was lined with a thin effete pencil mustache. Laurie could see Hatley had taken an instant dislike to his assistant. Most people did. Or maybe he just didn't like Westmoreland's question. Hatley had turned a rare shade of ivory.

"I thought you were going to ask me that." The major leaned forward and looked out the window at the yard with lonely dissipated eyes. "I received a call from a chap by the name of Michael Bower this morning. A junior inspector. He was here on Friday with another fellow by the name of Douglas to inspect the camp. You know, just a routine check. Seems he lost his wallet and National Registration Identity card. Thinks he might have lost them while he was here in the camp. Suspicious, wouldn't you say? Then on Thursday we had a soccer match. The Triggsdale Hall team against the naval base. We have a bit of a league around here. Six teams in all. An Ensign Beaumont from the naval base team reported his suit missing from the locker room. At first I thought nothing of it. We searched the camp but we didn't find it. I thought one of our players might have taken it as a joke. We were all very happy. We won the game. Put us at a second place standing, as a matter of fact."

"But then you assumed," said Westmoreland, his voice grating, "that Goerlitz would likely need a suit if his escape were going to be in any way successful, that anyone would spot him a mile away in his prison uniform. Very brilliant, commandant. Stunningly brilliant."

"Now, see here, Mr. Westmoreland, we hardly need your sarcasm. We're already horribly upset by Saville's murder and we don't need anybody around here with an unhelpful attitude."

"I understand Triggsdale Hall doubles as an explosives depot for the naval base in Barrow-in-Furness," said Laurie.

"That's correct, inspector."

"My specialists tell me U-512 was sunk by a homemade bomb. Do you suppose Goerlitz could have stolen some charges from one of the explosives sheds?"

"Absolutely not. Those sheds are guarded twenty-four hours a day, year round. Any prisoner coming within fifty yards of them are shot on sight."

Laurie looked at Westmoreland. Westmoreland simply shrugged and finished the rest of his gin.

"Well, do you mind if we have a look, commandant? Just so we can be sure?"

"By all means, go ahead. Lieutenant Carberry, take these gentlemen and show them around the explosives sheds."

There were three explosives sheds in all, made of tar-paper covered plywood and corrugated tin roofs. Each one had a sign above the door: DANGER. EXPLOSIVES. SMOKING STRICTLY PROHIBITED. Westmoreland inspected the first one, Taylor the second one, and Laurie the third one.

Laurie entered the third shed and looked around. Boxes and crates lined the walls, each stamped with a War Ministry stamp, and each was stencilled with what kind of ammunition or explosive they contained.

At first Laurie noticed nothing suspicious and still thought it might be a good idea for Taylor and Westmoreland to continue compiling their list of suspects from the naval base. But then he detected a slight chipping on the lid of one of the plastic explosives crates. Also, one of the nails wasn't hammered all the way in. He attempted to pry the chipped board away from the top using both his thumbs, but it wouldn't budge. So he tried to find something in the shed that might help him, and rounding a skid of Torpex, saw a board pried loose from the top of a crate containing percussion caps. One of the thick asbestos-padded bags inside the crate had been torn open and several dozen of the small mushroom-shaped detonators were scattered over the other asbestos-padded bags.

He knocked the loose board off and used it as a lever to pry away the top of the plastic explosives crate. Plastic explosives had come into use only a few years ago and were in great demand by the demolition crews of the Engineers' Corps. It came in five-pound blocks, each block coated with an oily grey wax to protect it from the damp. One of the blocks, he saw, was clearly missing, because the pile was incomplete by one block. He thought of the other things someone might need to make a bomb. Some kind of triggering mechanism, like a firing pin, would most definitely have to be included in the design. He looked around some more. Sure enough, a box of D-style firing pins had been broken open.

●

After these discoveries, the investigations of suspect naval personnel were suspended. Laurie asked John Hopcraft to reconstruct, on paper, the kind of bomb used, based on the size and shape of the hole it had blasted through the submarine. The materials described in the armaments and munitions expert's one-page report and diagram closely resembled those materials stolen from the explosives shed at Triggsdale Hall. The report added that the construction of such a bomb would need a thorough knowledge of explosives and explosive devices. Upon examination of camp records it was discovered only one man had such knowledge. Heinz Ballerstedt, the former armaments and explosives officer aboard U-93. Ballerstedt, of course, would be closely interrogated, but all in good time. There were more important things to do right now, especially if he were going to fly to London tomorrow with his report for Admiral Carson.

He had posters of Goerlitz, with a description of the commander, printed at the naval base printing plant and distributed to all the police departments in the area. The prisoner was of medium build, 5'10", broad shoulders, blue eyes, and was wearing a double-breasted brown suit with a torn lapel. He was most likely calling himself Michael Harvey Bower. Laurie sent posters not only to police departments but to all local public establishments, as well as the local reserve and Home Guard units.

He then requested, through the offices of the Naval Intelligence Department in Whitehall, all files and related material on Goerlitz, and ordered the distribution clerks to have the material on the afternoon's mail plane.

The files arrived shortly after four. The Naval Intelligence file wasn't that helpful and read more like a history of Commander Weiss's U-93. What was surprising, and most certainly alarming to Laurie, was the existence of an extensive file on Goerlitz from the MI5 Registry, the government's counter-espionage department of the intelligence services. Laurie began to believe that this case was far more serious than he had first assumed.

The *Abwehr* had recruited Goerlitz at the age of nineteen, in 1934, upon completion of his second year as a language major at the Sorbonne in Paris, the file said. In fact it was Canaris, head of the *Abwehr* and an old friend of the Goerlitz family, who had personally recruited the young Hermann as a great potential talent. Goerlitz had completed training at the *Abwehr's* school outside Hamburg with a specialty in cryptanalysis. By the age of nineteen, Goerlitz, like his father, had a masterly command of both English and French, and spoke some Russian. He had gone to school in England during his early teens, attending a private grammar school in the London suburb of North Finchley for two years. All in all, an impressive record, and at least to Laurie, a dangerous record. Impressive family, too. His father was an honored and respected linguist, though he had been dismissed from his post at the university by the Nazi authorities for anti-fascist grumbling. His mother, before she died in 1929, had established a successful drapery business.

Goerlitz seemed perfect by his training, temperament, and high degree of native intelligence to be an *Abwehr* agent, even more so a cryptographer, yet, in one of the wild swings that seemed to have characterized his life, he had joined Admiral Karl Doenitz's fledgling *Unterseewaffe*, apparently against his father's wishes, and took part in the now notorious and sly war games of 1937 in the Baltic where the *Rudeltaktik* or wolf-pack theory was proven an effective strategy in submarine warfare.

At this point the MI5 Registry file was marked NFA, no further action, and there was a note directing the reader to the NID file, the file from Naval Intelligence. What alarmed Laurie most were the fabulous discrepancies and inconsistencies in Goerlitz's life. Here was a man who had studied at an English grammar school far away from the influences of German fascism during the formative years of his young adult life only to return to Munich to promptly join the highly Nazified *Jungvolk*. Then, just as suddenly, he left the *Jungvolk* to study languages at the Sorbonne, then returned two years later only to join the *Abwehr*, which was essentially an arm of the highly feared Nazi institution, the Gestapo. Then he joined the *Kriegsmarine*, the least Nazified wing of the armed forces, and at a time when there were virtually no Nazis in the *Unterseewaffe*. Yet the MI5 Registry file contended Goerlitz was an ardent National Socialist, even though he had been arrested in occupied Paris one night for shouting anti-Nazi slogans. This was cross-referenced in the NID file, which concluded Goerlitz was a fervent supporter of Hitler. And this was what bothered Laurie. An intelligent Nazi, especially one with *Abwehr* training, was far more dangerous to British national security than the more common breed of Nazi.

By six o'clock, Laurie had received two calls from people who said they had seen Goerlitz. One was a waitress in the small village of Laughton-in-Furness. Accordingly, he drove out to interview her, and though she described Goerlitz perfectly, how he had tipped her, how his suit had been covered with mud, she wasn't that helpful, or at least helpful only so far as she confirmed the prisoner's attempt to reach Barrow-in-Furness and subsequently the submarine pen on the east harbor road.

The other call was from a man by the name of Joseph Rowden, a seventy-one-year-old camera shop owner in Barrow-in-Furness. It was with a grim and mounting apprehensiveness that Laurie interviewed this man in his musty old shop.

"Had a funny kind of accent, he did. Mean-looking fellow, too. Looked as if he hadn't slept in a day or two. Usually we like to be friendly with our customers. But this man — this man was ice. So it was business, you see, and we really didn't talk to him."

"And you're absolutely sure the man you saw was the man in this photograph?"

Rowden had another look.

"As certain as you're standing there."

"And what kind of camera did he buy?"

"Well, he seemed to know a great deal about cameras." Mr. Rowden walked along the counter of his shop. At Laurie's special request he had stayed in his store past closing. "He bought one of these new Larisas. Made in Manchester, and a fine camera it is, too, sir. A thirty-five millimeter fast-action range-finding camera. Top of the line, sir. Oh, he knew his cameras all right."

Mr. Rowden handed the Larisa to Laurie. Laurie examined it carefully. He had a fair working knowledge of cameras and he knew enough to see he held a solidly built, beautifully designed, rugged piece of equipment. He snapped the accordion-style lens into the main body and handed the camera back to Mr. Rowden.

"Did he say anything else?"

"Not much. As I say, he wasn't exactly a friendly man. Very business-like. Bought two rolls of film. He said he was going to use the camera for portraits and landscapes."

"Thank you very much, Mr. Rowden. You've been a great help."

The implications of this new information were only all too obvious to Inspector Laurie. Portraits and landscape quite clearly meant documents and installations.

He drove back to his field office by the submarine pen, arriving there around eight o'clock. No more leads had come in. He placed a call to Admiral Carson. He wanted to let the admiral know of this latest development. But Carson had left his office for the day and Laurie decided it could wait until tomorrow morning when he flew down to London to present his report.

He took his papers back to his hotel room and began writing it up. The only military installation besides Triggsdale Hall around Barrow-in-Furness was the naval base, and Laurie had to conclude that the camera was purchased for the purpose of photographing the base, the arrival and departure lanes in Morecambe Bay, and any barriers meant to obstruct enemy U-boat access. It was a dismal conclusion, but knowing Goerlitz's background, the most likely possibility. He wrote his report with a grave and troubled recommendation to catch *Korvettenleutnant* Hermann Paul Goerlitz before it was too late.

The submarine was one thing, and as much as he hated to lose such a revealing piece of German technology, he couldn't help thinking that this was by far a much larger catastrophe. If Goerlitz did indeed get back to Germany, the consequences could send the Royal Navy teetering. Goerlitz, with his *Abwehr* training, and as an experienced naval officer, would easily be able to determine the strengths and weaknesses of such an important base as Barrow-in-Furness. He had to be stopped, as soon as possible and at any cost. The NID's contacts throughout Europe would have to be alerted in case he should try to flee to one of the neutral countries like Spain, Portugal, or Switzerland. Laurie would have to make Admiral Carson understand the urgency of the situation. Barrow-in-Furness was such an important staging area for convoys that a major strike against it could cause a disruption of vital materials for several months, if not up to a year. Never mind the thousands who would be killed in the initial attack. What bothered Laurie most was that several parts of Britain could possibly go hungry, and that many might virtually starve, the way they were in Leningrad.

Chapter 14

Jillian Gregory was a weak woman. Goerlitz knew that the moment she asked him to stay. And her weakness could be acted upon, used and exploited. By the most joyful of coincidences she had two bottles of schnapps in her liquor cabinet.

They sat in front of the fire, she with her sherry, he with his schnapps. She was somewhere in her forties, dissolute, desperate, and lonely. He didn't want to think about Liverpool. He just wanted to rest. As she talked on and on about the death of her son, as if death were something only she could understand, he only half listened. Damon Gregory had been a fighter pilot, a bad one. He had been shot down on his second mission. Goerlitz wore one of Damon's fashionable double-breasted suits from Bond Street. His own suit was in Damon's bedroom drying.

Jillian had undoubtedly been an attractive woman at one time, and for her age, she still was. She had a horsey English face with long teeth. Her shoulder-length hair was ashy blonde with only a dozen or so strands of grey.

She had ripe full breasts and she reminded him of the prostitutes he had slept with while on shore leave in Paris. She could be used and exploited, and through her, he might possibly find a way to Liverpool. Yet he felt sorry for her, pitied her because she seemed so sad and lost, abandoned by the world. Five years ago he would have found her easy to hate. She was an Englishwoman and he had been taught to hate the English. What's more, she was a corrupt and dissipated Englishwoman, an object for scorn and ridicule; yet, inexplicably, he felt the need to comfort her.

"Have you ever had someone die, Michael?"

"My mother's dead. She died a long time ago, when I was fourteen."

"I suppose it's different when a parent dies. Of course, it's still tragic, but you expect them to die before you, don't you? With a child you expect to have them forever. It's been almost two years and I can hardly talk about it. Even now. You're a most understanding man, Michael." She looked at him with her big greyish eyes. "I hope you don't find me, well, too confiding. I guess I've always been the trusting kind. I really haven't talked about Damon with anyone. He and I were very close. With his father away all the time I think we had a special relationship."

"It must have been very hard on you."

"Yes, I think it was. Damon was my lifeline."

Talk to me about death, he thought. You know nothing of death. He thought of Ludendorff and of all the other fine U-boat men he had seen maimed, mangled, wounded or drowned. She looked at him with a longing in her eyes. He felt sorry for her, not because she had lost her son but because she didn't know how to cope with death. Try watching your mother waste away from cancer for two years. Try watching your mother die when you are fourteen years old. He leaned forward, poured

170

her another sherry, and schnapps for himself. The fire popped and sparked, and outside he heard the north wind blow through the trees. She put her hand on his knee. His body stiffened then relaxed. He knew what she wanted, and he knew he would do as she asked. Sex was a weapon. Sex was the greatest weapon of all.

"How do you feel?" she asked.

"How do I feel? I'm dry and warm, and I'm very tired."

"Do you find me attractive at all?"

She leaned forward, sticking out her chest.

"Yes," he said. "You're quite pretty."

"Oh, Michael," she said, "You don't have to be such a gentleman."

For a moment, he found himself in a lecture hall outside Hamburg with a lot of other *Abwehr* trainees. Colonel Peter Hashagan stood at the front explaining what he disdainfully referred to as psychological persuasion. She rubbed his thigh. He looked away.

"What about your husband?" he asked.

"Does that feel nice?"

"Yes."

"You don't have to worry about my husband. Leslie and I have this agreement. Do you want to do this as much as I do?"

She rubbed his penis.

"Yes," he said.

He turned toward her and nibbled experimentally at her lips. Forgive me, Ute, but this Englishwoman might be one of the steps that lead me back to Munich. She responded by putting her arm around his shoulder, then unzipped his fly. His blood began to flow, the way it had in Paris when he knew he was no longer in a submarine and that he had at least a limited lease on life. He felt himself growing hard. She was like a rotten peach, he thought. More important, she was showing ultimate trust and he could use this to his advantage. The British might be scouring the countryside but they would never find him here. For now she was a comfort. She moaned as he undid the buttons of her blouse. She pressed her lips against his and forced her tongue into his mouth. His hand crept around her back and undid the catch on her bra. Her big breasts flopped across her ribcage.

From there, it was much like any of the times in Paris. In Paris, only the fat, ugly, old, or desperate prostitutes slept with the Germans. Jillian was old and desperate, just like the slightly plump forty-year-olds in Paris who hoped face paint would make them look twenty. She was on top, her legs astride him, her pelvis grinding furiously. He reached up and took a breast in each hand. He began to lick her right nipple, finally taking it in his mouth and sucking on it. Her breathing grew faster. He felt slightly ill as she came.

When she had finished, he had her bend over the couch so he wouldn't have to look at her face, and pumped her from behind. He came in a matter of moments. That was that. She moved away, moisture dripping down her thigh. She seemed embarrassed.

"I'm exhausted," he said.

"That was wonderful," she said. He could tell she was the kind of woman who felt this kind of comment was appropriate after making love. "If you don't mind, I'd like to sleep alone. I sleep better that way. My husband and I have always had separate beds."

"Whatever you prefer."

"I hope you don't get any ideas because of this, Michael."

She pulled on her panties and wrapped her blouse around her shoulders.

"Of course not."

"I suppose it's the war."

"It must be."

"People sometimes act differently in wartime than they do ordinarily."

"It was fun," he said.

She smiled. This seemed to be what she wanted.

"It was fun," she said. "It was damn good fun."

She led him upstairs to Damon's old room. The bed was made and there was a fresh pitcher of water on the bedside table. He said goodnight, closed the door, and listened to her footsteps as they retreated down the hall. He turned on the lamp and looked around the room. He opened the closet and discovered a lot of Damon's old clothes. A rich family, he thought, just like his. He remembered some of the suits he had worn before the war. Beautiful suits, just like these. He was tired. He didn't have the strength to search the room now. He pulled off his undershirt and slipped under the blankets. The bed was soft, cushy, unlike anything he had slept on since joining the Weddigen Flotilla in the Baltic years ago.

•

Laurie was the only one in the antechamber adjoining Admiral Leo Carson's office in Whitehall the next morning, and as usual, whenever he visited the Director General of the NID, he was oppressed with a sense of emptiness and gloom. Outside, a light rain fell from a pallorless sky. Five coal-grey pigeons huddled on the window ledge, crowding each other, trying unsuccessfully to keep dry. The report on the destruction of U-512 and the escape of Goerlitz was in his briefcase. The light above the admiral's door hadn't gone off yet. The walls were green or grey, he couldn't tell which, cadaverous in any case, and on them hung Royal Academy portrait's of Carson's predecessors, Sir Joseph Lingard and Sir Mark Arnott. The room smelled of cigar smoke and moldy overcoats.

He was gazing out the window watching two lorries haul rubble away from the Southwark side of the river up toward Trafalgar Square when, out of the corner of his eye, he saw the light above the door go off. Whatever confidential material Carson had been working on was now cleared from his desk. Laurie entered the admiral's office.

Leo Carson sat behind his large bare walnut desk in his green leather swivel chair gazing at Laurie with a sour expression of displeasure.

"Well, Gerald," he said, "what have you got for me?"

Laurie opened his briefcase, pulled out the stapled thirty-page report, and tossed it on Carson's desk.

"It's all there," he said.

The admiral took the report in his square-fingered hands.

"Leo, would you mind if I stepped out for an hour or so? It's going to take you a while to read that thing. I thought I might visit my wife in the hospital. By the time I get back you should be finished."

"Of course, Gerald. I quite understand. Give the dear my best, won't you?"

After twenty minutes of battling rush hour traffic, Laurie arrived at St. Mary's Hospital on Knightsbridge just after six. He took the lift to the fourth floor where she shared a room with three women, and was just passing the nursing station when someone called him from behind.

"Mr. Laurie." It was Dr. Aldershot, the young doctor who tended to Heather. He hurried up the corridor past a group of roll-away stretchers, his white lab-coat gently flapping behind him, his stethoscope swaying from his neck. "Mr. Laurie, do you have a minute? I was told you were out of town." He joined Laurie and shook his hand. "Did you get the message I had Mrs. Moss send you?"

"No. No, I didn't. I haven't been talking to Mrs.

Moss. Why? Is there something wrong?"

The doctor looked away, and to Laurie, there was something ominous in his expression.

"I'm afraid your wife has had a relapse. As a matter of fact I was going over the progress notes from Dr. Unsworth's clinic and there seems to be a pattern of — "

"A relapse?" At first Laurie thought it had something to do with her broken leg. "What sort of relapse?"

"A mental relapse, Mr. Laurie. One of the nurses found her crying to herself and hitting herself over and over again with her good arm. I'm afraid I had no choice but to give her a sedative."

For a moment Laurie just stared at Dr. Aldershot. He couldn't believe this. Heather had been doing so well.

"Is she conscious?" he asked. "Can I see her?"

"Oh, she's conscious, but I don't know whether she'll recognize you. The relapse was a rather serious one. But come this way. We'll see how she's doing."

They walked down the corridor past the porter trolleys and linen buggies until they came to room 401. The three other women who shared Heather's room, their bed curtains open, stopped talking when Laurie and the doctor entered, and it was apparent to Laurie that they had been gossiping about his wife. He pulled Heather's curtain aside and he instantly recognized the old Heather, the Heather who had made their lives so difficult for all these years. Her leg was in traction and her head was propped up by some pillows.

"Heather?" he said. He could feel the pain of all those years welling up in his chest. "Heather, can you hear me?"

Heather turned to him, her eyes half closed and glassy, a beatific and uncomprehending grin on her small delicate face.

"She may be able to hear you," said Dr. Aldershot, "but I don't think she knows who you are. I had to give her a rather strong sedative."

Laurie's jaw stiffened. His feelings walked a tightrope between anger and despair.

"When did it happen?" he asked, his tone clipped.

"Around eleven-thirty this morning. I tried to get in touch with you but I — "

"I was on a plane at eleven-thirty this morning. Has Dr. Unsworth been in to see her?"

"No. He'll be coming tomorrow. If you like, I can arrange for you to see him then."

"I'll be back in Liverpool tomorrow," he said, more firmly than he intended. "I'm afraid I'm on rather important government business right now."

He gazed at Heather for several moments, his face hardening. Was this what he had to look forward to for the rest of his life? He didn't know whether he would be able to endure it much longer, the role of nursemaid to a mad wife. He just wanted to get away from it.

"You seem so surprised by this, Mr. Laurie," said Dr. Aldershot. "After all, there's been a pattern of recovery and relapse for quite some time now."

"What pattern? Dr. Unsworth never mentioned any pattern."

"Perhaps Dr. Unsworth was just trying to cushion you, and you misunderstood him. His progress notes clearly indicate that after every recovery there's been a relapse, usually more severe than the last."

"Now, wait a minute. Her recovery seemed so complete. I was sure we were finished with it once and for all. Dr. Unsworth said that might be the case."

"You can never assume anything about mental illness, Mr. Laurie. We simply don't know enough about it."

Of course the doctor could be perfectly impartial about this, thought Laurie.

"You say each relapse seems to be more serious than

the last. Does that mean she's getting worse?"

"I was talking to Dr. Unsworth on the telephone just before you got here. With this new episode we've both concluded that she does indeed seem to have some form of progressive disease." A bedside expression came to the doctor's face, and he turned to Laurie with sincere, well-meaning eyes. "I'm sorry, Mr. Laurie. It's rather grim news, isn't it? But yes, she is getting worse. I think that's the only realistic prognosis. And I'm afraid Dr. Unsworth concurs."

Laurie drove the Hillman back to the Naval Intelligence Department like he might have driven the Bentley, with a wild shifting of gears and a sharp cornering the small car's shocks weren't designed for. He was upset. He was more than upset. What a fool he had been. He had so firmly wanted to belive that she was better. He wanted to believe that the accident had made her sane, that such serious injuries might have acted as a shock treatment, like the electric shock treatments Dr. Unsworth gave to some of his in-patients. But now he saw that he was wrong. The Bentley. No more than a piece of scrap metal. Why did she have to do it to the Bentley? And why did she have to do this to him all over again? He felt as if his family, despite his monumental efforts, had disintegrated, and that now all he had left was his career.

When Laurie got back to the NID he found Admiral Carson waiting for him in his office gazing pensively into the grate where a small fire smouldered away. He looked up at Laurie with fixed and steely eyes then took the report from the coffee table and straightened up the pages.

"Heather all right?" he asked.

Laurie's face remained impassive.

"She's fine," he said. "The doctor says she's mending quite well."

"Pleased to hear it," he said, but Laurie could tell Carson's mind was already back on the report. "You've written a very disturbing report, Gerald. And a convincing one. But are you sure your assessment is accurate?"

"My assessment is a hypothesis, Leo. But so far the evidence seems to support my hypothesis."

"And this espionage business on page twenty-six? I admit, you seem to have the facts to back it up, Gerald. But are you absolutely sure?"

"I think we should act as if I am. Why the camera, Leo? Goerlitz isn't here as a tourist. I believe he intends to get as much information as he can about the naval base at Barrow-in-Furness, and that he will try to get back to Germany. You know if accurate information reaches the German High Command, Morecambe Bay would be highly vulnerable to submarine attack. The results could be disastrous."

"Disastrous?" said Carson, his eyes widening. "The results would be catastrophic. Absolutely catastrophic. Now, see, here, Gerald, let's try and keep this thing under wraps. I'm going to soften up this report and bowlderize it as well. I don't want the Admiralty tracing it back to you. Let's see if we can get this all cleared away before anybody really has to know about it, shall we? Good God. If the Germans have the same kind of information they had about Scapa Flow, then one U-boat flotilla could destroy as much shipping in one day as the entire Western Fleet could destroy in a year. Despite all our electronic gadgetry. . .It would be a slaughter."

"Yes, Leo, I'm aware of that. And that's why I think we should widen the investigation. We'll certainly have to alert some of our foreign agents."

"Who?"

"Well, Luis Jimenez in Spain, for one. And Gabriel Malaquias in Portugal for another. Possibly even Burton Madgett in Berne. And maybe we should ask for MI5's help. Maybe one of their Double-Cross agents can ensnare Goerlitz and we can take him before he tries to leave the country. Maybe we should even ask — "

"Absolutely not. This is strictly an NID matter. If we involve MI5," said the admiral, "the true color of the situation will get back to Downing Street. Mark my words, it certainly will. And heads will roll, Gerald, heads will roll."

Laurie looked out the window at the grubby, soot-smeared buildings across the street.

"Yes, Leo, I suppose they will."

"And what about the other matter, Gerald? The manhunt. It would mean separation from Heather, of course. And from what you've indicated about this German, it could be dangerous. Are you the man for the job or shall I get someone else?"

Laurie gave Carson a far-off smile.

"Well, Leo, since I started the investigation I believe I should finish it."

•

Jillian listened until all sounds in her son's room had stopped. Then she sat up and read for a while, scanning through the back pages of the *Times* until well past eleven. Ten-pin began to snore around midnight. She pulled on her dressing gown and crept down the hall to Damon's room. The wind outside was strong and caused a steady rush of noise around the house. She turned the doorknob and pushed the door open. Over the wind she heard steady and deep breathing. She saw his face in the light from the hall, eyes shut in profound sleep. Why was he so tired?

She crept closer and looked carefully at Michael Bower's face. He was pale. He looked as if he hadn't seen the sun all summer. Now that she had had her fun, she just wanted him to go. She had enjoyed him and she felt the score was even with Leslie, and she regretted having asked him to stay for a few days. Leslie might come home early. He groaned and moved his head. She had enjoyed him like a hot fudge sundae, and she could tell Leslie how certain things simply couldn't be helped. She didn't entirely trust Bower. Handsome men, she knew, could never be trusted. She lifted his duffel bag and crept down the hall to her own room. Ten-pin wheezed in a dead sleep like a broken accordion.

Inside his duffel bag, she found a flashlight, a pair of pliers, two pairs of wet underwear, a damp undershirt, a soggy map, a butter knife, a camera, and a roll of film. She found his wallet which contained just over twenty-one pounds. That reassured her. Money always reassured her. She checked his I.D.: a library card, a security pass for a junior standards inspector, a driver's license, all of it in the name of Michael Bower. So he was a standards inspector. Well, that was harmless enough. Twenty-one pounds in the wallet of a standards inspector wasn't outrageous, especially if he were on holiday. She reached into the duffel bag once more and pulled out a National Registration Identity card. She opened it. Michael Harvey Bower, 5'11", age thirty-one, brown hair, blue eyes. Well, his hair was more blond than it was brown, rather a light brown with a few streaks of grey. She reached into the duffel bag again and pulled out something carefully wrapped in wax paper. She picked away the tape and unfolded the paper. She found a photograph of a young woman inside, roughly twenty, with blonde hair braided around her head in a series of layered hoops. The studio imprint in the lower right hand corner read *Hossenfelder*. She turned it over and discovered some German writing on the back, written in the angular and Gothic hand of woman who at one time or another had gone to a Catholic school.

Für Hermann,
> *Der Mann von dem ich immer traumte!*
>> *Ute, Munich, 1940*

She didn't understand the writing and only recognized the names Hermann and Ute. Her heart began to beat faster. Who in heaven's name was Hermann? This woman in the photograph was presumably Ute, but who was Hermann? She wrapped the picture in its wax paper and put it back in the duffel bag. What did that German mean? And why did he have a photograph with German writing on the back of it in the first place? Calm down, Jillian, you're getting much too excited over this. After all, was it so strange for a Pole to have German writing on the back of a photograph? All those mid-Europeans spoke one another's languages, and the photograph was dated 1940. That was three years ago. Hermann could be anybody. Ute could simply be an old friend of Bower's. And all his other identification said Michael Bower. And he spoke English better than any German could. Still, he would have to go. She would have to tell him politely but firmly in the morning that she had had a change of heart, and that she was afraid her husband might come home early. Any reason at all, as long as she got him out of here.

She put the photograph back and, foraging around once again, pulled out a black leather-bound notebook that looked as if it had seen better days. She opened it randomly to what she instantly recognized as a map of the east and west harbors of Barrow-in-Furness, with Morecambe Bay stretching beyond. More German writing, with ticks, markings, and numbers she didn't understand. That scared her. She flipped through the pages and found yet more German writing. There were dozens of maps, all of the Morecambe Bay area. A creeping dread eased into her stomach like a big lead ball.

She continued to flip through the pages. The German writing looked ominous to her. It was written in a neat crisp hand, the long, long words following one after the other with a deadly precision. She had to do something about this. Was he a fifth columnist, she wondered? She had heard about those. Maybe she shouldn't do anything. Better to put the duffel bag back and pretend nothing had happened. Be perfectly charming toward him over the next two days, even have sex with him, if that's what he wanted, then let him go without raising suspicion, and never say anything to anybody. Suddenly, before she could stop them, tears filled her eyes. She was frightened. What had ever possessed her to invite Michael Bower into her house? What was she going to do? Ten-pin, still fast asleep, rolled over onto his left side.

She looked in the duffel bag one last time but there was nothing else to be found. She didn't know what to believe. Was he Michael Bower or was he somebody entirely different? The book of maps and notes scared her. In fact she was so frightened that she had to do something, anything, just so she could put her mind at ease. She slipped the notebook and photograph under her pillow then returned to his room with the duffel bag.

He was still sound asleep. She put the duffel bag back and moved nearer to his bed. Now that she looked closer she thought he definitely looked German. His face was pale, so pale, and yet strong. His hair was thick, now that it had been washed. A pleasant face and yet a hard face, and in the repose of sleep, a mysterious face. She didn't know what to believe. What an absolutely beastly thing to happen to her. How was she supposed to know what to do in a situation like this?

She backed away slowly, careful not to wake him. Closing the door quietly, she looked up and down the hall where, through the open door of the master bedroom, she saw Ten-pin, now sitting up on the bed, looking at her.

"Go back to bed," she whispered.

The chihuahua blinked and turned away, as if it had been insulted.

She started toward the stairs. If nothing else she could at least phone the Carlisle train station and enquire about Michael Bower's luggage. That was bound to confirm something. She pushed her way into the kitchen, letting the door swing on its spring hinges. The black wall-phone stared at her tauntingly. I dare you, the telephone said. You haven't got the stomach for something like this. Maps? Pages and pages of German writing? Jillian, who are you trying to fool? This man is some kind of German fifth columnist. Morecambe Bay. Barrow-in-Furness. Wasn't there a big naval base down there? Oh, come on, Jillian, you can't kid yourself about this man, you simply can't.

She reached for the half bottle of sherry on the counter and nervously lifted it to her lips, drinking three gulps. She wiped her lips. No more booze, she thought. No more booze, and she took another sip. She needed energy for something like this. She opened the fridge where she saw one last piece of French nougat left. Leslie would be bringing her some more this weekend. She ate the nougat quickly. There were also a few pieces of rye bread which she ate in huge bites, washing them down with yet more sherry. There were two loaves of whole-meal, but she decided against that. She was disgusted with herself. She looked at the telephone once more. At least she could call the Carlisle train station. She had the stomach for that.

•

In his dream, the U-boat sank stern first. Commander Weiss yelled at Schlabrendorff to take her hard up but they were just about out of compressed air and one of the saddle tanks had a three-foot gash, and meanwhile the depth indicator reached 300, then 350, then 400. In a desperate attempt to even the boat, Goerlitz and a few of the others ran frantically through the forward bulkheads to the torpedo room, hoping to shift the weight to the bow. All the time Commander Weiss cried hard-up and engines full ahead. The U-boat continued to slide backwards. Goerlitz ran back to the control room. Weiss was wide-eyed with terror. The depth-charges exploded far above them. The depth indicator read 500, 550, twice as deep as a Type VII C U-boat should go. Metal began to creak. Rivets popped out as the pressure became too great and the supports began to bend. The double hull wouldn't take it much longer. The depth indicator reached 650. Suddenly there were small leaks everywhere and they were showered with a fine mist. The conning tower caved in and a huge cascade of sea-water filled the boat. The men screamed. The lights went out. Death. The submarine broke apart and the heavy water squeezed him like a fly, puncturing his eardrums and sucking the air out of his chest. Darkness. He shot like a bullet toward the surface. The rapid change of pressure rent his insides. Darkness everywhere. Not a sign of the surface.

He woke up sweating. For several moments he didn't know where he was. Then he heard a gust outside, and remembered he was in a big house on Lake Windermere. The hall light shone underneath his door, illuminating the rug on Damon Gregory's bedroom floor. He looked out the window where he saw the dim shadows of branches blowing in the wind and rain speckling the grass. Stupid dreams, he thought. Why did he always have those stupid dreams?

He was just about to close his eyes again when he noticed his duffel bag wasn't in the same place. He had left it beside the desk and it was nowhere near the desk. Pulling the covers aside, he swung his feet out of bed and walked across the rug with a mechanical weariness. He lifted the duffel bag and brought it back to his bed. Both the photograph of Ute and the notebook of dispositions were gone.

He tossed the duffel bag aside. What could he do? He hadn't expected this. There was really only one option. He scratched the back of his head, got up, and walked to the door. He listened for a few moments but wasn't able to hear anything. He didn't want this. She was making herself into a victim. He should have been able to see her distrust, even when he had made love to her. He opened the door and looked up and down the hallway. The downstairs lights were on. Her bedroom door was open. Ten-pin stared at him from the end of the bed.

He walked quietly along the hall and listened from the top of the stairs. The kitchen tap went on, then off. He heard her lift the telephone receiver and dial the operator.

"Yes, operator, I would like the train station in Carlisle. This is Windermere exchange 223-3971."

Goerlitz descended the stairs, stopping halfway, hoping the wind would cover the sound of the creaking steps. She was complicating matters.

"Hello, is this the stationmaster?" Outside, waves broke against the shore. "Yes, I'll wait."

Goerlitz listened.

"Yes, is this the stationmaster? Yes, this is Jillian Gregory over in Windermere."

He heard Ten-pin trotting along the upstairs hall.

"I just wanted to enquire about some luggage. The name is Michael Bower. I was wondering if it was there yet?"

Ten-pin stared at him from the top of the stairs.

"I'll call any time I please," said Jillian. "Please check

for me. Bower is the name. Michael Bower."

Ten-pin walked down the stairs and sat on the step next to him. Ten-pin began to wag his tail. The dog thought it was a game.

"Nothing in his name?" said Jillian Gregory. "Are you sure? He was coming from Barrow-in-Furness."

Ten-pin lay down on the step and closed his eyes.

"Eight o'clock? Fine. I'll check again then."

He heard her put the receiver down. The tap went on again. She was washing a few dishes. She had had something to eat. He gave Ten-pin a small hit and sent him scurrying back to the master bedroom. He got up and descended the stairs as she continued to wash the dishes. Perhaps it had been a mistake to accept her invitation after all. But she had seen the notebook and there was only one thing he could do about that now.

He pushed the swinging door of the kitchen open. She turned, startled, dropping a knife into the kitchen sink.

"Where is it?" he said.

She gave a vague shake of her head, her face turning red, her body shrinking in fear.

"Just tell me where it is," said Goerlitz."

She took a few frantic breaths.

"I don't know what you're talking about. I was just up having a late night drink."

"Where's the notebook? You know what I mean."

"What notebook? I don't know what you're talking about."

She looked away, the color draining from her face. Outside the waves lapped against the shore with dull repetitive thuds, and the wind grew erratic, catching the branches of the plane trees with a rustling hypnotic rhythm. Ten-pin wandered in from the doorway leading to the dining room and looked up at them.

"And the photograph," he said, taking a few steps

toward her. "I want that photograph back."

She backed away.

"Get out of here," she said. "Get out of my house. I don't know who you are but get out of here before I call the police."

She reached into the sink and pulled out the knife she had dropped. Goerlitz frowned.

"Don't make it any harder for yourself. I know you've seen the notebook. Give it to me. That's all I want." He smiled, trying to frighten her into giving him the notebook. "Or shall I be obliged to use force, *fraulein*?" he said.

She backed away some more.

"You're a German," she said. "You're a German spy, aren't you?"

He advanced ominously.

"The notebook, please."

He lunged for her. She brought the knife over her shoulder in a wide arc, but he caught her wrist in the middle of her thrust and she dropped it to the floor. Tenpin started prancing around, barking, tail wagging, thinking they were going to have some horseplay. With a strangled shriek, Jillian broke away from Goerlitz, her face pale with terror, to the other side of the kitchen table.

"Get away from me," she cried.

"I won't harm you," he said. "Just give me the notebook."

She dashed away from the kitchen table and bounded out the door to the front hall. He chased after her, his face hardening with determination. She was dead, he thought. There was no other way. She was dead, and he would just have to steel himself to the unpleasant task that lay before him. She clambered up the stairs, half losing her balance, frantic little cries escaping from her lips. He ascended the steps two at a time after her. She ran down the hall to the master bedroom and then slammed the door behind her. He pushed against the door but it was locked. He gave it a firm hit with his hip and it burst open.

"Please," she cried. "Please, go away."

She backed against the wall on the other side of the bed. He glanced around the room and saw a glass statuette of a dolphin on the ledge above the bed. She was crying, shaking, absolutely terrified. He approached her slowly, examining her in the same way a scientist might examine a laboratory animal.

"No," she said, her voice now no more than a dry rasp. "Please don't hurt me. I'll do whatever you say."

He took a few more steps toward her.

She reached behind her, lifted the bedside table lamp, and threw it at him as hard as she could. He dodged and the lamp crashed to the floor with a big blue spark. He grabbed her arms and swung her down onto the bed. She cried out. With an iron grip he twisted her left arm behind her back and started to apply the pressure. She was crying uncontrollably now. Ten-pin walked into the room, unsure of what was going on, then hopped up on the bed to watch.

"The notebook," said Goerlitz. "The notebook or I'll break it off."

"Please," she said. "I was nice to you. I took you in. Please, I — "

He gave her arm a vicious push. She groaned as sweat covered her forehead.

"If I give you the notebook will you leave me alone?"

"Yes," he said.

After a few more moments she reached under pillow with her right arm and pulled out both notebook and photograph. He snatched them from her, opened the notebook quickly, making sure none of the pages had been torn out. He looked down at her, still holding her arm. She lay on her stomach, her hair spread out over the blankets, her right temple exposed. He glanced again at the glass statuette of the dolphin.

"You saw this?" he asked.

She gave a weak little nod and sniffled.

"Did you look inside?" he demanded.

Again, a nod.

"Do you know what this is?"

"No," she said, her voice desperate. "No. I have no idea. I swear to God I don't."

Goerlitz simply shook his head. The things he could do in the name of the *Unterseewaffe* and in the name of the Reich. Still holding her arm, he reached for the glass statuette of the dolphin, lifted it high in the air, and brought it down as hard as he could against her temple. Her body jerked as her skull crushed beneath the heavy blow. He brought it down again. Now she only twitched. He brought it down a third time and the twitching stopped. Blood trickled out her ear. She was dead.

Ten-pin gave him a puzzled look, whimpered two or three times, then hopped off the bed and sat on the floor. Goerlitz lifted Jillian, carried her out of the room and down the stairs. He opened the back door and lay her on the deck in the rain, shaking, feeling sick to his stomach, then went upstairs and emptied the contents of his duffel bag onto Damon's bed. Taking his duffel bag and flashlight, he hurried outside and looked under the deck where he found several large pieces of slate and an old twelve-pound anchor. He stuck these into his duffel bag and their combined weight was so great he had to drag the bag across the lawn to the boat-house.

He went inside the boat-house, unsnapped a portion of the canvas cover away from the boat, crawled inside, and pulled the duffel bag in after him. He hurried back to the house. Ten-pin sat shivering on the doorstep watching him. Goerlitz was tired, but he couldn't stop now. He dragged Jillian's body across the lawn, tearing the wet grass in places, and after a struggle, got her into the boat. He pulled the drawstring of the duffel bag tight, then fastened the other end securely to her wrists. He tugged on the drawstring many times to make sure it wouldn't come loose, climbed out of the boat, and pulled open the big boat-house doors. He got back in the boat, started the motor and reversed slowly into the lake.

Lake Windermere, though extremely long, wasn't that wide, and he was afraid it wouldn't be deep enough, at least not deep enough to conceal her body.

But when he dumped her overboard a small distance up the lake, she sank without a trace in a cloud of bubbles and a final flash of pale skin into the green murky depths.

He slept for another few hours then got up to have some breakfast. He found some leftover salmon, two loaves of whole-meal bread, a half-finished box of chocolates, and a magnum of champagne. He made a breakfast of bread, cheese, salmon, and butter, and brewed a strong pot of tea. The cream was on the turn but he used it anyway.

When he was finished he started searching the house for anything he could use.

He chose two of Damon Gregory's finer suits, a pair of slacks, and a wool sweater. He found a small suitcase in Jillian's closet. He checked all of Damon Gregory's drawers and found the dead pilot's National Registration Identity card. Then he went to Lieutenant-Colonel Gregory's study.

The study was sumptuously decorated with mahogany furniture, four red leather club chairs, and a minutely intricate Persian rug. The walls were lined with bevelled glass bookcases. He opened the center drawer of the Chippendale desk and found a billfold containing two-hundred-and-fifty-four pounds. Next to it lay a revolver, a six-shot Enfield .380, and a box of bullets.

Though the temptation was strong he left the gun where it was. He took all the money. On the desk there was a framed photograph of a young man in a Royal Air Force uniform. As he gazed at it, he heard a bicycle bell ring outside in the lane.

He looked out the second floor window of the study where, through the wet leaves of the plane tree, he saw the postman put her letters and newspaper into the mailbox. The postman rode away. Goerlitz closed the drawer, took one last look around the study to make sure everything was in order, then went downstairs to get the mail.

His prison photograph and three inches of column detailing his escape appeared on page three of the London *Times*. Any sightings were to be reported to Inspector Gerald Laurie at a number in Barrow-in-Furness. The escapee was known to be wearing a brown double-breasted suit with a torn lapel, and was most probably carrying a duffel bag. He was last seen, according to the article, by a waitress in Laughton-in-Furness, and had assumed the name of Michael Harvey Bower.

He would throw his brown suit and Michael Bower identity card into the lake. He would become Damon Gregory, with a clean checkered suit, hair combed back and dyed brighter with some of Jillian's hair color, and the mustache he had grown for Bower.

He phoned the train station at Kendal — he didn't want to be seen leaving from the Windermere train station — and learned there were Liverpool-bound trains at 1:35, 6:15, and 9:05.

He stayed in the house until dark, resting, eating, and making sure everything was in order. He wiped away the most obvious spots where his fingerprints had been, but they were all over the place and it was just a matter of time before somebody would discover one. He went upstairs and checked her bedroom. There was blood on one of the pillow slips, so he took it off and burned it in the fireplace, replacing it with a fresh one he found in the linen closet. He cleaned up the broken lamp and threw it off the end of the dock into the water. Lieutenant-Colonel Gregory would be home on Saturday night. And by that time he would be in Liverpool, possibly out of the country. And by a week Saturday he would be standing in front of Admiral Doenitz with a notebook of British naval dispositions in his hands, or even resting, at long last, with Ute in Munich.

Ten-pin approached him and began to whine for food. Goerlitz had forgotten about the black and tan chihuahua. He filled Ten-pin's bowl to the brim with dog chow, took it outside to the deck, put it beside the door, then wiped his fingerprints from the bowl.

Best to let Ten-pin stay outside for the next couple of days. If he ran out of dog food he might be able to find something to eat in someone's garbage.

"Ten-pin, come on, dinner time."

The chihuahua trotted out and ate the food gratefully.

The rain had stopped but the clouds were low and menacing. He took one last look around, closed everything up, made sure the cottage was locked and, with his suitcase, identity card, and now what amounted to two-hundred-and-seventy-five pounds, got on Jillian Gregory's bicycle.

He discarded the bicycle in a ditch a mile outside Kendal and walked the rest of the way. He was a minute early for the 9:05 train to Liverpool.

While he was on the train he began to think about Jillian Gregory. Three or four years ago he wouldn't have thought twice about killing her. Yet now he regretted having had to murder her, and was angry because it had been necessary to murder her, and angrier still because he had been forced into a situation where killing her had been necessary. But war was war, and had he let her live he would have left a vivid signpost for his trackers. He

192

gazed out at the dark English countryside as the train rumbled over the tracks toward Liverpool. War was war. The justification seemed hollow now. So much of the old life seemed hollow, all the drills and routine, the patrols, the rules and regulations, the courage and the will, the forced camaraderie of U-boat life, all of it seemed a sham when he thought of the small trickle of blood running from Jillian Gregory's ear.

Chapter 15

The inmates of Building C stood to attention at the end of their bunks. Weiss kept a grim face. Major Hatley walked slowly forward, hands behind his back, gazing at each one of them. For the first time in as long as Weiss could remember the major looked sober.

"Gentlemen," began the major, in German, stopping beside Schlabrendorff, "I'm sure you're all aware of recent events here at Triggsdale Hall." The major started rocking on his heels. "I'm speaking, of course, about the escape of Commander Goerlitz and the murder of Sergeant Terry Saville." The major looked around, weighing the effect his words were having. "The Naval Intelligence Department will be investigating the sergeant's murder. They will also be conducting an extensive manhunt for Goerlitz, and we've been asked to assist them in any way we can. We've come to the conclusion that Goerlitz couldn't have possibly escaped without your help, and this, in my view, gentlemen, is a grave breach of the trust I have shown you, and must be punished."

Weiss couldn't help gloating. Gloating was one of the

pleasures of war. Weiss had had his doubts, but now he was absolutely certain of Goerlitz. It was just a matter of time before his former chief torpedo officer would hand over the crucial dispositions to a waiting Doenitz. Patterson had again taken mail for them this morning. An envelope, sure to pass British censors, would be sent to an obscure address in Lisbon, and from there to Lorient, where it would reach Admiral Doenitz. At last the plan he and the admiral had devised what seemed like a lifetime ago would finally become a reality.

"And I will punish you, one by one, starting with you, Weiss."

The major came up to him, uncharacteristically brave, stood with his nose six inches from his face, and gazed at Weiss with steady eyes.

"You've been fooling me all this time, haven't you, captain? You've been plotting behind my back just when I thought all my leniency and generosity were beginning to pay off. I thought you were glad I was making your life livable, Captain Weiss, and that after two years you would reciprocate by cooperating with me. But I can see you've just been pulling me along by the nose all this time."

The major turned away, walked a few paces toward the back window, then stopped and stared out at the hill for ten or fifteen seconds.

"I can't be having my guards killed, Captain Weiss. Oh, no, I certainly can't. Terry Saville was a very close friend of mine and a very good friend to all of us here at the camp. But not only that, he had a wife and two children, and Goerlitz has killed him."

"Excuse me, commandant," Weiss said in English, taunting Hatley, "but do you have proof that Goerlitz killed Saville? No, commandant, I do not think you do."

"Weiss, I thought surely you would have played by gentlemen's rules," said Hatley, continuing in German.

"It was Goerlitz who stole the suit. We found several good copies of his fingerprints on the bench below where the suit had been hanging. I don't know who robbed Michael Bower, but he shall get his turn in the box as well. But first you, Weiss. Then Ballerstedt. Then Schlabrendorff. And Frischauer, you'll have your holiday around the end of October, just when the box becomes a very cozy place. In England we don't believe in torture, but after all, I'm not responsible for the weather, am I? Of course you think me sentimental for having trusted you, but I did. I'm not sentimental any more. Is ten days in the box long enough for you, Weiss?" said Hatley, his German stilted but nevertheless understandable. "How about one meal a day? You shall have no blankets. I'm pleased to say, Captain Weiss, that we're expecting frost tonight."

Weiss was escorted by Jenkins and Patterson down the steps of Building C and up the wet fairway to the box. They walked him fast, shoving him part of the way. What a difference death made, thought Weiss. The fairway was blotched by yellow plane tree leaves and the grass was slippery.

They opened the steel door of the box and pushed him inside. No blankets, no food, no water, just his thin prison uniform. Ten days of freezing, he thought. Well worth it. He was strong, he was invulnerable, he could take pain, the cold, almost loved pain, loved to endure physical discomfort. Ten days of freezing. Such a small price to pay for the Reich. The door shut, the bolts slid back, and he heard them walk away, their boots splashing through the grass. He was alone. Well worth it, because even from here, far away from Barrow-in-Furness, he would be able to see the star-shells burst across Morecambe Bay, lighting the sky for miles around, hear the distant thunder of torpedoes and depth charges. He had done all he could. It was now up to Goerlitz. It was out of his hands now, but his hot kernel of revenge, that object of beauty he had for so long nurtured with his anger and hatred during his two long years of captivity in Triggsadale Hall, would be eased and soothed, and his long impatient wait would finally be over.

•

Lieutenant-Colonel Leslie James Gregory's train arrived at Windermere station shortly after eight o'clock on Friday night. Gregory was in a foul mood, made fouler by the sinewy over-cooked piece of beef that lay undigested in his stomach. You simply couldn't get a good piece of meat in England these days.

He had the station's porter, an old man by the name of Cedric, load his luggage and the box of food he brought every week for Jillian onto the dolly, and wheel it into the station. A bad week, he thought. Several orders had been mixed up, and his superior officer, Colonel McNab, had lectured him for close to an hour this morning. He had drunk too much whiskey last night and his head still throbbed. Cecilia had caught him with Julia, and Julia had caught him with Helen. He had caught Helen with Peter, and now he was back at square one, and square one was always Jillian.

For the first time in a long time he was actually looking forward to seeing her. He walked to the wicket. George, the stationmaster, got up from his chair behind the counter.

"Evening, sir. Home early, aren't we?"

"Hello, George. Yes, I found London frustrating this week."

"I'd find it frustrating any week."

"Can I borrow your phone? I want Mrs. Gregory to bring the Rolls around."

"Certainly, sir."

The stationmaster put the phone on the counter and

returned to his seat. Gregory dialled the cottage, thinking how happy she would be to have another bottle of champagne and a fresh box of French nougat. The phone rang and rang. Can't just one thing go right for me this week? He hung up.

"She doesn't seem to be in," he said. "Keep an eye on this stuff for me, will you, George? I'll run down and get the Rolls myself."

"Right you are, sir."

All the lights in the house were off. Maybe she had gone over to Mrs. What's-her-name, the widow who lived in the old grey house across the lake.

"Jillian?" he called "Jillian, it's me. I'm home."

No answer. Oh, well, he needed some time to unwind by himself before he saw her anyway, time to ease the dyspepsia that had plagued him for the past two days. He went to the kitchen, mixed a glass of seltzer, and gulped it down quickly. He burped, a burp tasting of horseradish, then heard a scratching at the back door. He opened the door. Ten-pin stood there shivering, wet and miserable, staring up at him.

"Ten-pin, what the devil did she put you out there for?" Gregory lifted the dog and brought him inside. "Come on, old fellow, we'll put you inside where it's nice and warm."

He took the Rolls back to the station, picked up his luggage and the box of food, then drove back home.

She still hadn't returned, and now he began to feel irritated with her. Not that she could have known he would be home a day early, but he still felt irritated. What was that woman's name across the lake? Jillian's bicycle wasn't in the garage so she had obviously ridden over. Healy, or something. Or wasn't it Pealy? Yes, that was it, Mrs. Thelma Pealy. Now where did Jillian keep her little telephone directory? In the drawer of her bedside table. He climbed the stairs. That was funny. She usually left the upstairs hall light on. Kept the prowlers away, she said.

He stopped just as he entered the bedroom. There was something not quite right here. The room looked different somehow. Shouldn't there be a lamp on Jillian's bedside table? He just didn't know. He was here so seldom. And she was always rearranging the furniture. Probably put the lamp somewhere else. He found her directory in the bedside table drawer and telephoned Thelma Pealy.

"Hello, Mrs. Pealy. This is Leslie Gregory. Is my wife there by any chance?"

She wasn't there. Thelma Pealy hadn't seen her since Monday.

The house was breathlessly cold. Obviously, in typical Jillian style, she had forgotten to order coal for the furnace. He went out to the boat-house where they kept the firewood, and brought an armload of kindling and three logs back. It was so cold in here. London seemed to insulate itself. Ten-pin lay shivering on the ottoman by the hearth. He put the wood down on the slate platform surrounding the fireplace, turned on the light, and pulled the fire curtain open. What was that in the grate? It appeared as if she had been burning some kind of cloth in the fireplace, but hadn't succeeded in burning it fully. He took a closer look. What was that? He reached in and picked out the unburned portion. It looked liked the end-piece of a pillow slip. Why would she want to burn a pillow slip in the fireplace? He began to worry. Ten-pin outside. Jillian not home. And a piece of burned pillow slip in the fireplace. What did it mean?

He went to his study. Where else would she go? Now that all the summer people were gone there were only one or two possibilities. The Merrins and the Bradshaws. But those friends were too far away for a bicycle ride. He opened his desk drawer for his own telephone directory and immediately saw that his reserve money was gone. His body slowly went cold with fear.

•

Constable Statham of the Kendal Police Department understood Lieutenant-Colonel Gregory's point clearly. It did indeed look like murder. Two-hundred-and-fifty-four pounds had been stolen. Also Damon Gregory's identity card. And why the burned pillow slip?

"Just calm down, now, Colonel Gregory, and pour a drink for yourself. Nothing's been proved."

"But no one's seen her for five days, constable. I phoned all of our friends in the area."

"There could be any number of explanations. Really, Colonel Gregory, there's nothing more to do. We'll have our team here in the morning, so just leave everything to us. If you want something to do, you can check the house to see if anything else has been taken. I'm going outside to search the garden and the boat-house. I don't have to tell you, colonel, that you should be as thorough as you can with the stolen items."

It was almost dawn, and the low clouds shone with a dull grey sheen. Constable Statham turned on his flashlight and went out the back door into the pre-morning gloom. He aimed the beam at the fountain, and then the boat-house. There was something definitely all wrong about this, he decided. The burned pillow slip bothered him. Why would someone burn a pillow slip?

He walked past the fountain, shining his flashlight for any sign or clue, and noticed that some of the grass had been torn. Heavens, there hadn't been a murder in Windermere for the last twenty-five years. A missing sheep, perhaps, but nothing like a murder. He went into the boat-house and found a life preserver on the deck.

The boat seemed in order for the most part. Some of

the canvas cover was unsnapped. Statham scratched his jaw, stretched his top lip over his upper teeth, then stroked his mustache, one side with his thumb and the other with his finger. Only that burned pillow slip. The murderer had been careful. He smiled. What murderer? That was absurd. Murder didn't happen in Windermere. But supposing it had been murder. If the murderer had been trying to dispose of the pillow slip as a piece of evidence, he would dispose of the body as well. And what better place to dump the body than the lake? He shone his flashlight into the water beside the boat. A school of minnows darted away and hovered around an algae-covered support. It might be a good idea to have the lake dragged.

He went outside and walked to the end of the dock. The wind was up and the waves lapped at the floating deck twenty feet out in the water. He shone his flashlight across the lake thinking he might see some clue, then swung it round to his own side and scanned the shoreline. The beam traversed the rocky slope then quickly passed into a small inlet no bigger than the boat-house, where reeds and bulrushes grew. What was that, hanging on that log? It looked like a coat or jacket.

He hurried down the dock. Cold out this morning. Should have worn his other cardigan.

At the inlet he pulled the log to shore with a stick and picked the coat from the log. Just a piece of junk, he thought, cast toward shore by the high waves. A brown suit, double-breasted by the look of it.

"Constable Statham," called Gregory from the back deck.

"I'm over here by the marsh."

He waved his flashlight at the lieutenant-colonel.

"I think some of my son's suits are gone."

"All right, I'm coming."

"And a few other things."

He looked at the brown suit. The lapel was torn. It took

a moment to register. A torn lapel. More missing suits. He looked at his watch. 6:22. Constable Statham hurried into the house, pulled out his notebook, found the appropriate page, and dialled a number in Barrow-in-Furness.

•

By early Saturday morning no further leads had developed, and though Gerald Laurie was frustrated by the way Goerlitz had so completely covered his tracks, he was more determined than ever to catch him. Laurie was a stubborn man, stubborn to a fault, and the more difficult the obstacles, the stronger his determination. He and Westmoreland were driving out to Triggsdale Hall. The interrogations would begin today. Ballerstedt, because he was the most likely collaborator, would be their first subject. They had done everything else they could do. They had sent a thousand more posters out on Thursday and had run a story in the *Times* and half a dozen local papers. They made no mention of possible espionage activities on the part of the escaped prisoner. They didn't want to alert the powers in Whitehall just yet.

It was a bleak and windy morning. As they rounded the copse, Triggsdale Hall came into view. Laurie was tired, had lived on cigarettes and coffee for the past two days.

Major Hatley met them in the large chandeliered front hall. He showed them up the back stairs to the butler's bedroom. There, Ballerstedt waited, expressionless, his black wool cap pulled low over his forehead, guarded by both Patterson and Jenkins.

"Thank you, gentlemen," said Laurie to the guards. "Please wait outside. We'll call you if we need you. Major Hatley, could you please stay here? Mr. Westmoreland has a good command of the German language, but I'd prefer it if we had two German speakers on hand."

And so the interrogation began. It wasn't a brutal

affair, nor was the subject tortured or abused in any way. It wasn't the English way, and torture, especially in the British intelligence services, was abhorred. It was, rather, a civil and polite conversation, designed to put Baller-stedt at ease, to trick him into saying something, through sheer friendliness and politeness, he wouldn't otherwise say. Ballerstedt answered all the preliminary questions truthfully. Yes, his name was Lieutenant Heinz Johann Ballerstedt, the armaments and explosives officer aboard U-93, and yes, he had joined the *Unterseewaffe* as one of Karl Doenitz's early hand-picked men, and yes, he and Hermann Goerlitz had been good friends aboard U-93.

But when Laurie steered to the central question, did you build the bomb, Ballerstedt denied any involvement. The interrogation went round in circles for almost an hour until there was a knock at the door. It was Corporal Patterson.

"Telephone call for Inspector Laurie, sir," he said, addressing Hatley.

Hatley looked at Laurie. "Inspector," he said.

Laurie went downstairs to the commandant's office where the call was waiting for him. It was Taylor phoning from the field office. He said a Constable Statham from the Kendal Police Department had telephoned from Windermere. The constable said he had found a brown suit jacket with a torn lapel washed up onto the beach of Lake Windermere. The discovery had been made under grisly circumstances.

"They think Goerlitz has murdered a woman by the name of Jillian Gregory." said Taylor. "Name mean anything to you?"

"Not really."

"Apparently she moved in the highest social circles of London a few years back. Husband by the name of Leslie Gregory."

"That rings a bell."

"He's with the War Office. Purchasing department. He says his wife hasn't been seen in five days. There's been two-hundred-and-fifty-four pounds stolen and two of his son's suits. His son's identification card as well."

"How old's his son?"

"Twenty-one when he died. He was shot down over East Sussex in '41."

"Build?"

"Statham says 5'10", medium."

Laurie thought for a moment. "Was anything else taken?"

"No. Statham's men are still making a search of the house."

This was exasperating news to Laurie. He couldn't begin to imagine the kind of damage the Kendal Police Department could do to any existing evidence.

"Well, see if you can reach Statham. Tell him not to disturb anything until we get there. Call Jarmon at the base and tell him we'll need two experts to dust the place. We'll also need sailors to drag the lake, just in case he's dumped her there. I'll get the fingerprint file from Major Hatley. We're leaving right now. We'll pick you up in a half hour."

The interrogation of Ballerstedt was suspended. Whatever lead there was in Windermere had to be followed immediately before the traces of Goerlitz vanished under the well-meaning but inexperienced hands of a provincial police department.

They picked up Taylor, and the three of them motored along the winding ill-kept roads of the low Lake District mountains. Taylor had made the necessary arrangements with Jarmon, their district conduit to naval resources. They travelled along the pot-holed roads, through the small villages with their slate walls and thatched roofs, following a circuitous route over the endless hills. Laurie's mood was desperate. His enmity toward Goerlitz had deepened. Goerlitz had sunk his submarine. He had murdered two British subjects. Worst of all, he had bought that camera. That camera with the accordion-style lens. Goerlitz seemed to be getting away with this.

Constable Statham was waiting for them on the drive of the Gregory's beach-front cottage when they arrived shortly after nine o'clock. The sky had brightened to a pale shade of grey and it looked as if it might rain any minute. Their greeting was perfunctory. Statham showed them up the drive to the cottage. It was a big cottage, in fact, more of a mansion.

A black and tan chihuahua sat in the front hall looking up at them with a sad blank face.

"Where is he?" asked Laurie.

"He's upstairs," said Statham. "Working on a bottle of gin."

"Any chance he did it?"

"No. We've checked his alibi. He got in from London last night. He phoned her from the station and she wasn't here. Already checked it with the stationmaster. Gregory's been in London all week, and no one's seen her for five days."

"Could you send for Gregory, please? We want to talk to him in the kitchen. And could you have one of your men make some coffee?"

Constable Statham's face reddened. "Of course, inspector," he said. "Of course."

While Statham went to fetch Gregory, Laurie heard four jeeps pull up the front drive of the cottage. He walked down the hall and went outside. Large menacing drops began to fall from the sky. His two forensic specialists were here, as well as sixteen sailors with dragging equipment. He ordered the sailors to commandeer any civilian vessels they might need, and set the forensic specialists dusting the place for fingerprints.

Gregory was waiting for him in the kitchen. He asked

the lieutenant-colonel all the textbook questions, having him describe his movements for the week, obtaining numbers and addresses of people who could verify his movements, a surprising number of women among them. Gregory told Laurie how he had arrived home last night, how there had been no answer when he had called from the train station. He told them about the missing bicycle. Missing bicycle? Laurie immediately organized two search teams to comb the area for the bicycle. He then took down an accurate description of the suits that had been stolen, a checkered one and a pin-striped one, as well as a pair of slacks and a wool sweater.

By this time he could hear motorboats out on the lake. He concluded his questioning of Lieutenant-Colonel Gregory, allowing Gregory to console himself with his gin, and went outside. He was convinced Gregory was innocent.

He walked to the boat-house where the brown suit jacket with the torn lapel hung on a hook drying. He would get Ensign Beaumont to identify it later.

They dragged the lake well into the afternoon and evening, and Laurie, Taylor, and Westmoreland made a supper of French nougat, hard-boiled eggs, and champagne, the only things they were able to find. Around seven-thirty one of the search teams came back with the bicycle in the back of the jeep. It had been found a mile outside Kendal.

A half hour later the forensic specialists, using the sample from the prison camp, positively identified Goerlitz's fingerprints on a glass statuette of a dolphin they had found in the bedroom.

At this point, Laurie asked Lieutenant-Colonel Gregory the names and addresses of all the local train stations. Because the bicycle had been found outside Kendal, the Kendal train station was the most obvious first choice.

The assistant stationmaster, a middle-aged man of about forty-five, short, pale, wearing a brown vest that looked as if it could stand a washing or two, was on duty. When they showed him the photograph, he recognized Goerlitz immediately.

" 'e came in 'ere around nine o'clock last night. Bought a one-way ticket on the 9:05 to Liverpool, 'e did."

"What was he wearing?"

"Very swank, I must say. A checkered suit. You could tell it was quality just by looking at it. And an 'igh-class portmanteau, too. Genuine steer'ide leather, it looked like."

They got back to Windermere just before eleven. Statham and a few other officers from the Kendal Police Department stood on the dock smoking cigarettes and talking. Navy personnel continued to drag the lake looking for Jillian Gregory's body. Liverpool, thought Laurie. It was the obvious choice. It was a tremendously large port. If Goerlitz was going to find a way out of the country he would certainly find it in Liverpool. It was with some weariness that he decided his next move would be to seal Liverpool as effectively as he could, given the resources he had. If Goerlitz had taken last night's 9:05, he would already be there. The difficulty lay in stopping Goerlitz from leaving Liverpool.

They found Jillian Gregory's body just after midnight. One of the sailors waved from out on the lake.

"We've got her," he called. "We found her."

When they finally laid her on the deck, Laurie was glad Lieutenant-Colonel Gregory was in his study still consoling himself with a bottle of gin. Her body was bloated with water. Her lips were open and her nicotine-stained teeth smiled disdainfully. The right side of her skull had been crushed and her hands were tied to a duffel bag full of slate. Let him drink gin, he thought. He didn't have to see this right now.

207

Chapter 16

Goerlitz's train pulled into Lime Street Station just past midnight. He got his small suitcase from the overhead rack and worked his way through the crowd. When he was clear of the platform he looked around the station for a news stall, saw one by the exit, and bought a street map of Liverpool. A large group of sailors stood around the clock, most of them smoking cigarettes, one playing a harmonica, and a few others gazed at something high in the rafters, a pigeon, perhaps.

There were several taxis lined up in front of the station, and he climbed into the back seat of the nearest.

"Where to, sir?" the driver asked.

"I'm not sure. This is my first time to Liverpool. I have business down by the river tomorrow. Perhaps you could drop me at a hotel near there."

"Well, the Chadwick might be to your liking."

"Fine," said Goerlitz.

The taxi pulled away from the station and headed toward the river.

Entire blocks had been destroyed by German bombers

a few years ago, still not cleared by military road graters and dumpers, and where houses had once stood, there were only piles of rubble and the odd re-minder — a charred bathtub, a dusty sofa, a section of wall papered with a flowery design — of a once orderly and thriving working class neighborhood. Every four blocks or so they passed an anti-aircraft gun manned by three soldiers of the reserve who were by day most likely butchers, clerks, or dockyard workers. He and his father had had great arguments over the bombing of civilian targets, though Liverpool wasn't strictly a civilian target, not with six-and-a-half miles of docks along the River Mersey. A front-end loader, even at this late hour, cleared the mess away while three military dump trucks waited in line for their fill-up. A rusted old typewriter lay on its side against a splintered window frame. A filing cabinet, looking as if it had been torn as easily as tissue paper, had been collected along with an old sink and a refrigerator into a separate pile, and would most probably be melted down. His father called civilian bombing senseless and barbaric. Goerlitz called it an inevitable result of deepening animosity between enemies who no longer played by the old rules. Now he was inclined to think his father was more right than wrong.

The Chadwick, a begrimed seven-storey structure that looked like a wedding cake, was three blocks from the river. Piles of rubble had been gathered into large mounds on either side, and there was a charred and rotten smell in the lobby's smoky air. The clerk, an overweight woman in her mid-fifties with curly grey hair, a bilious complexion, and sturdy-rimmed bifocals, gazed at him with a look of hopeless boredom as he approached the desk. He asked for a room and she handed over the key with a desultory fatefulness.

The next morning he was up early and had a breakfast of fried potatoes, eggs, and bacon in the hotel cafe. He paid the waitress and walked up Water Street past the town hall, turned left at the next corner, and caught the bus down to Mann Island.

The offices of the Mersey Docks and Harbor Board were housed in a large building about a hundred yards from the River Mersey, not far from the canning dock, next to the Cunard Building. As he expected, he found shipping schedules posted on dozens of bulletin boards in the building's main office. He started with tomorrow's. He had to assume that by now they were searching for him and that Liverpool would most certainly be one of the first places they would try.

It took him well over an hour to read Friday's and Saturday's schedules, and the prying eyes of the junior controller, a man of about thirty-five with thin hair and a blue uniform his stomach had outgrown, annoyed him continually. The junior controller finally rose and came to the counter. There was no sign of the *San Julian*.

"Can I help you, sir?"

Goerlitz played dumb. "I'm looking for a captain."

"Well, do you know the ship?"

"I'm not sure of the ship."

"Well, then, I'm afraid you're looking for needle in a haystack, sir."

"That's what I thought. Sorry to trouble you."

It took him another half hour to find the *San Julian*, belonging to Ribalta Shipping Services Incorporated, of Barcelona, Spain, captained by Marcelo Gil Robles, and bound for Barcelona with a shipment of livestock. So Weiss had been right, he thought. The *San Julian* was where he said it would be. Had there ever been a doubt? She was berthed at pier twenty-seven of the Garston Docks and was scheduled to be convoyed at eleven o'clock on Sunday.

He reached the Garston Docks late in the afternoon. The clouds hung low like a funeral pall over the River Mersey, and a penetrating rain beat on the pavement. It was dark when he reached pier twenty-seven. Warehouses rose in a jumble of oblongs and angles around him. The *San Julian* was moored in berth nine, at least that's what it said on the shipping schedule, but to his dismay he discovered that berths six through twelve had been bombed. A sign told him it had happened three weeks ago and that he should check with the Mersey Docks and Harbor Board for changes of berth placement and schedules. What was left were only a few ragged ends of reinforced concrete, and three or four pier supports standing like pale tombstones in the dark water of the River Mersey.

•

Cameron Washburn, a junior controller for the Mersey Docks and Harbor Board, was in love with Antoinette (now Toni) Boissonneau. In 1940 she had lived in one of the lesser chateaus along the Loire, officially *Langres* but known to the locals as *Le Grenier*, which was what Toni called it, because of its barn-shaped appearance. When the Germans occupied that part of France in August, they requisitioned *Le Grenier* for a communications depot. M. Nadeau (her late father's dear friend and owner of *Langres*), her young cousins Marc and Philippe, herself, and the cook whom she simply referred to as *l'anesse* because of her rude manners, were forced to live with three officers, four technicians, and nineteen enlisted men of the *Wehrmacht*.

It was discovered one day that Marc had tried to poison two enlisted men with rat poison. They lived. Marc was executed by firing squad. The rest of them had been forced to watch. Toni escaped *Le Grenier* shortly after that with money her aunt, who lived in London, had sent her.

Tragic circumstances, thought Cameron. He looked at the clock. Should have been out of here hours ago. But they always stuck the junior controllers with everything, which meant these days, at least, making bedfellows of the merchant and naval fleets. Convoys. Convoys had been responsible for headaches, sour stomachs, insomnia, and anxiety. Thank God he had the next few days off. Tragic circumstances. But at least some small good thing had come of the tragedy. A thirteen-year-old French boy shot to smithereens by a half-dozen nineteen-year-old German boys. If it hadn't been for that dead French boy there never would have a been a Toni and Cam. She had left her stuffy old aunt in London, as she put it, because she couldn't resist the temptation to infuriate the old cow anyway she could. Toni had a cruel streak. That's why everybody liked her so much.

The next four days off. With Toni. Alone in a cabin in the mountains east of Inverness next to a loch. Where no one would find them. Alone at last. In a village called Colcabock. Who had ever heard of it? She was something to be proud of. They had a lot to celebrate.

He looked up. The man he had seen earlier, the one in the checkered suit who had been looking for a captain without a ship, came up the steps and through the door. What was it about that man, he thought? One topper of a suit. Bond Street, most probably. Like to have a suit like that himself. Obviously a Londoner. But not like most Londoners Cameron knew. The man went to the same bulletin board and peered at the list. He simply didn't look as if he belonged here.

"Excuse me," said Cameron, rising, "but could I help you with anything? You're here awfully late. The office is actually already closed."

"I'm looking for the *San Julian*. Marcelo Gil Robles is the captain. It says here she should be tied at berth nine of pier twenty-seven, the Garston Docks, but the pier has been bombed."

Funny kind of accent. Couldn't quite place it.

"Well, can't you read the sign underneath the schedule?"

212

The man looked. "What sign? There's no sign here."

Cameron frowned and craned forward. "Oh, Christ, they've torn it down again. They'll do anything they can to make my job impossible. Just a moment, sir." Cameron pulled a large master schedule from the shelf. "Could I have the name of the ship and captain again, please, sir?"

The man stepped forward to the counter. "The *San Julian*. The captain is Marcelo Gil Robles."

"Right. Here she is. She's docked over in Birkenhead. Pier four at number five."

"Birkenhead?"

"That's across the river, sir. You'll find any one of a half-dozen ferries going over every hour."

•

Goerlitz boarded the ferry to Birkenhead just after eight that night. A slow sticky rain was still falling, permeating everything with a damp cold, and through the mist shrouding the river he heard the occasional foghorn bellow low and heavy, like a dirge. He sat on a bench in the corner of the cabin away from the other passengers. His muscles were tight and his eyes felt sore from reading so many schedules. They had decided to list the schedules by time, not alphabetically, and as he had only a rough idea of the *San Julian's* departure time, the task had been a taxing one. He was tense, on edge, and hoped the *San Julian* would be where it was supposed to be this time.

The ride across the river was short, and he was in Birkenhead in less than fifteen minutes. He stopped a couple of merchant sailors walking along the river-front and asked them where he could find pier number four. After a moment's discussion they gave him directions.

As he neared pier four he squinted, gazing into the gloom, trying to pick out dock number five. It was with growing dread he saw that, except for a dozen sea gulls

213

sitting along the side like a row of marshmallows in the mist, berth number five was unoccupied. He stood there looking at the empty water for several minutes, as if he had been paralysed, wondering what he was going to do.

Finally, he went to the other docks along the pier, checking to see if the clerk at the harbor office had made a mistake, hoping that the *San Julian* might be berthed at one of the other docks, but she wasn't. There was only one thing he could do. Go back to the Mersey Docks and Harbor Board the following day and have another look.

He went back to the Chadwick in a dull and heavy mood, the more so because he was feeling something akin to remorse. He had brutally murdered two people over the last four days, what the Reich would have called needful exterminations, something he should have felt no remorse over. He took off his suit, draped it over the back of his chair, then lay down on his hotel bed. He shouldn't feel remorse but he couldn't help thinking of Saville's face and the way the chalky water had drained, almost oozed, from his mouth, around his cheeks, and down his neck. Or the small seemingly insignificant ribbon of blood which had flowed from Jillian Gregory's ear. The Nationalist Socialist cant said killing an enemy, especially killing an enemy to forward the causes of the Reich, was an honorable thing to do, even dignified. But he didn't feel honorable. Nor did he feel dignified. He felt small and cruel, sick from an overpowering sense of helplessness, and cynical because of the war. He felt the only things that mattered now were Ute, his father, and his home life, such as it was, not the so-called bold dream he had followed for the last six years. War is a great enterprise, Admiral Karl Doenitz had once told the crew of U-93 in Wilhelmshaven one night when they had returned from a particularly successful patrol. Two years later, in a private moment, just he and the admiral drinking schnapps while they waited for some aides to arrive,

Doenitz, contradicting himself, said war was the puniest of human acts if it were waged without justification. That's what was missing now. The belief, the patriotism, the absolute conviction that he was doing the right thing. That disappeared when they gave him a crew of green recruits.

He hated this waiting. The longer he waited the less likely — as the British net closed around him — he was to get back to Lorient, and ultimately to Munich. Over the past couple of days the goal of returning to Munich had superceded the goal of reaching Lorient with the naval dispositions. He wanted to get back so he could explain things to Ute, to patch up whatever damage had been caused by his callous comment. Only farm animals have miscarriages. Why did he have to say that? And what was he going to say to her? He suddenly laughed out loud. How could he explain things to Ute when he had hardly explained things to himself? Why had he been so mortified and embarrassed by her miscarriage? Miscarriages happened all the time. He sighed. He knew the answer. Because he had wanted his child to be among the elite of a superior race, and Ute had shown him that, after all, they were all just human beings, even Germans, not Neitzsche's supermen, but susceptible to human frailties, and in the case of himself, susceptible to human delusions.

And yet how he had believed, so ardently, that Hitler had been the savior of the Fatherland. In the first years of the Reich the New Order seemed to unfold with ubiquitous beneficence over the entire land, turning a tired, corrupt, impoverished Weimar Republic into a miracle of statecraft, as if divinely inspired. During that time his own life had never been better. To be a U-boat man in Germany was to be something special, a hero, to be idolized and praised, to be respected. There had been nothing but optimism, and optimism had inspired arrogance, and that arrogance had become dangerous after a while, producing, as arrogance always did, a misplaced over-confidence. In those days it had never occurred to him that Germany might possibly lose the war. And he had been arrogant along with the rest of them. How he hated that arrogance now. His confidence had been shaken. The Fuhrer no longer seemed in control of the war.

His father contended Hitler suffered from an inflated sense of his own worth and a pathological need to con-centrate ever-greater amounts of power into his own hands, a typical tyrant, so much power that it was even-tually impossible for him to control. And when a tyrant reached that point, his father said, despite all the good he might have done, he became dangerous, and like a rabid dog who had no sense of itself, had to be destroyed.

He slowly fell asleep thinking of his father's argu-ments, and how his father's prognostications of ultimate destruction seemed to be coming true.

•

The first thing Laurie did when he reached Liverpool was to alert the city's bus and train terminals, its air-fields, and its port authorities. He then telephoned the Liverpool Police and was guaranteed one-hundred-and-fifty men by the commissioner to join the man-hunt. The naval base in Barrow-in-Furness could provide another seventy-five.

He now felt as if he were closing in on Goeritz, that he had effectively sealed Liverpool, and that it was just a matter of time before he had the U-boat commander in his hands.

They went to the police commissioner's office to see if any leads had developed while they had been travel-ing. The sky was still grey, though in certain sections the clouds were thin enough to see the barest outline of the sun. Ghostly tentacles of mist advanced like a phantom army from the River Mersey into the town.

The commissioner of police was a long-faced man of about sixty-two, wore an expression of supercilious surprise, as if the undignified way in which the world conducted itself was a constant source of astonishment, and had the kind of cheeks more closely associated with basset hounds than with humans. He wore a navy blue serge uniform with big brass buttons. Descriptions of Goerlitz had been circulated to all the various transportation hubs in the city, and printed photographs were to follow. Even so, there was only one lead. From the Mersey Docks and Harbor Board.

"A junior controller with the board by the name of Charles Overholt thinks he might have seen him yesterday," said the commissioner. "Two of my officers questioned him last night, and the description fits fairly accurately."

They phoned the harbor board office and determined that Charles Overholt was indeed on duty that afternoon. They drove down to the river in a patrol car, leaving their own car parked in the station lot.

Charles Overholt was in his early thirties, possibly late twenties, with sandy-colored hair, freckles, a pleasant and mild face, and a large brow of almost Neanderthal dimensions. Overholt's supervisor understood the need for discretion in this matter, so he gave them his office to use. Laurie sat down, crossed his legs, took out his cigarettes, placed one expertly at the corner of his lower lip, lit it, inhaled, blew a cloud of smoke toward the ceiling, then looked at Overholt, sizing him up. He seemed like a sensible young man.

"Mr. Overholt," began Laurie, "can you describe to us the man you saw?"

"He was about 5'10", with short blond hair combed back, and, oh, I don't know, he had big muscular shoulders, and I think he had blue eyes."

"Could you tell us what he was wearing?" asked Taylor.

"A double-breasted suit. Checkered with large lapels. Very dashing. It must have cost a fortune."

Taylor and Laurie glanced at each other.

"Mr. Overholt, he didn't buy that suit. He stole it."

Laurie reached in his breast pocket, pulled out Goerlitz's prison photograph, and showed it to Overholt.

"Is this the man you saw?"

Overholt looked at the black-and-white glossy of Goerlitz.

"Yes, that's him. Had his hair different, but that's him."

"You're sure."

"I'm sure."

"Can you tell us at exactly what time he came here?" asked Westmoreland.

"He came here twice. Once about three-thirty in the afternoon. And once just as we were about to close, oh, about quarter past seven."

"Were you speaking with him at all?" asked Laurie, his cigarette bobbing in his mouth.

"I wasn't. Cam Washburn was, though. I was on harbor traffic yesterday, not scheduling."

"Is Mr. Washburn here today?" asked Laurie.

"No, I'm afraid not. In fact, he'll be on holiday for the next few days. He went up to Scotland with his girl."

"Would you happen to know exactly where? It's very important that we get in touch with him. He might have information we need."

"No, he wouldn't say. He said he didn't want people to bother him. Can't say as I blame him, really. You work here a few weeks and you'll see what I mean."

At the conclusion of the interview, Laurie asked the supervisor if he knew where Cameron Washburn had gone.

"All he told me was somewhere near Inverness."

Laurie then had the harbor board's personnel department dig out Washburn's file. Laurie dialled the who-to-phone-in-case-of-emergency number, which happened to be his widowed mother in Taunton, and his call was answered after three rings.

Mrs. Washburn said she had been so busy with her volunteer Red Cross work that she hadn't spoken to her son in over three weeks and knew nothing of his holiday. She was nevertheless pleased, said her son worked too hard and that he deserved a rest. Laurie left her a number to call in case her son should phone any time over the next seventy-two hours.

He left the same number with the controllers who worked the front desk and told them to call it the moment they saw anybody who even remotely resembled Goerlitz, or in case Cameron Washburn should call from wherever in Scotland he might be. He and Westmoreland then drove to the Washburn's flat on Oxford Street and after showing the landlord their identification, searched the controller's dwelling for any clue, no matter how slight, of where he may have gone for his holiday.

It was a small flat — two rooms with a hot-plate, kitchenette, and a shared bathroom down the hall — and was so sparsely furnished they were able to search it thoroughly in less than half an hour. They found some sexy women's undergarments hanging in the closet, and an expired French passport belonging to Antoinette Boissoneau. So, Washburn's girl was French. Overholt had already said as much. He opened the passport to her photograph. Westmoreland looked over his shoulder.

"What do you think?" asked Laurie

"She's quite stunning, isn't she? Wouldn't mind taking her away for a jaunt in Scotland myself."

"Yes, quite stunning," agreed Laurie. He dropped the passport on top of the bureau in frustration. "Unfortunately, it's not going to help us one damn bit."

219

Chapter 17

By morning the cloud cover had broken, and great rents of blue could be seen in the sky. Goerlitz had breakfast in the hotel cafe, then went back to his room. He opened the window so the milky light of morning shone evenly through the pane, without glare, against the small table there. From this window he could see the Mersey wind into the Pool. Some ships were anchored there. He opened the small suitcase he had stolen from the Gregorys and took out the Larisa and his notebook of naval dispositions. Opening the book to the first page and setting it on the table so the lighting was just right, he loaded the camera with a new roll of film. He then adjusted the focus and photographed the entire contents of the notebook. His reasoning was simple. No one like Jillian Gregory was going to discover the notebook again. And if he were stopped for any reason, a couple rolls of film were a lot less suspicious than a notebook full of maps and German writing.

When he was finished, he took the roll of film out of the camera, put both camera and film in his suitcase, and slid his suitcase under the bed.

Around six o'clock, when dusk was beginning to settle over the city and a heavy fog rolled in off the Irish Sea, he had a bath, dressed in his checkered suit, ate supper, then walked down to the Mersey Docks and Harbor Board. It was his intention to find out exactly what had happened to the *San Julian* and if need be, find another ship. He looked at the controllers behind the counter. The one he had spoken to yesterday wasn't there. Instead, a man about his own age, with sandy-colored hair and a large brow, sat behind the counter.

Charles Overholt recognized Goerlitz instantly. At first the junior controller wasn't entirely sure what he should do and was so startled and excited he hardly noticed the fine film of sweat that had suddenly covered his forehead. Goerlitz approached the counter, then seemed to change his mind, scanned the bulletin boards until he found the one marked Special Notices. Overholt picked up the telephone receiver, and, trying to make it look as if it were an everyday part of his clerical duties, dialled the number Laurie had given him earlier in the day.

Goerlitz decided he would try the bulletin boards first before he asked for anybody's help. He hadn't noticed how Overholt's face had turned red, or the fidgety nervous movements with which the junior controller dialled the telephone. Much to his relief, there was a notice about the *San Julian*. The inbound convoy in which the freighter had been travelling, the notice said, had come under German U-boat attack off the coast of Brittany, and had been forced to change course by over a hundred miles. The result was an eighteen-hour delay. The *San Julian* was due at pier four, number five of the Birkenhead Docks at one o'clock. In other words, the freighter had arrived just six hours ago.

Laurie answered the phone. Overholt was breathless.

"He's here," he said. "He's here right now."

"Are you sure?" asked Laurie.

"Positive."

"What's he doing?"

"He's reading the schedules."

"All right, now, listen, Mr. Overholt. Try and keep him there as long as you can. We're sending four patrol cars right away. If he looks as if he's about to leave, do anything you can to stall him. Is that clear?"

"Yes." Overholt was jittery, apprehensive. "Yes, I'll try."

So Overholt watched Goerlitz, a little too closely because after a while Goerlitz, with his combat-developed sense of danger, began to feel as if he were being watched. Goerlitz glanced over to the counter then quickly back to the schedule. Yes, the controller with the sandy-colored hair was clearly watching him. Goerlitz read the schedules for another few moments then began leaving the building as inobstrusively as he could.

"Excuse me, sir," called the controller from behind the counter. "Excuse me, sir."

Goerlitz's muscles tightened with the tension of a spring coil. He turned and looked at the man with the sandy-colored hair. The man was smiling somewhat foolishly.

"Excuse me, but don't I know you from somewhere?"

The man's voice was tremulous. Something was going on.

"No," replied Goerlitz, his voice as cold as stone, "I don't think you do."

"I'm sure we've met. Wasn't it in Tunbridge Wells last summer, at the annual Kent motor derby?"

Just then Goerlitz heard a number of cars pull up outside, and glancing out the windows of the front door, saw police.

He sprang at the man, knocking him down, and ran toward the counter.

"Stop him," cried the controller, rising to his feet. "Don't let him get away."

Goerlitz placed his hands firmly on the counter and swung his feet up and over, landing gracefully on the other side. He didn't know where he was going. All he knew was he had to run, and run fast. Another controller approached, tried to stop him, but Goerlitz swung out and punched the man in the mouth. The man fell back, landing hard on the desk, knocking a typewriter to the floor. A dumbfounded murmuring broke out among the people who were reading the schedules. Goerlitz ran around desks and chairs, heading for a back passageway he had seen earlier behind the office area. He looked back just in time to see a throng of policemen led by a man in a grey overcoat, a fedora, and a tartan scarf, burst through the front doors. It was Laurie, the man who had questioned him at the camp.

Goerlitz sprinted down the hallway, passing doors on his left and right, until he came to the door at the back of the hall. He threw it open. Stairs. He rushed down the stairs, taking three at a time, his shoes banging against the metal steps. He heard voices shouting behind him. After two short flights he came to another door. A sign on the door said: EMERGENCY EXIT. ALARM WILL SOUND IF OPENED. He kicked opened the door. Bells began to ring throughout the building.

He was outside, in an open area about a hundred feet from the river. He ran across the open area toward some riverfront tenements, hoping that the dimness of dusk and the fog rolling in off the Irish Sea would hide him. Adrenalin rushed through his body. A few shots were fired from behind. They were shooting at him. They were trying to kill him.

He heard a distant screeching of tires as he reached the tenement buildings, and the sudden wail of sirens. He bolted down the street, his legs pumping furiously, but stopped when he saw a patrol car skid to a halt up ahead, blocking his way. He turned around and headed in the direction from which he had come but stopped again when he saw another patrol car at that end of the street. Laurie got out, followed by four policemen. Goerlitz looked up and down the road. Policemen were running towards him from both directions.

"Hold it right there, Goerlitz," shouted Laurie. "Hold it right there or you're a dead man."

Goerlitz turned and ran to the nearest tenement house. Gunshots exploded through the evening air and bullets ricocheted off the pavement and the drab brick walls of the tenements. So it would be Laurie he would have to contend with, he thought, that unthreatening number in the newspaper, that face at the camp, a man whom he knew absolutely nothing about. He pushed the door of the tenement house open and went inside.

A man of sixty, two women in their forties, and a girl of about seventeen with tawny-colored hair sat in an over-cluttered parlor, the large cabinet-radio playing some kind of music hall variety show. They stared up at him, wide-eyed with alarm. The old man rose.

"What in the bloody name of hell do you — "

He pushed the old man down and went for the girl. He yanked her to her feet, put his arm around her throat, breathing hard, sweating, and dragged her out to the hall, grabbing a letter opener he saw on a side table as he went. He pulled her up the stairs to the second floor. The girl started to tremble.

"Mims," she cried. "Oh, Mims, he's got me."

Her family followed her out to the hall, terrified.

He pulled the girl into the back room on the second floor and pushed her down on the bed. He then shoved a rickety but heavy old Edwardian armoire in front of the door. He heard a lot of shouting from the first floor, and boots coming up the stairs. He wedged a chair against the armoire, kicking the back so it would tighten against the floor.

The girl had become weak with fright and he was able to pick her up as if she were a rag doll. She moaned as he put the point of the letter opener to her throat. He backed away from the door until he was at the window. Below him, not more than a jump away, flowed the black waters of the River Mersey. At this point the river was extremely wide, almost a mile across.

Someone tried to break the door down but the armoire and chair held.

"You might as well give up, Goerlitz," a voice called. It was Laurie. "There's no way out."

"Go away," shouted Goerlitz. "Go away or I'll kill the girl."

Another vicious thump against the door. He pressed the point of the letter opener against the girl's jugular vein. And then he froze. What was that fragrance? The fragrance of the girl's hair. Fresh and warm, dry and clean, like the fragrance of Ute's hair. It was as if time were suspended. The smell of apples, he thought, in his father's orchard, the smell of fresh cut hay, the smell of cream over raspberries, and the morning sun shining through the trellis-work of the gazebo, and Ute's tender vibrant smooth skin, like the skin of this innocent girl he was going to kill. Another thump against the door. The chair bounced away and toppled to the floor. The sound of the brass band in the *Hofgarten* and the taste of Ute's apple strudel, and hot strong coffee on Sunday morning. What had happened to his nerve? He couldn't kill this girl. He looked out the window. Water, a hateful refuge.

"What's your name? asked Goerlitz, almost tenderly. The girl didn't respond. Another crash at the door. The armoire started to give. Goerlitz shook her.

"I said, what's your name?"

"Lisa," said the girl, tears standing in her eyes.

A final thud. The armoire toppled, the clothes spilling out across the floor. Laurie entered the room and pointed his revolver at Goerlitz and the girl. He was followed by four uniformed constables. Laurie was a tall man, this, his true enemy, around thirty-five, and had strong cheek bones. For a moment they just looked at each other. Goerlitz heard the women crying from down the hall. Holding the girl tightly with his right arm, Goerlitz opened the window with his left.

"There's no point, Goerlitz," Laurie finally said. "Give us the girl and come along peacefully. We won't harm you if you surrender."

"Lisa, sit up here on the ledge with me," said Goerlitz.

Lisa did as she was told. It was a wide ledge. Goerlitz brought his legs up, holding the girl in front of him as he put his feet on the sill, and crouched in the casement. It was quite clear that if they tried to shoot Goerlitz they would likely kill the girl as well. Goerlitz took one last look at Laurie.

"*Auf Wiedersehn*, asshole."

And he jumped.

Even before he reached the water he heard gunshots. He cleared the embankment by over five yards and splashed into the river. Cold. Very cold. But silent and sweet. Jet streams of bubbles — bullets — pierced the surface. So he swam deeper and further out, until he began to drift with the flow of the river.

In the water. Alone. A sanctuary. He saw himself clinging to a large crate in the middle of the English Channel after U-93 had been rammed and sunk by the *Krajenka*. Three days without food or water. Then a German E-boat appeared over the horizon and dragged him from the slowly undulating Channel. They had written a story about it in the *Völkisher Beobachter*. He stopped swimming and allowed himself to float to the surface.

Bullets ripped through the air all around him and he dove again. Surely the fog would soon hide him and he would be able to stay on the surface long enough to catch his breath.

He pulled off his jacket and let it drift away. There. That was better. Now he could swim freely. He broke the surface, gasping for breath. They had brought the patrol cars around and were shining what little light came from the painted-over headlights into the water. Another volley of gunfire. The bullets stitched a constellation of small splashes around him. Then the bellowing of a fog horn. Right beside him and so loud it shook his bones. He turned. A cry escaped from his lips. A mountain of a freighter, maybe three storeys high, plowed toward him, almost on top of him. In one moment he saw his death, but in the next he saw his salvation.

A series of metal handholds went up the side of the ship. The idiots. They were shooting at his jacket. With supreme effort he rolled in the water just as the furrowing wake of the ship began to lift him. Bullets banged against the side of the ship, causing sparks. He cleared the water from his eyes and kicked fiercely until he was against the side of the ship, then reached up and grabbed the lowest handhold. The difference in speed, from a stationary position to a sudden seven knots, was wrenching. But he hung on, even though the handholds were covered with barnacles and were cutting his hands. He hung on and the freighter dragged him downriver into the thickening fog and out of bullet range.

The men on shore got in their cars and started following the freighter along the riverfront, sirens howling, but it was awkward because the road soon branched away from the river and they had to follow a circuitous route to keep up with the freighter. Goerlitz took his chance when the patrol cars were out of view. He let go of the handhold, swam away, but not fast enough. As the boat widened he was smashed against the hull. He stroked furiously, his arms flailing, and he was suddenly caught by the enormous wake. This forced him away from the freighter and he used the impetus of the wave to swim well clear of the boat.

By the time the huge propellors passed, he was safely out of the way. He stopped and turned around, treading in the cold water. He watched the ship disappear into the fog downriver, then breast-stroked back to shore and dragged himself up onto a small jetty where a few tug-boats were moored.

He stood up and pulled out his wallet. The Damon Gregory identity card was beyond repair but the money — he had two-hundred-and-twenty-three pounds left — printed on heavy Royal Mint paper, was wet though eminently usuable. He smiled, but it was a hard mirthless smile. It was the same kind of smile he had when U-93 had successfully torpedoed an enemy ship. A gloating smile. He should have felt some kind of satisfaction from this gloating, the way he would have three or four years ago. He didn't. He walked along the jetty toward the dim laneway nearby, the water dripping from his suit.

Certainly he felt relieved that he was safe, and that he still had a chance to deliver the dispositions to Admiral Doenitz, but he couldn't help thinking of the girl, Lisa, and how he had hated frightening her so much, and how she was still probably crying while her family tried to comfort her. He shook his head, unhappy with himself. From out on the river he heard a small fog horn hoot twice, and a larger deeper horn respond with a long low bellow.

Had he become a coward? He kept close to the buildings, hiding in the shadows. Not a coward, no, but there was something different inside, something he didn't necessarily trust, something he would have to guard against if he were ever going to get back to Munich alive.

228

Chapter 18

The night clerk was absorbed in a magazine when Goerlitz finally got back to the Chadwick Hotel, and he was able to climb the stairs without being noticed. There was no time to lose. He pulled off his wet clothes, had a quick bath, then dressed in Damon Gregory's slacks and wool sweater. Though his shoes were soaked he had to wear them because they were the only ones he had, and all the shops were closed. He took his camera, his notebook of naval dispositions, and his money, left the hotel and walked to the river, where he tossed both camera and notebook into the river. He had all the information he needed on the two rolls of film in his hotel room. He didn't want to carry the film around with him unless he absolutely had to.

His ferry arrived in Birkenhead just after nine that night.

The *San Julian* was there this time, docked at four of five, a freighter of about seven thousand tons. She had two 88mm guns mounted at the bow and stern. Two stevedores and a derrick operator loaded bales of hay for the livestock into the hold. Goerlitz walked up and down her length, inspecting her carefully. Great rust pocks splotched her bridge, her foredeck fixtures had weathered badly over the years, and her hull was caked with barnacles. The kind of ship that might make ten or eleven knots at best, one that would straggle in convoys, a rogue of a ship that should have gone to the bottom long ago. She listed to port, and two of her crew bailed out the forward hold with a gasoline-powered pump. He studied the two crew members who worked in the light of the kerosene lamp. One was short, with thick sturdy legs. The other was tall, lanky, and had a thick bushy mustache. He examined the ship more closely. Barely seaworthy, he thought. As long as she made the trip to Barcelona one last time. There was a German consulate there.

The lanky crewman stood up from his crouched position beside the pump, and, raising the kerosene lamp, walked down the gangplank toward Goerlitz.

He found out from the crewman that Gil Robles was at a pub called the Empire. They spoke in French because it was their only common language, and when the crewman, who introduced himself as Ramirez, offered to take Goerlitz to the Empire, Goerlitz accepted.

Birkenhead had been just as badly bombed as the Liverpool side of the river. As a German soldier he should have gloried in the destruction of his enemy's cities, but the sight of splintered beams, broken glass, and the smell of smoke in the air sickened him.

They kept along the river front until they came to what had once been a shopping district. Not many buildings were left standing. The few that remained stuck up like charred nubs in the surrounding desolation. The charred nub the second mate took Goerlitz to, the Empire, smelled rotten and was full of drunken seamen, prostitutes, and smugglers. It was just the kind of place Goerlitz had expected.

Inside, it was noisy, crowded, and smoky. A merchant sailor tried to stick an ice cube between the breasts of a woman who wore a dress with a low neckline, a waiter was mopping up some broken glass, and the publican poured foam off a pint glass of Guinness and refilled the mug with the precision of a surgeon.

Gil Robles sat at a back table by himself with a bottle of, miracle of miracles, Holland schnapps. Half the bottle was gone. He looked up and smiled dreamily.

"Ah, Ramirez, you've brought a friend to join us," said Gil Robles, in Spanish.

Ramirez nodded to his captain and, glancing toward Goerlitz, simply said, "*En Français.*"

"A Frenchman," Gil Robles said in French. "Go away, Ramirez. Go away so I can talk to our Frenchman."

Ramirez withdrew and ordered a double whiskey at the bar.

"Your name is Gil Robles?" asked Goerlitz.

"It might be. It depends on what yours is."

He was about fifty, looked as if he hadn't shaved in a week, had a small chin and mouth, and a complexion close to olive green.

"That's not important right now," said Goerlitz. "I understand you sail for Spain tomorrow. I wish to buy passage."

Gil Robles stopped his schnapps halfway to his lips. The corners of his weak mouth hardened and he leaned forward, putting his schnapps glass down.

"I suppose, *mon petit Français,*" he said with some sarcasm, "that there is a problem that stops you from travelling on the commercial lines."

Three sailors entered the tavern, arms around each other, singing an out-of-tune version of *Berkeley Square,* drunk and stumbling, slurring the lyrics. An old man, the front of his pants all wet, waved the sailors away with an angry snarl, then continued to drink his beer sullenly.

There was a sudden shrill laugh as the sailor who had been trying to get the ice cube between the woman's breasts finally succeeded. The captain stared at Goerlitz, waiting for some kind of explanation.

Gil Robles took a sip of his schnapps.

"You are not French, and you are not English, and, *monsieur*, you are certainly not Spanish. Could it be you are German?" asked Gil Robles, as if he had known Goerlitz were German all along.

Goerlitz cast a nervous glance around.

"Come," said the Captain, "let us go for a stroll and we shall discuss this thing."

Fifteen minutes later they walked along the river front, and in the distance Goerlitz saw the warehouse next to pier four of the Birkenhead Docks. Goerlitz looked at the captain with cool unrevealing eyes.

"My name is Hermann Goerlitz," he said. "I'm a German U-boat commander. My government is willing to pay you. The name I am to give you is Helga Weiss. Does that name mean anything to you?"

Gil Robles smiled.

"Ah, so here it is, what I have been waiting for. Of course it does. I wasn't sure you were the one I was to expect because you were so evasive in the tavern. But I understand now. One can't be too careful these days, can one, Herr Goerlitz, and your caution is most commendable. Let us go to my ship."

•

Gil Robles, once they boarded the *San Julian*, spoke with Goerlitz for another hour. When Goerlitz left just past midnight, everything had been arranged. The captain of the *San Julian* watched the German U-boat commander walk down the pier and turn left toward the ferry docks. Gil Robles walked up the companionway to his cabin. He would either have to telephone or telegraph

Miguel Ribalta before the *San Julian* weighed anchor tomorrow at eleven o'clock.

In his cabin, he opened his desk drawer, took out his 9mm Luger pistol — one of the many guns he and Ribalta had pilfered from German forces during the Civil War — checked the magazine, and for the first time in several months, took the safety catch off, making sure it still worked smoothly, then snapped it back on and examined the gun closely. When he was sure it was clean, and in perfect working order, he loaded it with a fresh magazine, and put it back in his drawer. He could trust the Jewish girl on his ship, but he wasn't about to trust this German U-boat commander.

•

Miguel Ribalta stood on his tailor's stool with a cigarette clutched between his lips regarding himself in the triptych of mirrors. The tailor measured his waistline, his inseam, and his shoulders, smiled obsequiously, then backed away. It was hot. They were both sweating. Barcelona could be hot in September. It would take a while for the rose-colored material to arrive, his tailor said, but he would do his best to hurry it up.

"That's quite all right," replied Ribalta. "I'm in no hurry."

He had too many suits as it was. He stood there absent-mindedly on the stool letting his cigarette turn into a long tube of ash, thinking about the telephone call he had received from Liverpool last night. Gil Robles said the man's name was Hermann Goerlitz, a U-boat commander who had escaped from a British prison camp. One thing about war, refugee trade always boomed. Three weeks ago there had been the young Jewish girl, Anna Liebel. There had been the Polish family, the Italian brothers, the Czechoslovakian couple from Lidice, and now there was the German U-boat commander. He had yet to hear back from the Germans, and he wondered why they were dragging their heels. It might be time to consider a discreet call to British Naval Intelligence to inquire what kind of posting they had on this man.

"Now, señor," said the tailor, "would you like the cuffs above or below the ankle?"

"Below."

"Very good, Señor Ribalta, very good."

There was an interesting picture here, mused Ribalta, there usually was, and an interesting picture always meant interesting money.

•

It was just after eleven the next day, a cool misty morning, and Laurie was sitting with Taylor and Westmoreland in the Liverpool offices of the Naval Intelligence Department nursing a tall glass of bicarbonate and smoking cigarette after cigarette when the telephone rang. All three men stiffened instantly. Taylor answered it. After a moment he looked up at Laurie.

"It's Charles Overholt again," he said.

Laurie nodded and took the receiver.

"Go ahead, Mr. Overholt."

"Is this Inspector Laurie?"

"Yes it is."

"I hear Goerlitz got away last night. Jumped into the river."

"Yes, he did."

"Any chance he drowned?"

"Unlikely, Mr. Overholt. As a U-boat man he's a highly trained swimmer. And we've had harbor police scouring the river since six this morning. They've turned up a soggy piece of identification on one of the piers. Damon Gregory's."

"Oh. Oh, I see. Then he's still at large."

"It would appear so."

"Inspector Laurie, I think I might know where Cam Washburn might be. He gave me the key to his locker before he left. It's laundry service day today. We're having our uniforms cleaned and I was supposed to toss his in with the rest of them."

"And?"

"I emptied his pockets before I threw his uniform into the hamper and I found a slip of paper with the name of the place I think he might be staying."

Laurie leaned forward and snatched a pencil from the desk.

"Go ahead, Mr. Overholt."

"Strath Errick Inn and Wilderness Cabins, North Durham Road, Colcabock."

Laurie hastily scribbled the information down.

"Is that it?" he asked. "No telephone number?"

"I'm afraid that's all there is, inspector. Nothing else."

Chapter 19

On the morning of their departure, Captain Gil Robles stood at the railing of the *San Julian* while two British customs officials came aboard, middle-aged Englishmen who were obviously in a hurry, behind schedule. They wore big blue overcoats and peaked caps, and carried clipboards under their arms. Gil Robles showed them down to the livestock hold where they made a perfunctory count of the sheep and cattle, then took them to the hard goods storage hold, where the *San Julian* carried six barrels of lubricating oil, seven radios, and numerous other small packages, all of which they checked, then check-marked on their clipboards.

It was always like this. A quick inaccurate search by men who were too harried to care. They took a tour of the ship, told him he should consider having one or two of the bulkheads replaced, had him sign the papers, then marched down the gangplank, clipboards in hand, into the rain toward their car.

He stood at the railing and watched them walk away, saw them get in the car and drive toward the ferry docks.

Now was the time, he thought. The entire crew had been told, were ready to expect Goerlitz. Gil Robles climbed the companionway to the bridge and went inside. He walked to the helm and gazed out at the warehouse near the foot of the pier, knowing that Goerlitz and Ramirez were waiting for him behind the broken window on the third floor. He turned the bridge lights on and off three times, then waited. In a moment he saw a burning match shine through the broken pane. He nodded to himself. Good, he thought. Goerlitz had not been spooked. And the German U-boat commander had no need to worry. Now that the customs officials had gone, Britain was no longer legally responsible for the ship, and the cargo, seventeen Hereford bulls and twenty-one New Zealand ewes, was longer their concern. Any possible claim, now that the forms had been signed, would be invalid.

He went out to the walkway circling the bridge and stood facing the warehouse. After a minute or two he saw Ramirez and the commander come out of one of the warehouse's several doors, two dark shadows in the mid-morning fog. He wondered what Goerlitz must be feeling. Probably proud of himself, even victorious. Well, thought Gil Robles, let him feel that way until he sees there is no longer any reason to feel that way.

•

Goerlitz stayed below while the *San Julian* left the River Mersey. He had wrapped the two rolls of film neatly together in masking tape, had wrapped them again in wax paper, once more coiled it all around with masking tape, and had put the small package into his pocket. The crew, about nine in all, hardly noticed him, seemed used to strange passengers on their ship.

When the *San Julian* finally entered Liverpool Bay, a gentle swell began to rock the boat.

He climbed topside and gazed out at the Irish Sea. A stiff wind blew from the northwest through a churning grey sky, and the rain, though persistent, was not altogether unpleasant to Goerlitz. The sea was tossed by the wind and flecked with white foam.

The *San Julian* fell into ranks just before twelve with Convoy OB 217D, running last in the fifth column. There were about eleven columns of ten covering an area of just over sixty square miles. The escort strength, as far as he could judge, consisted of three corvettes, two frigates, and, alarmingly enough, seven American destroyers.

They remained stationary, the last ship in the fifth column, until half-past-two, when the engine suddenly heaved and climbed to nine or ten knots against obstinate seas. He began to think that he had made it, that it was just a matter of time before he would present Admiral Doenitz with his two rolls of film. Yet that really didn't seem to matter so much any more, not in the face of returning to Munich. He wondered if he was viewing things in the right perspective, as a soldier of the Reich should. He didn't know. He had lost his understanding of himself.

By that night, he had settled into a soothing ennui. There was no cabin space so they put up a cot in the pump room next to the cargo hold where he heard the bleating of sheep.

Ramirez brought him supper around eight o'clock, something with stewing beef in it.

He climbed topside again around midnight, having spent most of the evening dozing in the pump room, and gazed out at the dark sea. By this time they were passing the English Channel. The rain had stopped but the wind still blew cold. A dim red light shone on the bridge, and a dull white cross — a sea gull — passed through the darkness before his eyes. He could hardly believe that in just over a week he would be back in Germany. Back in

Munich. The first thing he would do was take his father to the beer garden in Marienplatz, order two pints of dark beer, a bowl of white salted radishes, and some of that spicy sausage from Regensburg. And he would take Ute to a concert at the Great Hall of Nymphenburg Palace. Back to all the things he had loved. Next month in Munich it was *Oktoberfest,* and it was something he wouldn't want to miss, especially the music and the dancing. There was nothing he liked better than pressing his body against Ute's, to feel the pressure of her back against his arm as he swung her around to a rousing polka. And there was nothing that warmed his heart more than to watch his father dance a foxtrot with one of the older ladies. This was his true Germany. It was sad because he couldn't help thinking this Germany had been lost forever.

From out of the darkness came the plaintive sound of a fog horn.

Had Munich been bombed, he wondered? He didn't like to think about it. Better to think of things that were easy to think about. Like his father, and Regensburg sausage. Like his clarinet and the ridiculous way he could massacre the Mozart *Clarinet Concerto in A Major.* Better to think of the Eau d'Orsay he splashed on his chin when he had a few days leave in Paris, of Ute all in one piece and not crushed underneath a shrapnel- embedded brick wall. He and Ute would go on holiday when he got back, to his father's country house, and they would take the cats with them, and they would just forget about the *Unterseewaffe* and the High Command. What was he going to say to her once he got back? He had been so arrogant and condescending toward her.

He had seen her so infrequently during the war, had seen Munich so infrequently, and had heard from fresh recruits coming from Germany that the city had been bombed many, many times. And why wouldn't they bomb Munich, the wet-nurse of Naziism, the city which fertilized National Socialism and gave Hitler his power base from which to gain ascendancy over the nation? Out in the field, fighting the hard underwater battles of U-93, and winning again and again until she finally went down under the prow of the *Krajenka*, had given them all the sense that they had superhuman powers. They were heroes. They were supermen. They didn't have time for wives and miscarriages, they didn't have time for silly foreign languages or sitting at a desk all day trying to figure out secret codes. They were the best. They were the bravest. They relished danger. And they were going to win. But now they were going to lose. And in the face of that, thoughts of family, of what he would do, naturally came to mind. And yet there was always the anger, the anger he had had all his life. He was Hermann Goerlitz and no one was going to beat him, especially not the British. But he was also Ute's husband, and he was also Otto's son, and that made a much greater difference these days than it had before the mutiny.

•

After consulting a map, Laurie determined that Colcabock was indeed just outside Inverness, lending strength to the assumption that this was where Cameron Washburn would be found. Yet when he checked the telephone listings for Inverness and the surrounding area he found no number for the Strath Errick Inn. So he phoned the Inverness Police Department and had one of their constables run out to the North Durham Road in Colcabock to see if such a place existed. The constable got back to him two hours later.

"Aye, sir, sure enough she's there on the North Durham Road, just as you said. A beautiful spot beyond the River Cairn. But I hate to be disappointing you about this lad Washburn. The innkeeper says he has no one registered there by that name."

"Well, are there any other inns in the area? This one had cabins."

"There were about six cabins, sir. Up in the hills."

"And were you talking to the innkeeper?"

"No. The innkeeper was away on business. I was talking to the clerk."

"Did you have a look at the guest register yourself?"

"Aye, sir, that I did. And there was no Washburn."

"Well, was there anything in the register that looked like a French name?"

"A French name, sir? Well, I'm not up on my French names, but no, I don't think there was."

"Boissoneau would be the name."

"No, sir. I saw no name like that."

When he put the receiver down Laurie looked up at Taylor. It was a thin lead but their only lead, this small village of Colcabock, and he reasoned that a young unmarried couple would likely register under an assumed name. He had the girl's passport photograph, and one of Washburn from the dock and harbor board files. His only choice was to fly up to Inverness and investigate the matter first hand. He had to get whatever information Washburn might have as soon as possible.

"Don, could you have Jarmon arrange a plane for us. One with pontoons if possible. I'm going up to Colcabock myself."

•

The rain stopped and the skies cleared during the next day. By the time the *San Julian* reached the Bay of Biscay the sun was out, the wind had died down, and the waves were small. He spent some time with Gil Robles, who had been a captain with the merchant marine since the age of nineteen. Marcelo Gil Robles had spent much of his early life plowing along the trade routes between Malaya, the Philippines, and French Indochina, and remembered the days when many ships in that part of the world were still powered by steam. The rest of the crew ignored him, except for Ramirez, who stared at him from time to time with the most profound malevolence Goerlitz had ever seen.

On the third night out, when the convoy neared Gibraltar, Goerlitz climbed topside to look at the stars. It was a moonless night. He picked out the major constellations. At quarter past ten he went up to the bridge, borrowed a pair of binoculars, and returned to the deck. With the binoculars he could see, just barely, the rings around Saturn. His father was an amateur star-gazer and had a twenty-five-times magnification telescope at his country house. They had spent many hours together charting the skies. He moved to the bow of the ship and scanned the horizon for Mars. He found it thirty-five degrees off the starboard side, livid and murky, like a dying ember sinking in the west.

Then, out of the ocean, between the fourth and fifth columns, he saw a sudden frothy patch of water. In the negligible light of the stars a thin stem, like a tube or pipe, rose above the surface. It couldn't have been more than five hundred feet away, directly to starboard. He pulled the binoculars from his eyes and looked up at the bridge. The third mate was on watch, sitting on the upper deck smoking a cigarette and reading a book in the light of a kerosene lamp.

The periscope traveled beside them at the same speed for several miles then slowly pulled ahead. The periscope began to dive. Goerlitz watched as the last bit of periscope dipped beneath the waves.

The U-boat remained submerged for ten or fifteen minutes. Goerlitz thought she was gone for good. But then she surfaced about a half mile ahead. Not just the periscope. All of it. He saw the U-boat's silhouette angling in surface trim to the proper firing position, aiming at a twelve-ton tanker, the *Johannesburg*. He glanced up at the third mate who was still absorbed in his book, then turned back to the U-boat. Fire, you idiots, fire and dive.

From the bridge he heard sudden radio chatter. A few minutes later the chief engineer emerged from belowdeck and rang a bell. The U-boat fired a spread of three torpedoes at the *Johannesburg*. The submarine kicked backward three times as Ramirez and the third mate scrambled with grumbling voices to man the 88 mm guns. The silver wakes of the torpedoes shot out across the water. Gil Robles stumbled up to the bridge, binoculars to his eyes. The chief engineer continued to ring the bell. More sleepy sailors emerged from belowdeck. Ramirez fired forty or fifty rounds, every fifth round a tracer, but the U-boat was too far away and the entire volley disappeared into the ocean.

The first torpedo went wide, but the other two struck the *Johannesburg* broadside. Fire shot hundreds of yards into the air. The submarine dove. Star-shells burst across the sky, illuminating the convoy for miles around in a glittering canopy of lime-white flickers. The American destroyers, making a methodical pass between the fourth and fifth columns, started firing hedgehogs and depth charges. Gushers of water burst from the sea with violent and lugubrious regularity while the star-shells continued to explode across the sky. The helmsman gave the *San Julian* a hard turn to port and zig-zagged toward the torpedoed vessel.

The *San Julian* reached the *Johannesburg* in just under twenty-five minutes. The *Johannesburg* tipped to starboard, and men struggled with lifeboats in the pale glare of the fire. A slick of burning oil spread from the punctured cargo hold. Other ships in the convoy zig-zagged while the American destroyers continued to pound the water with depth charges. The sea was covered with junk — a bunk bed, a foot locker, barrels, boxes, and crates, all floating in the oily water. Seven or eight crewmen clung to a capsized lifeboat. The water flickered with a smoky fire. Gigantic flames rose from the *Johannesburg* amidships. The *Johannesburg* dipped suddenly to starboard, casting many still on deck helplessly into the water.

Crewmen aboard the *San Julian* dropped a climbing net over the side and shot out several lifelines. Meanwhile the American destroyers continued to pound the water two miles off. Ramirez and the other gunner left the 88mm guns and helped the rest of the crewmen drag the survivors aboard. Without exception, every single survivor was covered with oil, and looked as if someone had dumped black paint over their heads. Goerlitz had never seen a more pathetic lot in his life. There was a huge creaking sound from the *Johannesburg*, and a relentless bubbling of water as she started to go down. Cries for help rose from the seven men clinging to the lifeboat. So this was what it was like, he thought, when a torpedo struck a ship. Fire and oil, and garbage and innocent men scrambling to save their lives. A few dead bodies floated nearby.

Then he saw someone waving for help forty-five yards off the bow, and since the others were too busy with the climbing net, Goerlitz grabbed one of the life rings, tied it to the end of a rope, and flung it out to the man. This was what it was like when a German torpedo struck a boat, but he wasn't going to let that man die if he could possibly help it. The man swam for the ring, and when he had a hold of it, Goerlitz pulled him around the bow to the climbing net.

A small explosion came from the *Johannesburg* and water boiled in a sudden frenzy around the ship as she collapsed completely on her side. Goerlitz could now see all her deck fittings, like a top view. Debris drifted toward her, lured by the great undertow she created as she started to sink. The seven men clinging to the lifeboat were overcome by the waves that shot from the ship. Some tried to swim away, panic in their faces, but they were drawn back. There were a few loud clunks, like metal beams breaking. The *Johannesburg* lurched in an effort to right herself, her bow jumped into the air, sending out an unbroken curtain of water, and she slid stern first into the ocean and disappeared beneath the surface in a matter of twenty seconds. The lifeboat went under. So did the seven men. There was a final bubbling, like a monstrous underwater explosion, and the sea grew still. Airplanes, sent from Gibraltar, now flew up and down the convoy with searchlights on. Goerlitz couldn't help thinking that this destroyed tanker wasn't going to get Germany any closer to winning the war.

In all, there were eleven survivors out of a crew of twenty. The *Johannesburg* itself, of course, was now no more than a headache for insurance brokers. Of the eleven survivors, six had serious injuries and had to be taken to other, more medically-equipped ships. Of the remaining five, two, as the only surviving ranking officers aboard the *Johannesburg*, were taken aboard a British frigate. That left two South Africans and a Pole. They were to be billeted aboard the *San Julian* until they reached Gibraltar, where they would be debriefed at the British naval base there.

Another cot was set up in the pump room beside Goerlitz's. One of the South Africans, an assistant engineer by the name of Pieter Van Gessel, a man of about thirty-five, tall, strong, muscular, with white-blond hair — the man Goerlitz had saved — was given the cot in the pump room.

This bothered Goerlitz. How was he going to explain

to the South African why he slept in the pump room, why all the other crewmen ignored him, and why he didn't speak Spanish when everybody else did? Van Gessel, thankfully, was a quiet man, and hardly wasted more than a few words — where's the mess, where are the latrines? — that was all. Still, Goerlitz went to sleep uneasily that night knowing the South African would sleep beside him.

The *San Julian* continued to zig-zag for over a hundred miles as he dozed in and out of sleep. He kept on having half-waking dreams about the destruction of the *Johannesburg*, of the bodies floating in the water, and of the oil-covered survivors. Sometimes he didn't know whether he was awake or asleep. At times he was oblivious. Then around four in the morning, his mental fog lifted, the haziness disappeared, he opened his eyes — he was completely lucid — and he saw Pieter Van Gessel gazing down at him. Gazing intently. Scrutinizing Goerlitz's face. Their eyes met briefly. The South African studied him as if he were reading a map. Goerlitz closed his eyes quickly. But in the fraction of a second before he closed them he had seen recognition flash across the South African's face.

•

Admiral Karl Doenitz stood in map room C of U-boat High Command staring at the big grid-coordinated map of the Atlantic, pensive, worried, and frustrated. September had not been a good month for the *Unterseewaffe*. First there had been the disastrous capture of U-512, one of his Type IX boats, and the imprisonment of her captain and crew in England. It was a small mercy that the submarine had somehow been destroyed while in port. No thanks to the *Luftwaffe*, he thought. And as of last night they had lost radio contact with U-720, Commander Staroste's boat. He stared at the red pin representing the last location of U-720, two-hundred-and-fifty miles off the coast of Labrador. U-720 had simply vanished. It was so often the case these days.

Schimmler, one of his aides, entered the map room, approached him, clicked his heels, and saluted.

"Sir, a special dispatch from our man in Lisbon has just arrived. I've left it on your desk upstairs."

"Thank you, Schimmler. Thank you. I'll attend to it at once."

Yes, it was so often the case these days. He turned from the map, walked slowly across the room and mounted the stairs to his office. Radio contact lost. How he hated those words now. One could only imagine what had happened. Radio contact lost certainly meant the grim and horrible deaths of countless U-boat men. The fatality rate, according to the latest figures, was eighty-five percent, and a U-boat man had a life expectancy of two weeks. Radio contact lost. None of it would have happened if they had listened to him. If he had acquired his three hundred U-boats in the spring of 1940, as Hitler had promised, they might have actually been able to win this war. Those in Berlin didn't understand the simple equation. Germany had to produce more U-boats than the Allies could sink, just as Germany had to destroy more shipping than the Allies could produce. But it was a lost game now, and the equation worked in favor of the Allies.

In his office he opened the dispatch from Lisbon. Inside the envelope, he found another envelope. The admiral saw that it was post-marked in England, Barrow-in-Furness, where the only prisoner-of-war camp for U-boat officers was located, Triggsdale Hall. He tore open the envelope and pulled out a single folded sheet. There were five English words.

Grateful for word of Helga.

And below it, two initials, G.W.

He put the dispatch down. Georg Weiss, he thought. A name from a time when the war was still young, and ultimate victory seemed a real possibility. He looked out his window where he saw the harbor and the giant bomb-proof submarine pens. French laborers worked on another. All kinds of submarines crowded the harbor, Type VIIs, Type IXs, two-man boats, three-man boats, minelayers. And submarine tankers, the so-called milk cows, giant submarines that provided fuel for combat U-boats out on station.

He was puzzled. He felt he should be remembering something, but his mind drew a blank. So much had happened since Georg Weiss had been captured. And now this note from Weiss. What could have triggerered it? He walked to the top of the stairs and called to Schimmler. In a moment his aide appeared at the bottom.

"Sir?" said Schimmler.

"Have we sent anything to Georg Weiss in England recently?"

"Yes, sir, as a matter of fact we have. His wife is to undergo a rather serious operation for her Crohn's Disease and the Red Cross agreed that it would be appropriate to let Commander Weiss know. They looked after it."

Doenitz shrugged. Everybody in the *Unterseewaffe* knew Weiss's marriage to Helga was a dismal failure.

"Thank you, Schimmler. That will be all."

He returned to the window, his hands behind his back, and gazed out at the harbor. He couldn't escape the nagging feeling he was forgetting something. Poor Georg. Two years in a prisoner-of-war camp. Oh, well, if he couldn't remember, then it probably wasn't worth remembering. And he had more important things to think about. Like U-720 and Commander Staroste.

Chapter 20

A patrol car waited for Laurie on the end of the pier when he and Westmoreland stepped off the seaplane at Inverness. Laurie couldn't deny the pressure now, nor how urgent the manhunt had become. Goerlitz seemed to have completely disappeared.

A constable drove them out to Colcabock on the North Durham Road, where they found the Strath Errick Inn and Wilderness Cabins.

It was situated on low-lying hills at the south end of a pristine loch, among pine trees and pastures of the last of summer's tarnished heather. The innkeeper, Mr. Ian Frawley, a stout man of fifty with a full beard, whose arms looked as if they had done their share of wood cutting through the years, told them what they'd already been told, that there was no one at the inn registered under the name of Washburn. Laurie showed him his NID identification.

"They would be a couple, Mr. Frawley. And the wife would have a French accent."

"Oh. You must mean Cam and Toni Convery, then."

Laurie pulled out his photographs and showed them to Frawley. He craned over the counter and had a look.

"Yes, that's them. Lovely young couple. They're up in cabin 6."

"Mr. Frawley, it's very important that I speak with this man. Could you please show me the way to cabin 6? It's really rather an urgent matter of national security."

As it had started to rain, Frawley lent both men big Mackintoshes, and then all three climbed the hill to cabin 6. The cabin stood behind some pine trees, rustic and pleasantly well-weathered, with the curtains closed and smoke billowing gently from the chimney pipe.

"They should be here," said Frawley. "It's a nasty day for hiking."

Frawley knocked on the cabin door. After waiting several moments he tried again. His knock went unanswered.

"Maybe they drove into town for lunch," suggested Westmoreland.

Frawley shrugged.

"No," he said. "Their car's down in the lot."

The big Scots tried again, this time louder. Still, there was no answer.

"Well, I've got the key," said Frawley. "No point in having you gents stand around in the pouring rain."

He put the key in the lock and opened the door.

The couple inside looked up in sudden alarm. Both were naked, the Frenchwoman bent over on a chair, knees on the seat, hands grasping the spindle back, the nipples of her breasts staring reproachfully at Laurie, Westmoreland, and Frawley. Washburn stood behind her in a thrusting position, his hands grasping her pliant hips, his cheeks glowing with a rosy flush, a film of sweat on his forehead. They disengaged instantly.

"What in the name of. . .of all the bloody impertinence," sputtered Washburn. "Frawley, what the bloody hell do you think. . .My God, I'll have you sued for this."

Laurie quickly pulled out his identification. The Frenchwoman hurried to the bed and pulled a sheet up to her shoulders, blushing to the roots of her hair. She looked to the ceiling and shook her head.

"I can't believe this," she said. "I simply can't believe this."

"There's no need to get quite so. . .I'm sorry we had to. . ."

"Are you police?" asked Washburn. "Now, see here, whoever you are, we were doing nothing illegal. You have no bloody right to barge in here like the bloody Spanish Inquisition and start — "

"I realize that, Mr. Washburn, and we quite apologize. But I'm afraid we really must ask you some questions." Laurie glanced over at Westmoreland. "Westmoreland, would you stop staring at the young lady so much?"

"Are you all right, Toni?" asked Washburn, pulling on a pair of boxer shorts.

"Who are these men, Cameron?" she asked.

"I have no bloody idea who they are."

"I'm Inspector Gerald Laurie, of the Naval Intelligence Department. Please, Mr. Washburn, I'm terribly sorry to interrupt you like this, but I must ask you some questions."

Toni looked up at the ceiling, then out the window, shaking her head again. "I just don't believe this."

Washburn glared at Laurie, regaining some of his self-control.

"Questions about what?"

"Perhaps we could sit down here by the fire."

"What's this all about? You better have a damn good reason for all this."

Laurie turned to the innkeeper.

"Mr. Frawley, you've been more than kind. I'm sorry

251

I've caused you so much trouble. We're going to have to ask Mr. Washburn our questions in private. If you wouldn't mind."

"Of course, inspector, I quite understand. Let me know if you need anything."

"Thank you, Mr. Frawley."

The innkeeper left the cabin.

"What in the devil's going on?" asked Washburn.

"Please, Mr. Washburn. Could we sit down? Miss Boissoneau, I'm afraid I'm going to have to ask you to wait in the kitchen."

"Stay where you are, Toni. She's not going anywhere, inspector."

Laurie shrugged, becoming annoyed with Washburn. He just wanted to ask his questions and get back to Liverpool.

"Very well, Mr. Washburn. Have it your way. But if either of you repeats anything we say, you'll be in direct violation of the Official Secrets Act."

"Official Secrets Act?" said Washburn. He sat down, still angry, but growing resigned, even a bit curious. "I'm afraid you've quite lost me, inspector. Are you sure you have the right person?"

"Yes." Laurie sat down, and Westmoreland took the chair next to him, withdrawing a pad and pencil to take notes. "No question about that. We're looking for a man, Mr. Washburn. We think you may have seen him. You were on duty at the harbor board last Friday night, weren't you?"

"Yes, I was."

Inspector Laurie took out a photograph of Goerlitz and handed it to Wasburn.

"Do you recognize him?"

"I can't say I do."

"He's about five-ten, light brown hair, blue eyes, could be wearing his hair differently, and could have a mustache. He was calling himself either Damon Gregory or Michael Bower."

Washburn took another look at the photograph.

"No, I'm sorry, I don't recognize him." He glanced over at the bed. "Are you all right, Toni?"

"Just get them to go, Cameron," she said.

"Please, Mr. Washburn, could we stick to the questions. We'll all get done quicker that way, and we'll be able to leave, just as the young lady wishes."

"Of course, inspector. Ask your questions. You're going to bloody well ask them no matter what I do."

"Are you absolutely sure you haven't seen this man?" asked Laurie. "This is very important."

"No ... no, I wish I could help you, I really wish I could."

"According to Charles Overholt he was at the harbor board looking at the schedules. He could have been wearing a checkered suit or a pinstripe one, or he could have been wearing pants and a — "

"Now, wait a minute," said Washburn, looking at the photograph again. "There was a man come in wearing a checkered suit on Friday night. Looked as if he just walked in off Eaton Square. He was reading the schedules." Washburn looked more closely at the photograph. "You know, I think it might be the same man. Had the same broad face. His hair was different, though. Brighter, combed back."

Washburn angled the photograph toward the light of the fire.

"Now that I look hard," he said, "I really think this might be the man."

"Well, when was he there on Friday?" asked Laurie.

"Twice. Once early in the day and once just before I locked up for the night. The first time he said he was looking for a captain but didn't know the name of the ship. I thought that was odd. He had a European accent."

"Did he mention the captain's name?" asked Laurie.

"Can't remember. Then he comes back — after office hours, mind you — and he's looking for some Spanish freighter on pier twenty-seven of the Garston Docks. Well, everybody knows those docks were blown apart three weeks ago. I told him he would find the ship over at the Birkenhead Docks."

"Can you remember the name of the ship by any chance?"

"Yes, I can, as a matter of fact. I had to look it up for him. The *San Julian*. I can't remember the captain's name but I know she left for Barcelona three days ago."

•

In Gibraltar, the naval authorities began what they thought would be a routine debriefing. A South African seaman with the merchant marine by the name of Pieter Van Gessel had gone down aboard the *Johannesburg*. He told the naval authorities he had been amidships on the second deck standing watch when he saw the submarine break the surface. She angled toward the *Johannesburg* and shot three torpedoes. He saw one going wide around the bow but the other two were on target, racing toward the middle of the tanker. Ringing the alarm, he ran as fast as he could to the bow. He had just reached the first deck near the front when the torpedoes struck. He told the authorities how the ship lurched to starboard and how he was thrown from the deck into the water, and how great chunks of metal splashed down around him. And the authorities were weary and bored — they had heard the same story so many times — and just wanted to go home for the night.

But then Pieter Van Gessel began to talk about the rescue ship, the *San Julian*, in particularly about a man who wasn't part of the crew, a passenger who hadn't spoken a word of Spanish and who spoke English with a European accent. Van Gessel thought he had recognized the man. So the naval authorities showed Pieter Van Gessel some photographs. The South African went through them quickly and pulled out a photograph of a German U-boat commander.

"Yes, this is him," said Pieter Van Gessel. "No doubt about it. Saw his picture in the newspaper about a week ago."

The two naval authorities looked at one another.

The short one mumbled something about there being a special alert on this man.

"Better give London a call," was all the other said.

•

The call from Gibraltar had to be routed through Madrid, then Lisbon, then the Azores before it reached London, and by the time Naval Intelligence put the call through to Liverpool, the voice, thought Gerald Laurie, sounded far away indeed.

"We have a chap here who says he's seen your Goerlitz," said the voice from Gibraltar, crackling over the wires. "Aboard a ship called the *San Julian*."

This was all the corroboration Laurie needed.

"Have you phoned the port authorities in Barcelona and asked them whether she's arrived yet?"

"Yes, we did, inspector, and, no, she hasn't. Should we take any action?"

"Pretty pointless for the Royal Navy to get involved now that she's no longer in international waters." Laurie paused. "We wouldn't want to cause any diplomatic friction with Spain by accosting one of her ships in her own territory. No, don't do anything, at least not for the time being. I'll look after things from here."

255

•

Gerald Laurie corresponded with a great many people. In the NID he was known for his huge number of contacts. One of these was Luis Jimenez. Luis Jimenez was the NID's man in Madrid and Barcelona, and had been contacted earlier in the week, after Laurie's meeting with Leo Carson, and alerted about Goerltiz. He had met Jimenez in 1940 during the height of the blitz at the Southdown Hotel in Bournemouth. Jimenez had been hired by a rich couple in Madrid to track their runaway daughter who they believed had come to England. Jimenez had traced her as far as Bournemouth, where Laurie had been stationed at the time, and with the help of Naval Intelligence — a favor, nothing official — Jimenez had been able to find the girl in a Poole boarding house. At that time, Jimenez and Laurie decided that it would be in their own best interests to keep in contact, and he convinced Admiral Carson to put Jimenez on the NID payroll.

The *San Julian* was well up the Spanish east coast when Laurie's call reached Jimenez in Madrid.

"I have to agree with you, Gerald," said Jimenez, once Laurie had filled him in. "It's an extremely sensitive situation. If we're going to catch Goerlitz now we'll have to violate Spain's sovereignty."

"Well, let's be discreet about it, then. Because one way or the other he has to be caught. Britain has a lot at stake."

"I understand. I'll do everything I can, Gerald. I'll get back to you as soon as I have more information."

It was just after five in the morning when Jimenez called back. Westmoreland and Taylor had long since dozed off, but Laurie was up nursing a pot of tea and listening to the rain.

Jimenez told Laurie he was in Barcelona now.

"And I'm afraid I've got some rather disturbing news. Ribalta's a bad one. It might be difficult dealing with him."

"How so?"

"Well, he's been convicted on several smuggling charges, of living off the avails of prostitution, and of passage brokering. Over and above that, he has a list of minor offenses that reads like a catalogue of petty crime. A man like that can't be trusted. We'll have to be careful."

•

Laurie flew to London that morning and arrived shortly after one o'clock, where he made arrangements with Naval Intelligence for a flight to Madrid, and then to Barcelona. He stopped in to say hello to Ted and Mrs. Moss, who were staying at the house in Golders Green now, and made sure that everything was all right and that they had everything they needed. Then he got in his second-hand Hillman and drove to St. Mary's Hospital to see his wife.

He found Heather outside in her special wheelchair in the small scrap of park that adjoined the hospital, a blanket over her outstretched legs, a nurse standing behind her. Dr. Unsworth had put her on clinical trials with several new drugs, since nothing else was working, and from the dozy look of incomprehension in her eyes, Laurie knew it would be highly unlikely she would understand anything he said. But it was his duty and obligation to try. He looked up at the nurse. She nodded and moved away, giving them privacy.

"Heather?" he said. She kept looking forward through half closed eyes. "Heather, can you hear me?" She gave no indication that she could. "Ted's fine. He's in good hands. Very good hands." He would just have to go ahead and explain to her, and hope that she would understand at least part of it. "Heather, I'm going to have to go away for a while. To Spain. I'd like to stay, but I don't think I'm much good to anybody here. They want me to catch a man, a very dangerous man. He's an escaped German; he's killed two British subjects and he's carrying information that will compromise national security."

He stopped and looked at her carefully. Was any of this getting through to her?

"Heather?"

She slowly turned her head and looked at him, her eyes focusing. She was silent for several moments. Over by the hedge a grounds-keeper was raking up leaves, and out on Knightsbridge a double decker bus passed by. Her lips tried to form words.

"Will you. . .will you carry a gun?" she asked.

He gazed at her intently for several more moments. It seemed like an odd question to ask. Yet not so odd because she had always detested it whenever he carried a gun.

"Yes, I'll carry a gun, darling," he said, though he could have been speaking to brick wall. The grounds-keeper came by and dumped the leaves into the bin. Laurie glanced in his direction and nodded a hello. "After you're discharged Dr. Unsworth will find a permanent spot for you somewhere. And don't worry about Ted. Mrs. Moss looks after him wonderfully." He leaned over, stared at her for several moments, etching her face in his memory, then readjusted her blanket.

"So now we all know what we have to do." He gave her a kiss. "We truly do, darling."

•

By nine o'clock that night the *San Julian*, now no longer in convoy, was less than three hours from

Barcelona. Gil Robles and Goerlitz sat in the captain's cabin drinking the captain's schnapps. They would reach Barcelona around midnight. The Mediterranean was calm, the stars were out and the sea shone with a green phosphorescence. He liked Gil Robles now. The fifty-year-old captain had a great and wide experience, and that was something Goerlitz had always admired in a man.

Gil Robles, who spoke the rough street French of Marseilles, had endless anecdotes. The star-shaped scar on his neck, for instance. There was a reason for that star-shaped scar. He had been assaulted with a pick-axe by a drunken Laotian money lender while transporting one-hundred-and-fifty Malayan workmen to Australia to build a spur line. Gil Robles explained how there had been a fight between the money lender and some of the Malayans over some lost silver dollars.

"It was never resolved," said Gil Robles. "It was believed that the Laotian decided to hold me personally responsible for the loss of his silver dollars, and came in the night to my cabin with a pick-axe he had stolen from the engine room to kill me. Well, *monsieur*, I heard him outside the door before he came in," said Gil Robles. "I got up but he was already in the room and, *Zut alors*, Herr Goerlitz, he had me in the neck with the pointed end of the axe before I knew what had happened. You have no idea what that feels like, *monsieur*. He broke my shoulder, my collar bone, but luckily he missed my jugular vein by an angel's wing."

"So what did you do?"

Gil Robles paused, pouring more schnapps for himself.

"I shot him, *monsieur*, of course."

Gil Robles lifted his new tumbler of schnapps and drained it.

"You shot him," echoed Goerlitz.

"That's right."

The captain opened the drawer of his desk and pulled out a Borchardt-Luger 9mm pistol, as if he were going to demonstrate on Goerlitz. Goerlitz thought it was some kind of joke. But then he saw that he was staring directly into the barrel of that Luger, and that the safety catch was off. He smiled but Gil Robles didn't smile back.

"What's this?" asked Goerlitz, still smiling but feeling alarmed.

Then Gil Robles lowered the gun and grinned.

"Have no fear, Herr Goerlitz, I am just teasing you. Come, it is time to go."

"Go? We're still three hours from port."

"And in port this ship will be searched by the authorities, and searched thoroughly. I'm afraid Señor Ribalta has been guilty of certain irregularities in the past, you see, and now the port authorities keep an eye on him. Come. Get your things. We'll go outside."

Outside, the air was warm and moist, and the swell of the sea was gentle. Off the port side he saw a sixty-foot cabin cruiser anchored a hundred yards away. After a moment he heard its engines start up and saw a man pull the anchor into the boat. The cabin cruiser turned away, making a large curve, then came alongside the ship from behind. She nudged against the barnacle-encrusted keel of the *San Julian* and stopped below the ladder. Goerlitz turned to Gil Robles. There was something odd in the captain's expression.

"Well, sir," said Goerlitz, extending his hand, "thank you for all you've done."

"You've no need to thank me, Herr Goerlitz," said Gil Robles, shaking Goerlitz's hand, "but you're very welcome. Very welcome in any case. Perhaps someday, when the war is over, we shall meet again."

Goerlitz grinned. "Perhaps," he said.

He descended the ladder into the sixty-foot cabin cruiser where he was helped aboard by a man who weighed at least three hundred pounds, and who smelled as if he hadn't had a bath in days. Another man in a pale rose-colored suit and a Panama hat came out of the cabin, a cigarette in his hand. He gazed at Goerlitz with a cold scrutiny, calculation in his eyes.

"I'm Georg Weiss's friend," he finally said in French. "My name is Miguel Ribalta, and I'll be looking after you from here on in. Please, you must come below. It will be safer that way."

"Yes," said Goerlitz. "Yes, of course."

He followed Ribalta past the wheel into the cabin below. They walked through a small kitchen with a sink, shelves of basic food supplies, a first-aid cabinet, and a propane-burning hot-plate. Ribalta pulled a curtain aside and they entered a large room at the bow of the boat. There were four bunks on either side and a table with chairs at the front. There were also some small portholes. He sat down and looked out one of the windows, where he saw the *San Julian*, now no more than a dim wedge with a few twinkling lights on the horizon, pull away from the cabin cruiser, leaving a frothy wake behind. He leaned back and looked at Ribalta. There was the narrowest fringe of mustache on his upper lip, a small roll of fat underneath his chin, and one-inch sideburns in front of each ear. Part of the man's rose-colored jacket had been pulled back — the man rested his arm along the top of the chair next to him — and Goerlitz saw another Luger, identical to Gil Robles's, stuffed into Ribalta's belt.

They had been traveling at nine or ten knots for about two hours when the boat began to slow.

"Ah," said Ribalta, "we are almost there. Why don't you come to the deck, Herr Goerlitz? Barcelona is a pretty sight. We are near the Santa Maria Yacht Club and we have no need to fear the authorities now."

"You will take me to the German Consulate when we reach Barcelona?" he asked.

"Yes, of course, Herr Goerlitz."

They went topside. The buildings and lights of Barcelona climbed a gentle slope. The city was beautiful. He could hear the sound of traffic, saw a few palms silhouetted against a new crescent moon, could smell the scent of lime flowers and salt water.

"Have you ever been to Barcelona, Herr Goerlitz?"

"No, I haven't."

"Well, here you find the true soul of Spain. The soul of the Catalonian. You find people who care about art and music and literature, Herr Goerlitz. Madrid might be the capital, but we are the heart of Spain. There are things in Barcelona you wouldn't be able to find anywhere else in the world."

Goerlitz looked at Ribalta.

"I'm sure there are, Señor Ribalta."

Weiss wouldn't send him into a trap, he thought. Ribalta said he was a friend, but now Goerlitz had his suspicions. He could sense something wasn't quite right. The cruiser slipped into the harbor where the water immediately grew calm.

They puttered along the canal for about ten minutes. There were several other pleasure boats docked around them. The Santa Maria Yacht Club, he thought. They took a sharp turn to port then slowed down. The three hundred pound man, whom he had heard Ribalta call Satrustégui, pulled the throttle back gently and eased the length of the cruiser against the automobile-tire buffer. Satrustégui took the key from the ignition and hung it on a hook just inside the cabin door.

There was a man waiting for them on the pier with a car, a four-door Spanish Seat sedan. The man helped Satrustégui tie the boat down, and then the four of them walked along the pier to the car.

Goerlitz sat in the back with Satrustégui while Ribalta got in the front with the driver.

They drove along the pier and finally came to a large gate. Satrustégui got out and opened the gate, they drove through, Satrustégui shut the gate and got back in. There was a statue of Christopher Columbus standing beside a replica of the Santa Maria. They drove about six blocks and finally came to a wide boulevard. Ribalta turned around.

"These are the Ramblas, Herr Goerlitz. And over there, down the way, is Plaza de Cataluña."

They finally turned right onto a lane-way off the Ramblas, where all the streets sloped toward Barceloneta Beach, and pulled up in front of a series of attached buildings, three storeys tall, with green decorative shutters, white stucco, and old hacienda style roofing.

They got out. The driver took the car to park somewhere. Goerlitz entered the building in front of them and walked up the stairs, Ribalta and Satrustégui behind him.

When they got to the third floor, Ribalta pushed open the door and they entered what Goerlitz instantly recognized as a brothel.

"Where are we going?" asked Goerlitz. "I thought you were taking me to the German consulate."

Ribalta smiled at him and pulled out his gun.

"No, Herr Goerlitz, not yet. You'll be staying with us for a while."

Satrustégui grabbed Goerlitz by the arms. An older woman dressed in a scarlet dressing gown sat behind a desk watching them, unconcerned. Half naked women lounged around what appeared to be some kind of waiting room.

One of the women, a tall dark-eyed beauty with the longest slenderest legs he had ever seen, caught his eye, and smiled. He looked at her as if she might have some explanation for what was happening. But Satrustégui gave him a little shove, propelled him down the hall to a back room. He took one last glance back. The tall dark-eyed beauty had risen from her chair and stood at the end of the hallway staring at him. This was a brothel, he thought. Satrustégui pushed him inside the back room and closed the door just as he caught one last glimpse of Ribalta waving the gun at him. This wasn't the German Consulate. This was a brothel. Goerlitz turned around and looked at the door. Weiss had been right about the boat, he thought, but he hadn't been right about the man.

•

It was late when Ribalta finally got home. The shutters had been closed, and Jala, his Moroccan maid, had left a lamp burning for him in the kitchen. He opened the refrigerator and took out the glass of goat's milk sweetened with sugar, cinnamon, and lime Jala made for him each evening. He sat down at the kitchen table and sighed. He didn't like this. He had checked into Goerlitz today, and through his wide network had learned that Goerlitz was one of England's most wanted men. This was big, and he usually liked big things. But Goerlitz was dangerous, he could see it in the man's eyes, and he would have to be watched and guarded carefully.

And still no call from the *Abwehr* yet. The English seemed to know more about this U-boat commander than the Germans.

Then he heard the soft shuffle of slippers coming down the stairs, and the light at the end of the hall went on. Jala, unaware that he was there, approached, her head and face uncovered. She looked up.

"You don't have to look so alarmed, Jala," he said. "I've seen your face before. You carry your religion too far sometimes."

"I didn't think you would be home tonight."

"Well, I am," he said. "Are there any messages?"

"Yes, there was one message. From a man named Jimenez. He wants to see you."

"I know no Jimenez. Did he leave a number?"

"No. He said he would get in touch with you."

He took a sip of his goat's milk, looking at her, admiring her. Maybe some day, he thought, they would be lovers, but not yet.

"Was there any message from the German Consulate?" he asked.

"No," said Jala. "Only Jimenez. No others."

Chapter 21

The *San Julian* was seized, impounded, and searched under the direction of Luis Jimenez by seventeen armed Spanish civil guards the moment she docked in Barcelona. The crew were rounded up and every last one of them questioned. They were shown a prison photograph of an escaped U-boat commander, and told that the British authorites would be grateful, and even reward any information leading to the recapture of this man. But every last one, right down to the third engineer, denied any knowledge of the prisoner.

The seventeen civil guards searched the *San Julian* thoroughly but failed to turn up any trace of Goerlitz. Captain Gil Robles knew Goerlitz was no more than a half dozen blocks away in the back room of a three-storey building off the Ramblas.

Luis Jimenez called off the search of the *San Julian* around four in the morning. He hadn't found Goerlitz, but after questioning, there had been two breaks. All the crew members remembered the tall blond South African, Pieter Van Gessel, and consistent with the South

African's story, there were two cots in the pump room. Jimenez looked at his watch. The night flight from Madrid to Barcelona would arrive in just over two hours. Gerald Laurie was on that flight. He could tell his friend that if the trail wasn't exactly hot, it was at least still warm.

•

Goerlitz walked from the bed and put his ear to the door, where he heard Ribalta talking to Satrustégui at the end of the hall and the muffled voices of women in the other rooms. It had been two days. He tried the door quietly but it wouldn't move. He listened for a moment more, and with a shrug, walked to the window. It was nailed shut with a two-by-four. An unnecessary precaution because he wasn't going to jump three storeys to the laneway below. He wasn't far from the harbor. He knew that now.

He turned from the window, sat on the creaky bed, and looked around the room. The walls were papered with a flower design of daisies and bluebells. A chunk of ceiling plaster had fallen out, revealing the slats below, and a water stain spread like a map of a new continent in the corner. Tawdry red curtains hung on either side of the window, a threadbare area rug covered the warped hardwood floor, and a portrait of the Virgin Mary, a cheap one bought in a bargain store, hung on the wall above the wrought-iron bed.

He stood up and took the two rolls of film out of his pocket. They were still safe in their wrapping of masking tape and wax paper. He pulled out the photograph of Ute, unwrapped the paper, and looked at her for a long time.

The woman in the photograph didn't look like the kind of woman he would marry, and now, as he gazed at her aquiline nose, bright blue eyes, and slender jaw, he wondered if his wife was really as he imagined her to be. He wanted a chance to find out. If only he had been able to break away aboard the cruiser. He couldn't help thinking of that crusier, how Satrustégui had left the key hanging on a hook in the cabin, how with that cruiser he would be able to get to Vichy-controlled France with no questions asked, and ultimately back to Ute.

How did Ute manage to be so pleasant all the time? If only he were lucky enough to have such gentleness. He thought of the boat rides they had taken along the Isar through Munich, how she had rested her head against his shoulder, and how, when the weather was cold, and the wind blew up the river, her cheeks began to glow with two doll-like pink spots. Munich. Was there any place so beautiful? There was only one Munich and there was only one Ute and that Ute was in Munich, and both were beautiful. She would have to forgive him. He would have to make it clear to her just how strong his feelings for her were, and they would have to solve their differences.

He finally put the photograph away and lay on the bed with his hands behind his head. He was powerless. In prison. He remembered the bitter argument he and his father had had the evening before he had left to join the Weddigen Flotilla in the Baltic, how he had defiantly claimed that by joining the U-boat arm of the *Kriegsmarine* he was gaining his freedom, fighting for the destiny of the Reich. Herr Goerlitz said it took a wise man to know the difference between imprisonment and freedom. The destiny of the Reich. How hollow those words sounded now, here in this bordello room in Barcelona. His father, in his guarded and elliptical way, had once called the Reich a prison of ideas. The older he got the more reasonable his father's suggestions seemed to become. Yet was he really in another prison, or tomorrow would he find the German Consul at the door ready to take him home? He had been here two days, had only been allowed to go out once, for a stroll up the Ramblas to Plaza de Cataluña and back, Satrustégui guarding him with a concealed gun. There had been strange men here last night, possibly police, but he wasn't sure, only that they weren't regular customers. It was just about time to take things into his own hands, he thought. He was tired of waiting.

Around three o'clock in the morning there came a soft knock at the door. He was still awake, trying to figure out what he was going to do. He sat up and listened. Again, there were three light knocks.

"*Señor?*" a voice called.

A woman, thought Goerlitz.

"*Señor alemán.*"

He got out of bed and walked to the door.

"Hello?" he said.

He heard a key slide into the door. The lock clicked, the knob turned, and door swung open. The same woman he had seen two days ago, the beautiful one, stood in the doorway. At the end of the hall he saw Satrustégui sitting at the desk talking to one of the customers. From the stairwell he heard the sound of distant music. The air in the hallway smelled of beer and cigarettes. The woman wore a red full-length negligee with black fur trim, a pair of high heels, and had a black purse around her shoulder. Nothing more. She was ravishing, in a way only Spanish women could be ravishing, her black hair pulled back from her face into a bun, red studs in her ears to match her shining red lips.

Before he could say anything she stepped inside and closed the door.

"What is this?" he said in French.

"*Qué?*"

"What are you doing here?"

She put her hand on his chest and gently pushed him

toward the bed, not understanding.

"*Un vaso de vino tinto?*"

He didn't understand her. Only when she pulled a bottle of wine from her purse was it clear what she wanted to do. He couldn't help looking at her breasts, perfectly visible through the thin red material. She took a corkscrew out of her purse and handed both corkscrew and bottle to Goerlitz.

"*Abierto, Señor alemán.*"

He could already smell wine on her breath. He opened the bottle and handed it back to her. She took a long swallow then gave the bottle to Goerlitz. He looked at the bottle, raised it to his lips, and drank.

They shared the bottle over the course of the next fifteen minutes, and he learned, among other things, that her name was Christa, that she spoke only Spanish, and that she had an hour or two off and thought he might like some company. But it was more than that, he saw, or else she wouldn't have come in here dressed the way she had. She sat next to him on the bed, her hip touching his thigh. She was sensational. During all his shore leaves in Paris he had never seen anything like this. And yet this was different than Paris now. She said something in Spanish, but except for maybe a word or two, he wasn't able to understand. This was different than Paris because in Paris he had never considered his responsibility toward Ute.

"*Christa,*" he said to her.

"*Si, señor?*"

"*Christa, no.*"

"*Si, señor?*"

She raised the bottle to her lips, for a moment not drinking, and cast a sidelong glance at him. The implication was more than clear. He reached up and took one of her breasts in his hand. Much larger than Ute's, and perfectly shaped, a dream come true, but lacking the electricity Ute had. Christa put the bottle aside and lay next to him. She reached under his wool sweater and began rubbing his chest, her hand finally working its way to his pants. She began rubbing him there. The sensation of the alcohol and her hand together was like an old friend, like those times in Paris, but better because Christa was so beautiful. He reached underneath her negligee, responding automatically, then searched for her lips. In a moment they were locked in a kiss. She slid her hand beneath his belt, soon found the uncircumsized hood of his penis and began stroking it. How beautiful, he thought. He hadn't been this hard since the last time he had made love to Ute.

But then he gave her a shove with his arm. He didn't need this. He didn't want this. He only wanted Ute. Christa backed off, suddenly fearful. He pointed at the door.

"Go," he said. "Please go."

She looked at him for several moments, as if she couldn't understand why this was happening, then gathered up her purse and high heels and walked to the door, where she turned and looked at him again. He could tell he had hurt her feelings, not a good thing, especially because he had been planning to use her somehow to get out of here.

Christa opened the door and let herself out quietly, locking it behind her.

When he was sure she had gone he got up and tried it. Locked. Once again in a prison. And it was sad because for a moment, with Christa in the room, a woman he would never see again, he had been, at least for a few moments, free.

•

At eleven o'clock the next morning, as pre-arranged by telephone call, Laurie and Jimenez found Ribalta among the pious old ladies on the steps of Valencia Cathedral, a flamingo among crows, feeding the caged cat the brethren of the cathedral kept as a mascot for their order. Westmoreland stood watch outside Ribalta's house overlooking Barceloneta Beach in case Goerlitz might leave from there. Taylor was outside the shipping office. And a contingent of Guardia Civil covered the German Consulate on the off chance Goerlitz might flee there.

"Ah, yes, Señor Jimenez," said Ribalta. "Thank you for your call. Captain Gil Robles was telling me about you. What can I do for you, sir?"

"I think you can do a lot for us, Señor Ribalta. This is Inspector Laurie, from British Naval Intelligence. Do you speak English?"

"Your friend is an Englishman? Well, perhaps he can meet me halfway. Can he speak French?"

"I believe he can." Jimenez switched to French. "Inspector, this is Miguel Ribalta. Could you manage your questions in French?"

"I think I could," said Laurie, in the precise academic French he had learned in grammar school. "We're looking for a man believed to have been aboard the *San Julian*. A German by the name of Goerlitz."

Ribalta leaned over and fed another bit of fish to the caged cat, who pawed at it ungratefully.

"So Gil Robles told me."

"There was a South African taken aboard midway through the voyage after his ship was torpedoed. He says he saw Goerlitz on the *San Julian*. We've had corroboration from Liverpool that a man fitting the German's description was asking about the *San Julian* at the dock board office. But Gil Robles says he's never seen Goerlitz in his life before."

"This is what I like about the British," said Ribalta. "So. . .so unconfrontational. So reasonable. Well, gentlemen. I must tell you, and please don't mention this to my captain, but Gil Robles is often a notorious liar."

"We know that." Laurie saw that Ribalta, a man in his early forties, was going to have his joke about this. "We also know that you've been booked on passage brokering charges in the past."

"I should remind you, inspector, that you're in the sovereign territory of Spain and that in fact you're breaking the law trying to apprehend Goerlitz on Spanish soil."

"Did you let him go?" interrupted Jimenez.

"Gentlemen, why don't we go for a stroll so we can talk this thing over?"

They descended the cathedral steps and made their way to the Ramblas in the heart of the old town where vendors sold their goods from open air stalls. To Laurie, it was clear Ribalta wanted only one thing. Money. So Laurie didn't procrastinate. There were many deep questions in life, he thought, but there was only one question Ribalta understood.

"How much?" asked Laurie.

Those two words changed Ribalta's behavior immediately. His eyes narrowed, his lips hardened, and as they walked up the Ramblas past the piranhas, lemurs, and snakes the pet vendors sold from their stalls, Ribalta began to barter, just as the vendors bartered with their customers. A price was set, half right now, and half when he delivered Goerlitz. They would meet tonight at the *San Julian*. No witnesses, no Spanish authorities, just the money and Goerlitz. And, of course, still time to hear something from the Germans.

"Gentlemen," concluded Ribalta in a tone that suggested he only wanted the best for everybody, "you won't be disappointed. Trust me."

Chapter 22

By seven o'clock that night drizzle had begun to fall from low-flying clouds. Having slept most of the day, Goerlitz paced before the window, fresh with nervous energy. From down the laneway he heard a tram clank along the Ramblas. He stopped pacing and looked out the window. Three dogs trotted by, urgent with purpose. If only there were some way he could get out of here. If only he could get down to that back alley somehow.

He gripped the two-by-four nailed against the window and, giving several good yanks, finally pried it away. He listened, thinking Satrustégui might have heard, but it was quiet outside in the hall. He pulled the window open and looked down to the alley below him. A pile of discarded boxes lay not too far away. If he could manage to swing himself from a hang-jump position so the boxes would break his fall. . .but that was stupid. The boxes were too far away. He would land on the wet paving stones and break his neck.

He walked to the bed and pulled the covers away, thinking he might make a rope from the sheets, but testing their strength he found they tore easily. He tried the covers but they were just as threadbare as the sheets and he was able to rip them without much effort. In growing frustration he walked back to the window, sat on the sill, swung his feet out, carefully turned around and, gripping the sill, slid halfway out, his knees scraping along the stucco of the building. A few pigeons flew out from under the eaves, startling him. It was too far, he thought. Now that he was halfway out he got a much better sense of how high it was. He would never make it. He would have to try something else.

Just as he was pulling himself back up he heard footsteps coming down the hall. He took a chance. Using his whole body he swung out from the wall to the left and let go of the ledge. He dropped fast, much faster than he had expected, much faster than the jumps they had been required to make at the U-boat training camp on the island of Danholm near Stralsund, and his stomach rose and pressed against his diaphragm in a nauseating dislocation. He tried to make a rolling fall into the boxes, managing to land just within the edge of the pile, but even sö, he banged his knee so hard it sent a tingling shockwave through his entire body. He huffed great whooshes of air, sprang up, and hopped around on one leg, holding his injured knee with both hands. He uttered a long uncontrollable string of German obscenities.

"Hold it right there, Herr Goerlitz," called Ribalta from the third floor window.

But Goerlitz began to hobble away as fast as he could. Oh, but damn, does that hurt. At least it was taking some weight. Which meant it wasn't broken. From a hobble he went to a limping run. He expected gunshots any moment but none came. A wave of exhilaration swept over him. Maybe he was going to get away with this. He scrambled up the alleyway, using the crumbling stucco walls of the buildings for support.

He turned the corner. And there was Satrustégui. Standing there with a three-foot length of two-by-four. Goerlitz turned and ran the other way, but he couldn't run fast with his hurt knee, and was no match for a giant like Satrustégui, who, though enormously fat, had a tremendously long stride. Suddenly a large arm was around his head and he was lifted by his neck off the ground. Satrustégui cast away the board, grabbed Goerlitz's arm, and twisted it behind his back. Goerlitz grunted as the giant pushed his wrist up his spine. Satrustégui marched Goerlitz to the front of the building and up the stairs.

Ribalta stood in the front room and pointed his gun at Goerlitz the moment Satrustégui dragged him in.

"I appreciate your determination, *monsieur*. But if I were you I wouldn't try something like that again. Now, then, do you drive, Herr Goerlitz?" asked Ribalta.

"Drive?"

It seemed like an odd question under the circumstances.

"Yes, drive. A car."

"Yes."

"Good. Keep your hands at your sides and come this way."

"Where are you taking me?"

"To the German Consulate, my friend. Your fellow countrymen have been very generous."

Goerlitz walked down the hall. Ribalta pointed the gun at his back and gave him a shove. A few of the girls looked out of their rooms. Then Christa came out of her room, a blue housecoat hastily thrown around her shoulders, her face red and angry, and marched toward him, almost crazily. She slapped him across the face as hard as she could.

"Christa?" he said.

She spat on the floor.

"*Vete a freir espárragos!*" shouted the woman.

Ribalta shrugged.

"I think you've offended her, Herr Goerlitz," he said. "Christa isn't used to being turned away." Ribalta jabbed the gun in his back. "Come on. Get going."

At the top of the stairs, Satrustégui and Ribalta spoke in Spanish for a few moments. Then Satrustégui went back inside and Goerlitz and Ribalta walked downstairs.

"*Très bien,*" said Ribalta, opening the door of his Seat coupe. He handed Goerlitz the keys. "You drive."

They got in the car. Ribalta had the Luger drawn and pointed at Goerlitz's chest.

Ribalta directed Goerlitz down a narrow side-street to the Ramblas, then along the Ramblas where the palms seemed to sweat dully in the neon light, to Plaza de Cataluña. From there, they meandered through the Gothic Quarter toward the docks. That's when Goerlitz knew Ribalta had lied about the German Consulate. The German Consulate, though it could be many places, was unlikely to be near the docks. A trap. A chill crawled over his back, like those silent moments aboard U-93 when the depth charges were about to fall. The uncanny, instinctive sense of danger.

He tightened his grip on the wheel. Up ahead there was a wide square with a statue and a fountain in the middle. As they came out of the laneway into the square, Goerlitz wrenched the transmission into fourth gear, stepped on the accelerator, and veered to the left. The car jumped over the curb toward the fountain. Goerlitz turned sharply right, smashing the passenger side into the lip of the fountain. Ribalta cried out as glass shattered all around them. Goerlitz jumped out of the car, unhurt, and ran across the square to a lane-way, running with a limp, his heart pounding. He looked over his shoulder. Ribalta was getting out of the driver's side. The Seat's engine raced on and on. The muffler billowed great clouds of blue smoke into the sky.

Goerlitz heard the *crack-crack* of pistol reports, then felt a stinging pain burrow into his back. Dumbfounded and disbelieving, Goerlitz watched as a gusher of blood erupted from his shoulder. He felt sick to his stomach and his legs began to wobble. There were more pistol reports. A bullet ripped into his arm. The pain from this wound, because of the extensive powder burn, was so fierce tears came to his eyes. He was out of breath from the pain, and his legs, now as rubbery as elastic bands, gave out from underneath him, and he fell to the wet paving stones, scraping his chin.

He closed his eyes and tried to quiet his breathing, his mind racing as he heard Ribalta's running footsteps approach him from behind. He held his breath and lay perfectly still. Ribalta knelt beside him, breathing phlegmatically. He muttered something in Spanish, something about the Virgin Mary, then shook Goerlitz by the shoulder again.

Goerlitz suddenly lashed out at the Spaniard, knocking him over, sending the gun skittering across the cobblestones. Goerlitz dove for the gun, but just as he was turning around to fire with his good arm, Ribalta, grunting, tackled him below the waist. The gun went off. The bullet shattered a large lead-paned window in the building next to them.

Goerlitz gripped the pistol tightly while Ribalta clung to his legs, and brought the butt down against Ribalta's temple. Anger overwhelmed Goerlitz. In relentless fury, he smashed the pistol butt against the Spaniard's head repeatedly and stopped only when Ribalta no longer moved. Goerlitz struggled to his feet, his teeth clenched, his eyes glaring, and looked at the Spaniard. He lifted the pistol and pointed it at Ribalta's head.

Three or four years ago he would have killed the man outright. Back then he believed the Spanish were just another species of *Untermenschen*, just as the Slavs were. But he lowered the gun without firing. In one last burst of anger, he kicked Ribalta in the stomach and stumbled away, weak from loss of blood.

•

Laurie grew anxious as the eight o'clock appointment time he had set with Ribalta came and went. He looked at Jimenez, Taylor, and Westmoreland. Their faces were composed and grim. As the minutes passed, Laurie began to pace. Eight-thirty, then quarter-to-nine. Jimenez had deployed some guards to take over watch from Taylor and Westmoreland outside the shipping office and Ribalta's house while the others still guarded the German Consulate. Something had gone wrong. There was no question about it.

His suspicions were confirmed when, at nine-thirty, Ribalta walked up the gangplank of the *San Julian* on shaky legs with the side of his head badly bruised and bleeding.

•

As Goerlitz stumbled through the back alleys of Barcelona, a dark red stain spreading over the left side of his wool sweater, he found it difficult to collect his thoughts or think of any definite plan. In the distance he heard sirens. He ran a few more blocks and finally crouched, exhausted, in a doorway not far from Plaza de Cataluña. He pulled the neck of his sweater away, his hand getting covered with blood, and looked at his shoulder. A clean penetration just below the collar bone, in his back and out his chest, too high to touch any vital organs, a dark red hole oozing blood. His shoulder wound was far more serious than the graze he had taken on the arm, yet it was his arm wound that bled the most, the flow of blood out-pacing the production of coagulant considerably. Pulling off his belt, he rolled up his sleeve, and tied a tourniquet. He watched his arm for several minutes until the flow of blood diminished and the edges of the wound grew gummy with a purple scum.

He put his sleeve over the belt then wiped his hands on the wet paving stones to wash the blood away. The drizzle had turned into a persistent rain and headlights from passing traffic in Plaza de Cataluña polished the street with a neon-reflecting gloss. He took a few deep breaths, and making sure the Luger was securely hidden in his pocket, walked into the square and hailed the next taxi.

He sat in the front beside the driver and asked in a mixture of French and what little Spanish he knew for the driver to take him to the German Consulate, that they wouldn't stop there but drive slowly by. Then he would decide what he would do. The driver, a jowly short man in his fifties with a black mustache and a dark green beret, looked at Goerlitz warily, fighting to conceal his alarm.

The German Consulate was a narrow building, five storeys high, squeezed between two others in what was obviously a better section of town. When Goerlitz saw the blood-red banner with black swastika on a white circle hanging from a flagpole above the door, he felt a mixture of pride and shame, pride for the things that could have been and shame for the things that were. They drove slowly past. Something wasn't right. There weren't any German guards around, just Spanish ones. A man came out of the consulate and one of the Spanish guards checked his identification. Guards stood watch across the street and there were two police cruisers parked nearby.

"Go around again," Goerlitz said to the driver, in a rough approximation of Spanish.

Goerlitz made the driver stop the taxi on the other

side of the block. Why were there so many Spanish guards standing outside the consulate and why did they check that man's identification as he was coming out? Could it be that the Spanish authorities were cooperating with this man called Laurie? It didn't seem possible. Britain had supported the Loyalists during the Civil War, and some of the Royal Navy's supply ships had been sunk in the Bay of Biscay in 1937 by the Nationalists, and even though six years had passed, this was still hardly grounds for cooperation. Yet the *Guardia Civil* were obviously there for a reason. He couldn't help thinking of what Hitler had once said about Spain, that she was irresolute and that she would decide her loyalties once the outcome of the war was clear. He glanced at the driver. He had a calm gentle face, looked as if he were a family man who went to Mass every Sunday. Goerlitz pulled out his Luger and pointed it at the man.

"Out," he said in Spanish.

The man's eyes widened and he looked at the gun. He said something in a pleading voice but most of it was incomprehensible to Goerlitz. Two years ago he wouldn't have thought twice about making a victim of this man, but now he hated it, pitied this man and pitied himself. The driver got out. So did Goerlitz. Using a *patois* of broken Spanish and French, and a series of gestures, he directed the driver to get in the passenger seat while he himself got behind the wheel. He drove slowly around the block, feeling weak and faint from loss of blood, trying to fight the pain of his bullet wounds, knowing that if he didn't have attention soon he would pass out or go into shock.

When he rounded the corner, a few *Guardia Civil* stepped from the sidewalk into the road and waved him toward the curb. Another drove his motorcycle-and-sidecar into the middle of the street as a kind of road block. Goerlitz pulled the taxi over and stopped. One of the guards came to his window. The guard saw the blood all over his sweater, drew his rifle immediately, and pointed it at Goerlitz.

"I would like to see the German Consul," Goerlitz said in French, hoping the guard would understand.

The guard replied in French. "Get out. We have a warrant for your arrest."

"It is my right to enter the German Consulate and see the consul. I am a German citizen and I have broken no laws in this country. I have every right to see my consul."

The guard locked his rifle, his eyes hardening.

"Get out," he said.

Goerlitz hesitated one more moment then slammed the car into gear. The taxi jumped away from the curb in a noisy screeching of tires. The guard on the motorcycle stood up in the sidecar and fired his rifle into the windshield, puncturing a spider-web like hole through the glass. The taxi driver cried out, ducked, crossed his arms in front of his face. Goerlitz kept his hands on the wheel and his foot pressed hard against the accelerator, driving straight for the motorcycle. The guard's eyes widened in horror. He dropped his rifle and jumped from the sidecar just as Goerlitz plowed into the motorcycle. The motorcycle tumbled out of the way as if it were a toy, rolling over three times until it landed on its side, sidecar wheel spinning slowly in the air.

Goerlitz shifted into second, then third, cursing because the old taxi didn't have the same pickup as his Mercedes-Benz sports coupe in Munich. Some guards fired warning shots into the air. The taxi driver slowly lifted his head and looked at Goerlitz with dull petrified eyes. Goerlitz felt sorry for the man. But there was nothing he could do about it now. Whether he liked it or not, the driver was coming along for the ride.

Goerlitz shifted into fourth. He looked in the rear-view mirror. Two patrol cars skidded out from the curb and began to follow him. One of the cars veered down a side-street while the other one kept after him. He thought they might be setting up an ambush so he took the next left in a squealing of tires. He had never been to Barcelona before and had no idea where he was going, only that he had to get to Ribalta's yacht. He followed the slope of the land like water following a natural drainage pattern and soon he recognized the harbor district. The single patrol car was still behind him and he couldn't understand why more hadn't joined the chase.

When he saw the statue of Christopher Columbus beside the replica of the Santa Maria, he knew where he was, not far from the yacht club where Ribalta's cruiser was docked. The engine started to make a funny sound and the taxi began to slow down. He looked at the driver. The driver shrugged nervously and smiled with weak lips.

"It is an old car," he said in English.

Goerlitz jammed in the clutch and shifted into third, but the gears didn't engage and the engine raced in a high-pitched howl as the car finally rolled to a stop. He had probably stripped some of the transmission with his reckless shifting of gears.

He toppled out of the car, dizzy from blood loss, just as the patrol car squealed in a fish-tailing skid behind him. The *Guardia Civil* got out, their rifles ready. Goerlitz drew the door of the taxi open, and using it as a shield, pulled out the Luger. It was a gun he could use well. He was an expert marksman with a pistol, especially the 9 mm Luger. He fired once, then twice, and one of the guards fell over, blood spilling from his mouth. The other fired a few rounds then waited in silence for several moments before he went over to help the wounded guard. Goerlitz looked at the taxi driver, who was cowering in his seat, his hands covering his face. To take him along on the boat would just complicate matters. He pointed the gun at the man.

"Get out." Then in English he said, "Put your hands on your head and walk towards them."

The man didn't understand. Goerlitz put his hands on his head then pointed toward the *Guardia Civil*.

The man put his hands on his head tentatively, then nodded.

Goerlitz nodded back.

The man got out of the car and, trembling, almost shyly, walked toward the patrol car.

"*Adios, amigos,*" said Goerlitz.

In a small and relieved voice the man said, "*Adios.*"

Goerlitz got to his feet and hurried away, stuffing the gun into his pocket. He had only one thought in mind. Ribalta's cruiser. The taxi engine raced on and on. Satrustégui had left the key hanging in the cabin. If there were enough gas he could easily reach France, where the Vichy authorities would make sure he got proper medical attention.

Chapter 23

The other patrol car had gone to the *San Julian*. From there, radio contact was established with the chasing car, and Laurie and the others learned of the brief fire-fight, and of the stolen taxi. Laurie, through Jimenez's interpretation into Spanish, assured the guard at the other end of the radio that an ambulance was on the way for his friend, and reminded him that no reports of this incident would be filed under any circumstance.

Then Laurie, Jimenez, Taylor, and Westmoreland loaded their Webley revolvers — in Jimenez's case it was a Browning Mark IV — got in the patrol car, and drove toward the yacht club.

"Remember, gentlemen," said Laurie. "Shoot on sight."

The ambulance was already at the other car when they passed by. The taxi's engine still ran on and on as the driver looked into the open hood. A tow truck was just pulling up. There was no sign of Goerlitz.

•

The key wasn't there. Goerlitz hammered at the ignition casing of the cabin cruiser with a crowbar he had found on the deck until he broke it apart. He would have to hot-wire the ignition. It was so dark he couldn't see anything. He felt his way into the cabin where he fumbled for a box of matches, finding them on the shelf next to the sink, then he went back to the boat's helm.

It took several matches before he could identify the proper wires, especially because the wind kept blowing the matches out. He yanked the two necessary wires. He made hooks out of the frayed end of each wire. His shoulder was growing stiff and his body temperature was dropping. He climbed like an old man over the side of the boat, weak and unsure of himself, untied her painters, climbed back in, and shoved away with an oar. The docks were deserted.

Groping the side rail for support, he struggled back to the helm, knelt beside the ignition, and joined the two copper hooks he had made together. Sparks flashed. There was a wheeze from the engine. He twisted the wires together, wincing at the voltage he felt in his fingers. The engine sputtered, then coughed into life. Goerlitz clutched the wheel with his good arm, stood up, and pushed the throttle forward. The engine heaved and the boat moved away from the dock.

He meandered through the harbor and reached the open sea ten minutes later.

The rain was steady, the surf was high and laced with white foam, but by no means unnavigable in a boat this big. He looked at the dials. He passed a few other luxury cruisers coming into Barcelona, probably because the water was too rough to enjoy. The gas tank was only half full. He looked at the compass. With the tank only half full he would have to stay close to shore. But even so he should be able to make it. He swung the boat north and headed toward France.

•

Laurie and the others were just nearing the Santa Maria Yacht Club when Ribalta pointed out to the channel, his eyes widening.

"That's my boat," he said in French. "He's taken my fucking boat."

"Are you sure?" shouted Laurie.

"Of course I'm sure. That's my fucking boat."

Laurie turned to Jimenez.

"Where's harbor police?"

Jimenez pointed.

"Just up there. They have a sizable cutter. We should still be able to catch him."

By the time they had filed their reports with harbor police, and the ninety-foot cutter was churning its way through the channel, rocking the anchored boats, Goerlitz was already several miles up the coast. He would go to France, of that Laurie was certain. And Laurie was confident that the harbor police cutter would be able to catch up to Goerlitz sooner or later.

•

Goerlitz kept his good arm on the wheel while the one with the gunshot wound hung limply at his side. The pain was searing, overpowering. He was faint and his stomach heaved uneasily.

The waves carried the cabin cruiser up and down, tossing it from peak to furrow in a ceaseless heaving of water. Occasionally a huge breaker crashed against the bow, cascaded over the cabin, and drenched him with a shower of salt water.

He was perhaps an hour north of Barcelona when off

the starboard side and maybe a mile behind him he saw a red light closing in.

After a few more minutes, he made out, through the spray and rain, an unarmed cutter of about ninety feet. The cutter was closing in fast and atop its bridge he now saw small radar apparatus. Goerlitz pressed the throttle forward and the boat churned a knot or two higher. But it hardly had the speed or power this cutter did. Still it took the cutter at least five or ten minutes to close the gap in any measurable way, and that gave Goerlitz time to think.

A crackling came over his radio and he heard a man's voice, the Englishman, Laurie.

"This is Inspector Gerald Laurie of British Naval Intelligence. You are to stop your vessel. We know you are wounded. Repeat. You are to surrender your boat. We can give you help. If you do not surrender we will ram you."

Goerlitz didn't respond. Instead he slowed the boat then put the engine in neutral and let it drift. He picked up the crowbar he had used to smash the ignition casing and went into the cabin. He turned off the small light, crawled into one of the narrow top bunks, and drew the curtains shut. The boat heaved mercilessly, now that she no longer had the engine to steady her, and in the dark, with no reference point, Goerlitz began to feel terribly sick. He took out his Luger and gripped the crowbar. He lay on his side waiting, concentrating, forcing the sickness away.

Soon he heard the cutter's engine. They must be puzzled, he thought. The boat would appear completely empty. They wouldn't be able to hear the murmuring of the idling engine over the heavy battering surf, and even if they did they would still be mystified.

Over the rush and noise of the sea he heard a megaphoned voice.

"Hermann Paul Goerlitz, this is Inspector Gerald Laurie of British Naval Intelligence. If you are there, please come out. If you are too weak, do not resist. We will come aboard and assist you. I repeat, do not attempt to struggle."

Goerlitz got up on his knees in the bunk and readied the crowbar in one hand and the Borchardt-Luger pistol in the other as he heard the cutter come next to the cabin cruiser. In a moment, he felt grappling poles tug the cabin cruiser alongside and heard some men jumping aboard.

"Goerlitz?" a voice called. "Goerlitz, are you there?"

He heard the cabin door open and through the thin curtains saw the beam of a flashlight flicker over the shelves of supplies and the fresh-water tank. Once again the adrenalin rushed through his muscles. He grew as hard as steel, and he forgot about his pain. He could make out the dim silhouettes of three figures, two in uniform, the other wearing a fedora, the ones in uniforms carrying rifles.

"Goerlitz?" The voice was almost a whisper. It was Laurie. The three figures moved slowly forward. "Goerlitz?"

Three bullets, he thought. He held the straight end of the crowbar. Ready. . .ready. . .the first figure was in a uniform. The hooked end of the crowbar would sink like a knife through butter into his skull. . .ready. . . .

But then his grip loosened and the crowbar began to slide from his hand as darkness and faintness overpowered him. The noise of the sea faded and the pain of his wounds came back and he tried to shake his dizziness away but he couldn't. The first uniformed figure passed him.

Goerlitz shoved the Luger deep into his pocket as the crowbar slipped from his hand. He groaned. Darkness enveloped him. He fell through the curtains of the bunk on top of Laurie and heaved a nauseated sigh as he slid to the floor.

All was silent. All was oblivion. But then the sound of the waves came rushing back, louder than he had ever heard them before, and he regained consciousness with an intolerable pain at the base of his skull. Animal instinct took over. He felt someone's hands trying to lift him under the arms. He saw, in front of him, the two guards looking down. His mind cleared, his muscles tensed, and with a sudden deadly quickness he pulled the Luger from his pocket. Two muzzle flashes lit the cabin in blinding succession. The bangs were deafening. The two harbor police toppled over, both dead. Goerlitz grabbed the edge of the lower bunk and pulled himself up. He turned around just in time to see Laurie reaching into his jacket for his gun.

Goerlitz snatched the crowbar from the top bunk and threw it as hard as he could at the Englishman's face. Laurie fell back, stunned, a grunt escaping from his throat as the crowbar hit his forehead. Goerlitz dove on top of him and started pummeling his head with the butt of his Luger. The seventh or eighth hit was a well-placed blow to the inspector's right temple and sent Laurie into semi-consciousness.

Goerlitz stopped. He was breathing violently and sweating hard but he no longer felt faint. Like so many times aboard U-93, when all had seemed hopeless, and death just a moment away, and they had been forced to work or fight for twenty hours at a time without rest, breathing only the thinnest oxygen, he again found that reserve of strength, astonishing and miraculous, that he always found. He gathered the harbor police rifles and Laurie's revolver while Laurie still lay semi-conscious on the floor of the cabin, and, smashing the glass in one of the small windows near the front, slid them out the jagged hole into the sea. He then yanked a moaning

Laurie to his feet and, jabbing the Luger in his back, knowing he had only one bullet left, put his arm around Laurie's neck and marched him out the cabin door.

The harbor police still had the cruiser pulled close with grappling poles. He saw Ribalta standing near the back of the deck in his pink shirt. There were three other men in civilian clothes. Five harbor police pointed their rifles at them. Goerlitz jabbed his gun harder into Laurie's spine.

"Tell them to go away," he said. "Tell them not to follow or I'll kill you." Laurie hesitated. "Go on."

"Taylor," called Laurie. "Taylor, Westmoreland. Go back to Barcelona." The waves knocked the boats together. "I'm going to have to handle this by myself. I'll radio you when it's all over. Go on. Let go of the boat. And don't follow."

For a man with a gun at his back, Goerlitz was surprised by Laurie's bravado. The harbor police let go of the boat and she drifted away. Goerlitz pulled Laurie toward the helm where the wheel twitched nervously back and forth in the frantic swell. The huge inboard motor continued to idle.

"Turn north and keep along the coast," said Goerlitz.

"And the minute you can't see the coast I'll have a bullet through my head. Is that what you have in mind?"

"That remains to be seen, doesn't it? You might live, Laurie. You just might live. I have no wish to kill you. I have no wish to kill anybody. But if I have to, I will. Now, get behind the wheel."

The English inspector got behind the wheel and shoved the throttle up. Ribalta's cabin cruiser veered away from the cutter. Goerlitz stood beside him holding the side rail, gun pointed at Laurie's head while he watched the cutter grow smaller and smaller. Soon all that could be seen was the cutter's red light, and after a while even that minute marker seemed to disappear in the swirling grey darkness of rain and spray.

Now that the situation was under control the adrenalin began to drain from Goerlitz's body. He sat down on the bench along the railing. If he could only stay awake.

He kept his eyes on Laurie as the boat pounded over the waves. Laurie was hunched over the wheel, his thin dark hair ravaged by the wind and rain, his teeth clenched in what Goerlitz saw was determination. Though his face was pale, almost cream-colored, like a portrait by Vermeer or Gainsborough, crimson spots had appeared on both cheeks and on the tip of his thin but rather long nose. His deep brown eyes shone with the intensity of a bloodhound or beagle on the hunt.

From time to time Goerlitz got up and checked the compass, making sure Laurie kept the proper bearing. The east coast of Spain loomed to their left as they plowed north over the waves, like a giant impenetrable bank of clouds broken only by the occasional sprinkling of lights. Goerlitz, exhausted, beyond exhaustion, started to doze, had bizarre half-waking dreams. He saw the parlor of his father's country house with its harp and grand piano, heavy red curtains, and bulky furniture, and the somber portraits of his ancestors — barons and counts from the days when things like aristocratic titles had mattered in Germany. His father sat at the grand piano while Ute stood in front singing Schubert's *Der Tod und das Mädchen*. But then the parlor disappeared, and his father and wife were out on the waves, transposed from the tranquility of the country house to the raging dark Mediterranean. And they were calling him. They wondered where he was. They were worried about him. This half-sleep continued for some time. He would always shake himself awake. He was cold, so miserably cold.

He was falling asleep. He saw Ute sitting in her favorite corner by the window with the box of geraniums in their Munich apartment on Liebigstrasse working on the sweater she was going to give his father for Christmas. She looked up, her blue eyes shining, and smiled. He missed her. He thought of her in her favorite dress, the blue one with the pretty white swirls, and how well it matched her eyes, of the pearl necklace he had bought for her last Christmas and how she had been overwhelmed by what she had called his extravagance. She still hadn't fully comprehended that the Goerlitz family had money. Her family, during the Weimar years, had always had to scrimp and scrounge.

•

Laurie glanced over at Goerlitz as he gripped the wheel of the cabin cruiser. He had to admire the man's endurance, his single-mindedness, but did he really think he was going to get away with this, that he would actually be allowed to escape to France? Why didn't Goerlitz raise the gun and shoot him through the back? Didn't he see that by keeping him alive, now that he was so close to achieving his objective, was the most dangerous risk he could possibly take? The U-boat commander was so desperately pale, like a ghost, looked as if he were going to collapse any moment, yet he hung on minute after minute.

If Laurie had the gun he would shoot Goerlitz immediately. And that was the problem. He had to somehow get the gun. He had to shoot Goerlitz. None of the naive compassion the German seemed to have developed in his delirium. He looked ahead through the wind-driven rain at the mountainous sea-scape of endless waves. He had to try something, mount a deception that would somehow get him the gun. He experimentally pulled back on the throttle. The boat began to slow. Goerlitz lifted his head instantly and looked at Laurie through bleary eyes.

"Top speed, inspector," he said. "We don't slow down now." He raised the gun. "Come on, move it."

Laurie had no choice but to put the throttle back up to maximum. The boat heaved forward. Goerlitz promptly began to nod off. If only he could get Goerlitz into the cabin for a few moments. He was certain it would mean the end of the U-boat commander.

•

"Goerlitz," called Laurie.

Goerlitz lifted his head and opened his eyes. He had fallen asleep. He looked at Laurie and raised the gun.

"What do you want?"

"I'm thirsty. Could you get me some water?"

He tried to keep his eyes steady on Laurie, but he was having a hard time, and for a moment the inspector grew blurry and indistinct.

"Goerlitz?"

Goerlitz moaned.

"Yes, yes," he said, annoyed. "I'll get you some water. But I'm warning you. Anything funny and you're dead."

The inspector nodded.

Goerlitz went into the cabin, stumbling over the two dead harbor police. He had just put a cup underneath the fresh water tank's spigot, when he felt the boat begin to slow and curve to the right. The idiot, thought Goerlitz. He put the cup down with a grim deliberation and started through the cabin.

When he opened the door Laurie was no longer at the wheel.

Goerlitz whirled. Laurie was on top of the cabin.

The inspector took a flying tackle at Goerlitz, trying for the gun.

"You idiot," cried Goerlitz. "I was going to give you a chance."

The Luger jumped out of his hand and slid across the boat to the back as they rolled to the deck.

"I don't want your idiot's chance, Goerlitz."

Laurie broke away from Goerlitz and ran after the gun while the boat careened on a fourteen-foot wave. Goerlitz tried to follow but the wave knocked him off balance and he fell against the side of the boat. He got up and made another run for Laurie, but he was too late. Laurie had the gun in his hands. He levelled it at Goerlitz's chest with extended arms and fired. But he fired as the boat skidded down the backside of the large wave, and the bullet went wide. Laurie fired again but nothing happened, no bang, no flash, no kick. He tried again and then again. Nothing. The Borschardt-Luger was empty.

Laurie's eyes widened in alarm. Goerlitz looked at him almost scientifically. Now it was no longer innocent helpless victims like Saville or Jillian Gregory. This wasn't the hordes of Jews, Slavs, and undesirables they crowded into the death camps. This was his true enemy, a Briton, and he felt legitimate hatred for this man, as legitimate as hatred can ever be, felt hatred for this Briton because so many of his friends had gone to the bottom at the hands of the Brits. But he was weak and disoriented and he didn't know whether he had the strength.

Laurie lunged for him, and Goerlitz fell back against the wheel. His elbow hit the throttle, shoving it forward to full ahead. The Englishman put his hands around Goerlitz's throat while the boat began to pick up speed. Without a helmsman the cruiser began to circle recklessly, its deck rising to a sharp angle. Goerlitz gave Laurie a firm jab to the solar plexus and Laurie buckled, suddenly winded, gasping for breath. Goerlitz got up, cupped both hands together, and using his arms like a bat, smashed the inspector against the side of the head. But it wasn't a good hit, with the deck behaving like a fun-house floor. Still, Laurie stumbled backward, unaware that his left

295

foot had become tangled in a coil of rope on the deck.

The Englishman regained his balance and came at Goerlitz again. He punched Goerlitz in the mouth once, then twice. He tried to knee Goerlitz in the groin but the out-of-control boat climbed another huge wave, almost tipping, and he fell over onto the bench against the rail. Goerlitz grabbed the wheel and steadied the boat. It was perilously close to capsizing. Laurie struggled from the bench as the cruiser evened out, and, putting both hands on Goerlitz's shoulders, tore him from the wheel. Goerlitz was consumed by a blinding rage.

He swung out at Laurie, punching him first in the chin, then the mouth, then the cheek, then the eye in a series of lightning blows that stupefied Laurie. Summoning all his strength, he landed a crushing blow to Laurie's forehead. Laurie went stumbling back, his eyes rolling up into his head, just as the boat climbed another wave, tumbling him over the side into the water.

Goerlitz jumped for the helm, in a daze, pulled back the throttle and gripped the wheel. He felt violently ill, and his blood was pounding hard.

He checked the compass and veered the boat northward again, then turned on the storm lamp. The sea was rough and the large cruiser seemed to labor. He inched the throttle forward, which helped a bit. There was a faint luminescence to the dark whirling clouds. The sky and sea were made blacker by the doleful glare of the storm lamp. The only sounds Goerlitz could hear were the wind, the crash of the waves, and the noise of the motor.

Chapter 24

The sea grew even rougher as night turned to morning.
Though the rain had stopped, there was so much spray
he had to keep the windshield wipers on. When he was
about one-hundred-and-ten miles north of Barcelona he
put the boat in neutral and, bobbing up and down on the
waves, lit the cabin light and searched the cruiser for
something fresh to tie his wounds with. The corpses of
the harbor police lay there staring up at him in a pool of
blood. He had a long drink from the fresh-water tank
then found some gauze bandages in the first-aid cabinet
at the front of the boat. It took some doing but he managed to tie reasonable bandages around both wounds.
He then went back to the helm and continued along the
Spanish coast toward France.

The bandages didn't seem to help much because over
the course of the next four or five hours he grew weaker
and weaker. He shivered, had to fight to stay awake, but
kept his good arm steady on the wheel as he headed
north over the waves. The sea was rough, but he had
seen rougher during U-93's Arctic patrols outside

Murmansk, when the waves had been twenty-five feet high and great blocks of ice had crashed over the submarine's catwalk. Still the constant thumping bothered his arm.

He kept two miles offshore, navigating by the lights on the coast, keeping his eye on the fuel gauge. Around quarter-past-five in the morning the needle reached empty, and taking a chance, he continued up the coast for another twenty miles before turning toward shore. He looked at the odometer. Since leaving Barcelona he had now travelled a hundred and thirty miles.

He was weak, had a biting headache, and the blackness kept crowding around from the edges of his eyes. He breathed shallowly. The flow of blood was starting to ease, and his wool sweater stuck to his skin. He had no idea whether the bleeding had stopped entirely, and pulled the neck of his sweater away to have a look. The gauze bandages were soaked but the blood looked as if it were beginning to crust.

If the odometer were right, he should be in the Gulf of Lions, French territorial waters, and the fast approaching coastline should be France, Vichy France. The waves became breakers and began to toss the cruiser about like a twig. Goerlitz kept her steady at slow speed and ran her aground with a violent thump twenty feet from shore.

The cruiser listed to port as the waves washed over the stern and Goerlitz tumbled against the wheel, his weak legs giving way. He clung to the wheel with limp arms for several moments, his eyes closed, shivering and sweating at the same time. The boat rocked up and down, and the sound of the tumbling surf faded from Goerlitz's consciousness. He was blacking out.

Through the water-speckled windshield he saw a village a quarter mile to the north. He cut the cruiser's engine, pulled himself away from the wheel, and tried to

steady his legs. His muscles had always been willing vol-
unteers, but now he couldn't control them. He forced
himself into the cabin, emptied a jar of sugar, put the two
rolls of film, Michael Bower's wallet, and the photograph
of Ute inside, and screwed the lid on tightly. He struggled out the forward door to the bow, and, holding the
jar high over his head, jumped into the Gulf.

His plan had been to push the boat back out to sea,
but he was in six feet of water and he couldn't get any
traction. He felt as if he were going to faint any moment,
and he had to keep the jar dry.

Then he felt something nudge against him.
Something soft but with enough weight to startle him. In
the pre-light of dawn a face appeared in the water and a
shoulder heaved against his chest, and in a moment of
darkest terror he cried out as the grisly face of Laurie
smiled up at him through the salt-water. The waves
swelled and the dead man's face brushed against
Goerlitz's chin. Laurie's leg bobbed crazily, still encircled
by the coil of rope. Goerlitz turned and paddled madly
away, clutching the jar, horror-stricken, overcome by
superstitiousness. He swam frantically for shore, gained
traction, and ran as if for his life up to the beach.

After the buoyancy of the water he could hardly
stand on dry land. He wavered there for a moment, and
turned around. He saw the rope hanging over the cruiser's side, and it slowly dawned on him that he had
dragged Laurie almost a hundred miles. He had been so
sure, so sure, that Laurie had swam to shore. He looked
at the inspector as he bobbed up and down in the waves
face down, sad because he hadn't wanted it to come to
this. He walked down to the water's edge, unsteady, and
he could feel a warm fog of unconsciousness overpowering him. The fool, he thought. Why couldn't he have just
stayed in England? Goerlitz thought he had seen the last
of Laurie the night he had crouched in the window case-

ment above the River Mersey. In sudden fury he picked up a handful of sand and threw it as hard as he could toward Laurie. You stupid, stupid fool, he thought. I didn't mean this. I never wanted this to happen. You made it happen. This whole sad ridiculous war made it happen. He stumbled into the water toward the English inspector. He wasn't going to have the French authorities pawing the inspector's body for evidence. He could at least give him that dignity.

He walked waist-deep into the Gulf, fueled simply by will power now, and waited until a wave washed the inspector's body toward him. He grabbed the inspector's foot and fumbled with the knot for several minutes, finally getting it untied. To the deep, he thought, where so many of his friends and enemies alike had gone. He dragged the corpse a little further out and gave it a push.

He waded back to the shore. He stood there watching, rocking back and forth like a man who has had too much to drink. The body rolled in the waves for a while, a bloated patch of white in the dark foam and curl of the surf, and was finally drawn out by the morning's retreating tide. To the deep. *Auf einem seemansgrab da blühen keine rose*, thought Goerlitz.

He calmed his breathing and stumbled up the beach to where some bushes grew and found an old stick that had washed ashore. Using the stick as a third leg, resting on it when he had to, he climbed the slope to the coast road. He followed the coast road to the village he had seen.

He soon came to a farmhouse just outside the village and walked up the drive, counting fence posts as he went. He was breathing hard, struggling against his faintness and the desire to collapse on the spot. At the twelfth fence post he threw the stick into the ditch and walked over to the fence. He dug a sizable hole through the sandy soil behind the fence post and buried the jar.

He stepped back and counted fence posts again, making sure he was twelve from the road, then walked toward the farmhouse.

A light burned in one of the small windows, and water, even though the rain had stopped, still trickled from the eaves. He knocked on the door as the patches of black began to creep in from the edges of his eyes. A young woman, perhaps seventeen or eighteen, opened the door, gave a little cry, and lifted her hand to her mouth. She said something but in his confusion he couldn't make out the words through their hastily spoken dialect. The last thing he saw was an old man coming from a back room, then the patches of black darkened his vision, his legs buckled out from under him, and he fell to the floor, unconscious.

•

He regained consciousness off and on through the course of the night, catching glimpses of a chronology that sprang into view for a few moments at a time before the blackness came again: the old man and the woman bending over him, the sound of a truck outside, a constant river of French, one voice modulating smoothly into the next. A long truck ride. Through his intermittent consciousness he noticed that the sky was gradually brightening. Then he was unconscious for a long time, oblivious to everything.

The smell of carbolic woke him when the sky was fairly bright. He opened his eyes and saw lightbulbs flicking by one after the other. There was a plastic tube attached to his arm draining clear liquid from a bag above his head. The quiet hubbub of French voices bubbled all around him. He was being pushed on a bed quickly along a hallway. He saw faces looking down at him. The lightbulbs disappeared and he saw Ute sitting in the gazebo of his father's country house outside Munich. Ute threw a handful of leaves toward him and they scattered like a flock of birds. There was sunlight everywhere, and the smell of hay. And Ute was there, lying beside him between clean crisp sheets, with the flush of recent lovemaking on her face. It wasn't this bed, not this bed with the hard mattress and the clean sheets, but the bed with the canopy, the flowered sheets and pillow slips, and the woman who was his wife beside him. The bed turned a corner and they wheeled him into a big room where men in green surgical suits approached. There was one big light overhead. Sunlight, he thought. Ute unfolded her knitting and continued to work on the sweater she was making Herr Goerlitz for Christmas.

Chapter 25

A uniformed officer of the Ministry of Propaganda stood in front of him when Goerlitz regained consciousness a day-and-a-half later.

"*Guten Tag, Herr Kapitän,*" said the officer. "My name is Colonel Wolfbauer. I was first mate aboard Peter Cremer's U-333 for a number of years before I left the *Kriegsmarine.*"

Goerlitz squinted.

"Yes, I've heard of you. At least I've heard of Cremer."

How pleasant to speak German again, he thought, even though he found something unnerving about Wolfbauer.

"Where am I? Am I in Germany?"

"No. No, you're still in France. We're in Narbonne right now, captain, not far from Gruissan, where you came ashore. We can't be moving you to Germany, captain, not in your condition. At least not yet. Do you feel strong enough to tell me what happened? I'm the Ministry of Propaganda's liaison officer to the

Unterseewaffe, and I must file a report."

Goerlitz told his story in a disjointed fashion to Colonel Wolfbauer, who listened intently, and occasionally took notes. For some reason, and almost without thinking, Goerlitz mentioned nothing about the two rolls of films. When he had recounted the capture of U-512, the mutiny, his escape, the destruction of U-512, his voyage on the *San Julian* to Barcelona, and his final flight to France, the colonel leaned forward and gazed thoughtfully out the window at the streets of Narbonne.

"Remarkable, captain. Remarkable. Tell me, was there nothing you could do about this mutiny?"

"No," said Goerlitz, his tone leaden. "No, nothing. They'd been breathing chlorine fumes from the battery leak all that time. They were spitting up blood. They were untrained recruits, and Bergen was able to talk them into it behind my back."

"But out of forty-two crew members, captain, surely there must have been some who supported you."

"Two, colonel. Lippe and Hossbach. Lippe tried to scuttle but he was beaten unconscious by the others. Hossbach tried to open the ballast tanks, but he was beaten as well and thrown into the brig. If Hitler hadn't shortened the training period to two months it wouldn't have happened."

"Now, captain, let's not blame the Fuhrer."

"I understand Admiral Doenitz opposed the training reduction as well."

The colonel put his note pad away.

"So did Grand Admiral Raeder, for that matter," he said. "But we can't be blaming Hitler. And I think we'd better not mention this mutiny, captain, for your own sake, if you don't mind."

"But the British papers have already mentioned it."

The colonel grinned. "And we all know the British papers are filled with malicious, self-serving lies, don't we? Please, captain, we'll just quietly bury it. It will be our secret. It will be the best for all concerned."

The colonel's eyes narrowed and Goerlitz saw that he was clearly being warned.

"Thank you, colonel."

"You're quite welcome. Anything for a fellow U-boat man." The colonel stood up and pulled on his white drill gloves. "I'm glad we understand each other, captain." He smiled. "It's these kind of understandings that make life a little easier for us all in these troubled times." Colonel Wolfbauer adjusted his gloves so the fingers fit just right. "Now, then, you'll be staying here for two days, then you'll have a week's leave. I imagine you'll want to spend it in Munich. Your wife and father have been told that you are here, and are awaiting your return shortly. Of course we'll have photographers there for the happy reunion. You will smile for the cameras, captain. Is that understood?"

"Yes, colonel."

"I'll see you off at the train station Monday morning. If you need anything, you can call the district *Gaulieter*."

"There's one thing I do want," he said. Goerlitz found it an odd sensation to lie to a superior officer. "A jeep or a motorcycle to take me to Gruissan so I can thank the girl and the old man for taking me in. I imagine they saved my life."

"Ah, yes, of course, captain. A driver will come by this evening, if you're sure you'll be strong enough."

"I'm sure I will be. Thank you, Colonel Wolfbauer."

"A pleasure, captain."

His driver, he was glad to see, wasn't German but French, a member of the Vichy Armistice Army of France. He came in a World War I vintage motorcycle-and-sidecar and wasn't the least bit interested when Goerlitz dug the jar out from behind the twelfth fence post.

On Monday morning he left Narbonne, his arm in a sling, on the seven o'clock morning train, dressed in the standard grey combat uniform of a *Wehrmacht* infantryman. It was the only thing the local German garrison had available. As the train clanked and rumbled around the Gulf of Lions, he grew terribly anxious about going home, and wistfully longed for the steel and grease of a submarine. He felt different. He felt changed, as if he couldn't go on fighting this miserable war any more.

He met some regular German troops from the Fifth German Army who boarded the train in Marseilles, bound for the fighting in Italy. Some had already been there and said they hated the warfare that had developed there, where the Allies fought the Germans river by river and line by line in the same kind of deadening struggle their fathers had waged in the Great War. It was impossible, they said, to hold Italy, now that the Italians had signed an armistice with the Allies. Yet Kesselring, one of Hitler's favorites, insisted he could hold the Allies south of Rome. Most of the troops on the train took Rommel's view, much more pessimistic than Kesselring's, that the German Army should withdraw to the Gustav Line, or possibly the Gothic Line, and hold fast there.

Twenty miles east of Marseilles the train slowed to a halt. Members of the French Resistance, he was told, had blown up the tracks. Troops would be sent south by truck convoy while Goerlitz would be shipped to Germany with a bus full of wounded.

He recalled an old argument he and his father had, as he climbed aboard the bus. His father maintained that resistance movements, covert operations, and industrial sabotage were far more cost-effective, killed fewer people, and were less indiscriminate than imprecise aerial bombing and armored mechanized fighting. His father argued that if every Frenchman pulled down telephone wires, changed road signs, blew up culverts, and if possible, sniped at Germans, occupation would be impossible. This was, his father contended, an unwinnable war. Exactly the kind of rhetoric that got his father dismissed from the university. His father didn't care. His father made more than enough money from his mother's old drapery business. In some ways he couldn't understand his father. His father argued against the war, yet his mother's old factory produced four-hundred-and-fifty uniforms every hour.

Goerlitz learned about the July bombings of Hamburg from the wounded troops on the bus. Hamburg had already been bombed one-hundred-and-thirty times since the beginning of the war, but the wounded troops said there had never been anything like this before. Mind you, they said, it was all just hearsay. The *Völkischer Beobachter* had kept a low profile on the story, but from what they had heard, seven-hundred-and-forty fighter-escorted British Lancasters dropped seven-thousand-five-hundred tons of incendiary, high explosive, phosphorus, and delayed action bombs on the city. Massive fires had occurred and German civil defense had collapsed.

The RAF had produced the first fire-storm in history, the wounded troops said, and this fire-storm had sent a shockwave of dread through the entire Reich. Individual fires had joined in a city-wide blaze, they said. Buildings collapsed and winds gusted to a hundred miles an hour, drawing fleeing civilians into the blaze. The fire sucked the oxygen out of air-raid shelters and the occupants were either suffocated or baked alive. Thousands of people, the wounded troops said, had simply vanished. When the attacks were finally over, the mercy-killings of the hopelessly burned had gone on for days.

He arrived in Munich Wednesday afternoon. Ute and his father, looking frightened and bewildered by all the photographers, approached him the same way they might have approached a stranger, and in all truth, he felt like a stranger. The station was festooned with Nazi banners. Soldiers in grey uniforms milled about the platform and a giant portrait of Hitler hung above the archway. Ute raised her cheek tentatively to his lips. She looked older, had put on weight. She definitely wasn't the same woman who was in his photograph.

"What's all this, Hermann?" she asked, looking at the photographers.

"I think the newspaper wants to run a story," he said.

He put his arm around her and smiled at the photographers. He felt desperate.

"Ute, I ... I don't ... you've changed so much."

"So have you," she said. "You've lost so much weight. You look a hundred years old."

His father took him by the shoulder.

"Welcome back, Hermann. How's your arm?"

"It hurts. I can't move it, but I'll be all right. How are you? Is everything all right?"

His father grinned, his wire-rimmed glasses climbing his nose.

"I suppose as well as they can be under the circumstances."

"You there," cried Goerlitz. "Finish up with your camera. I want to go home."

"We'll be staying out at the house," said his father. "They've made about seven raids on Munich since you were last here."

"What about the apartment?"

"It's vacant," said Ute. "The landlord is holding it for us. We'll go back," she said, "if things improve."

"Which they won't," said his father.

His father's country house was a gabled and timbered monstrosity dating from the middle of the nineteenth century and had belonged to Goerlitz's great grandfather. Of the fourteen servants his father had employed during the Weimar years only four remained.

Of the departed ten, four had been Jews, and the other six had been conscripted.

A small apple orchard stood to one side and a duck pond stretched to a distant copse beyond. It was just the kind of peace and quiet Goerlitz needed to talk with Ute. They spent hours in the gazebo and going for walks, getting to know each other again. The brightness and freshness in her personality was there, but her girlishness was gone.

By mid-week, the *Völkischer Beobachter* ran a story on Goerlitz. There was a grainy black-and-white photograph of the three of them at the station, and another of Ribalta's destroyed cabin cruiser sitting in six feet of water outside Gruissan. They titled the article A FRIEND IN BARCELONA. It told how Ribalta had actually helped him to escape, to the point of sacrificing his own cabin cruiser and spending a sizeable sum of his own money to buy off corrupt Spanish officials who had illegally allowed the British to search for Goerlitz in Spain. Ribalta was indeed a friend, the article said, and expressed the true sentiment of the Spanish people better than the Generalissimo's present undecided policy.

"But that's not the way it happened," said Goerlitz.

"It is now," said his father. "The *Beobachter* is never wrong."

To see these blatant lies, so nonchalantly passed off as the truth, was heartbreaking to Goerlitz, and destroyed his conviction in the Reich more than anything else. *A Friend in Barcelona.* He had to laugh. And yet it saddened him greatly.

The story of U-512 was altered as well. After two days of breathing incapacitating chlorine fumes they were finally forced to surface and were immediately overrun by seamen from a nearby frigate. Planes had pounded them with depth charges, and even the most valiant efforts (and here they mentioned Ludendorff) couldn't stop the attack. The crew had fought for the submarine yard by yard (they mentioned Lippe and Hossbach and how they had attempted to scuttle against the British). Captain Goerlitz had personally killed four enemy seamen with his sidearm before his boat was overwhelmed "by the grubby filth of the Royal Navy."

For the most part they recounted the destruction of U-512 accurately. The article concluded with a few editorial comments: that it was about time Spain realized who her real friends were, and that she should join the Axis powers and push into Gibraltar once and for all.

A telegram arrived at Otto Goerlitz's country house on Thursday morning. Goerlitz was to be awarded the Knight's Cross of the Iron Cross along with a hundred others at a ceremony in Berlin's *Kaiserhof*, the city's most prestigious palace, on Saturday. The medal, for outstanding valor in the service of the Reich, would be awarded by Hitler himself. Black ties and dress uniforms were required. Both Herr Goerlitz and Ute were invited.

Berlin surprised him. He had no idea the bombing had been so extensive. Berliners went about their business gloomily, expecting the worst, resigned, trying to dull themselves to the blow the Allies would inevitably deliver. He didn't feel comfortable in his dress uniform. His arm was in a clean white sling.

The ceremony was held in the vaulted hall of the *Kaiserhof*. Nazi flags hung one after the other along the mirrored entrance way and a heavy contingent of SS guards had sealed off the area for the Fuhrer's arrival. As Goerlitz stood in line on a raised platform — like a circus animal, he thought — with the other soldiers who were to receive medals, he craned and looked at the doorway and big glass windows, conspicuously sandbagged, of the palace, waiting for the country's leader.

He came in a big black armored Mercedes with an escort of six motorcycles and an armored personnel carrier full of SS men. The band struck up the *Horst Wessel* song, and everybody raised their right arm in the Nazi salute as Hitler got out of the car. The honor guard raised their rifles to their chests. Everyone began to sing the *Horst Wessel* song along with the band. The Fuhrer, dressed in a plain grey uniform with no medals, hatless, climbed the stairs slowly, talking to his aides and smiling at the cameras.

Hitler began at the far end of the line. Goerlitz had seen the Fuhrer in person once seven years ago at an outdoor rally in Nuremburg from twenty-five rows back. Two officials stood behind Hitler as he went down the row. The closer the Fuhrer got the more different he looked from his photographs, from his portrait on stamps, coins, and paper money.

Then the Fuhrer stood before him and gazed into his eyes.

"And you're Goerlitz," said the Fuhrer.

"Yes, sir, I am."

"A fellow Bavarian, I'm told."

"Yes sir."

Was this Hitler, thought Goerlitz? Was this the man he had so fervently pledged his allegiance to so long ago? He looked at the Fuhrer closely as the medal was pinned on his chest. The Fuhrer's pupils were unfocused and dilated. The same narrow stiff moustache, weak lips, and sweeping band of greying black hair, but Goerlitz couldn't help thinking that this was just an ordinary if somewhat objectionable-looking man.

Back in Munich he got his orders. And a promotion. He was now a rear admiral. All lies, he thought, all lies. He was to report to Lorient, France, as soon as possible, at Admiral Doenitz's personal request.

That's when he saw he had a decision to make about the two rolls of film. To deliver them would definitely prolong the war. And he didn't know whether that's what he wanted. To prolong the war would simply prolong Germany's misery. He developed the negatives in a dark room he had rigged in his father's country house, made a few prints — they were clear, sharp, and focused — and put the negatives in an envelope.

He had met and talked to Admiral Doenitz many times. Doenitz made a point of fraternizing with his officers and enlisted men. The tall, thin, stern admiral rose briskly when Goerlitz came in, escorted by two of the admiral's assistants.

"Well, Goerlitz, I'll be frank with you. Wolfbauer told me the whole story. And not the one in the *Beobachter*."

"Yes, sir."

"Don't be alarmed, Goerlitz. I'm not going to bite you. A sad thing, this mutiny. I warned the Fuhrer but the Fuhrer doesn't listen to men like me."

The Fuhrer never listened to reasonable men. He dismissed them from their posts, just as his father had been dismissed.

"At ease, Goerlitz. You don't have to be so stiff around me. I understand you met Georg Weiss in England."

For a moment, Goerlitz didn't reply.

"I did, sir."

"And how was he?"

"Holding up well, sir."

"Well, that's good. His wife Helga recently had an operation. I believe we had the Red Cross let him know. Did he get the message?"

"I wouldn't know, sir."

"It went well for the most part. One or two complications. Something to do with the small intestine, I believe, but she's recovering nicely. How's your arm?"

"The doctor says I shouldn't use it for a month or two."

"Then that works out well." The admiral leaned forward, pressing his hands on his desk with a spread of tight fingers. "You've been relieved of combat duty. Not because of the mutiny, of course, but because I'm running out of capable managers here. Rear echelon, I'm afraid, but you're well over thirty, aren't you?"

"Thirty-three in November, sir."

"Really? You look older, much older." The admiral shifted some papers on his desk. "You'll be stationed here in Lorient for, well, for as long as we can hold on."

That's one thing he liked about Doenitz. He was a realist. They would hold on here as long as they could. That was all.

"I guess that's about it. Unless you have any questions. What's the trouble, Goerlitz? Do you have something on your mind? Do you have something you want to say to me?"

Goerlitz hesitated. "No, sir," he said. "No, nothing."

"Well, all right, then. Dismissed. The warrant officer outside will show you your quarters."

"Thank you, sir."

"Report to map room C at 0900 hours tomorrow morning."

"Yes, sir."

Goerlitz turned and walked away, feeling only weary and a little sad.

"Oh, Goerlitz," called the admiral.

"Sir?"

"Last night, sitting with a shnapps and thinking about meeting you today, and then about Weiss, I remembered something about a plan he and I once discussed. I seem to remember — it's all so fuzzy — it might have involved you. Did he ever happen to mention it?"

Goerlitz could feel the envelope of negatives through the inside pocket of his fur-lined leather jacket.

"No, sir, he didn't."

The admiral looked at him with serious eyes and a

grim mouth. Then his eyes softened with understanding.

"It doesn't matter. I don't think it would have made any difference," he said in quiet voice. "Not now."

Goerlitz just stared at the admiral.

"Yes, sir," he said. A reasonable man, he thought, a man who perceived the war as it was, not as they saw it in Berlin and Berchtesgaden. "Thank you, sir."

The faintest grin came to the admiral's lips.

"You're a good officer, Goerlitz," he said. "Dismissed."

They gave him his own private room with a decently soft bed. After he had arranged his few items of clothing and had placed his photograph of Ute on his bedside table, he put on his jacket, zipping it up over his sling, and went outside.

The night air was cool and calm, though sizeable breakers crashed onto the shore. In the distance he saw a submarine, low in the water, coming in from patrol. He walked past the forty-foot-thick bomb-proof pens right to the ocean until the water washed over his boots and he could smell the salt. A large orange sun sank behind a smokey patchwork of clouds. Goerlitz took the negatives out of the envelope and tossed them into the waves one by one.